Cormac James was born in Cork, Ireland. A graduate of the UEA Creative Writing MA, he has published short fiction in *Columbia*, *Phoenix Irish Short Stories*, and *The Dublin Review*. His first novel, *Track and Field*, was published in 2000. He lives in Montpellier, France, with his wife and son.

Praise for *The Surfacing*

'THE SURFACING is an extraordinary novel, combining a powerful narrative with a considered and poetic use of language in a way that is not often seen these days. Reading the book, I recalled the dramatic natural landscape of Jack London and the wild untamed seas of William Golding. Cormac James' writing is ambitious enough to be compared with either.'

John Boyne, author of *The Boy in the Striped Pyjamas*

'The great topic of Cormac James' THE SURFACING is the reach of human possibility. The prose is calm, vivid, hypnotic and acutely piercing. James is attuned to the psychological moment: this is a book about fatherhood and all its attendant terrors. It's a remarkable achievement. . . . James recognises the surfacing of love in the face of solitude. A stylish novel, full of music and quiet control. This is a writer that I'd like to see hurry - I'm looking forward already to the next book.'

Colum McCann, author of
TransAtlantic, Let the Great World Spin

'Cormac James' writing is very assured, with a harsh poetic edge. His evocations of barren landscape, sea weather, pack ice and frozen skies are powerful and compelling.'

Rose Tremain, author of
Music and Silence, Sacred Country, Restoration

THE SURFACING

Cormac James

SANDSTONEPRESS
HIGHLAND | SCOTLAND

First published in Great Britain
Sandstone Press Ltd
Dochcarty Road
Dingwall
IV15 9UG
Scotland

www.sandstonepress.com

Commissioning Editor: Robert Davidson
Editor: Moira Forsyth
Copy editor: Kate Blackadder

The author wishes to thank the Arts Council/an Chomairle Ealaíon
for its generous funding during work on this book.

The publisher acknowledges subsidy from
Creative Scotland towards publication of this volume.

ISBN: 978-1-908737-98-4
ISBNe: 978-1-908737-99-1

Cover design by Jon Gray, London
Typeset by Iolaire Typesetting, Newtonmore
Printed and bound by Totem, Poland

for Cian and Laetitia

PART I

1850

25th May

They passed through belts the colour of mud, and belts the colour of mustard, that ran directly across the stream. They slid into banks of fog that stood dead on the water, that blanked everything but their voices, and slid back into the daylight as out of a steam room. Exiting one such bank, on the 25th, they met a queer-looking brig. They'd had the sea to themselves since Aberdeen, and hailed heartily, but she made no acknowledgement, slid silently by, into the fog aft, and they never saw her again.

Captain Myer insisted on a strict schedule, to tame the day. By seven o'clock. By eight. By half past. Bunks. Breakfast. Tubs. He wanted all mouths fed at the same time, whether they were hungry or not. At the fixed hour, he wanted them all abed, even if they were not ripe for it. He spoke of the ship as one family, one body, unified. Every noon without fail he could be seen reconciling his several chronometers.

On the 27th, finally, a coastline was cried out. The men all came up and stared at it as a wonder. Greenland, it was called. It looked like burned bog. There was not a single tree, or a single bush. There was no grass. Frayed and shabby at the edges, there was still snow on those hills that faced north.

At Disko there was no other ship. Well above the high water line stood a lone warped wooden house, with a line of huts behind, set directly into the hillside. The huts were roofed with sods level with the land, and from the ship, through the glass, the dirty bundles seemed to crawl out of a hole in the ground.

The whaleboat moved towards the shore with Myer standing at the bow. It was a pose he had admired privately. Already, crowds of women and children were waiting on the rocks. It was an open-air abattoir. Bones, waste, and offal everywhere. And everywhere strips of meat three and four and five feet long laid like frost-charred ferns on the bare ground, to cure. The air was almost sweet. To no one in particular, Myer announced: What a welcome. A carnival of the unclean.

Under the boat, giant grey tentacles, that looked more animal than vegetable, tried a lazy flourish. Lieutenant Morgan, the ship's second, stared down at them from the stern. The previous summer, he had swum in the liquid jade of Aegean. That seemed another world to him now, another man.

The governor's house was suspiciously clean, and suspiciously neat, as though something untoward had happened there, of which they hoped to eliminate every trace. It was a blatant rebuttal to everything seen on the shore. The floors were green, and looked freshly painted. The low ceilings were pale blue. The lady of the house was the governor's sister, Miss Rink. She was pale as an invalid, yet glowed with health. Her skin too seemed strangely clean.

They sat and stared at a grumbling stove and let Rink talk. He was struggling to pull the cork from a bottle. Near the fire stood an empty brass birdcage. The cork came away with a sound, knowing sigh.

You and your officers are all my guests, Rink said. As long as you are here.

We couldn't think of soiling your sheets for just one night, Myer said.

What does that matter? Rink said. Let her wash some sheets. She complains she is being bored most of the time.

We're really not so badly off where we are, Morgan said. Quite tightly packed, it's true, but comfortable nonetheless.

She asked outright how many they were, and Myer told her. They were six officers, ten men, one boy and one Greenlander, to manage the dogs and to translate, if need be. We couldn't possibly ask you to entertain us all, Myer said.

It's not often I have the pleasure of proper conversation, she said.

You see, Rink told them.

You must regularly have visits from the whalers, Morgan told her.

The whalers are a very particular, I almost said peculiar, class of man. I admire them greatly, but there are limits, I find, to their charms.

Her hair was blonde, pulled back very tight. There would be a great relief, it looked to Morgan, if all of a sudden the thing were undone.

Myer said they really could not linger, however much the hospitality of Mr Rink and his charming sister might appeal. Already they were behind schedule, he said. They had a rendezvous with other Admiralty ships at Beechey Island, in Lancaster Sound, from where they would disperse to various points in the archipelago, to begin the search, before the winter set in again.

I do not think so, Rink said.

The winter is slow going this year, she said.

We're hoping to get a good run through The Pack, said Myer.

You will be doing it well, Rink said, if even you get there at all.

That month alone, she said, three whalers had been crushed in Melville Bay. Out of Peterhead. Two more, crippled, had only just gone home.

Myer said he had not seen them, coming up the coast.

Did Myer really think there was still hope of finding them? Rink asked. Franklin and the two missing ships, he meant. Didn't he think it had been rather long, how many years was it now, with neither sight nor sound of them?

We must try, Myer said. We must make our very best effort, and we must not relinquish hope.

The drawing rooms of London will not tolerate anything less, DeHaven said.

Myer scowled. Pay no attention to Dr DeHaven's irreverence, he said. At every opportunity he runs down the entire enterprise, but I can assure you there is no more resolute man aboard. His younger brother is on the *Terror*.

Myer said he had a letter for Rink from the Directors of the

5

Royal Greenland Trading Company. He nodded at Morgan, who tendered the envelope.

What does it say? Rink asked.

Naturally I haven't opened it, Myer said. And even if I had, I believe it is written in Danish.

Still Rink refused to touch the thing.

His sister took it and broke the seal. She mumbled through the formalities, scanned for the essentials. Where possible, she read, we are to – she checked her translation – generously to supply the bearer's material needs.

Rink did not answer. He was staring out the window, seemed not to have heard. He had drunk half the bottle himself. The skeleton of a ship lay on the shore. A ship found drifting off the coast, abandoned, the previous summer. A strange story, Rink said.

The officers let the man talk. Every now and then Myer made a civil noise in his throat. Morgan caught the sister looking at him. She raised her eyebrows a fraction, her shoulders, and gave a silent sigh. Every year a package came down from Upernavik with the last of the whalers – however many sentimental novels the priest there had managed to beg from the captains that season. These and her brother's stories were all she had to shorten the winter nights.

Standing at the window beside him, Myer said he dared not imagine what it was like, inside the natives' huts. Rink led the way to the nearest one, and Myer followed eagerly. From the porch, they watched him pull aside the flap. They watched Myer lean forward, then jerk his head backward, as though he'd been struck. They live in a ditch, he shouted back to the house, and called his officers to come and see.

The officers all obeyed, but just as Morgan made to follow Miss Rink placed a hand on his arm. She shook her head. She made an ugly face. He did not go. They stood in silence, alone on the porch. Morgan watched her touch the tip of her cigar to the post and put what was left back into the case. Just as gently, she touched her fingertips to the drop of green glass hanging at her neck. This was as though it might not still be there – an elegant pretence. They stood and listened to the ice groan and stutter down at the shore. There was rain on the way. The low sky was a slab of stone.

Are you quite sure you cannot stay for dinner? she asked.

I would very much like to, he said.

They talked carefully. She said she had not so much as set foot on a boat or a sledge for five years.

Morgan made no comment. Rink and the other officers came back and stood up on the porch out of the rain. Myer was hounding him for supplies.

There were no supplies, Rink said. The most he could offer them was a few hares, a young goat. They could have all the codfish they liked, of course.

What about furs? Myer said. There was nothing he would not trade. Books, rum, beer – whatever Rink and his sister wanted most.

It made no difference. There were no furs. The reindeer, Rink said, sprawled his arms in a helpless gesture. The great days were gone. They should have stopped farther south.

But Myer refused even to think of going back. He was afraid of being late, of missing his chance, of not getting through. In the end, the officers all went back into the house and waited with the sister, and drank her coffee, while Rink did the rounds of the huts, confiscating what he could.

Through the window, they watched the rain flailing at the mud. The water ran red in the tracks, as though the whole country had been dyed on the cheap. They watched the mud fuming under the stampede until the hour was rung on the watch bell, out in the bay. Under the roar of the rain, the toll was cheap tin.

Even as they were throwing the furs into the boat, she came after them. She had brought him a bag of coffee, and a little bag of seeds. She had written in English on the folded paper. CARAWAY. The whalers swore by it, she said, for the blood. It needed heat, she said, but could be started off in the dark. Morgan told her to go back, quickly. The rain had eased off, but that would not last.

7

29th May

On the 29th they pulled out of the bay and swung north. The rigging was strung with salted cod. Water, ice and sky were the colour of ash.

Two days later, at four in the morning, Myer hustled all the officers out of bed and up on deck. Here, at last, forming a lee shore, lay the thing they had heard so much about: The Pack. In the early morning quiet, they listened. It crackled like a burning log.

After the rest had gone down for breakfast, Morgan remained at the bows with MacDonald, the chaplain. They stood side by side, like men hypnotized. Straight ahead, rising up out of the water, stood a block of marble about the size of the Taj Mahal. Each in his own way, the two men admired greatly its utter indifference to the constant fuss and clamour of the sea.

At lunch, MacDonald declared: In my sermon next Sunday, I am tempted to propose the iceberg as a symbol of the Almighty Himself, that is to say, the perfect embodiment of unlimited power held perpetually in reserve. An analogy of which Mr Morgan, I somehow feel, will entirely approve.

Not wishing to contradict you, Mr MacDonald, but I don't know that I'd see the thing in quite the same terms as yourself, Morgan said.

What terms would you prefer?

I don't know.

Come come, MacDonald said. We've all seen your book-shelf. We've all read your reports. You're an articulate man. Give us at least an idea of what you mean. Look, you have a captive audience.

I'm not being coy, Morgan said. I simply don't know how I feel about the thing. What we saw this morning. That is the simple truth.

The door burst open. It was Cabot, the cook.

Giorgio! He's disappeared. Over on the floe.

They rushed up on deck. Two hundred yards from the ship,

some fifty yards into The Pack, a group of men were standing on a giant pan of ice. The officers all rowed over, drove the boat as far in as they could, clambered out.

The boy had gone out with Petersen, to carry his rope and hooks. The Greenlander had spotted a seal, and they had gone to try their luck.

Only for the fun, Petersen said. He looked more annoyed than upset. They had been hopping from pan to pan, he'd been pushing on ahead, and when he turned around the boy was gone. The rope was floating in the water, in one of the cracks. The heavy grappling-hook, perhaps, had caught in his clothes and pulled him down. There was no other trace.

I want only the boy to see, Petersen said. I am telling him the story. He wants to see with his two eyes.

Hand over hand, Petersen drew the rope up out of the water. The gap between the two pans was barely a foot wide. Morgan watched the man coiling the rope nicely onto the ice. Inside him, a stupid hope had already bred, that the boy might still be attached to the end of it. He would come up laughing and spluttering, amused as much as relieved.

Perhaps Mr MacDonald would consider saying a few words, Myer said.

Of course, MacDonald said.

They gathered about the coiled rope. So close to the edge of The Pack, the ice was always alive, and already the crack had completely closed over again.

Greater love hath no man than this, that he lay down his life for his friends, MacDonald told them. Such has been our young shipmate's sacrifice here today. Our every action must henceforth stand in its shadow. His memory must inspire us to equal abnegation. Our brother Giorgio, I say, has shown us the way.

Afterwards, the whaleboat ferried the men back to the ship. As there was not room for them all at a go, Morgan and Cabot and DeHaven remained behind.

Not a bad way to go, when all's said and done, DeHaven said.

How do you mean? Morgan said.

A smile on your face, all is right with the world, and a minute later . . . bonne nuit.

He might have preferred a few more rounds of the carousel, all the same.

Perhaps. But I hope when my time comes it'll be as quick and as quiet.

I thought it was raging and cursing you wanted to go, Morgan said.

Under their feet and all around, the ice was awake. They listened to it fret. They stared at the spot. They did not yet dare to be bored.

The boat had ferried and unloaded its passengers, was coming back.

Well, DeHaven said, at least we now have an extra bunk. Maybe we could send Hepburn down with the men.

Geoff, Morgan said, the old man deserves a little comfort.

And the rest of us don't? We're living one on top of the other, the four of us, in that little cell.

Maybe we could send Hepburn down to berth with the crew, have MacDonald take his place, and MacDonald give you his cabin. Would that suit your convenience?

It would, DeHaven said.

They passed the Women's Islands early the next morning, the 1st of June. By breakfast-time the wind began to fumble, and falter, and even as he sat eating Morgan could feel the life draining from the ship. By noon the wind had died to nothing, left them sitting like fools in thick fog, amidst phantom fragments of the floe. They could not see fifty feet. It did not matter. Morgan knew exactly what lay ahead. They were making their way north as into an estuary, that had been narrowing from the off, since Disko. Miss Rink had told him what every one of the whalers had told her – that where Myer hoped to pass, up along the coast, they would find a solid white wall.

2nd June

They were set in a pane of glass, a mile from the shore. The surface was sprinkled with thousands of eider ducks, as far as the eye could see. The world was at peace, the morning impeccable, the bergs sparkling thoughtlessly in the sun. All day long, there had not been a breath of wind.

Morgan was standing alone in a boat by the shore. Even a mile off, he was sure he could smell the dried cod. The mists and showers had ruined it, but Myer still insisted it would do for the dogs. To shut it out, Morgan closed his eyes, felt the cool air creeping over him, down off the glacier. Then he heard the thunder. The entire face of an iceberg was falling away, to reveal the same face again, shed of its mask. At the ship, too, they heard the guns in the distance, and saw the birds begin to bob. The wave reached them minutes later, and set the ship in a lazy roll.

The next morning the canvas began to stir, and the light ice began to drift away from the wind, southward. They watched the pieces sail by. They spotted a seaman's chest. Morgan told Banes to row over and fish it out. The label was ruined for reading but they could tell it was neither *Erebus* nor *Terror*. Inside were last year's *Almanack* and a fine pair of riding boots.

That evening, from the Crow's Nest, free sailing was announced to the west, well inside The Pack, but from there stretching to the horizon. Myer declined to go up and see it for himself. He did not need good cause, only a good excuse. The next morning, he announced, they were going in.

4th June

All morning they forced their way through the mess, until they made what Myer had baptized The Open Water. They drove hard, free and unhindered, north and west. By noon, from the deck, they had sunk the coast.

From the Crow's Nest, Myer was shouting down directions. Brooks was at the helm. Morgan sat on a crate near the stern, smoking his pipe, trying to pretend he knew nothing of what was going on. But overhead Myer was bellowing like a school-boy. Ahead of them now was half a mile of water at most.

The ice was visibly nearer. Inside it, the little lead they were aiming for was the colour of ink. Another order was roared from above. Morgan watched the men heaving frantically at the braces. She turned shyly towards the gap.

The first contact put him lying on the deck flapping franti-cally at the cinders on his coat. All around him, fish were hopping off the boards. Far above, a man was screaming. It was a voice Morgan had never heard before. The shock was done, no more fish fell, but their dead eyes like dried peas rattled over and across the deck, as the ship ground and grunted, and bulled for an even keel.

Afterwards, Morgan brushed himself off and went to the bows, to see where their commander wanted to go. Even here at its widest it was a nice fit, and tighter still in the distance. Myer seemed not to notice, but called for a full spread of canvas, even to studding-sails, and ordered all hands out on the floe, with picks and pinch-bars, to work them farther in.

At dinner that night, Myer did not say a word, and his offic-ers did not mention the ice, or what they had been at. They leaned their elbows on the table, heads down, hunched under an invisible weight. They ate their food mechanically, but when Myer coughed, as though clearing his throat, all the forks stalled in mid-air. Still Myer said nothing. They kept eating, and the cutlery kept creaking and squealing on their plates.

After supper Myer sent Morgan forward to the crew's quarters to get Daly, their strongest man. Out on the ice, they watched Daly crouch down, to lift their smallest kedge. The thing weighed at least one hundred and fifty pounds. They watched him waddle. There was no protest or complaint.

Now then Doctor, Morgan said, there's a nice specimen for your collection. He could feel it inside him, the jealousy, now well awake. The man was of a different breed. The veins were standing out on his forearms, and the forearms looked carved from wood.

They watched him go. To his friend, quietly, DeHaven wondered about the wisdom of sending a man out over doubtful ice, carrying an anchor.

He is a sailor in Her Majesty's Navy, Myer announced, turning to face his accuser. If he is not so fond of danger, he should have stayed at home to dig potatoes.

From the bows, they watched Daly hack a hole in the surface with some class of hatchet. Into this hole he hooked the anchor. He threaded the hawser through the eye. The slack was wrapped round the capstan. The men got into place, three to each arm. It was now half past eight at night. They leaned into the bars. The hawser rose up off the ice. It began to tremble. Soon they could hear it crack and splinter, like wood. The object of their efforts was beautifully simple: to pry apart the two halves of the world with their bows, and drive themselves into the crack, where the danger was greatest.

They had not been heaving two minutes when Myer swore he'd seen a definite twitch in the floe. It was like a wedge being hammered home. Ten minutes later, when they paused to swap teams, Morgan saw that a crack about two inches wide ran crazily out from the bow for a hundred yards. That little gap, of course, was nothing and everything. Somehow they had managed to push apart two floes each as big as a nice-sized cricket field.

Quod erat demonstrandum, Myer announced, waving his hand grandly at the entire visible world. Proof of a principle I have cherished all my life, but never before been furnished with so perfect an example. That every force, however small, against opposition however great, must ultimately have its effect, if exercised relentlessly. Naturally – the hand dismissed the notion prettily – the orthodox mind insists the thing cannot be done. We are simply out of our depth, n'est-ce pas? He showed the sceptics his sorry specimens, and their surrounds. This against this. One was small and weak, the other giant and indifferent. Now the hand showed them the new crack in the floe. Was ever evidence more eloquent? he asked. It has been done. *We* have done it. That is why a man must never listen to reason. He must merely exercise his will unceasingly, and only afterwards stop to consider what he has achieved.

When they paused to swap teams again, Myer sent Morgan down to check the progress. He knelt on the ice to peer into the crack, to see how deep it was. To Morgan, the thing seemed no wider than before.

Put your hand in, said DeHaven, who was standing over him.

Morgan looked up, looked offended. Are you out of your mind? he said.

What are you afraid of? DeHaven said.

Put your own hand in. If you're so brave.

What are you afraid of? DeHaven said. The anchors are well dug in. The hawser is brand new. The tension is good. Or do you think someone up there is watching and waiting? Do you think this has all been contrived, just to trap you?

Morgan curled the tips of his fingers around the top of the crack.

Deeper, DeHaven said.

Morgan slid in his whole hand, to the wrist.

Deeper, DeHaven said.

He forced his arm almost to the elbow, until it was firmly wedged in place. He had to tug hard to get it out. The skin was striped, white and red.

Now you, he said.

DeHaven looked at him askew. Me? he said, perplexed.

14

Are you out of your mind? He was grinning superbly. Just how stupid do you think I am?

Up at the capstan, they leaned into the bars, and groaned, and cursed, and changed teams, and leaned into the bars again. For four long hours they stuttered forward, inch by inch. By midnight they had driven themselves quarter of a mile deeper, and the vessel stood motionless – dead centre of a vast, featureless plain. But for a few streaks of water, the world around them was now perfectly white.

13th June

Eighty-five feet high, Morgan stared over the frozen sea. Myer had sent him up to scout for a better lead. The order was perfect proof, if ever he needed it, that Myer was a fool. There were no better leads. To every point it now looked the same – proof, in turn, that the fool had led them into a trap.

They had warped all day every day for a week now without interruption, and today they were at it again. This morning, for no particular reason, the floes had relaxed a little, and it was a more polite affair than usual. From above, Morgan watched them strolling round and round. It looked like the *visites* of a French quadrille. The smart chatter of the pawls was music enough, he thought, after the strain of the previous days.

About eleven o'clock he saw that half a mile ahead the ice opened up into a kind of canal. From boredom, he called it out. Myer immediately hustled the men off the capstan and down onto the floe. The traces were passed down and every man rigged. They shuffled across the ice until the lines grew tight, and then they leaned forward, as into a stout headwind.

Unseen, Morgan looked straight down the length of the mast at Myer winding his chronometers again, and imagined putting a bullet straight through the top of the man's head. It would be an easy, undeserved end. He imagined the mess. He wondered what they would do. He himself was next in line for the command. He could always say he had been climbing down with the gun. He had been sure it was not cocked. It would be interesting to see who was willing to believe.

16th June

The last of the slack was brought in, and the men leaned into the bars. For the moment, Brooks let them make their own pace. After a few minutes stretching, tightening, threatening, the ship suddenly jumped forward, or backward, about an inch. It felt like the first jolt of a departing train.

Well now, DeHaven declared, maybe there's something in that house besides smoke.

Morgan, in his spoiled mind, wondered if the ice anchor was not coming home. The heaving began again, and soon it seemed to him, by closing one eye, and taking a bead on the bowsprit, that the ship was shuffling ever so slightly to starboard.

By now Brooks, the mate, was fearlessly goading the men as they filed past: Come on now boys and make a name for yourselves! Can't ye feel it, honeys? The meat is gone out from it entirely! Are ye Christians or what kind of men are ye? Will ye not heave then, for the love of Christ? Heave now and be saved!

The feet were starting to scramble. Myer pretended he did not see. Brooks took a step forward and addressed directly those at the bars:

My dear boys, what had ye for breakfast at all? White bread and fresh butter is it? Damn it all to hell, Mr Daly, is it idlers only they're breeding in the county of Cork these past thirty years?

He had the teams piped down every fifteen minutes, for a five-minute pause. He did not want them looking any farther into the future than that.

After watching them for an hour, Morgan removed his jacket and shoved in beside the men. Soon his legs were faltering. Faltering, he goaded himself with half-forgotten insults, and imaginary slurs, searching for strength in anger and shame. But by the time Brooks finally piped them down for their midday meal, he was stupid from fatigue.

Halfway down the deck was a long flat crate he could lie on, if he could get to it. He shuffled across the deck like a man chin-high in water. Every breath now was effort or relief. He sat down stiffly, with old age in his legs, and stared into the darkness of the hatch. The sunlight blared up off the wood worn to a sheen and he could see nothing. As he lay back, and his head touched the boards, a strangled sound came out of his throat.

A gentle breeze was flowing over the ship, teasing the dangling lines. From nowhere, the cat sprang up onto the roof of the galley, spotted him, and shrank. All around, the sullen faces were watching.

Eventually Morgan stood up again, shuffled to the gunwale, unbuttoned his flies, and began to piss over the side. It sounded exactly like a tearing sheet. He watched the hole widen and darken. The thing seemed so easy. The ice seemed impossibly soft.

At lunch, Myer told the officers that they must meet the difficulty head-on. They must not shirk for so much as a moment, nor seem even to think of it. They must try every device and example to buoy up the morale of the men.

17

All the same, it's little enough gain for so much sweat, Morgan said. The day before they'd named their progress in yards. Today they named it in feet. It might be as well, Morgan said, to wait for the ice to slacken a little, which it surely must, and spare their strength.

Mr Morgan, Myer said, in such an enterprise as ours, the one sure warrant of discipline is the faith of those below in those above. But if you prefer dismay, distrust and disorder, it is easily bred. You have merely to hesitate at the first difficulty, and the job is done. If ever you have the privilege to command, try to remember that.

After lunch, Myer decided to change the angle of traction, again.

An excellent idea, DeHaven said.

They watched the men tugging at the anchor, which had burrowed deep into the ice.

The finest naval mind of his generation, Morgan said.

You do realize, DeHaven said, that there are men now sitting in armchairs in London would give their right arm to be in your shoes. To be able to say they were right there in the thick of it, by Captain Myer's side. In Paris too, he said, pointing. Cabot had propped open the galley door, stood there watching with a pained look on his face.

Believe me, Morgan said, I feel it a privilege and an honour. I'm sure I've done absolutely nothing to deserve it.

The men began to heave again. Ten minutes later, there was a wretched rush of noise. The men leapt back. Something had snapped. The new hawser was actually smoking, as it surged from the snatch.

And that there now, DeHaven nodded sternly, is why Mr Gordon Myer is commander of one of Her Majesty's finest sailing ships, and you, my dear fellow, are merely . . . He fluttered his fingers nimbly.

A witness to history, Morgan said.

Brooks was ordered to dismantle the capstan, to find out what exactly had gone wrong. Myer waited to watch him knock out the first of the blocks, then turned towards Morgan and DeHaven. It was not possible he had heard. There had been too much noise.

Perhaps, Doctor, you think you would do better in my place, Myer said. He stood facing them both.

DeHaven held his stare. To be perfectly honest, Captain, I don't think I'd have got quite so far, he said. I don't think I'd have tried quite so hard. Certainly not along quite the same lines as yourself.

Luckily for all of us, my friend cannot aspire to command, Morgan explained. However much he might like to do so. There was a kind of regret in his voice, theatrical, but what he said was true. In certain arrangements, the expedition was not altogether regular. DeHaven was a civilian, under contract.

If life aboard a naval ship is too trying for Dr DeHaven, he can renege on his contract whenever he likes, Myer said. Though he'll find it's rather a long walk home, I think.

They watched Myer collect his coat, go down. Cabot had been listening at the galley door.

I suppose somebody has to be in charge, he said. It was a peace offering, to nobody in particular.

DeHaven turned his head, seemed to find something distasteful in what he saw. Somebody, not anybody, he said. In English there's quite a difference. Perhaps one of your friends might be good enough to explain it to you.

Cabot considered the man. He cleared his throat scrupulously and spat far out onto the deck, stepped back into the darkness. Then Brooks was beside them. The captain wanted them to go below, fore and aft, to check for damage.

They crawled as far forward as possible, with a single lamp. Between the bows it was a mass of timber, shores radiating from every Samson post, in every direction, and extra beams and knees added wherever they could be got in. The two men lay port and starboard, facing each other, each lounging against the bow's inner sheath.

Bravo, Morgan said. Another great diplomatic success. He nodded at everything overhead, the scene with Cabot, the scene with Myer. His friend could be resolutely, deliberately irritable at times. He seemed to enjoy it, as the assertion of a right.

In the silence, he could hear the ice fidgeting at the side of the ship, fussy but patient, only inches away.

You think I should keep my mouth shut, DeHaven said. Like you. And for why? For a broken-down horse soldier, that somebody somewhere one day decided to give a ship.

We were horse soldiers ourselves once. Both of us.

In a distant land, a long, long time ago.

Look, it matters not a whit what he or any one of us once was. Just now, he's the captain, Morgan said.

Is that who he is?

Morgan listened like a schoolboy, sullen. His friend seemed to think it courageous, such talk. At least, that courage was what others lacked. It was easy for him, of course. He risked nothing. At worst he could change ships at Beechey, as Myer said. Quite likely there would be a supply steamer there ready to return home. How much harder it was, though, to listen and watch and obey without a murmur.

He bowed his head, exhaled audibly. Geoff, he said. He was starting all over again. Look at it this way. From a purely pragmatic perspective. You are now on, we won't say friendly terms with him, but on both sides you're still able to keep up the pretence of civility. But go ahead, have it out with him, a real proper flare-up, and see where it gets you. Because afterwards, after you've worked up a nice head of steam, and blown it all off, who's still captain? Myer. Who's still judge and jury to every man aboard? Myer. Which is why not a man aboard will lift a finger to defend you, myself included, and we're damned right. Resign your service if you like. Who's still your lord and master? Myer. At least until he can set you down someplace. But take a look around. Wildly, he flung out an arm. At best it'll be Beechey, if the other ships are still there. But if they're not, what will you do? Because from there, if he decides to push all the way to the Pole just to spite you, that's exactly where we'll go. We could be two and three years out here yet without meeting another ship. So choose your mask carefully, Morgan told his friend. He was pointing at his face. Because if you ask me, you might well have to wear it awhile yet.

They fell into silence, as they crawled slowly back from the bow, searching for signs of an injury. From the other side of the boards, relentlessly, came a neat patter as of pegs on a plank floor.

Christ, DeHaven said, lifting the lamp. Look. You could put your finger into that.

A long crack ran right down the length of the sternpost. DeHaven thrust the light closer. He glanced over at Morgan, desperate to know what the thing was, and what it meant.

With the lamp they followed the thing down, all the way to the floor.

Jesus Almighty, DeHaven said. Down the bottom you could put your dick into it almost.

If you were so inclined, Morgan said.

If you were so inclined, DeHaven conceded.

These things deserve to be specified.

Indeed they do, DeHaven agreed. Indeed they do.

17th June

Morgan brought Myer down to see for himself. Myer called down Brooks, Brooks called down Cabot and Banes, the carpenters, and that evening they turned east again.

Halfway through dinner, DeHaven told Cabot to bring another bottle of wine.

I don't think we need it, Cabot, Myer said.

Cabot, you can get one from my own private supply,

DeHaven said. If the captain does not wish to make the sacrifice.

That is not the issue, Myer said.

I am going to have a drink, DeHaven told them. You are not obliged to join me, of course.

Are you mourning or celebrating? Brooks asked.

I am not yet sure, DeHaven said. Not yet having been informed what course of action our captain intends.

Myer laid his cutlery down. Mr Brooks, he said. Assemble the crew.

When they were all gathered on deck, Myer stood up on a crate. In a voice that was clearly satisfied, he delivered this speech:

It has been hinted to me lately that some little query may be alive in certain minds as to our course. You cannot doubt, I hope, that despite our latest reverse, our ultimate destination and purpose remain unchanged. Of course the greenest cabin-boy knows that without a functioning rudder we cannot take to the open sea, and it is for that end I intend presently to return to Disko and refit there as quickly as we can, and thence return to the North Water as soon as is at all practicable, before this year's freeze sets in. I tell you this in the confidence that not a man amongst you can conceive an honourable alternative. After all, I myself feel, and suppose every man before me feels, that we are exactly what we were at the beginning of summer. Will anyone contradict me?

2nd July

The sea was slopping its thick stew against the hull. Since coming out of The Pack, the men all seemed to feel it a comfort – the darling cradle, the gentle swell. Only Morgan did not like it. He felt brittle, almost sick. He felt the world unsteady again, shifting beneath him whether he moved or stayed still. He stood at the bow, looking into the bay, at the wooden house on the high ground, well back from the shore. All along the beach the whale carcasses were flecked with ravens. The starving dogs were landed and unleashed. From the bow, Morgan watched the rampage. He watched the whaleboat wheeling to come back. He was next.

Rink welcomed them like old friends. Morgan let the other men talk. They told him about Giorgio. Rink seemed to think it was to be expected, almost fair. This was how the man kept himself safe, Morgan supposed. There was no post for them, Rink said. The only whalers who'd called had all been going home. Morgan was glad. There was rarely anything good for any of them in any letter they received. Nor was there any word of the missing ships.

There was a cameo of a young woman on a stand on the mantel, that resembled the sister strangely. My wife, Rink said. She had shipped from Copenhagen at the end of May to come out, he said.

On what ship? Myer asked. The name of the ship meant nothing. Very quickly, Morgan counted up the weeks.

I expect her any day now, Rink said.

There were dirty faces at the window, looking in. Rink shouted at them, but they would not go away. They were shouting back at him, the words incomprehensible. Rink turned to the officers and shrugged. One of the native women was in labour, he said. Apparently it was not going very well. In the end DeHaven agreed to go and the others followed, all but Morgan, who said he had no stomach for that kind of thing.

He stood in the doorway of her parlour, at the back of the

23

house. Her hair was in a long plait, right to her waist. The thing looked like it was carved from a soft white wood.

I thought you might offer me a cup of coffee, he said.

Disdainfully, she dropped her knitting-needles onto her lap.

Is he gone? she said. Have we time to row out and cast off?

We can cast off, or we can have a cup of coffee. One or the other. There's not time for both.

It's a long time, I suppose, since you've seen a proper set of china, she said.

Unchipped?

Unchipped.

It is.

He waited for her to bring it to him. He heard her close the kitchen door. He'd let his hand settle on the back of her armchair. Now he fanned his fingers over the cloth, that still bore something of her shape. He brushed his hand back and forth, as though to smooth the fabric down. The cloth was worn shiny, and warm. A thousand winter evenings she'd been sitting there, waiting. He stepped around to the front of the chair and lowered himself to his knees. He looked up, to check there was no direct line of sight into the room. There was not. There was time. He would hear her coming out of the kitchen, and back along the corridor. A desperate glance again at the door. Then, with great formality, he bowed his face to the seat of the chair. He did not lift it up again. He was breathing deeply, with great relief. From the moment he stepped into the house, he'd been wading through her perfume. Now, with every deep breath, he was sifting through the layers beneath. Beyond the hint of powder, polite but righteous, and beyond the slightly charred smell of cloth, and the manly smell of soap. He was searching beyond flesh and even sweat, for something more earthy, beyond the animal – something more than the merely uncivilized.

I wouldn't even like to describe what it is I've been drinking these past few weeks, he told her, as she handed him the cup.

What that Frenchman does to it, I don't know and I don't want to know.

She caught him glancing at the cold grate.

A waste of coal he says. I occasionally get a little sun here in the afternoon. There now. You see.

They stood together in the narrow square of sunlight, listened to the petty quarrelling outside. She called the children to come and sing him the latest song she'd taught them. It was in Danish.

I didn't know your brother was married, Morgan said.

He's not.

Who is she then, the picture?

Some poor girl with pretensions. It was arranged. To keep him here. To let me go home.

It was a definite arrangement?

In his mind, yes.

And in hers?

Who's to know? Since the whole thing started he's had one short letter, though he himself wrote quite a few. Or rather, I did, on his behalf. She never answered.

An uncomplicated courtship.

The best kind, they say.

They say, Morgan said.

If you ask me, she has no intention of coming, she said. The one letter was last summer, when she wrote and promised to come, and never appeared.

This year too, for the past two months, Rink had been waiting for her ship. But the days were filing past patiently, politely, and he no longer took his walks on the high ground, to stare offshore.

You must have been in a rush, Morgan said.

He was looking at her chest. Her tunic had some two dozen buttons, solid little balls of bone. She'd slipped the right button but one into the bottom eye, and worked her mistake all the way up. With both hands he reached across the open space between them, took the thick thread of the eye between finger and thumb, and popped the first

25

button out. The cloth was thick, held its shape well, and even with the second button free he could see no more of her neck.

He pressed the top button into the top eye. It was a nice, tight fit. One by one, he began to undo and redo every button on her tunic, in the right order, lining them up the way they ought to be.

You'll be an expert by the time you get to the bottom, she said.

He was almost halfway down. The fit was snug, and he could feel the warmth against his hands.

Maybe I'm an expert already, he said.

In any case, you're doing quite well. I'm impressed. I would have thought sailors a little less . . . habile.

Sailor?

Seaman?

He shook his head. Seaman was even worse.

I've offended you? she said.

Greatly.

Can you ever forgive me?

He was not sure if he could. He would consider the matter. He returned to his work.

We must have caught you unawares, he said. And here's me thinking you'd be on the lookout for us, night and day.

I admit, I didn't expect you back so soon.

Yet here we are, Morgan said.

They've found them, and are now returning home to glory. That's what I said to myself as soon as I saw you round the cape. They've found the missing ships.

Alas, no.

They drank their coffee, calmly held each other's gaze. She asked him about The Pack, the efforts and obstacles, the accident, the return. She knew better than to ask if they now intended to go home. She knew well they wanted to start all over again.

Do you realize how many square miles it is, that we must search? he said.

I said nothing, she said. She looked at him curiously. He was harassing himself.

Get out the map, Morgan said. Even the best of them are half blank. Land or sea or ice, what's up there no one knows.

With a reckless flourish she drained her cup to the last drop. They were in the kitchen together, she was rinsing the cups, when the others arrived.

DeHaven ambushed him alone in the hall. Did she ask to come with us? he asked. The words were a hiss.

No, Morgan said. Saying it, he felt a rush of relief, and a rush of dismay. He was at DeHaven's mercy now, until DeHaven told him what he'd heard from her brother.

6th July

They began to refit the rudder as best they could, and to take on whatever they could find in the way of stores. Rink signed the bills without reading them, DeHaven looked at the worst of the natives, and that Sunday MacDonald held a service for the whole island in the tiny wooden church.

Afterwards, Rink set up a table of food for the officers, in front of the house. They stood and stared at the view, the ship. Myer had volunteered to take the watch alone, so that everyone else could attend.

In his arms, DeHaven held the infant he'd delivered – saved – the day they'd arrived, who now bore doctor's name. As though to celebrate, DeHaven had been drinking. On his head was Rink's hat, and now every time he opened his mouth, it was the governor's buckled English that emerged. He pointed his chin at the sailors down by the shore.

See these men! he ordered Morgan. I turn my back three minutes, they are pulling her off with her hair!

Down by the shore, the sailors were haggling and clowning with the native girls.

Not enough you are taking our furs, our dogs, our meat, DeHaven told Morgan, you want all the lock, stock and caboodle. So here – And he thrust the bundle straight at him, forcing him to fall in with the joke, quick, before he let go.

In Morgan's arms, right away, the thing began to squirm. Kitty studied him with a sour look. DeHaven, too, stood back to admire. Already he was sporting a lavish grin.

Richard, she said, but Morgan didn't answer.

A very pretty picture, if I may say so. This was Brooks, determined to enjoy the scene. I believe one of your plates, Doctor, might capture the moment.

Kitty took a step closer, peered into the bundle, offered it a finger. The eyes were screwed tight, with what looked like tremendous effort.

Fifty yards away, the sailors were chasing the girls into the sea. By now there was pushing, shoving, screams. The water was too much of a temptation. Morgan was watching them in silence, one in particular, and it wasn't long before she went in.

Elle n'aura pas résisté longtemps, DeHaven said. She didn't put up much of a fight.

Morgan was listening, nodding at whatever was said, but his eyes were still on the girl down at the water's edge. There she stood, arms wide, twirling, pagan. Under her shrivelled clothes, everything looked perfect. Everywhere you looked, something was straining to break out.

Can't you do something, Doctor? Kitty said. I'm afraid the poor girl will catch cold.

I'm afraid I couldn't possibly interfere with a sailor's entertainment, DeHaven said. He nodded at Morgan. Apparently it's an unwritten rule. There seem to be so many of them. Of course not being a Navy man myself, on these matters I must defer to a higher authority.

28

They deserve it, Morgan said. And no man more than Cabot. He's done Trojan work this past week.

I thought he was the cook, not the carpenter, Kitty said.

Cook *and* carpenter. Almost every one of us is doubling up.

Down at the shore, the girl's court began to clap. The performance was over, she told them, with a pompous bow.

What I'd like to know is where she got the drink, MacDonald said. I'd understood it was strictly forbidden the natives.

What makes you think she's drunk? Rink said, ready to be offended.

She's doing it out of the goodness of her heart, I suppose? Brooks said.

Of course, said DeHaven. Pep up the boys. You know how it is. The hard summer behind us, the long hard winter ahead.

Rink shuffled off stiffly towards the shore, to see what could be salvaged.

I can take him, if you like, Kitty said, stepping closer to Morgan.

But the baby was still asleep, and Morgan was afraid to shift it. The look on its face was one of total concentration. A mind in deep conspiracy with itself. Waiting to be disturbed, to be outraged. So that even the act of sleeping was just prolonging that possibility, that power.

I expressly forbid it, DeHaven said. The man must learn to assume his responsibilities.

Rink had set out a buffet for the officers, and in his presence they'd savaged it as politely as they could. Now he was gone, they were helping themselves again. But Morgan had his arms full and was missing out. She'd seen where he was looking, allowed herself to presume, and within seconds she was guiding a spoon towards his mouth. Perched on the edge was a lump of jam. That jam was the deep, quiet colour of blood. Her hand was trembling slightly, and he stretched his neck forward to meet it.

That night he sat alone on his bunk. The rest were all up on deck, and he did not bother to light the lamp. Sooner or later, he supposed, someone would open the door and jeer at him for sitting in the dark. The next day, he walked inland with her over the hills. In three hours of walking they did not see so much as a hare. The day after, Myer and Brooks announced they were taking a boat round the far side of the island, into the Waigat Strait. The cliffs there showed open seams of coal, and Myer wanted to know more of their quality, and the prospects for mining. DeHaven said he would accompany them, it would give him a chance to tend the sick. Rink, of course, insisted on going along to guide and translate, and MacDonald went to baptize. It all worked out perfectly.

10th July

He was standing at the upstairs window, watching the men below on the beach, at the tubs. The curtains were drawn, but he held them open a sliver, just enough to see. He could feel it stirring inside him, the wish to be down there with them, splashing and shoving and fooling about. He could have gone down, certainly. No one would turn him away. But he liked them wild and unruly, and in his presence they were tame.

It was all horseplay, naturally. The first man who rinsed himself off got a pat on the back from everyone, praising his frame, his strength. It was Cabot, Morgan saw. They let him go off to the towels, and waited for him to discover the crime. What they wanted, of course, was a blaze of curses, a mad wail.

Morgan watched him traipse mournfully back to the tubs. He'd thought he was done, but now had to get back in the water, to rinse off the soap. They welcomed him back like a long-lost son – hugged him and ruffled his hair, shook his hand heartily, begged him to leave them never more. Once he'd rinsed himself off, he stood up again to leave, but the others had already formed a guard of honour, that he had to pass through.

Cake! someone cried, and instantly every man was rubbing a hand up his own backside. Cabot tried to thrash his way free. He was too slow, too weak. There was a long howl of outrage as the hands were smeared all over him.

In the bedroom, behind his back, she'd seen him shaking with laughter and wanted to know why. She'd been stalking, for something to share. Down at the tubs, Cabot was roaring and flailing now, like a panicked child. Morgan watched him plunge back under the water, frantically scrubbing himself with soap. He looked like a man scalded or burned. Without even turning around, Morgan waved her away, shaking his head. Afterwards, Cabot tried to leave again, wearing a furious face for protection, and this time they actually held him down. The screams must have been heard all over the island; certainly she heard them there in the room, and came to stand beside him, to see what the matter was.

What are they doing? she asked. In her voice a hint of fear, like a faint foreign accent. Are they trying to drown him? Why don't you shout at them? You must make them stop.

Morgan merely flapped his hand again, to flap her away. His only real concern, for the moment, was not to laugh out loud. It was one of the voices he wanted her never to hear.

The third time, as a defence, Cabot rubbed his own backside and brandished the hand as he made his way out of the tub; then stood whingeing and lost at the bottom of the steps – holding the spare hand strangely aloft, wondering what to do with it.

Morgan pulled the curtains together and turned to face the twilighted room. They're just playing, he told her. It's been a hard enough haul for them, these past few weeks. They're just letting off a little steam.

He lets the towel fall to the floor, balances himself on one leg, and lifts the other over the side of the bath. As it touches

31

the water, he lets out a long, solemn breath. It is too close to scalding. Delicately, he dips the foot in and out, and each time tries to leave it in a little longer. Once the foot has learned to trust the heat, he should be able to lower it all the way; and once one part of him is ready, it should be easier for the rest. Finally, he forces his foot right to the bottom. Between his teeth, he curses the mother of God. In the mirror, he can see himself struggling to keep his balance, as he lifts the other leg. Now he is lowering himself onto his haunches, lifting and lowering again, and always able to bully himself into going back for more. The foam rises to meet him, almost level with the top of the tub. Unseen, the water rises too, begins to suck and slurp. Finally he touches bottom. He relaxes, carefully, lets himself spread out. He can still hear the men roaring and cursing outside. In here, he has surrendered to private pleasures and their disappointments. By now he is completely submerged, everything but his head.

Are you quite at home there? she says. She is standing in the doorway.

Quite at home, thank you.

You don't look like you'll ever want to come out.

Never, he says. Just bring me my meals and my letters. And a little hot water from time to time.

He watches her walk into the bedroom. Hears the springs take her weight. Through the doorway, he can see the legs stretch out.

For a time, the voice says, I thought you were actually going to go with the others. For this, she's waited until she's out of sight, safer.

Leaning back, he can see most of her body, but the head is cut off by the jamb. He watches her undo the belt of her dressing-gown.

Really, he says, you're underestimating your charms. Hot meal, warm bath, clean sheets . . .

And here was I imagining you were looking for something else.

Speaking, she is fingering the long hairs at the top of her

32

thighs. She's like a child in a game, who hasn't yet learned how to lose. She thinks he cannot see her, because she cannot see him.

A bit of good old-fashioned mothering, that's what I want, he says.

This time she doesn't answer. This time she lets silence do the work, so he tries to recast and redeem it. Louder, he says: Double windows and stoves in every room. Clean and bright. Plenty of privacy, and a wonderful view. If we could just manage to get rid of your brother, I might move in permanently.

As though to demonstrate, now he lifts himself up, gets his feet under him, steadies and stands. Maybe he'll meet a nice native girl up there and never come back, he says. A fairy-tale ending for everybody. Maybe even as we speak . . .

Mr Morgan, she said sternly, that's positively scandalous. Why, the man is engaged to be married. What kind of people do you take us for?

Now he's standing over the bed, looking down, at the way she's laid herself out. Now he's lying beside her, and before he's even had time to settle she has her hand on his chest. Systematically, she moves the hand back and forth, as though searching for a particular texture, a particular quality, that only she can appreciate. She lets the motion of the hand become a circle, and lets the circle grow, to bring more and more of him in.

The children gathered round him, almost as soon as they left the house. The sailors had given them a pack of cards and they touted it proudly. They wanted Morgan to show them how it was done. He fanned the cards out, faces hidden, asked the smallest boy to choose. She translated and explained as best she could. Morgan got her to blindfold him with her purple silk scarf. The chosen card was being passed from hand to hand. They were looking for a hidden sign. They did not want to give it back. They watched Morgan shuffle, still blindfolded. He gripped the pack and began to squeeze. The cards were spluttering into the air, then lying in disorder on the ground, half the faces turned up. He seemed to be searching through them the same as everyone else. The King. The Queen. The Ace. A few had fallen on the window ledge. And then they saw it. On the other side of the panes, between the inner and outer windows, somehow. The thing was impossible, but there it lay, with the dead flies. It was the Knave.

They stared at it in silence, suddenly afraid. They all wanted to ask the same question, in Danish or English or Esquimaux. She could ask it in any language she wanted. It was a secret he would never tell. It was the one thing he would leave behind that would not perish. It would grow untended, for years to come.

22nd July

At breakfast Myer told them to close their letters, any man that could write. The rudder was repaired. They were leaving tomorrow morning, to try again to force a way through The Pack.

About Giorgio, Myer said. Someone really ought to write to the family.

No one said anything.

Mr Morgan, Myer said. You knew the lad, didn't you?

As we all did, Morgan said.

What I mean is, you knew the father. Know.

He's my wife's cousin's brother-in-law, Morgan said. If the truth be known, I've never even met the man.

All the same, it was you brought the boy aboard, am I right?

34

I wrote the recommendation, that's all. I'm sure, sir, you've written plenty of those yourself over the years.

Are you refusing to write the letter? Myer said.

I'm not refusing, no sir, Morgan said. Merely, I would have thought the thing more the captain's privilege. And to be perfectly blunt, I would prefer not to be involved.

As a little courtesy by the ship's second to his captain, Mr Morgan. Is it really so much to ask?

Shouldn't it be the chaplain? Morgan said. Is that not how these things are usually done? I mean even for form's sake.

MacDonald knows the man no better than I, said Myer.

For godsake one of ye give me the address and I'll write the damn thing, DeHaven said. How hard can it be? Dear so-and-so deeply sorry to have to inform you, be assured it was but the matter of a moment and entirely painless. He had from the first impressed the officers and crew by his courage, diligence and good nature, was held in the warmest regard, et cetera et cetera, will never be forgotten by those of us who had the honour to serve at his side. How does that sound, Captain?

That sounds like just the thing, Myer said.

If you like, DeHaven said, I'll do you out a copy for future reference, should the occasion again present itself.

That afternoon Morgan rowed over to see her. Her brother stood brooding in the parlour. She said they would go for a walk. It was one of the first fine days of the year, and everyone was sitting outside, soaking up the sun. Before they could get beyond the last hut, they were surrounded. The faces looked hunted, shrunken, grey. The voices were imploring, and Morgan did not understand a word. He searched his pockets for something that might pawn them off. He brought out a little signalling mirror and the leader took it straight from his hands, put it down into his parka with barely a look. The voices were still pleading. They wanted something else, or they wanted more.

They strolled together along the coast. On the other side of the headland there was a little cove. Back at the settlement, a tuft of smoke was snagged on the chimney of her brother's house. The wind had all but died away, but still he caught a whiff of rotten meat. He scuttled down the rocks, nimble as a goat, then wandered along the beach, waiting for her to pick her way down. When he looked back she was sitting on a tree trunk up at the high water mark. He called out, called her to come and see. The cliff face had fallen away, revealing a dozen different strata of rock, like the layers of a cake. Here there was sand, here slate, here tiny fragments of shellfish, crushed almost to dust by an unimaginable weight, by an unimaginable lapse of time. But she made no move, and eventually he began to walk back towards her, trawling his feet through the coarse, heavy sand.

She told him again what she'd told him before. Regardless of what he decided, she said, she could not continue here. She told him Rink did not need her, did not want her, was ready to go home.

Where would you like to go? Morgan said.

Is that an invitation?

No.

She didn't care about the details, she said. The place was not important, the life. He would be surprised at how little she needed. These past few years, she had surprised herself.

He started to climb back up the rocks to the path. Sooner or later she'd follow. From that height, he kept an eye on her progress, step by martyred step. Below them the sea turned in its sleep, the waves boiled over like milk and sizzled on the shore.

He walked her home. In her brother's presence she didn't look at him once, but at the front door she asked if he would be able to call again, later.

We'll see each other at the ball, won't we? Morgan said brightly. I presume you'll keep at least one dance for me?

He walked down the front steps. He made sure not to turn around. Fear had put his heart in a gallop and it was coursing over every obstacle. Steadily, his boots chewed their way across the beach, the careless shingle, towards the whaleboat. Still he hadn't heard the door close.

For their last night, MacDonald held a special service in Rink's church. Morgan sat alone on the foremost bench. An invisible draught was toying with the limp flame. In the corner, a doe-eyed saint was pining. Behind him, the voices were singing in Danish or in Esquimaux, he tried not to listen, he didn't care.

Afterwards, as the men shuffled out of the church, MacDonald took hold of Rink's elbow and led him aside. He respectfully wished to disadvise his friend from unlocking the door of the dancehall. They turned their heads to look. It was too late. The crew were already prying it open with an oar.

About midnight, Morgan went outside to empty his bladder, and recognized a face in the shadows. It was DeHaven, sitting on a crate with one of the native girls. She was drinking straight from the bottle, her head thrown back. Morgan watched them groping each other awhile.

The hall was candlelit. Through the open door he watched the revellers lunging and tottering blindly. An old Irish jig had every one of them by the lapels.

The next time he went out, he met DeHaven again down at the ditch. Shoulder to shoulder, they stood in silence and listened to it sizzling on the ground. What in the moonlight looked like the same girl strolled past them, barefoot. Slung around her neck was a pair of their sailcloth boots, puppet-ting along to a silent march. DeHaven asked had Morgan anything left to drink. Morgan had brought over a dozen bottles of his own wine for the common table, and a bottle of brandy, which he'd kept for himself. DeHaven pulled the bottle from his friend's pocket, held it up to the moon, to see how much was left.

Rowing to shore earlier in the evening, there'd been the usual brave banter, and statements of grand ambition. Bastard thinks he's Napoleon, Morgan had said, and DeHaven had countered deftly, with a jibe about him and Rink's sister.

Later, the barefooted girl came and danced beside him. Morgan gave no ground, and soon afterwards she took his hand and led him outside. On his way out, he made sure to catch DeHaven's eye. Morgan gave him a stiff salute over the heads of the mob, glad he'd been seen, because it would give them something else to jeer him about.

She turned her long white back to him. A little later, she turned to face him again with a wise grin. He told her it was hopeless, she was wasting her time. He told her how much he'd had to drink, but the girl believed in her own special talents, and got down to work. Either she thought she knew better, or she simply didn't understand a word he said.

Afterwards, he lay alone in the sly midsummer twilight, listening. What he heard, all around him, was panic and surrender. Out on the ship, Myer had hoisted a red lamp to guide them home. Across the harbour, every window in Rink's house was liquid gold. Morgan was wrung-out, stupid, brittle, and ready to make the most of it. He would be calling on her for sympathy – a role he didn't think she could resist. Sympathy and forgiveness, of course, could easily be confused. Letting her see him in that state, with his guard down – she'd take it as an act of trust, and feel obliged, or allowed, to pay him back.

From a distance, later, DeHaven watched his friend trying to walk from the dancehall across the beach, towards the governor's house. He watched the man falter and dither, stagger on only to stall again, as if unsure of his bearings. Now he gathered resolve and lunged forward, swaying outrageously, like a ship in a heavy swell. Beside him, the sea glittered like silver foil in the moonlight, and slopped beery foam onto the sand.

At six o'clock in the morning, still singing, the men took hold of the capstan, and began to haul up. Some of the girls stood crying silently on the shore. About the ship, the gulls swooned and mimed in the wind. Morgan had been found and carried to the jolly-boat and laid along the bottom, and that was how he quit Disko – snoring, unconscious, almost forgotten, in a leaky boat trailed behind the ship.

Even as the last whaleboat was pushing off from the beach, Rink tried to convince them to wait. Myer was out at the ship, of course, and there was no one to appeal to but the drunken crew. They left him letters for the next homebound ship, whenever that would be.

25th July

All sails set, they ran along smartly under the cliffs. For two days now, a strong wind from the south had been driving them on. It felt like proper progress at last. On deck, Morgan listened to the jibes batted back and forth overheard. They were no more anxious, it seemed to him, than men making a jaunt from Kingstown to Holyhead. They seemed utterly indifferent to their own fragility, and that of their ship.

Up the coast the whalers were all gathered just off Upernavik, where the ice now pushed right in to the shore. Like them, Myer made fast to the floe to wait for an opening. Immediately, a boat came working its way towards them through the mess. It was Captain Parker, of the *True Love*. He had mailbags for them from Scotland, but no news of Franklin.

Myer insisted the man stay to dinner, and all through dinner interrogated him. True, the ice was fairly rotten, Parker said. But what did that matter without the wind to scatter it? No, he said, this year he did not think they would find a way. Neither their nor his nor any other ship. Of course, Parker told the table, I'm not a prophet.

Myer insisted on telling the man their own story, blow by blow, as though inviting him to approve or find fault. The long weeks trapped in the floe, the daily crush, the ice that simply would not be bullied aside. He'd left himself open to accusation, he was sure. Now, listening to him interrogate Parker, Morgan wondered was Myer looking for a way in or a way out. Coaxed by the lamplight, he felt something very like pity for the man. The weeks refitting and recruiting at Disko had done little for him. Since taking to sea he'd been tired and sick. He looked older, starting out a second time.

Afterwards, as usual, MacDonald retired to his cabin early. Now Myer too stood up, saying he was not altogether well. That left Morgan and DeHaven and Brooks, and Cabot clearing away, and Hepburn already in his bunk. They had all understood the conversation with Parker. As soon as the ice loosened any, they would begin to bore again. They would have to bore as far as they possibly could, for the sake of the log. Myer had even convinced Parker to sell them a sail and yards, that would let them add a main topsail to their spread.

Pure folly, DeHaven said, almost to himself. The ship and everything in it, he meant, or what was waiting for them in The Pack.

How do you mean? Brooks said. It was a challenge of sorts, a show of loyalty to the captain.

He means we're too late, Morgan said. He could not contemplate an argument. Like Myer, he'd been not a little tetchy since shipping from Disko, and in every half-heard word now felt some little barb. He would not be easy, he knew, until they entered the ice again.

It's still the middle of the summer, Brooks told him.

The solstice was six weeks ago, Morgan said. In a month it'll be September. He was tracking the calendar, counting the days. September, he said, as though that would settle the argument once and for all. It did not. It was only a word. It was still bright, close to midnight. Men were sleeping up on deck. All the evidence was against him, and it was pointless trying to explain. Nonetheless, they were too late. That was the simple fact. Even if the passage went fairly well, it had been a lost race from the start, having to return to Disko, leaving again late in July. This far north, the doors did not stay open long.

26th July

He did a round of the ship after breakfast, to distribute the letters from Parker's postbag. He handed each one over and quickly moved along. It was a poor life had sent most of them out, he knew, and precious little promise in it anywhere, no matter how hard a man looked, to tempt himself back.

He found Banes on deck, trying to tempt the cat with a frayed bit of rope. But Banes refused to take the thing. He needed Morgan to read it out.

Would you not prefer to go below? Morgan said.

I don't care who hears, Banes said. It's not me had the writing of it.

It was a single sheet. Morgan tore it open and folded it out. He began to read it aloud. First the formalities. Then: Well I bet you will be surprised to hear that Anna Lennon is married. She married James Dempsey the schoolmaster last month in Cork. They had a good day out. Everyone here was surprised at the news. I expect you will be surprised yourself.

Who was she? Morgan asked, wondering was the news proof or reprieve.

A girl I knew, Banes said. I know the fellow too, fairly well. Another of his conquests, many and varied, DeHaven jibed. Leaving other men to clean up his mess after him. Isn't that it, Dan?

That's it exactly, sir.

They had been ready for days. They were only waiting now for the word from above. Above, the canvas was slapping joylessly against the masts. The wind from the south was failing, that till now had held The Pack in place. Already the ice seemed a little looser. Tomorrow morning very likely they would begin to bore.

Myer was studying the whalers through the glass. One by one, he noted their names in his book. What it was proof of, Morgan did not know. After a time Morgan himself stood out at the bow and studied the land. At the far end of the glass, he saw another life and another age. The houses were all sod, walls and roof. He felt he was looking all the way back to Ireland, his father's estate, the life he'd left behind.

He watched until his eyes began to water and the world began to dance. He shook out his head and saw the vision was not merely private. Between ship and shore the air was dancing as over a stove. It was the warm air. It was like staring drunk through old glass. The men did not like it. They stood frozen at their tasks to watch the bergs being hoisted into the sky. Morgan stood on deck as rapt as any of them.

As evening came on, they heard a new song set adrift from Parker's ship. The voices were brazen against the rough silence of the sea. Cabot stood alone, listening, tears in his eyes.

That's not French, Morgan told him, as though to set him straight.

Basque, Cabot said. They used to rule the seas up here. All this. The first of the whalers. The bravest and the best. And all is left of that now is a few old songs. He shoved the butt of his hand against his eye. It will be a time before I will hear them again, he said.

You could teach them to us, Morgan said. Beef up the repertoire. God knows I'd be glad to hear a new tune.

It is not the same, Cabot said.

42

No, Morgan said. I suppose not.

There had been a letter for Giorgio, the cabin-boy, from his father. Morgan read it to the whole deck, with a sick taste in his throat. We had a letter from your brother Jim, he read. He told us he does not think you care so much for the life of a sailor. However much it may seem a hard life and a strange one to a young boy, you must put up with it now. Maybe you will like it more with time.

4th August

At midnight Morgan hauled his mattress up on deck and rolled it out. Still he could not sleep. Below it had been too warm. Here it was too bright. The moon overhead, and the stubborn sun, and both giggling below, in the long crazy lead they'd been ploughing through the floe. He got out his mother's letter again, that had been waiting for him in Parker's bag.

Dear Richard, it said. It is with deep regret I am writing you these few lines, in the hope that they may somehow find you, wheresoever in the world you may be. Your father was buried yesterday 28th. I am only after coming back from the funeral at Bandon, where all our people are buried as you know. He had a very happy death. You can rest easy on that count. It was a grand funeral. The bishop insisted on saying it himself, on your account I believe. 79 yrs he was according to the Bible. I am congratulating you on your birthday 19th July whether yet to come or already gone. I hope you will enjoy many more years. I hope too you have seen sense and are now living a better life than previously. The weather here is still very hard and cold. It is terrible hard on all the Old People, and there is plenty about the place I think will not see another winter through. I myself will be 71 years in September. I am going through life here alone now the best I can, but I am lonesome as I have not a single one of the family with me. That is not what I expected of you. I did not think ye would forsake me every one. I am very anxious to hear from you at least one last time before I die. I am lonesome here now after your father of course. To the end like myself he could see neither sense nor virtue in your pursuit of hardships and labours to which you were never bred. We could never neither of us ever comprehend why you went and quit the Land Service. I expect a long letter soon and don't forget it. God bless you and watch over you day and night wherever you may be.

He remembered his last visit home, calling to his father's room. He'd opened the door just enough to stick his head in, to ask was it a good time? The doctor was bent over the bed. The old man was getting his daily dose, the doctor said. Morgan chastely closed the door. Going down the stairs, his mother was coming up. He stepped back against the wall, so they would not touch as they passed. Afterwards he waited almost an hour down in the kitchen, warming himself at the fire, before he could muster the courage to go up again. For this, his last visit, he wanted the old man in a proper state – beyond the first flush of stupidity, the first grin of relief. He wanted him well enough to pretend he wasn't in too much pain. By extension, that he wasn't in pain all the time, that he hadn't always been in pain, more or less constantly, more or less unbearably, all his life. That it didn't matter his son couldn't do anything about it, was helpless, like a parent with a suffering child, because nothing more needed to be done, it had been dealt with, he felt considerably better now. So Morgan waited a long time at the fireside before going back up.

He had mentioned the letter to no one, and most likely never would. It was something he wanted to keep for himself, apparently. Why, he could hardly say. In so many things, he was a mystery to himself. Perhaps those aboard were not fit to share it, in his slighted mind. Yes, that felt right. That felt like a reasonable counterweight.

Now in the silence he could hear scraps of ice nibbling at the hull. Still he could not sleep, and in the end he climbed down and walked out in the queer twilight, under its spell. He could see clearly that the thing had relaxed. He watched the cracks breathe, felt he was standing on the back of a lazy Leviathan. All day there'd been a fair breeze blowing that worked with the tide to open everything up. They'd been boring a week now, were making much better progress this time round. He wondered would it last. He hardly cared, now, if it all closed up again. The prospect no longer vexed. Now he was simply glad to be back in the ice. Now he felt and enjoyed its preserve. On the open water he'd still felt too close to Kitty, to Disko, to home. Now he breathed deeply and freely, great lungfuls of cool, clean air. More than anything he felt relief.

10th August

In the officers' cabin, they all felt the breeze, and all lifted their heads. It was MacDonald, in the open doorway. Most likely there would be some extra duty for one of them, or something very like a reproach.

Mr Morgan, I wonder if I might talk to you privately, he said.

Of course, Morgan said. He turned his book face down on the table. It was something he would take up again exactly where he'd left off. But Hepburn and Brooks were already on their feet, and already stood between him and the door.

We're going to take a little turn, Brooks said. Stay where you are.

Too quickly, they were gone. Morgan was still sitting at the table, looking up.

There is someone wishes to see you, MacDonald said.

Here I am, Morgan said.

It would be better if you came with me.

Morgan studied the man's face, searching for the eloquent clue.

Trust me, MacDonald said. It was not an order but an appeal, and an offering.

Morgan got to his feet slowly, burdened. Do I need my coat? he said.

No.

MacDonald led the way, the few steps down the corridor to his own cabin. He opened the door and stepped aside, for Morgan to go ahead. Morgan stepped inside, and MacDonald stepped straight in behind him, closing the door. She was sitting on the bed, her legs folded beneath her tailor-fashion, her back to the partition wall.

Morgan stood there in silence. He needed a moment to let the information soak right the way through. To open himself up to it, physically.

Who else knows? he said, and heard himself saying it. That was what he finally managed to say.

Just the three of us here in this room, MacDonald said. No one else.

Three weeks you're stowing her in here, without one other soul in the know? I don't believe you. It's not possible.

Believe what you like, MacDonald told him. But there she is.

The man was right, of course. What he said was true. The proof of it was only three feet away, sitting on the bed.

She says she is carrying your child, MacDonald said.

Even as he heard the words, Morgan felt the planks under his bootsoles wavering, preparing to cede. A sickening lurch, as the entire solid world fell away. Suddenly there was no bottom, no solid surface to crash – crush – into, to give this moment an end. He reached for the post to steady himself.

She says, he said.

A woman tends to know these things, MacDonald said. Especially when it concerns herself. You're not going to contradict her, I hope. Or are you going to try to tell me that, how shall I put it, that the means were not put at her disposal, for such a thing to come to pass?

Morgan had been listening with his head bowed, penitent. He now reached out and opened the door, as if to go. In turn, MacDonald reached to take hold of Morgan's arm, to keep him, and oblige him to face full square his responsibilities. At the first touch Morgan's hands shot out and lifted the man bodily off the ground. He carried him out into the corridor, like a docker hefting a hundredweight sack of grain.

The officers' door was kicked open.

MacDonald was thrown into the room.

At the table, Cabot was looking up expectantly, ready to be amused. He'd come to collect the dirty ware.

Out, Morgan said, but Cabot stood where he was, faltering, unsure. MacDonald lay sprawled on the floor, panting, a hounded look on his face.

OUT! Morgan roared, and there was now great ambition in his voice.

Cabot scrambled past him. The door slammed shut. Morgan dragged MacDonald off the floor and held him up. He lifted a fist and the man whimpered like a child. Disgusted, Morgan flung him bodily away, as hard as he could, into the great man's mirror screwed onto the wall, in which he had so often studied his own sorry face.

You too, Morgan said eventually. It sounded like he was talking to himself. He sat down on the edge of his bunk. Get out, he said mildly. Get out of my sight.

He sat on the edge of his bunk, waiting for the news, like a condemned man in his cell. DeHaven was in MacDonald's cabin now, on the other side of the wall. Waiting, Morgan felt

47

neither fear nor impatience. What he felt was a curious kind of inertia, a physical resistance, his body's refusal to move. Strangely, he seemed to have been waiting for this moment for years. The braver part of him already knew it was true. In his mind he was already rehearsing the announcement, testing the words. The right words seemed not to exist. Somehow, to announce they were to have a child aboard. No, he thought, reaching for the brake. Not a child. A pregnant woman. It was not necessarily the same thing. No matter, these were words should never be pronounced on a ship. They were a betrayal. Of what kind, he did not know. He wondered who should be most disappointed with him. Who had earned that right. He himself was not particularly outraged. Merely surprised it had taken so long – thirty-six years – for such an indignity to come to light.

Sooner or later they would come to summon him, to appear before his captain. All he wanted now was for it to be done. The news unparcelled, set adrift, irretrievable. He sat staring at the calendar, giving it one last chance to prove her wrong.

The door opened and DeHaven stepped in. The man looked slightly ashamed, as though he had a tale to tell on himself.

Well? Morgan said.

She wants to see you.

Fine. But the examination?

She wants to tell you herself.

I've been waiting long enough.

She made me promise.

With an insubordinate sigh, Morgan stood up and strode out into the corridor, banged hard on MacDonald's door.

Who is it? asked a woman's voice.

He flung the door open and slammed it shut – but slammed too hard, and the door bounced back at him.

You don't need to tell me, he said. I already know.

He told you? she said. She sounded nicely surprised, nothing more.

If it was good news you wouldn't have asked him to keep his mouth shut.

48

She had nothing to say to that.

In any case, Morgan told her, she – they – would have to wait for the end of the month, the second month, whenever that was going to be, before she could even begin to be sure.

One week next Monday, she said, but Morgan hardly cared, the exact delay did not matter, all he wanted now was something to hold the danger at bay.

Well, we'll have to wait and see, he said. As though the decision ultimately resided with someone else, in some other place. As though no one aboard, not even DeHaven, had the proper authority.

How can he be so sure? he said, pointing at her belly. A quick examination like that? Just lying you up on the bed?

He's a doctor, she said.

That's what he keeps telling us.

Inconvenient, isn't it?

There was a knock on the door, and Morgan opened it instantly. Showing them that, from the first, he refused to hide.

It was Cabot. Dinner is served, he said, then turned his head slightly, to nod. Mademoiselle, he said.

They listened to him go.

Dinner is served, Morgan told her.

Go then, she said. Go and eat.

Morgan stood in the open door, behind Myer's back, as Myer ferried his soup spoon from bowl to mouth. MacDonald was sitting at the end of the table, head down. Myer would have been told, of course, but Morgan wondered would the man force him to make the announcement himself, here, in public. Myer finally set his spoon on the table and twisted round to face his second-in-command. Above all, Morgan saw, he did not want to seem surprised.

I suppose I should shake your hand, Myer said. But he did not stand up, or turn around properly, or reach out his arm.

There were two empty places waiting, fully set. One on each side of the table, at opposite ends. Morgan sat with his

49

back to the door, so that he would not be obliged to look up or ignore her if she came in. Cabot set a bowl of soup before him, almost as soon as he sat down. Apart from Myer, the others were all still eating when she arrived.

You'll remember all my colleagues, Myer said. He named them all, one by one. And of course Mr Morgan, he said. Gentlemen, you all remember Miss Rink.

She looked around. Very nice, she said. Very cosy.

Everything a man could possibly want within easy reach, DeHaven said.

And how many of you in here?

For the moment, four, DeHaven said. He glanced at MacDonald. It was hard to see how they might fit another one. The cabin was not much bigger than a penitentiary cell. Two berths on each side, each two and a half feet wide. The six feet in-between – 'the country' – was completely occupied by the hinged table and benches.

You'll have to excuse the cook, DeHaven said. He didn't know we'd be having company.

What is good enough for you all, she said. The thing felt like wet flour in the mouth.

She ate quietly, like a woman eating alone. There was the occasional polite inquiry from Myer. Was it warm enough? Not too warm? Had she had enough? She nodded obediently.

A bit rich tonight, Cabot, the sauce, MacDonald said.

The other men did their best to answer him, to chat. It was like the first effort at conversation between strangers. Only Morgan said nothing at all. They would have plenty of time in each other's company, he knew, to say what they wanted to say. So far into The Pack, so late in the season, there was no question of another about turn. Saving another accident, Beechey would be their next port of call.

You'd think the mushrooms would have come out stronger, wouldn't you? MacDonald said. He sounded puzzled. He was prodding the mess suspiciously, as though searching for something important, that he was determined to find.

She rose to go to bed early, said it had been a tiring day.

No one offered to accompany her to her cabin. Goodnight, MacDonald said, that was all.

As soon as she was gone, Myer downed his cutlery and pushed his plate away. Cabot, he said, lifting a phantom glass to his lips. His forefinger turned a neat little circle. For everyone, he said, even as MacDonald made to stand.

The measures were poured. With great formality, Myer lifted the little glass. The other men did the same. Some of the hands were trembling. Only Morgan had not touched his.

To Miss Rink and to her child, Myer said. Good health and a long life.

Several voices echoed him. Except Morgan, they all drank.

You're not drinking? Myer said.

I'm not thirsty, Morgan said.

I don't think he should feel obliged, DeHaven said. I think that's quite contrary to the spirit of the thing.

I will drink if you order me to drink, Morgan said.

The other men sat in silence, feeling it go down. Afterwards Cabot began to ferry the dirty dishes away, everything but Morgan's glass. Myer got to his feet and wished them goodnight. They watched him go. For the first time ever, MacDonald did not follow. He had been asked to move in with the other officers, and Hepburn to move down to berth with the men.

Morgan sat awhile in silence, studying the full glass before him, as though suspicious of the workmanship. In the end he handed it to Cabot, who threw it back in a go.

You know I said my wife was expecting another one? Brooks said.

Morgan nodded.

Well, there was a letter from her in Parker's bag.

False alarm? Morgan said.

False alarm or false start, I don't know what exactly women call these things.

I suppose she was upset, Morgan said.

I suppose, Brooks said. Still, it wasn't her first, and won't be her last, if ever I'm let at her again.

51

Morgan nodded to show he understood. Already one part of his mind was in riot, clamouring for the worst, the perfect solution. For her, he had to imagine, the grief would be an ordeal of definite length, like a body of water to be waded through, traversed, emerge on the far side.

12th August

The next day was Sunday. One by one, the whole ship came up on deck for the service, even their guest. They stood to listen, bowed their heads.

Even now, as much in station as in motion, MacDonald told them, we offer our heartfelt gratitude for the love and mercy of He who tempers the wind to the shorn lamb.

And of course I cannot let this opportunity pass without expressing publicly my congratulations to Mr Morgan and Miss Rink, MacDonald said, after his sermon.

There was a long, loud round of applause. To Morgan it sounded like a slab of meat slapped onto a sizzling pan. He kept his face blank, refused to in any way acknowledge it.

L'heritier, I think he meant, DeHaven said when it was done.

Ah, Morgan said. Is that what it was?

The entire ship is quite delighted for you, DeHaven said. As you must imagine.

Delighted for me, or delighted at the news?

They seem happy, that's all I will say.

Well, Morgan said, I'm glad I could be the source of so much joy.

Afterwards, he helped her down the ladder again.

A lovely service, she said. This morning.

I suppose it's a useful distraction, he said. It breaks the monotony, marks the passage of another week.

He looked around MacDonald's cabin. Already she'd made herself at home. The desk was swarming with needles, hairpins, spools of thread. Under the bed, a pair of her button-up boots. They looked brittle. They looked too small. They looked like things from another age, for another race.

Do you believe? he asked her.

No, she said.

Nothing of any persuasion? Morgan said.

No, she said. It was as simple as that. Talk of God, at even the greatest remove, merely irritated her.

You've played MacDonald fairly smartly then, he said. I wonder would he have been so quick had he known he was helping a heathen.

Nonsense, she said. He thinks of nothing but their salvation. Why else is he out here? Have you seen the way he hounds Petersen?

He has his work cut out for him there.

All those nights I had to lie here listening to his blather, she said. He used to read me passages from the Bible, von Kempen, all that.

Caught in a little nook with a little book, Morgan said. How lovely.

He has great plans for me, I fear.

Does he not realize you may have plans of your own?

They talked. They felt quite alone. It was noon. Almost everyone else had stayed up on deck, greasing their leather, worshipping the sun.

Did you say goodbye to your brother? Morgan said.

What good would that have done?

You can't leave him thinking you've just vanished off the face of the earth.

I'd wager he hasn't even remarked I am gone.

You're wrong, he'll be worried for you.

I won't go back, she said.

You may be obliged to go back.

I'd rather jump overboard.

Be careful or you'll break a leg.

I'm clear in my mind, she said.

I wonder will you be quite so sure of yourself by the time we get to Beechey. If we ever do.

She said her mind was fully made up. She said she'd already written her brother a letter, that she would send back from Beechey. She took it from her journal and held it out.

He looked at the name, the address. The devout schoolgirl's script. Then, with a feeling of foreboding, mortal, he slid his finger under the seal. She said nothing to stop him. The letter was written in prim little strokes on a watermarked sheet. It was only three lines long: Dear Edmund, it said. It said she was never coming back. He should not expect further news. There was neither thanks nor reproach. It said: I hope you will understand, but expect you will not. Your sister, Kitty.

Until now he'd always seen her as a coward, and a simple-minded one, who wanted nothing more than sympathy or admiration. That, he'd always believed, was why she'd left everything to come out to Greenland and look after her brother, for whom she'd never even registered on the scale. Now he saw quite clearly that this picture was too simple, and altogether false. She was much more original, and much more complicated than that.

13th August

You must have something on your conscience, said DeHaven's voice.

He'd been shaking his friend by the shoulders. For Morgan, the shaking had been a crucial part of his dream. His eyes searched the dark cabin for bearings. There was the taste of old age in his mouth. He'd been asleep for no more than an hour, after his watch.

You were talking in your sleep, DeHaven said.

Morgan sat up and sat there gripping the frame, holding himself in place.

I confessed everything, I suppose?

I couldn't repeat it, DeHaven said. Pure filth.

Morgan peered out the open cabin door, considered the corridor's twilight.

Did I mention any lady in particular?

Not by name, no. Unfortunately.

Blindly, his hand was groping the upright, for the little hook. But his watch was not where he needed it to be.

What time is it? What's going on?

Come and see.

What?

Come and see for yourself. Come on, shake a leg.

Scowling, Morgan stepped out into the light. As far as he could see, in every direction, the floe was alive, shivering. He lifted the goggles out of the way, propped them on his forehead. He was squinting fiercely, seemed disgusted with what he saw. The entire floe was covered with birds. Little auks. Tens of thousands of them.

Goggled, owl-eyed, the two men walked out amongst them, under the blind stare of the sun.

They stepped through the crowd in a silent pantomime, as though through a slumbering mass of bodies they were afraid to wake. Each man was carrying an oar.

Don't be afraid, DeHaven whispered with his kindest voice, as one wandered towards him. You won't feel a thing.

He lifted his oar. Shots would only frighten them all off, they had learned.

They killed all afternoon. Again and again Morgan raised his oar. Again and again he brought it down. Occasionally DeHaven stopped to watch him, the exhibition of rage. It was a release, sheer savagery – the force with which the blade came thundering onto each bird. Again and again, beyond mere killing, as though trying to drive it into the ice.

He kept at it until his arms were useless from fatigue. In the end he sat with his back up against a hummock, propped his elbows on his knees. He was too tired even to lie down. With a studied movement, he shoved his goggles up onto his forehead, to rub his eyes. Scraps of purple flesh went scampering down his smock.

He had destroyed as many as he was able, yet all around him he could hear them bustle, the horde as vast and as happy as ever, gloating noisily, crops gargling with shrimp. For all his effort, he seemed not to have killed – even frightened off – a single one.

It's not a good sign, DeHaven said. He flung another bloody heap at Morgan's feet.

It was true. It meant their summer was over. They were heading south.

14th August

In the officers' cabin, MacDonald was standing between the bunks, leaning forward, hands flat on the inner hull, as though to hold it in place. It was not enough merely to hear what was happening. The man needed to feel it, physically, every twinge.

For godsake sit down, Morgan told him. Sit down and eat.

But he too was starting to fret. The timbers were complaining freely now. It was a definite squeeze. The wind had swung round to the southward, was pressing the looser floes in on those ahead of them, that refused to cede. The ship was caught in the middle, and now being pinched very nicely indeed. It was nothing, he had told the men. It was merely the tides. The sun and moon would be in conjunction on the 18th, that was all.

Not quite the little jaunt you expected, he told the woman sitting opposite him.

She considered him closely, seemed to be revising some opinion in her mind.

Do you honestly think I didn't know what I was getting myself into? she said.

No I don't, Morgan said. To be perfectly frank.

The ship I came out on went down just north of Baal's River, she said. The *Kronprindsesse*.

She told them the story. They'd left Copenhagen very early in the year, and when they came round the southern tip of Greenland the ice was still in place, even that far south.

I had gone up on deck to drink my coffee, she said, because it was the first fine day of the whole passage. Seeing me up on deck, the captain invited me to the bow, to show how he could squeeze through even the tightest gap. He was all swagger, of course. Who knows how long before he'd see a white woman again?

That particular morning the gap shrank a little sooner than the captain expected, and the floes touched her exactly across the beam. She went down with Kitty's coffee still steaming in the cup, and they walked over the ice all the way to the shore.

A gorgeous day, she said. Hardly a breath of wind. You get a great many of those up here, believe it or not. The entire world seems at such peace with itself. Even the ice. Especially the ice. So quiet, so reliable. You're so ready to trust. I entirely agree with you, Richard, how hard it is to convince anyone has not seen the thing with their own eyes, that this is death.

Their cabin door was suddenly flung open, with a lovely pop. There was no one there. Brooks went to close it, and could not. The frame was skewed. It was the crush. The entire ship was trembling now.

Up on deck, the snow was fine as flour. The wind was freshening still. Morgan leaned over the taffrail to watch the next slab come. Carefully, the thing lifted itself onto its hind legs, stood there without the slightest stagger. He stood back out of its way, to let it fall.

All evening the men worked desperately to relax the squeeze – shoving the ice back as it rose up and readied to topple, and heaving off whatever they could not keep from falling onto the deck.

By the time she came up, the men were shirtless, and bright with sweat.

A nice spectacle, she said.

Do you mean the men or the ice? said Morgan.

They both have their interest.

I could order them to put on their shirts again, if you prefer.

The last thing I want, she said, is to interfere. You should do exactly as you would were I not aboard.

From their beds they listened all night to the ice grinding itself against the hull. Whatever was out there, it sounded stubborn and wise. In it was a promise he knew would be kept. Every now and then, he risked a glance at MacDonald, who had the top bunk opposite. The man lay there motionless, his hands trapped in prayer. For almost twenty-four hours he had not said a word.

17th August

Every dawn now was another miracle. Every morning, coming up out of the murk and the stench, for the first few minutes he felt he could start afresh. Before him he found a world stretched and flattened, boiled and starched, rid of every flaw and stain. For the first few minutes, it seemed, none of it had happened yet. He had only to shift his course slightly now and it never would.

But by mid-morning there would be a harsh, brittle beauty to it, and from then on the men kept below, out of its sight. It was like a visitor or shipmate they were desperate to avoid. It reminded Morgan of the tropics. The scorched, searing afternoon. Wherever he stood, wherever he lay, even in total darkness, he could always feel the weight of its stare. Outside, it was waiting for him.

By evening the glare would be more gentle, and often the men sat on the bulwarks in their shirtsleeves until midnight, to sew. They worked idly, chatting and mumbling, needles and threads sprouting between pinched lips. There would be a shout of dismay, and to a man they would lift their heads. A circle was already formed around the players, to enjoy the latest treachery. It was DeHaven again.

She's in there somewhere, he was telling Banes, goading. Just waiting for the right gentleman to come along.

They had chosen their hero. Night after night they stood peering over his shoulder, waiting to see him slap down that last, devastating card. They were never in any rush to return to their work. They had time. The long bright days would never fail.

Morgan sat nearby, pretending not to hear. There was news now in every overheard word, every careless threat, every jibe. Her cabin was directly under their feet. She was down there now, counting the minutes, taking DeHaven's blue pills, and aching for the end of the month. He had seen the date marked on her calendar, a reckoning. He too was waiting, in much the same way. A week before, he'd brought in a stone picked from the side of a berg, olive-green and almost perfectly round. Now it sat on the shelf in their cabin, wobbling constantly, alive. Every so often he found himself staring at it, or taking it in his hands. It was something solid, real, irrefutable. What the pregnancy might one day dare to become. A bald fact, that nothing could erode. But for the moment he felt nothing so sure. For the moment he felt as though he'd come into a familiar room to find the furniture shifted slightly, or something removed – and this in every room he came into, everywhere he sat or stood, except out on the ice. In everything there was some change now he could not quite put his finger on, knew only by his own unease. He looked up and down the deck, tried to remember how it had been. For all he could see, it had been much as it was now. Only his body told him it was otherwise.

When the ice was too tight they diverted themselves with shinty, cricket, and wagers against time. In everything it was the English against the rest. Today, with a spike and a length of rope, Morgan had them etch out a circle that made quarter of an English mile; they traced the line over with cinders the better to see, and he raced the men round and round against the clock.

Petersen had been watching them from a distance, and now called Morgan to come with his little grinder. The chronometer, he meant. Get your woman too, Petersen told him. She will like the show of it.

A mound of minced seal flesh had been slopped out onto the snow. It was two days' rations, and the dogs were frantic. Kitty and Morgan and Cabot watched from the deck. Petersen let slip the chain. He was grinning with a crazy pride.

A real cheat! Petersen roared up. But it is the only way how to help the weak.

Morgan glanced down at the sweep of his second hand. The dogs were still savaging the surface, too busy to turn on each other just yet.

She had forced herself to watch, but now hurried to the

side and leaned over. They heard her retching noisily. Cabot made to go to her but Morgan grabbed his arm.

She wanted to come out here, Morgan said.

Afterwards, the ragged trail of it ran all the way down the hull. Already the dogs were mopping at the snow, and the few feet above. Morgan told Cabot to leave the rest for the night, the freeze, the easier to scrape off in the morning.

22nd August

On the 22nd DeHaven came to her cabin again. He laid the calendar flat before her. The 12th of July was circled in red. She furrowed her brows, leaned forward for a better look. No, she said, irked at the inaccuracy of a man from whom she expected so much. The correct date, she said, would be the tenth.

It took Morgan a moment to realize what she meant. Already DeHaven was writing the date in his ledger. With considerable pleasure, no doubt. As though he were present at the actual coupling – the event, as he liked to call it – and looking on with a wise smile, already relishing the consequences of so frivolous an act.

DeHaven and Kitty sat together on the bed. The calculations were a promise of certainty, of proof. The voices were lowered, conspiring. Four feet away, Morgan was forgotten. He saw her better now, he thought, the woman he'd lain with. Eventually she noticed he was still there. She clapped the ledger shut. Either the affair was concluded, or there was something in it she did not want him to see.

DeHaven asked her how she felt. She complained of irritable skin. That was perfectly normal, he said. He seemed to know in advance exactly what she would say. They were merely making conversation now. They were running down the clock, Morgan saw. They were waiting for him to leave, for the sake of her privacy. He who had already seen everything, been there ahead of every other man. So he went and sat on the other side of the wall, and listened to the lock turning in the door.

From the off, DeHaven had told Morgan he would not intervene. Let nature do its work, he said. Give it time. He spoke with absolute authority, the catastrophes at his feet.

Twenty minutes later, he called Morgan back in.

There was nothing to be done now but wait, DeHaven said, and let things run their normal course. 'Now,' he said, as though it were a milestone they'd reached, and not one they kept passing, incessantly, all along the way. Le col est fermé, he said, with a nod. Anything delicate, in anyone else's presence, was now said in French. The 'col' was closed. 'Collar' might best translate it, Morgan thought. He thought of the notices in the newspapers, in Geneva, after the first snows. *Le Col Est Fermé.* Overnight, the blocked passes, the travelling season's abrupt end.

Sceptical, disapproving, Sir John Franklin stared down at them, from inside a gutta-percha frame. Theirs was too trivial an affair. A distraction – and a slightly sordid one – from more important things. It ought to have been beneath his attention, but was being played out right under his eyes, making it impossible to ignore. Once DeHaven was gone, Morgan reached over and faced the picture to the wall.

She lay on the bed, letting the news take her in its grip, tightening, to a perfect fit. He could see she wanted to celebrate, but did not dare. It was still too early. It was still not too late for everything to go back to how it had been before, as though the ship had never returned to Disko. Determined to keep that possibility behind her, she kept staring into the far distance, did not dare turn her head. She had not yet heard the gates clank shut behind her back.

What else did he say? Morgan said.

He asked me how is the father.

And what did you tell him?

I told him you were quite well, as far as I knew.

He wanted to take a bow. Not *a* but *the* father. It put him up on a stage. It gave him an audience, called for a performance, that would be judged.

DeHaven laid down his cards, and did not dare explain. Morgan stared at them in silence, with a puzzled look. He seemed not to understand. There seemed to have been some mistake. There was no appeal possible, of course. Fin de partie, Cabot said, apparently pleased, because for him there was nothing at stake. But Morgan was physically sickened and dismayed. This was sudden, unexpected proof of his own mortality.

DeHaven reached wide his arm and gathered all the cards to himself, properly tidied and stacked, and began to shuffle the deck. He worked devoutly, and neither Cabot nor Morgan dared interrupt.

She would have made a fine wife for a man, DeHaven said, watching his own hands at work.

I have a wife, Morgan said.

And still DeHaven was shuffling. For a full minute and more he refused to look up, as though he did not quite trust his own hands not to fumble or cheat.

Myer wonders if she's not a little mad, DeHaven said.

She hoards it well enough, if she is, Morgan said.

The hands began to share out the cards. The thing was done with a lazy, sinister proficiency – the movements quick and fluid, but ridiculously precise. Morgan watched the fingers suspiciously. They did not appear to be under control, but there was no doubt that this was their proper work. The entire performance – the entire scene – had been practised to perfection, seemed inevitable.

Afterwards, in his bed, Morgan wrote up his private journal for the day, and refused to mention her. This morning, he wrote, we found the canal cleared yesterday afternoon covered with a kind of thin paste. I invited Myer to come and look at it, but he declined. Day after day we haul and warp through a thickening stew, and only our captain seems not to notice the change. He has not the courage to concede defeat, and there is no greater guarantee, I believe, that we will never reach Beechey. I now look the thing in the face, with all the serenity I can muster, he wrote. We are condemned to pass the winter here in the heart of The Pack. With her, he wanted to write – with everything her presence and condition entailed. Myer, he wrote, insists there continues fair ground for hope. He says we cannot possibly stay ice-bound until the searching season had passed. Such appears to be the full reach of our commander's logic, namely, that matters as they stand do not quite suit his convenience, and must therefore change. He continues to hope for some unseasonal thaw, or some great commotion, that will liberate without destroying us. The man has great faults, but I think I am beginning to be jealous of his tenacity.

23rd August

He was up in the Crow's Nest, scouring again. A little earlier he'd seen something very like mist to the northwest. Mist meant water, in the normal run of things. They called it a water-sky. That would be Cape York, according to the charts. But it was too perfect, and he told no one. It was exactly the thing they were all waiting to see.

Eighty-five feet below, with sober triumph, Kitty was carrying herself up and down the deck. Her evening constitutional, that DeHaven had prescribed. Morgan studied her through the glass. Of the few dresses she'd brought, this was his favourite – well cut, and now quite tight. She seemed to have put on a little weight, and every ounce to her benefit.

She was chatting to Brooks now, and Morgan could hear every word. At first there were polite, reheated inquiries about where Brooks came from, how long he'd been at sea, and so on. Morgan was listening zealously, letting her voice do to him whatever it wanted to do. He let it warm and sway, and didn't resist.

You were never on the *Kronprindsesse*, Brooks told her.

Wasn't I? she said.

No, he said. The *Kronprindsesse* went down off Upernavik, not off Baal's River. Nor was it the year you came out.

Indeed, she said. What is your point?

My point is, you were never on a sinking ship. You don't know the first thing about life in the ice.

My story had its effect, did it not?

It did.

And there was nothing in it that was not true, as to the dangers of the ice?

No.

Well then, what does it matter whether I saw it myself or not? Can you even imagine how many times I had to listen to the whalers bragging about the like?

From the galley door, Cabot watched her go. He watched her bend through the hatch. Every stretch, of every stitch. Through the glass, Morgan read the man's face, staring mournfully at where she'd been. The ramshackle smile he'd used to greet her had long since fallen away.

24th August

The days were fine, with light winds from the south. These of course packed the ice tighter still. In the evening, from out on the floe, came the polite pop of ball against bat. Tonight again, Morgan was practising his French with Cabot. They watched Petersen coming in. He had rigged himself a harness, was trailing a young seal. He staggered past, leaving a tattered red thread behind him on the ice.

The liver, fried with bacon, Cabot said. He looked astonished. He closed his eyes and puckered his lips.

The next day Morgan asked Petersen if he might come along. But the man seemed to take it as an order, and Morgan was obliged to carry the rope and the grappling hook, to show it was not so. A mile from the ship, not a seal in sight, Petersen suddenly stopped and turned to face him. He brought his fist up against Morgan's chest. The arm jerked and thumped Morgan at the heart. Here, no good, he said. This was the first lesson, apparently. In the beef, he said, you lose a bullet, you lose a seal. But here, good. He raised the same hand, index finger extended, and touched the tip between Morgan's eyes. The gesture was a priestly one, an ordination. The pressure grew, but Morgan stiffened his neck, refused to cede even an inch. Then, with a jab of his arm, Petersen sent the ship's second sprawling backward, flailing.

They pushed on farther from the ship than Morgan had ever gone before. Finally, they squatted down in the lee of a hummock, by a fresh ice-hole. Petersen squatted down onto his hunkers. He had drawn his knife from his belt, was holding it point and handle and scraping the flat of the blade over and across the ice, as on a whetstone. This was a seal's flipper, apparently, scraping out a hole. After two or three minutes of that, he took up his length of bamboo. He slid one end into the ice-hole, put the other to his mouth. Much like a spoiled child, he began to whine.

Come on up, Morgan said nicely. Just for a second. Just for a little look. It's a wonderful world up here.

They waited almost an hour for the first one to appear. The young face was quite human, even to the tear-filled eyes. Morgan settled his stock, lined his sights, and pulled the trigger. It seems so easy, he thought, if you have the patience. The bullet went straight through the head, and it popped like a balloon.

Cabot says the liver can be quite a delicacy, if cooked right, Morgan said.

Petersen stopped what he was at with the grappling hook, and looked around. Cooked? he said. One day you will eat it raw, if you can get it. All of you.

26th August

They finally gained the sheet of water Myer had taken to calling The Lake. Up in the yards the sailors were roaring bawdily to each other, like sailors coming into port. Morgan made a point of timing how long before they touched the ice on the far side. 110 seconds of sail, he wrote. He had not been counting the seconds up, but counting them down. He wrote the figure where it belonged. He closed his chronometer, closed his notebook, and went to the bow to watch. Myer was already dancing about below.

He watched his captain thrashing at the ice with a steering-oar. The man was a lunatic. Suddenly, the lunatic disappeared. Where he'd stood just seconds before, there was now only a dented hat. The men stood looking in silence at that sacred spot. Finally Brooks bent to lift it up, to see was there anything underneath.

That night Morgan spent the whole of his watch aloft, searching the northern horizon again, until his eyes were full of water. He let down the glass, and with the naked eye saw something the size of the moon branded into the sky. What it was he could not tell. He came off his watch at four tingling with fatigue. He could not remember when last he'd had a good, full night's sleep. It was the unfailing light. All day now he felt as though he'd been drinking strong coffee, and too much of it. His skin felt shrunken, tight, like the skin of a smaller man.

On his bunk, he turned his face to the wall, shut his eyes, let slip the moorings, and begged the current to draw him away. But even with his eyes closed and his back turned, he could not ignore the light. He could feel it coming for him. This past week, coming off the middle watch it was always the same. Myer had ordered the hatches and bull's-eyes all left open, and by the time Morgan lay down a grey mould was already creeping over the floor. By now it would be creeping up the walls, up the legs of the bed. By now the rind of light about the cabin door would be grown to a brilliant thrill. He knew well how it would end. Soon or later the bell would strike, and boots would march across the deck. He would hear them march down the ladder, and along the corridor. He would hear the door-handle turn, and the light would come flooding in.

27th August

Cabot came carrying the breakfast plates to their table. Morgan could see he had something he wanted to say. Even after they'd finished eating, Morgan and DeHaven lingered, until Cabot came back to clear up.

Put your goggles, Cabot told them quietly. And come.

He led them back to the edge of The Lake.

Watch, he said.

He took a coin from his pocket, bent low and flung it away. They watched it skip neatly over the water. The thing was well launched, and the life in it refused to die. In the end it stuttered and failed, but did not disappear. It lay there on the surface. Cabot stood grinning, proud. The ripples settled. Morgan crouched down for a closer look. Beneath the bright veneer, there was young ice.

It was the proof he'd been waiting for. The gates were closing, one by one.

The next evening, DeHaven and Morgan and Kitty went to watch the men skate over The Lake, where The Lake had been, where the ice was least likely to hold them. They were playing tickly-benders. The rules were simple. A leader skated over a thin patch and if he managed to cross without a collapse cried 'I survive!' The brave followed. The more men passed over it, the weaker the ice became.

More light than heat, DeHaven liked to say, and he was not wrong.

She touched her boot to the surface, in a half-hearted test.

It's perfectly safe, Morgan said.

Why so are you not out there?

As though to prevent her from falling, he gently took hold of her arm. The grip tightened. He began to push, to pull. The soles of her boots were scraping along the edge. DeHaven was smiling. He looked as happy as he'd ever been. She let her legs buckle and let herself sag, but instantly both men had their arms under her, to lift her up. They swung her back and forth. She hung weightless at the top of the arc.

She sat panting. Morgan was afraid she was going to cry. They watched her tramping sullenly back to the ship.

She spends too much time in her cabin, DeHaven said.

She's making herself a whole new set of clothes. What for, I don't know. I haven't seen the slightest change. Sometimes I wonder if she isn't just pulling our leg.

It won't be long coming, DeHaven said. Eight weeks next week. What he meant was, it was almost time to examine her again.

I'll take your word for it, Morgan said.

I'm simply going by the dates she's given me, DeHaven said. He was offering Morgan a chance to contradict, to withdraw.

Morgan made no answer. He refused to regret or protest. It was still far too early in his mind. There was still too far to go.

Yet when he went later to call her for dinner, the clothes were all laid out on the bed, on display. They were not all the same size. They were for now, and for later. They had a story to tell. I see you've been working, he said. And before he could object she was in her shift, shuffling one of them over her head. It was in the Empire style, flaring loosely from under the bosom, with plenty of room farther down. She took a cushion from the bed and slid it up under the dress, paraded her new self across the cabin, those few little steps, and back again.

29th August

It was mid-afternoon. On the other side of the wall, in their tiny washroom, she was taking a bath. He could hear the water rattling against the sides of the tub. It seemed to him he'd not heard the splashing of water in an age, since Disko.

The hatches were open, Cabot had a lump of bear in his oven, and the smell of roasting rosemary and fat was rampaging through the ship, would ambush her as soon as she opened the washroom door. In it there was nothing she could complain of. It was the smell of Sunday roasts, of Christmas, of home.

They sat together in her cabin. She was fiddling with a ball of wool. He was paring his nails. They were waiting for the dinner bell to ring.

She showed him the thumb and forefinger of her right hand.

About three inches, she said. He says.

That's not three inches, he said. That's more like five.

Already, he thought. The ambition. As though the numbers were in some way a measure of herself. He reached and took the seamstress's tape from the sewing-box, rolled a foot of it out on the spread. With forefinger and thumb, he showed her what she had showed him.

She considered him hatefully. His useless precision. Regardless, she said, it's growing bigger and bigger every day.

He brushed his parings into his cupped hand and stretched to sprinkle them into the stove-box.

He's a handsome man, Morgan said.

Who? she said.

Cabot. Myer. Banes, Morgan said. Who do you think?

I will openly admit it, Dr DeHaven has a handsome face.

More handsome than me, Morgan said. Don't you think?

I suppose that would be a matter of personal opinion, or personal taste.

And what's your personal opinion?

Well, he's a little younger than you, I suppose. He certainly has that in his favour.

I'm July, he's December. The same year.

You wouldn't think it, she said.

He's led a very sheltered life. Compared to me.

That must be what it is.

We've known each other since we were boys, Morgan said. We were in the same class, all through school. Afterwards, we were in India together, for a little while. Our families are still neighbours. The story has it we even shared the same wet-nurse. Sucked at the same teat, if you will.

He obviously sucked a little harder than you, Kitty said.

71

I'd have made more of an effort, Morgan said, had I known at the time it would make such a difference.

What's done is done.

Indeed.

I thought once a man went Army or Navy, he had to stick with it for life.

Usually, but I managed to wriggle out of it. One of my father's friends.

Another false start.

One of many, Morgan said.

Is it true his brother is on the *Terror*?

It is. Even so, it was no easy matter getting him signed up. I had to pull a few strings. More than a few.

So he came out of his own free will?

Yes and no. Likely he feels that somebody somewhere forced his hand. That he had to at least make a token effort, for his brother's sake.

I wish he wouldn't rail about everything, all the time, she said.

That's just his character, I'm afraid. He's always been a man who's very easily unimpressed.

30th August

They had another storm. All day and all night MacDonald lay on his bed, listening to the noise. He felt very alone. As often as he could, he thought of Christ in Gethsemane. This was how He must have felt, he told himself. He liked the comparison. The effect was calming. He reached for his Bible, read the passage over, though he knew it by heart. Each word was where he'd left it, in exactly the right place.

In the early morning, Morgan went up to admire the wreckage. The floe had been shattered completely. Still the wind was blowing hard, but now swinging round to the southeast. Immediately he heard that, Myer gave the order to cast off their ice anchor, set their mainsail, and begin boring, due north.

Morgan steered through the clutter as best he could. Some of the slabs in their path were ten feet thick. The hammering sickened him, but Myer insisted he keep his course. They would not haggle their gift, Myer said. Everything depended on riding this slant from the south, as long and as far as they could.

By afternoon their precious southeasterly had settled and stilled, and they were stuck exactly as before. Morgan stared hatefully at the web, that stretched to the sky on every side. The wind had done its work well, jamming all the pieces together again.

That evening Morgan climbed above, as though to get out of range. And from on high, inexplicably, he saw a solid shadow on the northwestern horizon. He had often dreamed of it, from out of the sky the wicked voice crying Land! Land! And here, now, was something very like land, to the northwest. But he held his tongue. He confirmed it through the glass. After a time he got out his pipe and knocked it out, let the ash fall and flare. It did not matter who was below. Nothing else mattered at the moment. There was a single consequence now, that drowned everything else. They would get through.

When his watch was over he went down again, sat on a crate. Myer was gone. It was Cabot to deal. The hands moved clumsily. The cards came one by one, rationed out.

What will happen now? Cabot asked, tilting his head towards the bows. The closing ice, he meant. Their latest impasse.

Morgan did not offer an opinion. He'd said nothing to anyone yet of what he'd seen from above.

73

Don't worry your little head, DeHaven said. I have it all figured out. It's not the ice is holding us back, it's the ship. He showed it to them, proudly. All we have to do is get out and walk.

That's fine for us, fine mints of men one and all, Morgan said. But what about her?

She's the one wanted the life of a rover, DeHaven said. He considered MacDonald, and pointed him out. There's the man brought her aboard, he said. I wonder does he think now was it such a wise choice.

I'm sure we can all understand the inconvenience, MacDonald said. At least as far as Mr Morgan is concerned.

Not only me, Morgan said. The entire ship.

Her presence seems to me to have had little effect thus far. A general improvement in manners, perhaps. Perhaps you begrudge her the extra bed, and the extra food?

I begrudge her nothing. You know well that's not what I mean.

Afterwards, Morgan spelled it out, the future that Cabot saw. If we're caught, he said, we may well tough it out till the spring, the thaw. Other ships have done it. Or – He stamped his boot loudly on the boards, then turned up the sole, to let them see. Underneath was something that had been alive, with a definite shape, only seconds before. Now it was pulp.

He had decided to play, to enjoy his reprieve. They were no longer condemned. From the foretop he'd seen a definite shadow beyond the mist. At Beechey Island all the other expedition ships would be waiting, and they could put her on the supply ship, the steamer, to bring her back to Disko, or England, whichever she preferred.

Then our geese, they are cooked? Cabot said. The lilt made him sound almost hopeful. He threw down a worthless club.

Our goose is, MacDonald said.

My goose, his goose, our *geese*, Cabot insisted.

Absolutely spot on, DeHaven said. He showed them his card and gathered his trick. My goose, his goose, our geese.

74

Are all cooked. Good man Cabot. We'll teach these bastards a bit of plain English yet.

That night, Cabot served the officers up a Salmis of Auk.

Dugléré himself would be proud of it, DeHaven said afterwards, and Cabot actually blushed.

If you've ever had the pleasure of Muscovy duck – , Morgan announced. He jabbed a finger at each of his accusers. He had forgotten what he wanted to say. Only seconds before, it had been of the utmost importance. He was very drunk, with no obvious occasion. It was the water-sky he had seen to the west. Still he had shared the news with no one, not even DeHaven. He needed time, to figure out how to enjoy it properly.

Now that it was over, he managed to think – and instantly corrected himself. Nonetheless, what he felt just now was more than relief. It was almost a thrill. They would get through. For the first time in months, he felt certain. The thing felt solid, and he liked the weight of it. Nothing his mind could concoct had spoiled it yet. They would get through. They would catch the other ships at Beechey, where they could be rid of her. His drinking tonight was a celebration, he supposed.

Now musk ox, he declared, with time, respect, and the right marinade – He did not finish the phrase. They were drinking gin. He could no longer pronounce the word 'palatable.'

The clock sounded midnight. It was another day, another month. The world was an older place.

September, DeHaven said.

It was something that had been dropped on them out of the sky. Sadly, Cabot nodded his head. The faces were sullen. They were slowly working their way through another bottle of wine, as though determined to leave nothing behind.

10th September

Starboard, ruined pyramids were scissored into the sky. That was Greenland, sweeping down again from the far north. On the western horizon, from the foretop, Morgan had yesterday seen great masses of smoke, that meant open water, that looked like a city in flames. That was where they wanted to go.

The night before, they had tied up to the land floe – a frozen ledge lipped far out over the sea, like a vast, silken sweep of white sand. According to the whims of wind and current, the outside floe battled against this shore, or was sucked away from it, to open up a treacherous canal. This was the only way forward now.

The outside floe was fifteen feet thick, a mile across, and moving north now at a rate of two knots. A hundred yards ahead of the ship, the canal was slowly narrowing, to nothing. Gently, the outside floe came in to kiss the land ice. The land ice did not cede, and the outside floe did not stop. It simply cracked and buckled and began to rise. The first marble table rose up at a sharp angle, like a drawbridge. When at last it broke, it did so with a lazy, wretched rip. Behind it, the outer floe advanced at exactly the same rate as before.

From the bow, Morgan watched it come. From the helm, Myer was shouting at him for instructions, as though there was something yet to be done. Still the ice advanced. Morgan stood facing forward, saying nothing, both hands on the gunwale to steady himself for the shock to come. The train-lamp was swinging back and forth beside his head.

Overhead was a slate sky. Wreaths of snow were lifting up off the ice, hovering magically. Finally the ice touched the bows, and began moulding itself to their shape, as though to get a better grip. Morgan could feel it tightening about his own heart. Underneath him, he could feel her starting to lean to landside. She was tilting hard, and he could feel himself starting to slide. She began to whimper, to groan, trying to back out of the vice. Behind him, the dogs were all howling now with a single voice.

In the end she popped out like a pinched orange pip. The gate was closed for now, but it did not matter, he had seen the smoke. The next tide would draw the floe back and reopen the canal, and they could start inching forward again. They would push through. He was no longer in any doubt.

11th September

Then it was the 11th. The 12th. The 13th. The winds wheeled about and died. The tides swung back and forth. Mechanically, the canal opened and closed, and they scraped their way along the coast. Progress was slower every day. Every new morning they had to push through a brittle skin an inch thick, that dragged at their sides like broken glass. In Morgan's mind, it was still a race against the clock. If they arrived too late, the supply steamer might be gone home, and they would be stuck with Kitty aboard all winter, and perhaps beyond.

The hatches were always closed now, even at noon, against the cold. The bull's-eyes too had been boarded up. But it was still far too early, Morgan told Myer, to set the stoves and ventilation pipes. After all, if by some late freak they did not get through, they would need their coal.

She lay in her bed, with a sick stomach. She felt she was being slowly smothered, she said. She meant the stench below. The walls were closing in. By the time they got to Beechey, Morgan told himself, she would be glad to go.

He went to see her. She was sick, and weak, and perhaps he thought there was benefit to be had. A chance to brag or be cruel, perhaps. Perhaps he hoped it might be a first goodbye.

I had a dream, he announced.

Well done.

I don't have them that often, it seems to me.

You have as many as the rest of us, she said. You don't remember them, that is all.

Well, I remembered this one. Even as I was dreaming, I was telling myself, don't let this one go.

What was it?

I was out on the ice.

Original.

Hauling something on a sledge.

Perhaps you were posing again, for one of our good doctor's plates?

What wit, he said. How ever did the Danes let you go?

What was it you were hauling?

Some kind of box.

Big or small? Narrow or wide?

Long and narrow.

A coffin, she said.

I don't think so, no.

You're not sure?

It was a dream. How would I know?

You make it sound like it happened to someone else. It sounds like a coffin, she said.

Then maybe it is.

Ah! The plot thickens, as you like to say. And what was inside?

Your guess is as good as mine.

You didn't open it?

No.

And then?

Nothing. That's the dream.

Nothing actually occurred? she said.

No, but I was very fearful. That I do remember. Of what might be in the box.

What do you think it might be?

It's hard to say.

Do you think it is a body perhaps?

Perhaps, he said.

Your father?

Perhaps. Or perhaps my mother. Or perhaps my wife.

Saying this last word, Morgan made sure to keep her eye.

It was a full-sized coffin? she said, unblinked. Not a child's?

No, I don't think so. But I can't rightly say. Such things are often unclear, in dreams. Perhaps deliberately so.

Might it be me?

I hadn't thought of that, he said. Then: No.

Might it be you yourself, future, present or past? Might that be who it is, in that box?

I don't know.

We're not getting very far, are we? she said, now with something brighter in her voice.

If I felt one of your answers rang more true than another, I should say, he said. Or do you want me simply to give you a good answer, to keep you quiet? Is that it?

If you wanted me quiet, you wouldn't have come in, she said.

He didn't answer. They listened to the men's voices through the wall. To Morgan, they were a summons he did not always know how to resist.

You say you felt fear, she said. Nothing else?

Both fear and relief, oddly enough.

She let him talk. He seemed less drilled, just now. It was a strange tangent they'd taken, but the farther they followed it the more something in him seemed loosened, undone.

It seems strange, he said, staring at and addressing the wall. It seems there has been some definite occurrence, perhaps even a death, as you say, yet I have no definite feeling about the thing. Perhaps by dreaming it I was testing myself, to see my reaction. And I honestly can't tell you, did I pass muster or fail.

Why don't you unhitch yourself, she said, and walk on without it?

How can I, if I don't know what it is? Why don't I simply open it up?

It might be many things, she said.

I must want to keep it.

Perhaps. Or perhaps you like the definite burden, which you can unload and leave, eventually, in a definite time and place.

But how can I mean to unload it? he said, now with protest in his voice. I've hauled it down the gangway and set it on the sledge, and hitched myself up, and presently I'll trail the damned thing behind me out over the ice.

You seem determined to think of it with resignation, as something . . . perpetual, she said. I don't see why. As I said, it may be you're merely bringing it away from the ship, and will come back alone.

There are some things you can never rid yourself of, he said.

But you said you felt relief.

I did. I don't understand it, but I did. I'm not much of a witness, I'm afraid.

Out in the corridor, familiar footsteps passed. They both paused, to let Myer get to his cabin. They waited to hear his door shut.

Is it me in the coffin? she said.

He didn't answer. He was thinking, visibly. To hide the fact, he had started to rummage through the mess on her desk. He was admiring her woman's implements, one by one. One of her stray hairs, she noticed, clung to the back of his coat.

I have a set of possible answers, he told her mirror. No one of which . . . He paused again for a long time. He was peering at his own face, leaning in, tweezers at his nostril, poised for the kill. Here is one answer which occurs to me, just now, he said. Whether it be true or false is hardly for me to say. My mother is in the coffin. That's what I think.

Now you've surprised me, she said. The first time you've ever done that, I believe. Suddenly she felt herself scrambling, flailing for a sure hold. You've never so much as mentioned the lady before.

Enjoy it while you can, he said, with lashings of charm. You might never hear her mentioned again.

The tweezers gave a little jolt and he waited for the pain to come; it came, did its worst, then quickly moved away. Carefully, he emptied his lungs, his eyes filled with water, and he breathed again. Only then did he turn to face her. He stared her straight in the eye, unblinking. For the moment, she knew, she wasn't meant to look anywhere else.

But do you really think that's true? she said, determined to get him talking again, not let him fritter the moment away with his little act. Do you really think it's her face you'll see, if you remove the lid?

He thought again, and she refused to interrupt him.

Here's what I think is the right answer, he said finally. He had laid the tweezers down, and sat round to face her full square. I myself am in the coffin, alive. That's who it is I'm dragging through the world. Perhaps that's it. She could hear, now, the first note of retreat in his voice. Or perhaps that's merely a nice fantasy, he said, that has just this minute occurred to me.

I'm surprised you are so ready to talk about this, she said. Any other man I'd take for drunk.

Drink tends to have the opposite effect, I'm afraid. It shuts me up.

I've noticed. Perhaps you're drunk in the dream, she said, offering a smile. Perhaps that's why you insist on leaving the lid on. Perhaps you're not curious at all. She was half joking, and half wise. She wanted somehow to be careful and carefree, all at once.

Another possibility is that the coffin is empty, he said, as though he'd not heard.

Would that be good reason not to want to open it? To be afraid?

Perhaps it is not a person. Or not only. Perhaps it is not a specific thing.

What could that be? You've mentioned your mother. You've mentioned me. Who or what remains?

81

Maybe you're all in there together, he smiled. Having a ball.

Perhaps you're in there with us, she said. Perhaps you're in there with her, alone.

An interesting proposition, he said.

Perhaps what is inside the coffin is a moment. A moment in time.

For half an hour that afternoon there had been progress. Then the wind had died again. That gave them time to dismount and grease the capstan, to be ready for the next ebb. That was the banging that came again now.

You must have many happy moments from your boyhood, she said. Every child does.

He seemed physically to recoil at that, if only an inch. But he was suddenly quiet and still, and stayed quiet for some time. As usual, she supposed, he was making all his concessions in advance. Agreeing to whatever judgment he thought she would reach for. He seemed to take a particular pleasure, always, in imagining the worst. Confirming every slight he'd ever felt. How often she'd imagined him doing what he'd done today – coming down to talk to her. How hard that seemed to be. She saw the scene unfold. Morgan walking down the corridor to her door, everything narrowing. Savouring the indignity he was about to undergo in there – in here, as he seemed to be undergoing now. Her every misplaced word less like a wound than a surgical incision. Specific and precise. The effect not pain but relief.

It feels like two different people, he said finally. That woman, and that boy.

Your mother, you mean?

I can remember her cutting my hair, when I was very small. That wasn't something she usually did. I can remember long days at the beach. She's upright, walking comfortably, in her dayclothes. There's nothing remarkable about the thing, no special warmth or affection, but nothing cold either, no distance. It just seems – seemed – a regular part of the everyday.

What came afterwards?

82

Afterwards, it was different, he said.

How so?

He suddenly stood up to go. That's it, he announced. I've said far more than I meant to say. I don't at all know how you managed to get so much out of me, but bravo.

The session is adjourned? she said, as lightly as she could.

The session is closed.

16th September

Under a clear sky they stood to the westward. They were sailors again, riding the waves, canvas bragging overhead. Already they had forgotten. As in the old days, there was shouting across the spars. The insults were brazen, but glanced off the new armour harmlessly. They were invincible now.

I hate to piss on the fire, Morgan said, but I think we're going to be a little late for the party.

We're not late, we're *last*, DeHaven said. Which is far, far worse.

They had lost too much time going back to Disko. The other ships had passed this way long before.

God knows where they're going to send us, DeHaven said. Where nobody else wants to go, I suppose.

Surely a commander of Myer's stature, Morgan said, but the joke was stale. What his friend said was true. There was no telling what part of the map the *Impetus* would be assigned. Arriving last, they would have to fall in with what had already been decided in their absence, by other men.

In the evening they stared over the water towards the

undying sun, that they were too eager to serve. Beneath it were what looked like ink-spills on cotton wool. That was Devon Island, Myer said – the great northern pillar of their gate.

For a day and a night they galloped through thick fog with men hanging from every tree, scouring for danger. They were sailing blind, but Myer promised they had entered Lancaster Sound, the last leg to Beechey.

It was the 17th of September, first watch. They were making eight knots. Suddenly canvas was called out. By the time Morgan got up they were alongside. She was a schooner, with a queer little lug foresail, pitiful small, being bounced like a barrel by every wave. A man in an oilskin clung to the mast. As they came alongside, they saw him open his mouth, roar. Myer stood at the stern with a bull-horn and they bellowed back and forth across the wild sea. The voices, in shreds, drifted by on the wind. He was barely audible, impossible to understand, but they were all cheered by the sound of a strange voice.

Near breakfast-time land was announced to the north. Myer wrote his guesses in the log. Cape Warrender? Cape Bullen? He could not keep away from the map, but they did not really need it. They needed only to follow the coast, until it turned north into the Wellington Channel, at Beechey Island.

PART II

20th September

Three headboards were planted in the slate of the eastern shore, to guard three mounds of shale, shovelled from the ground round about. They lay in a neat row, facing east. Each had an inscription burned into the wood. Morgan took out his little notebook and wrote them down verbatim. They were all three much the same. The name and the ship, then the date and the age. William Braine RM. HMS Erebus. Died April 3d 1846 aged 32 years. John Hartnell AB. HMS Erebus. Died January 4th 1846 aged 25 years. John Torrington departed this life January 1st AD 1846 on board of HM ship Terror aged 20 years. Choose Ye This Day Whom Ye Will Serve, said Braine's marker, the marine. Consider Your Ways, said Hartnell's. Torrington's had nothing but the bare unbending facts.

Down by the shore, Austin's men had found hundreds of food tins, filled with shale. Ballast, Morgan said. To bring them home. All about the island they'd found scraps of paper, canvas, cloth. Spent and unspent matches, heaps of cinders, heaps of nails. Austin had found a cairn, too, on the island's highest point, and dismantled it to the last stone. They'd found nothing near it but a tiny silver key, as for a trinket-box.

Grouped together, so many clues could be made to mean something, Myer told his officers. Morgan knew better than to contradict him. His captain obviously could not think straight for hope and sympathy and ambition.

A raked patch of ground showed rows of mountain sorrel and saxifrage, all shrivelled and black, years old. It was a garden, Myer announced. And no one plants a seed but expects to tend it, or later to harvest. It was an anchor, Myer went on. Or a marker to come back to. In either case, it spoke of journey's end.

Mr Myer, your reasoning is quite sound, DeHaven said, but neutered by plain fact. Farmer Franklin, where is he now?

Later that day, Morgan and DeHaven walked the island alone. Coming over each new hill, Morgan expected to find something waiting for him. He was not sure what. He'd been to Easter Island, and a hundred times had met that stern, unflinching stare. It followed you around the landscape. It remembered everything, and could not be appeased. It had decided where exactly to lay the blame. Somehow, he expected to meet similar sentries here.

Afterwards, the two men walked to the isthmus that led inland, north. They were like tourists on a schedule, visiting the sights. Next, the famous sledge-tracks, that Austin himself had found. In places, the bootprints of those who'd hauled it could still be seen in the snow, that freeze and thaw had turned to stone. Gently, Morgan placed his foot in one of the frozen prints. It had been made by a foot much bigger than his own.

21st September

The *Resolute* was Austin's ship, the expedition commander. She sat well inside Beechey's bay, alongside the *Intrepid*, the *Assistance*, the *Lady Franklin*. There was also a supply steamer, the *North Star*. Myer had not brought the *Impetus* in to join them, but dropped anchor just outside the mouth of the bay. He's shy, DeHaven said, but Morgan knew it was the shoals Myer was afraid of. With all the other ships watching, hoping he would run aground. At first, Morgan had been pleased with this new embarrassment, that might distract a little from his own.

This evening, for the reception, they would have to row all the way over, in heavy rain.

Am I invited? Kitty asked Morgan, when she saw how he was dressed.

Your name wasn't mentioned, Morgan said. As far as I can recall. Besides, the reception is not only a matter of pleasure, he told her. They were also going over to discuss where the *Impetus* was to search.

You could just turn up with me on your arm, she said. It would give them a nice surprise.

I'm not sure the humour would be to everyone's taste.

Are you ashamed of me?

No I'm not.

You're ashamed of yourself, maybe? Is that it?

In the *Resolute*'s stateroom, there were charts on the table, prints on the walls. At Morgan's back, the room was crowded with the other ships' officers, all waiting for Austin to appear. Since coming down he had looked no one in the eye. He knew none of them, and was not willing to presume. In any case, he supposed, they had only a single subject they wanted to discuss. With unusual attention, one by one, he was studying the framed pictures screwed to the wall. He was desperate to have something to do with his hands.

At eight bells, Austin stepped through the stateroom door. One by one he greeted those present, and came finally to Morgan.

Careful Captain, said a lieutenant, grabbing Austin's extended arm, they're still in quarantine. The man was nodding west, towards the mouth of the bay. Everyone laughed. It was a joke they'd been waiting for.

They're keeping it to themselves, another man said. Their own private hareem.

And would you blame us, DeHaven said, what we'd catch, if we started sharing it around?

A whole shipment, I heard. Donated by a kind-hearted London Madame.

The last of the laughter trickled away.

Austin put his hand on Morgan's shoulder, gave it a little pat. Good to see you, Dick, he said. He was an old friend of the family, of Morgan's father. Still a junior, Morgan had

89

served under him several years, and always liked him well enough. It was thanks to him he'd managed the swap from land to sea.

Let's get our business over with, Austin said, then we'll have a drink and proper chat.

There was a handshake for Myer too, and polite inquiries about his ship, his supplies, his crew. But already Austin was unrolling a chart of the Wellington Channel. Morgan watched him drag a finger along the coastline, towards the blank spaces farther north.

He asked what difficulties Myer envisaged in an exploration of that particular sector. Myer said he couldn't see any insurmountable obstacles. Self-belief, of course, sounded better than prudence. Morgan watched Austin make a mean little scribble in his book, close it over, stand up. He came round his desk and again shook Myer's and Morgan's hands both.

Now, he told the room, let's have that drink.

Outside, the storm was worsening. Beyond the glass the rain flapped and gathered its vast grey sails, and the wind was keening in the yards, like wind in a bottle. Alongside, on the *Assistance*, he could see men dashing for haven across the deck, damp cloth shrivelled around their thighs. To the west, out past the mouth of the bay, their own ship was solid black, flat and deep against the glow of the sky.

He was listening to Myer explaining something to Brooks, just a few feet away. Myer's voice said it was the luck of the draw. Their assignment, he meant. Brooks nodded politely, but the lie and the truth were too blatant, and soon Myer was calling it other things. A necessary evil. The most daunting of all the sectors. A rare opportunity. A true test. They had been assigned the Wellington Channel, to the north of Beechey, and whatever they found in the blank spaces to which it led.

By now Morgan's eyes were sleepy with drink, and he raised his hand to wipe away a false tear. But as he moved another arm moved, outside the window, beyond the blur of the glass and the fuss of the rain. He bent forward the better to see, and a figure bent towards him, equally cautious, equally curious. He paused, and it paused, in a strangely familiar posture. Out there, at an uncertain distance, it seemed in its silence more scrupulous than he would ever be.

Slightly unsettled, Morgan turned away, to face the room, where the bodies were all swaying back and forth as in a jolly singalong. Most of the other ships had already managed two months' searching before returning to winter here, and the whole evening he'd been listening to Austin dish out the praise.

He turned his back to all that, and there was that man again in the darkened window pane, still looking out, still looking in. There was a frailty in his stance, a cowering, that was troubling to look at and would be troubling to recall. It seemed to say he knew exactly what to expect, and was already disappointed. He seemed perfectly formed and positioned for reproach. And the reproach he was making, whatever it was, it felt like he'd been making it all his life. He had looked away, and now refused to look up again, to face his accuser. He felt he had to resist, and at the same time felt it was already too late, that he'd already been tricked, into an intimacy he had not sought and didn't deserve. Still he didn't move. He knew that whenever he chose to look, that face would still be waiting to stare.

Morgan didn't know how long he stood there like that, staring at the floor, refusing to face his reflection yet leaning towards it, as towards the answer to the question its presence seemed to pose. Between them, the wind was flinging buckets of sleet against the window panes. Overhead, the gutters spluttered and coughed. Still he could hear Austin's voice, somewhere behind him, ploughing through it all. That voice, those words of sumptuous praise, whose depth could never be sounded – for a moment, Morgan had convinced himself they were part of a distant, deluded past. It was a lie. Even now, he was soaking up every word.

91

Have you decided yet how you mean to spend your prize-money? Austin said, when finally they found themselves face to face.

I've given it a great deal of thought, naturally, Morgan said.

A new brougham? Austin suggested. A new bitch pack? A house in town?

All of that, Morgan conceded. But first off, I'm going to take a long holiday.

Anywhere in particular?

Somewhere hot. And dry. Somewhere the sun sets after dinner-time, and rises before breakfast.

I thought you wanted shot of all that. You really must make up your mind.

It was typical banter from Austin. It was what he was renowned for – his familiar humour, his easy charm.

How do you like your remit? he asked.

I'm sure Captain Myer is best placed to give you an opinion on that.

I've asked Myer, Austin said. Now I'm asking you.

They had a long talk. Morgan tried not to listen too closely. Outside, the tide was yearning under a layer of paste.

Of course, Austin was saying now, there's nothing like the scent of glory for making a captain brave.

By brave you mean foolish.

Austin shrugged. Brave men think they're the equal of everything, he said, and that everything will go in their favour. That the winter will hold off. That spring will come early. Some of the things I've heard, Dick, even here tonight, it beggars belief. Men who've been north before, who should know better, and they talk as though the summer will never end.

Even now, standing before him, Morgan reproached himself the attention he paid the man, the craving to please. His supreme commander. He felt like a junior all over again. He could feel all the old fantasies coming alive, like seeds planted long before and forgotten until now. He could almost physically feel something pushing up under his skin. And once he felt that, all he wanted was to get away.

I've seen it time and again, Austin said. Always the youngest and oldest officers are the worst. Those on their first or their very last chance. They want to go as far and as deep and as long as they possibly can. The young ones always say they want to test themselves. Prove themselves, is what they mean. Personally, I've always judged how far a ship might comfortably go, in reasonable conditions, and made that my rule. Without living on fresh air and fine speeches, if you see what I mean. Because up here, of course, you never get the reasonable conditions. Or never for very long. A good commander won't be afraid of reminding his officers that sometimes, well, ambition can be a very dangerous thing. Of course, and this is between you and me, sometimes it's the officers may have to do the reminding. Doesn't sound very glorious, does it, any of that? Not the kind of a speech will sell newspapers, I suppose.

After a time, DeHaven wandered by, with full hands. He showed them his plunder. My compliments to your chef, he said. Dick, you're not eating? He was sucking sugar from his thumb. He's afraid he'll owe you something, he told Austin. He's afraid of how it is you'll make him pay.

Morgan watched a line of jam dribbling out through the fingers and onto the floor. He watched DeHaven swallow, extravagantly.

I heard about your passenger, Austin said when DeHaven was gone.

I think everybody has by now.

Unfortunate.

For me or for her? Morgan said.

For you both, I presume. Inconvenient too.

That's one way of putting it.

What are you going to do with her?

Morgan shrugged, almost helplessly. It was a half-hearted protest against the question itself.

She can't come with us, obviously, he said.

Obviously, Austin said.

Even if she wasn't in her present condition. Even if she was in the very full of her health.

93

Obviously, Austin said.

Out there, Morgan said. In the winter. He lifted his face towards the ceiling, exposing his throat. You know what it's like. And I can't go back with her, obviously.

So, Austin said. Taking all that into consideration. What are you going to do with her?

With your permission, I'd like to send her back on the steamer, Morgan said.

Tell me this, Austin said. I'm not saying you have the answer, but you're likely better placed than most to make a good guess. Why did she come after you?

Morgan shrugged. I suppose she was trying to get me to face up to it. She didn't want to be just left behind.

Holding the baby.

Holding the baby. I don't blame her. In fact, I rather admire her, if the truth be known. Between ourselves. The sheer balls of it.

Rather put you in a spot though.

Rather.

Morgan gave a quick glance through the window. There was a band of mussel-blue on the southern horizon. That was all there was left of the day.

Do you really think the *North Star* will be able to push down the coast? he said, as nonchalantly as he could. It's not too late?

Yes I do, Mr Morgan. I think you can rest easy on that point. Speaking of which, Austin said, she has a postbag for you from England. She had only arrived a week before.

Wonderful, Morgan thought. In that bag, there would be nothing good for any of them. Censure, death, silence. That seemed to be what letters were for. As second officer, he would have to hand them out, wait for the echoes, go to see the men concerned.

22nd September

This time it was Cabot, the news that his little boy had died. It was just the kind of thing Morgan was afraid of, touching port. Another reason he always preferred to get and stay away.

Morgan was onshore when he heard of it, from Brooks. Cabot was out on the ship. He let Brooks go back alone. He needed time to prepare something to say. It would have to be something meaningless but unimpeachable. It did not much matter, he supposed, once it sounded familiar. The man could be offered a few concessions, of course. Ask if he preferred to be relieved of his duties for a few days. But otherwise, what to say?

Morgan knew well it didn't matter what he said. Very likely the man would barely hear it, would have already heard the formula twenty times. Only the fools tried to say something memorable, thought the words could get through, might find or force a way if well chosen and well deployed.

The man would be the centre of attention for a while, Morgan thought. For a while he could do more or less as he liked, and no one would dare complain. In grief he would be a freer man, that no one wanted to meddle with. Because no one could be quite sure how deep the current ran.

At dinner that evening, Morgan didn't think Cabot would come. In Kitty's cabin, he himself deliberately took his time, asking her how she was, telling her how she looked, helping her button up.

Did you hear about Cabot? he asked. He was afraid to look her in the face.

I did, she said. Poor man.

In the officers' cabin, Cabot and the others were seated almost in the dark. No one had dared turn up the lamp, but that merely created an air of intimacy – for Morgan, the feeling that he was invading a private space. There were only three men sitting with him. DeHaven, Brooks, and MacDonald. Myer had sent word that he was not feeling well.

Morgan squeezed past to the chair at the far end of the table. Kitty was still standing over them. She put her hand on Cabot's shoulder. Morgan found he did not like it. It was the first time he had ever seen her touch another man.

I'm sorry for your little boy, Kitty said. She didn't offer anything more. She looked him straight in the eye and held it, determined to be recognized. Cabot gave a single nod, that was all. There was no word of thanks. He'd heard what Miss Rink had said and was acknowledging the fact, and the other fact, no more. No one else had spoken. The subject had not yet been evoked, apparently. They'd been waiting for the right cue, for permission of some kind.

Cabot gave out a tired, pneumatic sigh, and something seemed to slide from his shoulders.

Oui, he said, and it was a concession. C'est la vie. Et c'est de la merde.

The other men nodded in agreement. They knew exactly what he meant. You soak it up. You have no choice.

Kitty asked him how his wife was. The question was a great risk, Morgan thought. Who knew what it might open onto, that door. Cabot shrugged. There seemed so little room for manoeuvre. He turned up two empty hands. What did they expect?

God is good, MacDonald said. She is in good hands. He will not forsake her in her time of need.

Cabot nodded vaguely. She believes, he said. And that will get her through it, I imagine. I hope. To be honest, I am glad I am out here, and not at home.

Kitty stepped round the table and sat down. Cabot nodded again. For the moment, that was all that could be said about the thing, without betraying it in some way. Then the shoulders lifted and stiffened – the shrug in reverse. Cabot was holding himself straight again.

So, he said brightly. He was putting it back up onto the shelf. It had been acknowledged. The pain and the loss, and the pain to come. Now he wanted them to talk about something else.

96

He ate little, left as soon as he could. The others listened to the door close. Still they said nothing. They were waiting until they heard the door close at the far end of the corridor.

Mr MacDonald, Kitty said. If you had the slightest respect for that man's loss you would have kept your mouth shut.

There was total silence in the room. MacDonald turned in his seat to face her properly.

I can see you feel very strongly about the matter, Miss Rink, he said. And I suppose considering your condition we should none of us be altogether surprised at the fact. Nonetheless, you must admit that in such a trial religion can be a great comfort.

To whom? she said. To you, perhaps.

I am merely quoting Cabot himself, what he said, the succour he expects his wife to find in her faith.

He said that to shut you up, Kitty said. It's a ready-made answer, that's all, your faith, as you like to call it. What do you actually know or care about Cabot's wife?

MacDonald nodded in concession. I am prepared to write to the good woman if her husband thinks that might be of some comfort, he said. Someone would have to translate, of course.

Did you write to Giorgio's father? she said.

No, I did not, MacDonald said. I ought to have written. I will readily admit that.

Why didn't you?

I have to say, Miss Rink, I am surprised at your rather belligerent attitude towards me this evening. If nothing else, it reeks of ingratitude, considering all I have done for you, and at no small risk to my own position, I might add. I can only allow that the sad news we have had has touched a very tender nerve in you.

23rd September

In the late evening, in the cracks the sea was now the colour of port. On the land, the shadows of the headboards reached far across the snow, for home, and Mecca, and Jerusalem. The wind was due west. The ice grumbled against the hull. At night Morgan lay and listened to it burrowing in through the planks, searching him out. A cabin was being cleared for her aboard the *North Star*, but still Myer had not gone into the bay, to join the other ships.

What is he waiting for? DeHaven asked his friend.

It was the 23rd of September. The last traces of summer were gone. To the north, the Wellington Channel was a wreck, a new kind of wilderness. Morgan had never seen the like.

Think of it as sugar, DeHaven said, who had caught his friend staring again. A million sugar loafs. Ten thousand shiploads. A lifetime's supply, gratis. It's a child's paradise. Why would anyone in their right mind want to go anywhere else?

That makes me feel immeasurably better about our prospects, Morgan said.

Here and there a lead still threaded its way through it all, for Myer to look at longingly. They would not last. Even here at the mouth of the bay, the ice was now closing up.

Finally, the *North Star* was ready to go home, the next day if all went well. Morgan expected a scene, when he went to her cabin, to announce the news that she was being transferred.

You managed to get this far, Kitty, he said. And for that, I tip my hat to you.

She did not answer him. She seemed not to have heard.

Even if I wanted you to stay, he wanted to say. Myer was against it, and DeHaven. A medical doctor. He was ready to plead. He had all his arguments ready, and all his rage, but she didn't say a word. She stood with her back to him, folding up her petticoats.

Afterwards he sent Cabot in to help her with the packing, and went to find DeHaven, and together the two men rowed over to the land to walk about, not to be aboard when the time came to take her off. They walked up to the stone house now built as a refuge for Franklin, or any other shipwreck. Morgan stood in its shadow and found the ship with the glass. He watched the stiff farewells, watched her climbing into the whaleboat. A small trunk was handed down. MacDonald was sitting beside her. Daly and Cabot at the oars. They started to pull.

I should have brought champagne, DeHaven said.

Liar, Morgan said. A blind man could see you're sorry to see her go.

I admit there are things I'll miss.

A woman's presence, you mean, Morgan said. Her civilizing influence.

Exactly.

That and her scintillating repartee.

Now now, DeHaven said. She gave it to MacDonald the other night very nicely indeed.

True. I didn't think she had that class of beef in her.

Another few months and she'd have had us all marching in line.

At one stage I thought she was actually going to bite him, Morgan said.

I'd say it was stewing a long time. Can you imagine being cooped up in that little cabin three whole weeks, with just him and his Bible? Thanks be to God he's moving back, is all I'll say. Another week of his lectures and I'd be cutting his throat in his sleep.

Morgan lifted the glass to his eye, watched the whaleboat go round the far side of the *North Star*. He did not find her again.

I could smell her in the washroom this morning, DeHaven said reverently. He lifted his sleeve to his nose. I think I even have her on some of my clothes.

Why don't you go along, if you're going to miss her so much?

Don't encourage me.

You wouldn't dare, Morgan said. You wouldn't leave me alone out here with this circus.

DeHaven lifted his other sleeve, pushed his face into it, inhaled deeply.

What happens between a lady and a lady's doctor, I wish not to know, Morgan said.

She's a fine-looking woman, DeHaven said. I'll give you that.

Is that a compliment to me or to her?

And the approach of motherhood has done her no harm. No harm at all.

I know, Morgan said. He sounded quite bereaved. I never before knew what they meant when they said blooming, but the word is wonderfully apt. These past few days there's been an actual glow off her. I shouldn't be surprised, perhaps. Her personal physician has been marvellous with his care.

That afternoon, Myer told Morgan they might now unpack the organ. He had them set it out in the men's mess. Almost to himself, Myer spoke of the benefit to the men's morale, even their health, whilst Petersen worked the pump, in something like a trance. Both his head and Myer's nodded mechanically. Morgan watched them both, and wondered which man – which persuasion – he hated most.

The music funnelled up through the hatch, drifted fragrantly across the still air of the bay. It was an old, familiar hymn, and on each of the other ships men began to appear on deck. There was no rush, no commotion. They were like the ragged figures he had often seen in the fields, pinned in place by the angelus bell. They stood there like sleepwalkers, revelling sullenly, snared in the dream. There was no more hammering, no more heaving, no more coiling of rope. The communion was general. The scene had been arranged long before. To a man they stood without moving, without a sound, staring towards the west. Morgan too had finally heard the call. He stood half hidden behind the galley, staring towards the *North Star*. She did not appear, but he remained where he was, as fixed as any of them. As the handle turned, he forgot his spite, felt the hymn unravelling inside him, note by note. The machine was not pumping music into him, but drawing it forth. Stubbornly, strictly, he had always refused to believe in the words, but now he could feel his lips forming them silently. He had learned them all as a boy, and no amount of work could ever scrub them from his heart.

When he went down to dinner that evening, he found MacDonald sitting alone at the table.

This morning, Morgan said. No hitches? No trouble?

No trouble at all.

Thank you, Mr MacDonald, Morgan said. I'm sincerely grateful to you for that.

During dinner, Myer insisted on discussing the winter ahead. In any case, he said, we are well set to meet whatever trials the climate can bring. In our outfits, our outlook, and our health. Dr DeHaven, do you not agree?

DeHaven said nothing. Water was dripping from the beams down onto floor. A drop landed on his plate, left a little crater in the cold sauce. It was like the first drop of summer rain on a month's dust. DeHaven hung his head for a moment, like a man in private prayer. He kept a tight grip on his cutlery. Then he opened his eyes, exhaled audibly, and raised his head to look directly at his commander.

I do agree with you, Mr Myer, he said, that it is quite remarkable how well the thing has been planned, the guarantee of idleness and boredom, and futility and danger, for the next six months of our lives.

My plans, sir, are to persist, and to endure, and to be ready to serve whenever the chance presents itself, however soon or however late. Is that too ambitious for you?

Ambitious isn't the word that comes to mind, DeHaven said.

I won't be interrogated, sir.

101

Now now, Mr Myer. No one is interrogating you. I simply presumed you would appreciate a frank, honest exchange of opinion between gentlemen. I underestimated your vanity, it seems.

Shut your mouth sir. God damn you. I won't be interrogated by a mere . . . supernumerary. Myer's face was almost purple. He looked like a man with a disease.

Supernumerary, yes. Subordinate, no, DeHaven said calmly, the way one would explain to a child. He gave every sign of enjoying the exchange. Take a good look at my contract, he said. You have no more authority over me than –

I don't give a damn what your contract says. You'll obey or you'll be made to obey. Ship's surgeon or not.

I'm not one of your cabin-boys, Myer. Remember that. These men here – he pointed around the table – are all witnesses can be made to take the stand, if you so much as lift a finger against me.

We're a long way from London now, Doctor, Brooks cut in.

There was perfect silence. Myer had not taken his eyes from his rival.

Be careful what you say now, DeHaven told him. And don't go making any promises you can't keep. It won't raise your stock any. Au contraire, as our French friend would say.

Myer's silence continued. He had a decision to make. To remind him of the fact, there came a tepid knock on the door. It was Hepburn's stupid, guilty face.

I think you should come up to take a look at this, sir, he said.

Hepburn went out and Myer turned to face the table again. They were still waiting. Nothing had changed. Finally he announced:

You will pack your bags, sir. Tonight. You will leave behind all medical supplies, including your own instruments, for which I will be happy to give you a receipt, and for which I have no doubt you will be more than generously reimbursed. You will also surrender to me your private diaries and journals, which are ship's property, I think you will find. If you have any doubt on that point, you can consider your contract. You are so fond of referring to that document I presume you have a copy of it within easy reach.

You're welcome to them, DeHaven said, smiling sourly. I'm not going to need them, when people ask me about my time under Captain Gordon Myer's command. Because what I've seen on this ship, I'll never forget. What I've seen these past few months bears not the remotest comparison, I can tell you, to anything I've seen in all my born life.

Myer was gone. A stack of journals slammed onto the table, startling the plates.

Something for you boys to read, in the long winter ahead, DeHaven said.

Brooks was staring at him in silence, exactly as Myer had done.

What are you looking for, Brooks? DeHaven said. Someone to blame, I suppose. For all the uncounted malheurs to come. Well, voila. Take a good, long, last look.

Brooks continued to stare zealously.

The Sound and the Channel are completely clogged up, DeHaven said. He was answering questions that had not been asked. Can we at least admit to that? Can we at least recognize the facts? For the life of me I can't see why we're not already hauling into shore to make ourselves safe for the winter. What is it he's waiting for? I tell you, it'll be a blessing – no, a miracle – if the *North Star* manages to get out.

Brooks looked at him incredulously. He nodded at the wall. The season's not closed yet. Not completely, he said. There might still be plenty of sailing to be done.

Mr Brooks, DeHaven said, obviously our opinions as to Mr Myer's abilities diverge. So be it. But even I do not think the bastard sufficiently stupid that he would propose leaving a safe winter harbour to go north through soup ten feet thick, into uncharted waters, at the end of September, and the

103

mercury heading for zero Fahrenheit, twenty-five degrees shy of the Pole.

Perhaps we should scupper the ship here and now, Brooks said. It sounds like that would suit you best.

Go easy with the acid, Mr Brooks, Morgan said.

Plenty of sailing, DeHaven said. Just let him try it, I say, and see how far he gets.

What are you planning, Doctor? A mutiny? Mr Morgan, I trust you are taking note of this.

The word had been pronounced. Everyone was listening now.

Nothing so grand, I'm afraid, DeHaven said.

Are you afraid to call a spade a spade?

Mr Brooks, if a commander shows himself unfit for command, mentally, morally or physically, it is the duty of the medical officer to record and announce the fact. However disagreeable the task might be. Take a commander proposing a course of action that serves no useful purpose whatsoever, yet endangers the lives of every man aboard, and the ship itself. Questions should be asked about the sanity of such an individual, I think you'll agree. It wouldn't be a question of usurping his command, merely relieving him of it. There's quite a difference, from a legal point of view.

Morgan was smiling at all of this, enjoying the audacity, the outright refusal to submit. DeHaven had that talent, and had that luxury. In a matter of hours he would have packed his bags, be ready to row over to the *North Star* tomorrow, to go home with her. These past six months would have been nothing more than an interruption for him.

And that's a letter it wouldn't take me too long to compose, DeHaven was telling them. It's quite a while now I've had that little testimonial by heart.

You're all wind, Brooks said. You've done absolutely nothing this whole trip but whine and whinge, and now it's roughing up a little, you're deserting.

I'm not deserting, Mr Brooks. I've been discharged.

Perhaps. But I've never seen a man so glad to go. So write

your letter. Write it and nail it to the mast, to give us something to remember you by when you're gone.

DeHaven patted the stack of ledgers on the table. Don't worry, he said, I don't think you'll be forgetting me for a while yet.

23rd September. Midnight

Morgan touched the edge of the blade to the hawser, began to saw it back and forth. It was their best bower anchor, and his best skinning knife. An hour before, he could not have imagined the act. Now it felt like something he'd been planning for years. The first strands curled into the air. Long smooth strokes, he told himself. The full length of the blade. The thing was firm but yielded something under every thrust. It felt more like cutting meat than cutting rope. A minute or two more was all he needed now, without anyone coming up. Like a piston, the knife shuttled smoothly back and forth. His arm was starting to tire. On each side of the blade, the rope-ends were flowering beautifully.

Then he was standing alone at the bell, sounding midnight. He could hear them singing below. So she had to climb the mast, they sang. It was DeHaven's farewell. They had been at it for four hours solid now. He sat and watched the light flickering in the seam of the hatch door. He had left a few strands intact on both hawsers, and wondered when exactly they would cede. Lately he had often thought of Cabot, opening the letter that brought the news his boy was dead. Morgan could not help imagining it. That first, irreversible moment of understanding. The definite downward pull. Under the man's

105

own impossible weight, the surface of the world suddenly paper-thin. Under Morgan's own bootsoles now, that was how the deck felt. They were about to launch. The entire ship was ready to tilt.

Below, he stepped through the doorway with a definite stride. DeHaven was wearing a tricorne hat. A naked sword lay on the table before them, amongst the bottles and the cups. The cat too was up there, licking at a plate.

Here he is, DeHaven announced, pleasantly surprised. Our lost sheep. We were going to send out a search party. He stood up and offered his hand. Geoffrey DeHaven, he said, by way of introduction. Ship's surgeon, dentist, coroner and midwife.

The others were laughing. The words were perfectly pro-nounced, and Morgan wondered how much more they'd had. It was half an hour since he'd slipped away, and the lack of drink now was making him drunk, showing him just how much he'd already had. He was no longer distracted by the momentum.

Remind me what exactly it is we're celebrating, he said. Her departure or your own?

Mr Morgan, DeHaven said, did you honestly expect the lady to travel without a chaperone?

24th September

He was lying in the bottom of a rowing boat. From time to time it bumped gently against the wall of the quay. He did not let it wake him. He knew exactly what was wrong. Smiling harmlessly, he let himself drift off and drift under again. Afterwards, who knows how long he slept. Hours perhaps. And even when he woke fully, he did not get up. The sound of DeHaven's lusty breathing was floating overhead. Something had dared him to open his eyes, and now dared him to smile again. They were on the move. He was sure of it. More than anything, he felt relief.

By the time DeHaven finally woke and charged up on deck, they were well out in the Channel, being driven west. Already they were sinking Beechey, and rising the southeastern coast of Cornwallis Island.

One by one, backs flat to the wind, the bergs came cruising past. Myer and Morgan and DeHaven stood shivering at the stern, watching the procession. To the south and west, the ice surpassed anything he'd ever seen. Beside him, DeHaven stood hypnotized. The man was no sailor, but even he must know there was no point trying to turn back. Even if they managed the manoeuvre, and swung her about, it would have been into the teeth of the gale. They would try to make fast to the Cornwallis shore, or the shore of Griffith Island, if the drift carried them that way, as it now seemed inclined to do. And there wait out the storm as best they could.

That night it blew a lunatic gale straight down the Sound, and the mercury dropped to 14°. It was a new record. They were in new territory. They had managed to make fast to the southeastern tip of Griffith Island. Their small and best bower anchors were gone, but they still had the two kedge, and somehow managed to attach themselves to the land floe, a cable fore and a cable aft.

For no more than a minute Morgan stood up against the

galley and watched the slack racking along the ground – the snow drawn out into long thick tendrils, swaying endlessly, alive. It reminded him of his youth. It reminded him of the sandstorms of the Afghan plains.

At eleven o'clock the stern-cable finally gave. Her rump swaggered left and right. But at the bow, for no good reason, the cable refused to cede. Afterwards, it was a sobering night for all aboard. All through the small hours Morgan lay awake on his bunk. DeHaven lay four feet overhead, mute. He had said nothing since bolting awake that morning, to realize that Beechey was behind – beyond – them, and that very likely he would now winter aboard the ship, with everything and everyone he despised. Morgan lay in the dark just as silent and still as his friend. For once he made no effort to defend himself. He let the bunk under him melt away, till he had all but merged with the floe. To the roots of his teeth he could feel it scouring, sounding, working with a purpose. If they broke loose now, they would be rushed straight out into the mayhem. It would not matter what they tried. Whatever happened would happen as it did to other men. They were helpless, paralysed. Their rigging was solid with ice and rime.

All night he lay awake listening to the carnage. In the early morning, he wrote: We cling by a thread to a scrap of floe, itself but perilously fixed to a barren island out in the Sound, home to a million blocks of marble in total riot. If havens the locality has, they are unmapped. Mapped, they would be unattainable, against contrary winds, and with the ice as it is, prospering on every shore.

All morning DeHaven sat at the table with his head in his hands, in despair, as if despair could somehow annul the defeat. Cabot and Hepburn made it four. At noon the door opened. It was Brooks, down from his watch. He shucked off his greatcoat and left it steaming on the boards. He stood dripping. At the table, in perfect synchronization, the heads bobbed and dodged like boxers. The mast mercury was down to 11°, according to Brooks. To every horizon now, it was a solid sea.

During the night, miraculously, the wind died a little, and wheeled around more to the south. Next morning Myer ordered the ship flogged. They were going back, he said. If they could get her soft enough to steer, and steer her round and into the lee of Griffith Island, he had determined to try and work their way north, then beat their way back to Beechey.

Bravo, DeHaven said. It was the first word he'd said in two days. A cup was rattling uselessly back and forth across the floor.

By noon they were boring their way round the southern tip of the island, through the narrow lead that had opened up between the fixed ice and the drift. But even there a new scab was forming fast. Morgan at the helm, and Myer conning from above, they rammed their way north, and refused to count the cost. Time and again the ice looked too close to pass, but Myer roared at Morgan to plough on. Anything that was not a solid mass of the main pack, he had decided to ride it down.

The wind wheeled one way and another. The tides swung back and forth. Mechanically, the canal opened and closed. Hour by hour they ground their way north in the lee of land, then swung east again into the channel between Griffith and Cornwallis Islands, and began to box from tack to tack. Everything to the west was now a single solid block.

They bore east as best they could, through the young ice, that was stiffening by the hour. Morgan tried to sleep, but could not manage to slight it – the dull, lumbering rounds of the millstone, up against the hull, two feet from his head.

They staggered on. The rigging was wrought iron. The wind was failing, and the mercury falling still. Now they stalled, now they limped a little farther. A little farther, they stalled again. They staggered on, erratic, almost petulant. The clockworks were wasted. It was a half-hearted struggle by now.

In an austere silence, he listened to footsteps overhead,

footsteps on the ladder, then along the corridor. The door flung open. It was DeHaven. The face looked nothing like the safe, brazen face of his old friend. Defiance, effort, ingenuity – they had all run their course. Morgan wrapped up again and went to see for himself. Myer was alone out on the new ice, twenty feet ahead of the prow. It was a final proof, he seemed to think, that the skin would now take his weight. Overhead, every sail was big with wind, straining, and they could not move another inch.

28th September

For the next three days, the ship lay swaddled in veils of mist and fog and falling snow. Their world was shrinking, dissolving. Time and again Morgan went up on deck to study the show – the way each layer feathered seamlessly into the next, and all were constantly renewed, and constantly on the wane. He went up again, and could not be satisfied. It was a world without ground or horizon, with no resting point for the eye. The affinities were endless, and endlessly shifting. Out there, nothing could impose itself for long. Some other world was whispering to him from beyond.

For three days he studied the show, and all that time a gentle cradling of the ship warned they were not altogether fixed in their block of ice – their pedestal, as DeHaven called it. Either that or the ice itself was on the move.

That Sunday Myer prayed aloud that the wind might haul around to the north. The wind continued strong from the south. Every night Morgan lay awake listening to the carnage. There was a new voice now in his head. At last, it said.

1st October

The officers' cabin door was open, and the cold air was charging in. MacDonald, dripping, stood at the threshold, but did not step inside.

Mr Morgan, he said. I wonder would you mind coming with me.

Morgan closed his book and pushed himself to his feet. What now? he said. It had been MacDonald's watch. He reached for his oilskins, the stiff empty moulting hanging from a hook on the wall.

No need for that, MacDonald said. He was still out there in the dark corridor. Please, the voice said. You need to come with me.

A minute later, Morgan was standing in silence in MacDonald's cabin, staring at the physical block of her, laid out on the bed. She seemed not to have heard him enter. He watched her blink, and blink again, impossibly slow. He looked her up and down, head to toe. The evidence was irrefutable.

Without a word, he began to turn away from her, towards the man who'd betrayed him, again. He was turning, and watching himself turn. Both feet swivelling on the spot, the way he'd been taught. Twisting at the knee and then at the hip, the shoulders coming round last, the momentum flinging the arm out, his fist pulling his whole body with it, towards a point where he would lose balance – a point just behind MacDonald's head.

The arm moved out and back, out and back, as a piston would. The shock of it had to go straight through the wrist, and straight through the elbow. The force of it had to come from the shoulder.

Don't hit the head, he coached himself. Hit *through* the head. Drive *through* it to what's on the other side. That was the secret. Imagine a man just behind the man. A head just behind the head. That's what they told you at the gymnasium. That's what you were aiming for.

He'd been boxing all winter, stuck in London waiting for the ship to come down from Aberdeen, and his arms were as good as they'd ever been.

From time to time he shook out the hand, making sure to fold the fingers over right, to tuck in the thumb, to make the whole thing a single solid block of bone. He wanted to be sure and not break anything. Already he could see DeHaven's smile, when the news was announced. He did not want to give him the chance of a smile extra. He did not want to have to go and ask him for help. He took a step to the side to hit another part of the face. Little by little the head was loosening up, rolling from side to side, like a puppet's head. He could feel the whole arm warming up nicely, getting stronger at each punch, more relaxed. The arm kept moving in and out, towards what was left of MacDonald's face. As though reaching for – or through – the pain. The thing was quite messy by now, but that mattered none. Bettered or worsed, the face would never be his own. It was something he'd been born with, and born to. It was merely something the world looked through, to see the resemblances. The faces of those who'd made him. That's all it was. That's all he'd ever be. Leftovers. That's all you got.

Between his feet was a bucket of snow, that he'd asked Cabot to bring down, when they came to carry MacDonald away. The snow was for his right hand, what had been his fist, and his fist was pushed deep down into it, red hot.

He sat on the edge of his bunk without moving, alert to every sound aboard. He could hear nothing but the shy whisperings of his bucket of snow. The ship had been abandoned, it seemed. He wondered how many stitches DeHaven would have to work into the face. He wondered was the light good enough to work in, below. He saw MacDonald laid out in the main mess. Cabot holding the lamp. The whole ship leaning in to get a closer look at the new face Morgan had given him, trying to look through it to see the face he had before.

He looked around. From the moment he'd stepped into MacDonald's cabin, the ship had definitely changed. The distance between the walls, the height of the ceilings and doors – everything now seemed ever so slightly compacted, a mere inch or two. It felt like a house revisited for the first time since childhood. Nothing you'd notice with the naked eye, but the proportions no longer felt quite right. Even the size of the bunks and tables and chairs seemed to have been tampered with, deliberately, to make a man feel ill at ease. He'd spent months organizing it for himself, for the longer winter ahead. All those places to hide and tidy things away, offer himself the impression of order. The partition walls, purpose built. The shelves fitted around posts. His own desk in the corner, not three feet square, but which he insisted remain undefiled by the rest of the world and its business – a clean, uncluttered space for his mind. Now, in an instant, that was all something to be defended, against an invasion guaranteed to succeed. Before, she had merely been a passenger, from Disko to Beechey. Now she would begin making the ship her own. She would bully out all the space she wanted for herself and her baby – of that he had no doubt. She would make herself a home. And he – like every one of them – would have to take a step backward, to make way.

When he heard the door-handle turning, Morgan drew his hand up out of the bucket of snow. To the wrist the flesh was pink, and tingling. DeHaven stood before him, looking slightly ashamed.

Well? Morgan said.

He'll be even uglier than before, DeHaven said. But no permanent damage. Apart perhaps his pride.

I'll have to be punished, I suppose, Morgan said. After all, we can't have that kind of thing aboard. If everyone suddenly started smashing everyone else's face in, who knows where it might end?

Don't worry, DeHaven said. Myer needs you. Now more than ever before. I'd like to look at that hand.

That's true, Morgan said. He needs me. He does. I hadn't thought of that. Poor Myer, I'm afraid I've put him in something of a spot.

DeHaven flapped the thing to and fro at the wrist. Does that hurt? he said.

What I don't understand is *why*? Morgan said. What does she think she has to gain?

Women, DeHaven said. Always the first to cry, and the last to give up hope.

He found her presenting her profile to MacDonald's great man's mirror, hands flat on her hips, stretching the cloth tight. She seemed utterly immune, protected, chosen.

Proud of yourself? he asked.

Yes, she said.

You want to be bigger, don't you? he said. Her waist was perhaps a little thicker, but he really could not say. Had he not known she was with child, he would have noticed no difference at all.

Yes I do, she said.

A belly just like Banes. That's what you want.

Only Banes isn't great with child. He's fat.

An imposter.

Exactly.

Why did he do it? Morgan said.

Banes? What did Banes do?

You know well who I mean. Why did he bring you back?

Do you think he forced me?

But what's the good of it?

I suppose he wanted to punish you. Force you to face your responsibilities.

So you get to see me squirm a little longer. You and everyone else aboard. I hope you all enjoy the spectacle. I hope it's worth the trouble. Because now you're stuck out here. A woman in your condition. Drifting north, and winter coming on. What a wonderful idea that was.

So it was for my own good you sent me away? Is that what you're saying now?

Was it for your own good you came back? Or was it merely to punish me?

The bell shyly summoned them to dinner. She seemed not to hear. She was stroking her belly with the flat of her hand, owning it. It was a habit by now, almost a tic. At Disko, he seemed to remember, she used to twist the stray ends of her hair.

DeHaven says I shouldn't be surprised, Morgan said.

Does he now?

Do you know what he says about women? He says they're always the first to cry, and the last to leave. This from your best friend, your closest ally, Morgan said. He was testing, prodding, to see where the armour might cede.

She refused to react. She had returned to the glass. It was an audition, for a new role. She was a debutante before the ball, fluffing herself up.

What do you think? she said.

To be perfectly frank, he said, they look much the same to me.

Don't worry, you'll have plenty more to admire soon enough.

He didn't answer. The future, for him, was not something they would share.

I don't mean to offend you, he said, but if I wanted a woman with an ample bosom, I imagine I would have chosen someone else. I think that's the least we can say.

I suppose I could take that as a compliment, if compliments were what I was after.

Still she was staring into the mirror, where admiration was guaranteed. Now there was a loud bang on the door.

Coming! Morgan roared.

Don't shout, she pleaded. It's bad enough for him as it is, with all this other noise.

I should go get the organ, should I? A little lullaby, to send him to sleep?

Precisely, she said. That's precisely what we need.

This, now, was the newest word in her vocabulary. We. It was an alliance, that she wanted him to join.

In the officers' cabin, he stood in the open door in silence, behind Myer's back, as Myer lifted one spoon of soup after another to his mouth. MacDonald was sitting at the end of

115

the table, head down. There were two empty places, fully set. One on each side of the table, at opposite ends.

Miss Rink is not eating with us tonight, Morgan said. She's not feeling entirely well.

Myer had stalled his spoon, but he did not stand up, or turn around.

Mr MacDonald, Morgan said. I am sorry for your face. I was angry. I hope you can understand.

Well, Myer said. That's being very much a man about it. Mr MacDonald, I'm sure you'll accept the apology. Cabot, I think we're ready for the meat.

2nd October

He went to see her again. As long as the storm lasted, there was little else to do. But, standing outside her door, something told him not to knock, to linger. There were voices at the far end of the corridor, in the main mess. He stepped closer, stood and listened to DeHaven explaining everything to the men. He was explaining – insisting – that if Myer let the ship drift any farther north, he would pronounce the man unfit to command. All along Morgan had thought they were merely mocking their situation, their helplessness, themselves. But now he saw DeHaven actually believed there was someone to blame, and something to be done.

On medical matters, my word is final, DeHaven told them.

Myer will say you were against him from the start.

Paranoia, DeHaven said.

It was call and response. The man had already decided – imagined – everything. Morgan was to assume command, turn the ship about, push as far south as possible, and find a safe spot to wait out the siege. That was all he had to do. That was the new role they'd written for him.

And come spring, DeHaven was saying, the first chance we get, Disko, and then home.

They were all idle promises, useless threats. They were drifting north. They had already drifted too far. In command, Morgan would be no more able to direct the ship than any other man. It was as well to let Myer in charge. They had crossed an invisible line. Only DeHaven and his disciples were able to pretend otherwise.

That evening he reread his wife's letters, those he'd brought along. He even reread some of his own, that he'd never sent. They were an old history book taken down off the shelf. Forgotten wars, pointless campaigns. They had been so important then, to those involved, and now read like childish spats, where everyone seemed absolutely determined to fight.

3rd October

At four he rose to take the watch with Cabot, and found him waiting in the galley, huddled up against the oven, and sipping at the jug of the spirit-lamp. They put on their hats and hoods and veils, their mittens, their furs, and each took a last warm breath, and together they stepped out. In the moonlight the floe looked like a slab of granite dropped from a height, that had shattered very nicely indeed. Underneath, the Kraken were brawling. They watched the ice shift. They watched the narrowing gap. Gently, the first slab touched the wood, and began to squeeze.

They watched it rise, and watched it pile. Unseen, he knew, slabs were also being driven downwards, and prying the ship up, as a crowbar would. He wondered how that sounded below. He wondered how it sounded in her cabin, inside her.

She began to groan. She began to tremble. Still the ice kept grinding itself to pieces against the hull. She weighed over one hundred and fifty tons, but now actually leapt up out of the vice. It felt as though she'd struck a rock, and Cabot's hand shot out to catch Morgan's arm.

Cabot, he said, I do hope we'll not have any show of unmanly emotion.

Of course not, Cabot said from behind his veil. He'd lost his balance, that was all.

Morgan smiled at the explanation, but something had tightened in his heart. It would be a long night – three hours more – trying to keep the man calm, trying to convince him the ship was not about to be crushed to matchsticks. In the end he said nothing, because there was nothing he could say that was not a blatant lie.

The second their watch was over, Morgan went down. Very quietly, he opened her door. She seemed at peace, harmless, but then opened her eyes. Somehow she'd heard him come in. He asked how the night had been, how she felt. A little tired, she said. A little thirsty. He brought her a cup of tea. He watched her sip at it cautiously. They talked awhile, and he tried to describe how it was outside, above.

He sat flapping through one of her magazines, looked up again. She had closed her eyes just for a moment, and dozed off. The cup was balanced on her belly. Inside it, the tea was echoing invisible shocks. Through the hull he could hear the noise of another world, the working parties and the ice, the rival industries. It seemed impossibly far and dangerously close.

He took and set the cup on the locker. She did not wake. He leaned back in his chair and let himself stare. She looked no bigger than before, but the clothes definitely seemed tighter. Whenever she left them, the eyes followed her all the way out the door. Watching them, Morgan was watching himself, back in Disko, all those months before.

He stared awhile, but his own eyelids wanted to come down. She had by far the warmest cabin aboard. He tried again to hear the hammering from a distant, safe place. The noise dulled and blunted by a wall of flesh. Like a distant knocking at the gate. He felt a certain solidarity. Alone with her in the cabin. Trapped in and shut out. At times he felt he was studying her through the glass, watching her move farther and farther away from him, day after day. The day before, he'd watched her stepping out of her bath. She had insisted on his staying with her, saying she was afraid she might slip. He knew she wanted to be admired. She stood there with the water running off her, the skin slick and shining and tight. Flaunting what it was she'd done to herself. He'd struggled not to stare. This was not the woman he'd known in Disko. This was someone else.

All through the morning, hour after hour, the ice rose up relentlessly, to the level of the deck, then level with the bulwarks, then higher again. They worked like horses through the afternoon, every man, with shovels and oars and boat-hooks, trying to keep the slabs at bay. Early in the evening, taking pity, the ice slackened its grip. There were a last few whimpers about supper-time, then nothing more. Most of them were too tired to eat, too tired to undress, fell onto their bunks. Morgan, like the rest, slept in his boots, and that night he dreamt he was alone in a house, naked, with wardrobes full of women's clothes.

4th October

Cabot was sitting alone in the galley when they came in. Between his forearms sat a plate of cold mush. In his hand was an empty glass. The stove was crowded with dirty pots. Morgan and Kitty sat opposite. He'd not yet spoken, had barely moved, but to Morgan it looked like his evening was already well under way. He was drinking more now, in a quiet, dedicated way.

I'd say he has a young thing in every port, Cabot said suddenly. He'd been prodding his food with his fork, as if he hadn't even noticed them arrive.

Hopping from one bed into the other, I'd say, Kitty said.

I hope you're taking good care of him, Cabot said.

Very good care, she said. The Pasha in his hareem is not better served.

I'd say she's good, Cabot told no one in particular. I'd say she knows well enough where to fit the spout. As you say.

Morgan knew well he wouldn't leave it at that. He was in one of his states. He'd keep going until they wouldn't put up with any more or until he couldn't come up with worse. Soon he was talking about his wife, and what she liked. Drunk, he could think of nothing more daring than confidence.

A real lady you think, when you meet her, Cabot said. But I tell you, once when you put a little wine into her, she's a dog.

We all have our crosses to bear, Morgan said with a smile, but he pitied the man, his near horizons, and how little he had left to defile.

In the end Kitty said a few quiet words, trying to calm him without giving him an excuse to flare up. Cabot gave no sign he heard. He checked the level of his glass, filled it up. Then the saltcellar was somehow knocked over, and Kitty reached for a pinch, to flick over her shoulder.

Leave it, Cabot said quietly, still staring at his plate.

It's bad luck, she said, smiling. Her hand was stalled in mid-air. She still had a smile between her teeth, but she'd heard the iron in Cabot's voice.

Cabot lifted his head and looked her straight in the face.

Bad luck? he said, and he sounded confused. That means things could get worse? Is that what you mean? He looked her straight in the eye, waiting for the explanation. Go on, he said. I'm listening. I am only ears, like you say. Allez! He was shouting now, wild-eyed, choking on the words, spit spraying in all directions.

Day after day, week after week, he stood in the galley punching holes in metal tins. Ever since the news of his boy, all he wanted to do was drink and sleep. He had grown thin. Overnight, he had grown old. Now he looked like he'd been whipped. Eventually he blew himself out. He'd been tired and shamed and determined to make the most of it. Morgan felt sorry for him, and embarrassed, because he hadn't yet learned how to hide behind himself.

A little later Cabot swaggered off to empty his bladder. He's just drunk, Morgan told her. Because of his little boy, he meant. She'd just been in the wrong place at the wrong time, Morgan told her, but there was more to it than that. From the day she came out of MacDonald's cabin, Cabot had been watching her. Tonight she'd set her swollen body opposite him, began to manoeuvre it, and dared him not to admire.

Where do you think he's gone? she said. He still had not come back.

There's a fair chance he just lay down on the ice, Morgan said. Unless one of his friends goes out to get him, he'll fall asleep and freeze to death.

Apparently a rather pleasant way to go, she said.

Apparently so.

5th October

Crushed and blind, it was hard to imagine they were still being driven north; they'd had no observation now for three days, and Myer refused to believe it, as he refused to believe that winter had definitely set in. Except for her cabin, he still refused to let them set up the stoves, as though this must necessarily stave off the worst of the cold.

Then, early on the morning of the 5th, to the west, through thick fog, Morgan thought he spotted something like a headland. Their last bearings had put Beechey more than fifty miles to the south. They tried sounding, but could find no bottom, even with the hundred fathom line. They could not say where they were.

The barometer was falling. The deck was covered in snow as dry as eiderdown, knee-deep. On the galley roof sat a lone raven, huddled there in stern judgement. It was one of their old friends from Beechey, the one with the cloudy eye – the only one who had not yet abandoned them.

They hove to and bore up about breakfast-time. Morgan thought he'd snatched another glimpse of something solid through the veils, due west, but could not say for sure. They ran on until mid-morning, until the fog started to come off. Something very like a coastline was pushing through. The rest of the fog came away, and he told the helmsman to stand off, until he could properly fix the ship. But the headland opposite resembled nothing on their charts.

Inland, there was rock and ice and frozen snow and nothing else, as far as the eye could see. As bleak a country as I have ever seen, he wrote. Beside it, Disko is a pleasure garden.

A nice prospect, DeHaven said. He was too impressed, and trying to stir up a little scorn.

Morgan did not answer. It was too soon to summon a front. He stood there marvelling morbidly. It was a dismal spot, without the slightest tint to the sterility. This would be their refuge, if they were crushed.

By dinner-time the sun had dropped low enough to block

out something like a line of hills much farther to the north-west. It was more of Cornwallis, or some northern reach of Devon Island, or an altogether new and unknown part of the globe. Between the ship and it, there was a wall of ice the colour of granite. In the log, Myer was already calling it The Fixed Ice, as though to reassure himself they could go no farther, that this year's limit had finally been set.

8th October

It was the 8th of October. The air was alive with a million specks of light. The sky was remarkably clear, and Morgan spent all morning aloft, scouring for anything that was not white. Far out in the Channel he could see the black lines, the great rivers like open wounds, the steam rising from every one as from a hot spring. Down on the deck, they could see none of that. They were down there now, laying bets with Petersen on what they could get the dogs to eat.

By noon the southern skies were ablaze. The low sun caught the masts to the root, and their shadows stretched farther north than he could see. He let the shadows lead his eye, and at the very edge of the northern horizon spotted something being carried through the air. He watched it drift over and beyond the ragged line. It looked like a courier balloon. But who would have sent it up, and to what end? Franklin, he knew, had been equipped with several, as they themselves were. Still, he did not call it out, or call anyone to come and confirm what he thought he saw. This was a secret he wanted all to himself.

He'd done his sums. He'd made his observations. Three

more days, his sums said, would carry them right to the edge of the map. By now Beechey Island was more than eighty miles off. He felt a strange sense of achievement. He had read every account of Arctic voyages, and no ship had ever let itself be trapped so far north so late in the year.

Overhead the rigging stuttered. The mast thermometer gave 13°. Beside it, the galley blow-hole billowed ginger steam. Beside that, the hatch door was now the door of a sauna, as though fires were everywhere raging below. There were not. Miss Rink's apart, not a single stove had been set. No matter. Walls and ceiling alike were slick with sweat, and that sweat dropped onto their faces as they read or ate or slept. They slept and woke, read and wrote, ate and drank, and kept themselves inside now as much as they could. Proud atop their pedestal, they drifted north and northwest.

After lunch Myer summoned the officers to a conference. He had made a decision, Morgan supposed, and now wanted it confirmed. He gave them each a sheet of paper to complete. They worked in silence for a minute or so. Myer shuffled and squared the papers into a pile, went through them in silence, one by one. Their quickness had taken him by surprise. Morgan stared at the untouched cup of tea on the table before him. The surface was troubled, trembling. They were drifting again. Finally Myer cleared his throat and began to read aloud:

Mr Morgan. Direction South, Inshore, Practicable or Not, Not. Offshore, Not. Direction North, Inshore, Not. Offshore, Not. Dr DeHaven. South, Inshore, Not. Offshore, Not. North, Inshore, Not. Offshore, Not. Deliberately, proving his point, Myer went through every sheet, every answer, and the answer was always the same.

After dinner he had the men gathered, and announced his decision to winter locally, rather than attempt a return to Beechey.

The situation of the lost ships makes inconceivable any

immediate attempt to extricate ourselves from our current impasse, he said. Those inclined to doubt that obligation need only imagine our own situation should we continue in our drift, cut off from all communication with the civilized world, and all proper source of provision, in these latitudes during all the coming winter, and the five winters following. With that in mind, I believe the most useful course of action for us now would be to get in with the land and find a safe anchor for the coming cold months, all the more readily to commence exploring in the spring. That is the very best we can do for our friends, I believe, at the present point in time.

10th October

DeHaven was pointing at the sky. He let Morgan find the marvel. It was a pigeon, perched on the Crow's Nest, looking as perfectly stupid as ever a pigeon looked. No one moved. No one spoke. They were afraid of scaring him off. They set out a heap of crumbs and a saucer of warm water, to tempt him down.

Immediately he saw it properly, Morgan saw their mistake. He looked glum. The hope had been overwhelming, of what the world unbidden might have sent out to find them. But it was one of their own – a bird they themselves had sent out two days before, to give the world their latest news.

What were you expecting? DeHaven said. An olive branch?

Beyond the gunwale the ice looked solid, deeply bruised. They watched Morgan hustle the unhappy thing into a corner of the deck. He gently cupped it in his hands. He flung his arms into the air. He'd already done this a dozen times. He might as well have flung a crumpled news-sheet at the horizon. The thing flapped once and spiralled slowly onto the boards. In the end they gave it to Cabot to cook. Afterwards, below, the men were unusually silent, almost sad. They would be last to leave the dance.

It was the 10th of October. Twilight in the morning and twilight in the afternoon. They came to rest somewhere along the northeastern curve of Cornwallis Island, just outside a little inlet that Myer said would make a perfect refuge. They tried to bully their way in, and could not quite manage it. They were fifty yards short, no more. They anchored their last cable to the rocks and tried warping. The ice was too thick. They hardly gained a yard. Already Myer was talking of cutting a canal to get themselves in. In the meantime, he ordered the cable left in place, for security. They drew it as tight as they could, and the very first night the thing froze. Thick as a man's arm, stiff as iron, and slumped in mid-air. Morgan could see they would never coil it again.

That night, as usual, he lay awake listening. Apart from the dripping water, it was strangely quiet, and he liked it no more than he had liked the noise. Ordinarily, the crush – the collisions – sounded like heavy artillery. Now, from far out in the Channel, they sounded like distant surf. Immediately about the ship there was no more than a murmuring. All the aimless days, the abandoned efforts, now had a single, specific goal. Looking back, it seemed not to matter if they'd done any one thing or its contrary. The final amount was the same. All their struggles, and all their concessions, had brought them to this spot.

11th October

Now that they were fixed for the winter, Myer ordered Banes to build a porch around the hatchway, and ordered Morgan to see it was properly done. After a while DeHaven came up to keep him company. He had been down with Kitty again. These past few days she'd not been well.

How is she? Morgan asked.

Worse, DeHaven said.

They stood on the open deck in their furs. From out in the Channel, they could hear the workings of the old mill. On the southern horizon, the frost-smoke was the colour of tobacco. At their feet, the steam was seeping out through the chinks in the boards.

Another nice day, Morgan said.

Calm, DeHaven offered.

Dry.

It could as well clear up as come down.

It could.

Day by day, they were honing the performance.

You making any progress, Banes? Morgan shouted. For the moment I don't see much to show for all that noise.

None at all, sir.

You just banging those planks to keep yourself warm, is that it?

That's about the size of it, sir.

That afternoon, the two men made a three-hour tramp over the land, and returned without having fired a single shot. A month before, at Beechey, time after time the Brent geese had come lording down over them in great braying flocks from the north, stirring up loons and divers to flatter the air.

There's got to be something somewhere, DeHaven said. She needs fresh meat.

As they turned back for the ship, they saw a single flock of snow bunting trembling in the air, far out over the Channel, pointing south.

*

The next day Morgan headed out alone over the ruins of the floe. Inside the ship, he knew, she was waiting patiently, purring almost. Later, she would say nothing of his long absence. She never did. She knew well he had to come back.

He squatted down in the lee of a hummock. The snow was impeccable. The water in the ice-hole was a pool of ink. An hour later, a nicely-bloated calf struggled up onto the ice. He settled the stock, pulled the trigger, and watched the thing wobble back into the water with a neat splash. His powder had been spoiled by the cabin damp.

He began the long tramp back to the ship. Coming back, he could hear a dog far out in the wilderness, complaining pitifully. One by one they ran off, in the hope of a better life elsewhere. One by one they came back. It was not a good sign, Petersen said.

He tramped all the way back to the ship, and dried his powder in the galley, but did not have the courage to go out again. So close to a warm cabin and a warm meal, he felt too cold, too sorry for himself, and for every other living thing. He could still see the one he'd missed. The head rising straight up out of the ice, to stare in wonder at the new world. An expression both eager and innocent, it seemed to him now.

From their bunks they watched him marching on the spot. He was stamping hard, in a cadet's drill, trying to revive his feet. It was no use. It had been too cold to stay still so long, and in the end he had to ask DeHaven to cut off his boots. Kitty too was there, and knelt to help. She bent to take his feet in her hands and let out a yelp. The socks were stiff. They crackled and splintered as she peeled them off. Underneath was exactly what he did not want to see. She went to put some water to boil, and brought back a plate of food. Carefully, spoon by spoon, Morgan began to transfer the mess into his mouth. He chewed it as best he could, and forced it down.

My compliments to the chef, he told Cabot. Or chefs. Wheresoever they may be.

Of course, we understand, DeHaven insisted. A man of your talents, after all, can hardly be expected to thrive in such

128

conditions. He flapped a hand at the ceiling, the galley. It was another scene from their repertoire.

It is all part of the adventure, Morgan said. As I keep telling Miss Rink here, if you wanted luxury, you should have stayed at home.

They were all grateful for the banter, the act. They all knew it could not last. It could not hope to compete with what was on the way. Under the table, she'd put his two corpse's feet to stand in a basin of warm water. For the moment, they looked and felt like two feet carved from wax. But soon she would take them in her hands and begin to massage them again, to try to bring them back to life.

13th October

By now Myer rarely left his cabin. Except for dinner, Morgan suspected that some days he did not even leave his bed. He had no encouragement to do so. No one invited him to join them in their walks. No one sought his opinion on anything anymore. There were times Morgan forgot he was still aboard. Then, to remind them of everything they hated in the man, after dinner on the 13th Myer called together Petersen and Cabot, and all the officers, and told them he had an announcement to make.

It has occurred to me, Myer said, that we would all of us sleep easier if someone else knew precisely where and in what manner we were set. The easiest manner would be to send a communication to the ships at Beechey.

A communication, DeHaven said. It was a strange, new word.

A sledge party of five, victualled for twenty-eight days, Myer said.

Morgan listened to Myer reveal his plan. He had poured himself another glass of wine, and now held it up to the light. It glowed handsomely. Suddenly it seemed too precious, too sweet. He was afraid to put it to his lips.

I'll leave it to yourself, of course, to choose your men, Myer was telling Morgan now.

I'll give you one piece of advice, DeHaven said. Keep my name off the list.

You're afraid of a little hardship? Brooks said. What a revelation.

If I was afraid of hardship, what would I be doing out here? Me and all these other fools?

Do you refuse outright to go? If Mr Morgan selects you?

I don't refuse to go, but if I go, and get within striking distance of Beechey, I'll refuse outright to come back.

Morgan did not even look up. He was tired of being a spectator to their spats. He cupped his hands about his glass, warming it. They had found it frozen in the bottle, given it to Cabot to thaw.

In any case, DeHaven smiled, how hard can it be? Nice and snug in your furs. Perched on top of the sledge, admiring the view, cracking the whip at the dogs every now and then.

It is too rough, Petersen said, from Morgan's bunk. He was nicely installed. He had been listening. He was awake.

What is? DeHaven said.

The ice. You smash it up, you freeze. Ten times you do this, then it is too rough.

Too rough for *what*? DeHaven said. The man's stupidity seemed deliberate.

The dogs. You see it with your two eyes. Dogs they do not pull all together, not like men. Straight and flat, they are very good. But for ice rough like this? No. They will make a big knot and that's all.

But that is what they are *for*, the dogs, DeHaven said. That is the sole solitary reason we brought them along. To haul the bloody sledge. Dick, are you listening to this?

It is too rough, Petersen said, without even bothering to open his eyes.

There was total silence in the cabin.

You don't like it, good, Petersen said. So take the dogs. Make your big knot. See it for yourself.

Pemmican aside, Myer said, in boiled and boned pork alone, I have calculated our essential needs at one hundred and eighty pounds. It was as though he had not heard Petersen speak.

Our, DeHaven said. So you're going with them? Bravo, Mr Myer. And here was I thinking you only ever ventured other men.

The manufacture of which will consume in excess of two hundred and seventy-five pounds of raw meat, Myer explained, as though someone had insisted on having the details. It causes me no small pain, I can tell you, to sacrifice such a quantity of provision.

Listen to him, DeHaven said. You'd think this whole lunatic scheme had come from someone else.

Of course, Brooks cut in, five men away from the ship, for however many days, makes that much less necessity aboard. He was using his most reasonable voice. We do recognize that, he said, and we have, in our calculations, taken that into account.

Dick, don't even listen to them, DeHaven said. They're trying to cut down your food, plain and simple.

Myer started over, patiently. It's a very particular kind of economy, Doctor. They can only haul so much per day per man. The more they bring to eat, the more they have to haul, and the hungrier they are at the end of the day. The equation may not be quite as simple as you think.

The more they talked, the farther off the voices seemed to Morgan. By now he was thinking only of the suffering, the slavery. There had already been the first flicker of pride, that he would be equal to it, that he had been chosen. At last, he thought, a proper test.

131

14th October

Myer had other ideas too, about the sledge, and the lamps, and the tent. About how a man might survive out there, if separated from the rest. For instance, he said, it would be interesting to see what hospitality there was to be had *under* the snow.

Hospitality, DeHaven said. For whom?

A man. Evidently.

What man?

Any man. It doesn't matter. The whole point is to ascertain what refuge a man caught alone out on the ice –

You yourself, for instance.

For instance. Or indeed you, Doctor. If you're not too . . . frileux.

But I'm not going out there. I'm never going to need it.

Nor am I.

The next morning, three burrows were dug out of the snow.

How big? the shovels asked.

Just big enough, but no bigger, Myer explained.

Morgan wriggled in as best he could, on his back. He shut his eyes, listened to them piling the snow at his feet, packing it down. Opening them again, he expected at least some little hint of twilight, and found total darkness. If he lay there calmly, he told himself, there was no reason he should not imagine himself lying in a vast hall. Then he lifted his arm, it struck the solid wall, and instantly his heart was pumping panic through his veins. He opened his mouth and emptied his lungs, noisily. He sucked them full of air again. He wanted to hear himself breathe, to show himself he could do it as slowly and calmly as he liked. It was not good, he knew, that he had already started to fret. He did not yet feel any particular cold. That was the first thrill of fear, he guessed. The cold would come later, once this opening bluster had died away.

They were all out there, already grinning probably. It would not surprise him if Brooks decided to let the clock run on. It was no surprise the man had not volunteered himself, for all his brash talk. He thought of the full hour ahead. The devices that might help him weather it. Clench and unclench the hands and feet. Paddle the arms and legs. Roll the head. Let himself shiver wildly, if the shivers came. Always remembering that there was a thermometer somewhere near his feet, that he would have to try not to break.

Under his furs, against his skin, he was wearing his silk undershirt, that Kitty had made for him. If nothing else, she had fine taste in clothes. He would always remember the first time he'd seen her, the vision, the woman with her fists on her hips, standing by the mantel in her brother's front room.

A chunk of snow slapped onto his forehead and his entire body leapt up off the ground, with a yelp. Afterwards, he wondered if they could have heard. Would the outer shell remain, if the insides collapsed? Would he choke to death before they got to him? Probably not. Probably there would be peals of laughter as they dragged him out. He lifted his head an inch, tucked chin to chest, narrowed his eyes to stare furiously at his feet, at where his feet should be, where there was most hope of light. He could see nothing, of course, except what he already saw in his mind. The boots, he told himself. Think. He needed some mind-trick to pass the time. Go through it carefully. Say it out loud. Who. Where and when. Why. The boots, he told himself again. They had all warned him off leather, but he'd brought them along anyway. They were a relic of better times. The night of his marriage he'd ended up in the cellar with DeHaven and Roche and Roche's brother-in-law – he forgot the name – and there in the lamplight he shot a hole in a cask of French wine stood against the wall, and all night long the four men drank from their boots. His wife had often mocked him for it since, but he was glad he'd done it, it was something his own father had done in his day, and he would never have a better chance to pander to its appeal.

He could no longer feel his legs. That meant nothing, he knew. It happened often enough, lying in bed under the

133

heavy blankets, listening to the riot. It was easy enough to lose track, if you lay still long enough. Why could he not pretend he was merely under the blankets now? He lay there absolutely still, afraid. There was no need to be afraid, he told himself. All that fretting, those memories – they were precious minutes passed. Any second now he would hear the first distant scrape. He must not panic, that was all. What you needed was not courage, merely to trick yourself into staying calm. Gently pick yourself up, then put yourself down again in a place you would like to be. The corner room, upstairs, that faced south. That was where he was now. It sounded like the old charm. There had once been a great ease to him, able to convince himself of his right to whatever he desired. He was a more sceptical audience now, almost always hard to please. Rink's house, Disko, he insisted, to bring himself back. Upstairs, the corner room, that looked over the bay. A blue glass trim to the bedstead. In a room directly adjoining, a tall enamel tub. A room that conferred rights he had nowhere else. Afterwards, that last time together, he lay there wide awake. The late afternoon sun roaring behind the blinds. Shifting in her sleep, somehow she'd managed to wind most of the sheet about herself. The shadows were deep in the folds. On her forehead, a lone damp hair, like a crack in porcelain. Something was still alive just under the eyelids. It would be over as soon as she woke. His head only inches from hers, he blew gently – breathed almost – into her ear. He saw it all again, as clearly as ever. The nose twitches, annoyed, but she doesn't wake. The next time, she jerks away, and her tits jerk out of invisible sockets, shiver back into place. He lets her settle in again, and he gives her time. Then he takes the corner of the sheet between his fingers, and very gently begins to pull. Noiselessly, the sheet slides off her thigh. It takes a few seconds for the cold air to register. She rolls onto her other shoulder, and the hips follow, dragging the sheet out of his hand. Turning away, she has turned her face to the window, and has to bury her head in her pillow to shut out the light. He takes hold of the sheet again and pulls until he can see some flesh. He lets her start to fret and bother, trying to cover herself again. They go through the routine a few more times. All he has to do, to be sure not to wake her, is stop at the first sign of resistance, then leave her to her own devices for a while. Even asleep, she is an expert at wiping the slate clean. This time she tightens her fingers about the sheet, and tightens the fingers into a fist, and clasps the fist stiffly under her chin. It's something she wants to keep safe, for later. That fist is welded to the end of her arm. The elbow and the shoulder, too, are of a single piece, so that tugging at the sheet he is tugging at her body entire. It's like pulling at something on a string. He is no longer curious to know how she will react, because each time her reaction is the same. What he wants to know is how long it can continue. How many more times can be just like the first? On the bedside table, his watch is ticking shamelessly. Beside it, in the ashtray, there is a charred matchstick, and a shrivelled cigarette butt, which they have shared. For two full days the house had been empty, yet at any moment he expects to hear voices, footsteps, a knock on the door. Now that he's noticed it, the ticking is getting louder. Soon it sounds like a dripping tap. Eventually he stuffs the watch under his pillow. For a few seconds, it sounds like the smothering has succeeded. But from the very start he suspects it can't be quite so easy. From the very start his mind has been rooting, and probing, and it's not long before he finds its hiding place. There it is, a little farther off, but just as stubborn and scrupulous as ever, working away in the background all the while.

17th October

He went in to pass a little time with her, before he went away. She raised herself up a little to greet him. Her head sank back into the pillow with a well-earned sigh. It was not fatigue. It was the relief of someone who has finally arrived.

Look, she said.

She pushed away the blanket, lifted her nightshirt. Whatever was inside her had grown. It looked like one of those shallow bulges in the India-rubber boat. It looked like one of those bumps in their iron plates.

You know, Morgan said, all things considered it might have been better if you'd gone back.

It's a little too late for that now, she said.

It is.

Unless you're asking me to come along?

I wouldn't think that particularly prudent.

Are you concerned for my safety, or for the safety of your child?

For the moment I hardly think the distinction useful.

He remembered kneeling over her. Lying flat on her belly, eyes closed, face pressed into the bed. The careful unravelling. The shy moans. The spit too, draining from her half-open mouth. The stain growing, where her lips were pressed into the sheet.

How long do you think it will take? she said.

Myer says we could be back within three weeks, if we are prepared to do ourselves some little violence. You know Myer. Personally I think we'll be doing very well indeed if we make it in a month.

You're not afraid? she said.

Morgan shrugged. I can see his logic, he said. If anything happens to the ship, it's probably best someone knows where to find us. Look at what happened to Franklin. As much as it pains me to admit it, for once he's probably right.

He had found a way to agree. The night before, in private, he'd made a list of the facts. More often than not, he wrote, we are enveloped in impenetrable fog. The ice is quite closed

136

as far as the eye can see, north and south, inshore and off. Even if it were not, for southern sailing the winds are consistently foul. For the foreseeable future, then, we must remain where we are, in isolation. Of our position, our consorts in the search have not the first inkling, no more than we have of theirs, unless they be still at Beechey.

You want them to know where to find you, don't you? Morgan said.

Who?

The Three Wise Men.

She lay under the covers, flapping nonchalantly through a magazine brought from Disko. *Godey's Lady's Book and Magazine*. The open page: *Infant's Frock For Knitting*. The instructions were an entire page of minuscule print. Another complicated dream, he thought, to keep herself occupied. She could dream as prettily as she liked. Out here they had no crochet cotton, no muslin, no cotton braid.

Sometimes I think I can feel a little flutter, she said. Probably it's pure invention.

He considered the blanket, expecting to see something visibly alive underneath, struggling, like a rat in a bag. As though the outside world were closing in and the thing was determined to resist, to fight for its own space, regardless of the damage done. As though trying to break out, to face him squarely, unrestrained. He saw nothing, of course.

Perhaps by the time you come back there'll be something to see, she said.

Wouldn't it be funny, he said, if it started to shrink, day by day, until in the end everything simply reverted to normal, and you were no longer pregnant, and our lives resumed as if none of this had ever occurred?

He set his clothes on his bunk. The folds were meticulous. At the foot of the bunk, his open bag. Once again he began to weed, as an example to the other men. They needed to see themselves striding ahead, unencumbered. They needed to imagine themselves travelling light. It made the voyage easier to face. From the far bunk, MacDonald watched him fingering out some essential calculation. One less shirt, one less pair of socks. And always the nagging voice in his ear: later, out there, this will still be far too much. The answer was simple, even brutal. Courageous, if that was what he needed to believe. Shed every useless ounce. Nothing that does not pull or help to pull its own weight.

What do I need, absolutely? This time Morgan said it out loud.

A hot-air balloon, DeHaven said.

MacDonald and Brooks laughed, and Morgan paid them no mind at all.

What can you simply not do without? he asked himself. It was no longer mere curiosity, but an interrogation. Forget *like*. Forget comfort. What is the absolute minimum you need to remain alive?

It was their last night. Dinner was something that looked like roast beef, and something that looked like roast potatoes. The kind of meal you like to feel you've earned, Morgan said. They would earn it afterwards, he supposed. They were drinking champagne, from DeHaven's private supply.

Are you really so glad to see the back of us? Morgan said.

I'll have no one to drink it with when you're gone, said DeHaven.

Cabot, chapeau, Morgan said sternly. He pointed his knife at the ruins. I'm starting to have second thoughts, he said, about leaving all this behind.

There were flamboyant toasts, and soft, searching jibes. There were second helpings, and third, until they were scraping the bottom of the trays, and reaching in chunks of biscuit to mop them out. It was dinner as it should be.

The drinking was not light-hearted. Very likely, Morgan thought, they would not have a chance to do this again, all together, as they were now. He watched Cabot lift the glass to his mouth, tilt it, hold it in place. He watched the throat working. The man looked like he was trying to catch up.

138

They were chewing their way through the cheese, mould and rind and all. The conversation lurched from side to side. The voices were being piled up now, one on top of the other. Tonight the past was buffer enough for almost everything. The wrack lay before them, a prize, an accomplishment. They were proud of their work, every sip and every bite. He almost wished some stranger could walk down the corridor and look in the open door, to admire. Then Cabot stood up and reached for a dirty plate, but Morgan put a hand on his forearm.

Not tonight, he said. For once, someone else could clean up after them.

He refilled Cabot's glass, and refilled his own. It was a refusal to end. Later, it would be over long enough. For now the work went on, lowering the levels time and again. As though determined to leave as little as possible for those who stayed behind. It looked a cheerless task. Like men who have given everything, they would stumble to their beds.

18th October

Petersen was stripped to the waist, rubbing melted blubber into his arms and chest. On the bench beside him, Daly was winding a length of bandage about his foot. Banes and Cabot were rubbing hog's lard onto their eyelids, their noses, their lips. Morgan watched the layers go on. Outside, waiting for them, was the primitive world. No one spoke. Each man was readying himself for something new. Morgan too was at it, clearing his head, flushing it free of all rivalry. Everything was cheapened now but the trial to come, the furnace, the tempering.

Brooks appeared in the doorway. Myer was up on deck waiting, he said. Banes stood up, stood over the bucket, and roughly hacked up what sounded like a solid chunk. It was one thing less he wanted to bring along.

Your proper adversaries are neither the climate nor the geography, Myer told them, rather such doubts as you may carry with you as to your own capacity to endure. I myself have no such doubts, he told the gathering. Beneath him, the men stood bareheaded, shivering. A wicked little wind sent snow flickering down on them from the yards, and chopped Myer's speech to pieces. Morgan watched the mouth moving, and did his best not to hear. Relief. Reward. Duty. Those were the words that stood out.

At first they kept out from the coast, to cut a straight line to the next headland. They had the wind at their backs, and for a long time could hear the dogs howling back at the ship.

Six hours that day they walked and waded and crawled across the snow-covered ice. They flailed over year-old hummocks, slickly glazed. They marched over new snow as soft as cotton wool, and snow that looked well tough enough to bear them, but soon set them in drift to their armpits. By midday Banes's ears had turned to tallow. Petersen took off his gloves, rubbed the ears back and forth until Banes was whimpering with the pain. They drove on, always up to their knees, often middle-deep. The traps had all been nicely laid, and nicely disguised. They had no way of knowing what would hold and what would swallow.

On the beach, the ice looked like flour, was hard as rock, lay scattered like rubble at the foot of the cliff. A few minutes of that and they felt they were walking over broken stone in their socks. Mist was now pouring down over them from the land. The mist was welcome, it meant they could not be seen through the glass, and as soon as they got in under the headland Morgan had them set up camp. It was only just four o'clock in the afternoon.

By five the men were in their bags, sitting up, around the

conjuror. For their first day, he knew, this was enough. There was no gain in driving them too far too soon. These past few months, they had learned how to be lazy. It would take a few more starts to teach them again how to sweat.

Cabot doled out the food. Finest Quality Pork, the label said, but it was all bones and gristle and fat.

More money the quartermasters threw away, Banes told the whole tent.

Morgan looked up. Hand me your tin please Mr Banes, he said, reaching across the other men. He scraped the whole of Banes's dinner on top of his own, flung the tin back onto Banes's lap. He began to spoon the lukewarm mess into his mouth. Out of the corner of his eye, he could see that Banes was staring at him. Morgan swallowed extravagantly, forcing it down.

Banes, he said. Maybe you haven't noticed, but you're not on the ship anymore. There are different rules out here.

The second day the hauling was no easier. He would almost have welcomed a gale, its hard frost, to fix the road. There would be easier hauling, he told them, once they got out from under the lee of the land. Still he gave them no encouragement, let them stroll along at their own easy pace, close under the cliffs. He would not let any man single himself out yet, strong or weak. In the traces, for the moment, he refused to lead. With Cabot, he put himself in wheel, behind the younger men, Daly and Banes. Petersen out front, scouting the best road. This early, the effort was still something to be shared. An old man like me, he said. Thirty-six years old. Never hauled in my life. Any kind of a load. A nod in that direction now and then would let him lead and harry later on.

In any case, he was not quite as spry as he'd hoped to be, setting out. Leaving the ship, he thought he would feel physically relieved, unburdened. It was not so. Still he felt a definite weight slowing him down, driving him into the ground.

That night they made camp in one of the stone circles

that punctuated the shore. The ground round about was scattered with whale bones, which Banes was sure would burn. Petersen scoffed, but Morgan wanted to let Banes try. The man was going to be a troublemaker, once the shows of strength lost their charm, and it was always useful to prove a troublemaker wrong.

Inside the tent, Morgan decided to give them their first dose of rum. It was a brand new bottle, and the cork whimpered its way free.

Slow, Petersen said, but in one reckless gesture Cabot poured the whole of his dose down his throat. Petersen himself had barely wet his lips. Banes and Daly too were sipping carefully at their cups. Only Morgan had done more, to disguise his friend's need, and already he could feel it working its way down, exploring every opening it found. Then Cabot jerked himself upright, strangely alive. The fright made Morgan almost drop his cup. His friend was already scrambling across the floor on all fours. Through the tent wall, they listened to him retch.

As though jealous of the sympathy, Banes began to carp, that his eyes were burning. Like live coals, he said. Burning right a way into my head.

What do you want me to do about it? Morgan said. DeHaven had given him plenty of drops, but it was far too early to start using them up.

Banes did not answer. He was still sulking about the bones, which had showed no interest whatsoever in the flame. Outside it had begun to blow. Morgan looked hatefully at the flap. In another minute or two he would have to go out there, to drag Cabot back in.

He was standing on the headland, high above the little tent. The air was strangely clear. The gale had swept all interference away, and through the glass he could see the ghost of Devon Island – a headland much like his own – directly opposite. Immediately north of that, however, was void. No visible coastline, and no lines on the map. Myer's orders were clear. They were to push up into that empty space. Just a day or two, Myer said. If it was not the outlet Myer dreamed of, they were to about turn and push south to Beechey, inspecting the coast along the way, whatever its trend.

It was now eight o'clock in the morning. Morgan stood watching a tiny spot of ink on the beach, a few miles away, in the direction of the ship. The spot had definitely swollen. It was a man. They would have to wait.

Grog and cold tinned pork in an unspoiled setting, he shouted as he came in, gesturing grandly. How could I stay away?

There was not time to quiz him. The men were already crawling out. They had heard the shouting. They all shook his hand heartily.

Aren't you going to show me round the château? he said. He seemed not a little giddy, perhaps from the cold.

He crawled into the tent, and Morgan followed.

You need a new maid, he said, when he saw the wreckage.

Well, Morgan said, it's just impossible to get good help these days.

The men were standing just outside, could hear everything. Morgan asked him what he would like to drink. He had made his decision instantly. He had no way of forcing him to go back, and out here he could not risk having an order refused.

What are my options? DeHaven wanted to know.

Well, just at the moment I'm afraid my cellar is a little understocked. He rooted out a bottle from one of the bags. The label says cognac but it's lamp oil. You can have that or you can have rum.

I'll have whatever you're having, DeHaven said.

A wise choice, sir, if I may say so. Grog all round then. Bien corsés, as Cabot says, and to be honest I think I prefer the French notion of straight-laced to our own.

One by one the men were crawling back inside. It was too cold to stay standing out there for long. Morgan lit the conjuror himself. DeHaven stretched his hands towards the flame.

143

That day it was almost eleven o'clock before they packed up the tent. Banes had begun to complain again, louder than ever, for DeHaven's sake. Alone, Morgan would have let him suffer, but did not interfere now as DeHaven saw to his eyes – rinsed them and wrapped them up. Afterwards, Morgan told Banes to rig up beside him, at wheel. Today he rigged them in unicorn, and put DeHaven in lead, the hardest slot.

They watched Cabot wriggle out over the ice, down on his belly, arms by his side. The others crouched behind the sledge, Petersen ready with the gun. She came across the floes at a fearless stroll. Neither paused nor hurried, nor acknowledged her admirers in any way. The frost-smoke lay in loose bales beyond her.

Just as Petersen had told him to do, Cabot kept honking, wobbling, flapping his elbows. And still she came steady and straight. And still no one said a word. Finally they heard Petersen's hammer cocked – a smart, elegant sound. She hoisted up onto her hind legs, pompously sniffed the air. Then turned and set off in a blundering run, back the way she'd come.

At lunch, he watched Cabot eat. In his tin was a small lump of mush. Cabot prodded it with his fork for some sign of life. He put a forkful in his mouth but didn't bother to chew, didn't swallow. It was in there, slowly melting. Morgan sat opposite.

I still say we should have shot the seal, DeHaven said.

They say it tastes very like man-flesh, said Morgan.

Mix it up with a tin of soup, you wouldn't know the difference.

One less mouth to feed, Morgan said. Now that we have a mouth extra.

Less matter to haul.

More space in the tent.

A bigger share of the prize.

And what better proof, to those at home, of the extent our trials?

Still Cabot showed no sign he heard.

Sighting that tiny fleck in the far distance, Morgan had been fearful. His first thought was that someone had been sent to call him back, to prevent him from leaving her behind. Hearing DeHaven's voice, he had been relieved, and the relief had surged through him as the fear had, through the selfsame channels, showing him what he had refused to see clearly until then, that part of him did not want to return. Perhaps it was because he secretly wished to do the same that he had not immediately condemned DeHaven for abandoning the ship, for wanting to push on with them to Beechey, and remain there.

The advantages were too obvious to push from his mind. But it was hard to see how it could be managed with five other men at hand, for witnesses. He would not know how to explain it. He barely dared explain it to himself, the thing was so simple. He did not want to go back to her, that was all. He did not want to be present when it arrived, for her to hand it over, the debt he could never discharge. He had not asked her to follow him. That was not what he'd come out here for. That was not the trial he'd planned.

He wondered in what way precisely he would be misunderstood, what would be the terms of the judgment, if he did not return. The worst they could say, of course, would be that he'd been using her – it – as an excuse, a chance to escape the hardship of a long winter in the ice. That would be the most ingenuous version, and the most cruel. He did not think he could stand it. The mere thought of it was a challenge to go back, regardless of all the promises calling him to Beechey.

The day was bright again. Today he rigged them in unicorn, with Banes in lead. Leading, you could not merely blink your eyes open now and then and feel a way with your feet.

All day they pulled towards the Devon Island shore. Three times they watched Banes stumble and fall, and each time Morgan had to grab hold of Daly's arm, to stop him helping the man to his feet. With the wind in their faces, they scraped

145

all the way to Cape Osborn, the nearest point of the Devon shore. By evening, Banes's eyes were swollen shut. They propped him against the cliff and unwrapped the head. On each side of the nose, the tears had trickled into his beard and frozen in a little lump.

In the tent, he watched DeHaven dribbling the spoon into the blind man's mouth. The lips were shrivelled and cracked like old varnish in the sun. Afterwards, they put him into the blanket bag, in a hood.

Unwrapped, the other faces too were anguished, sorrowful, yearning – seemed less in physical than in moral or mental pain. Inches from their heads, the tent was rattling frantically. Outside, the grumbling ice. Legs folded under him tailor-fashion, Morgan hunched over his bowl. He was studying them secretly, his slaves.

The cold tunnelled through to him early. It was Sunday. Overhead, glazed with breath, the canvas was frozen stiff. It was a wedge driven into the wilderness, with walls that were wafer-thin.

After breakfast, as it began to brighten, he left the tent. From the top of the headland, he named the points north and south. He named the capes and the inlets, and the tiny islands, some that were little more than rocks. Others had always named such things after fellow officers and ice-masters, retired captains, sponsors, the Lords Commissioners of the Admiralty. The lights and shadows they wished to walk in. But Morgan named them after his wife, and his wife's sister, his mother and his father, his dead cousin, his favourite dog. His forgetful friends, his first wound, his first whore. He was bringing them out here with him, and finally fixing them in a definite place, from where they could no longer follow.

Had the lost expedition travelled this far north, up this par-ticular channel, he wrote – He wondered how best to state his case. There were certain conclusions he had to avoid, try not even to steal a glimpse at them. In their place, he would have left some definite sign of his passage, and would have left it precisely where he was standing, here, the highest point for miles. There was nothing, of course.

From Cape Osborn they would now haul round to the north. Those were Captain Myer's orders, he reminded them – to haul round to the north and inspect the adjacent bay, about which Captain Myer entertained some considerable hope, that it might in fact be a passage back east to Jones's Sound, and the head of Baffin Bay, from whence they had come.

I'm impressed, DeHaven said. You're already on short supplies, you've an extra man to feed, and now you're going to stretch yourself even further for that fool? Chapeau. He was blindfolding Banes with a length of boot-hose. You haul straight down the Channel for godsake, write it up how you like in your journal, and who'll ever be any the wiser?

The idea was tempting, but Morgan did not yet want to turn south. Turning north, he was putting his decision off.

If you want to go south, go south, I'm not going to stop you. That's why you came out here, isn't it? Morgan said. DeHaven, he knew, could not reply. With no tent, no heat, and no supplies, he would not last two days.

How many searchers have been lost, down through the years? DeHaven asked him, straight out.

A great many.

More than the number of those they were searching for?

Undoubtedly, Morgan said. He thought of his heroes. Franklin, Parry, Ross. Many was the night he'd turned the pages, sifting through their torments, their failures, that he hoped to rival with his own.

And what did it ever get them? DeHaven had asked. All their backbreaking labour and all their lost fingers and toes?

Morgan did not know what to say. He did not know why, even now, away from the ship and everyone in it, within safe sledging distance of Beechey, he wanted once again to veer north. He did not know why so many men had come to chasten themselves so high up in the world.

147

They had a hefty breakfast of tea and rum and pemmican. They had provisions remaining for twenty-two days. North of the headland the flat beach stretched as far as the eye could see. Every mile or so a line of rubble ran straight out from the land.

It was the 24th of October. All night long the wind had been roaring over the beach, sweeping everything off the surface, hosing it horizontal. They lay there in the dusk, smoking their pipes, murmuring conspiracies. Banes in silence, behind his mask. DeHaven seemed to be asleep.

How does it look? Cabot asked. There had been another lull.

Once more Morgan poked the glass through the flap. This time it snagged on what looked like the ghost of a cairn, far to the north. He made the mistake of telling them what he saw. Then watched Daly begin to bother himself with hope. Who else could have made it, Daly said, but the men they were searching for? Morgan could not contradict him. If cairn it be, its appeal was made directly to them, the searchers – first imagined, afar; now real, and so close.

The conjuror was lit for their midday meal. The heat woke DeHaven. Morgan watched the steam come off the man. He watched Petersen picking at his ear, and admiring the extract. Outside, the scouring was merciless. They had half an hour to kill, waiting for the food to thaw and warm. Waiting, they watched DeHaven rigging little lengths of wire to two bones he'd found at their last campsite, what looked like the upper and lower parts of a jaw.

Some species of whale, he said. Stiffly, he closed the contraption, with a decorous clack.

With teeth? Morgan said.

There are whales with teeth. Petersen will tell you. Tell him, Chinaman.

There are whales with teeth, Petersen said.

Each bone held a long neat row of them, tiny as a baby's, but razor-sharp.

The pelvis, DeHaven told them. That's the key. The keyhole, if you prefer. He set the jawbones yawning on his lap. He held aloft one of the bread bags, queerly stuffed and tied. Head up, head down. Back to front, back to back. Those are the possibilities, he said. He was gently wrestling with the doll. Head down and back to front would be best, he said, for mother and child alike.

Morgan wondered had he done anything to deserve an alternative. He could not say. He did not know how he registered on that particular scale.

DeHaven was holding the doll against his torso. Below, the open jawbones lay waiting on his lap. To DeHaven, apparently, the thing was going to be ridiculously easy, ridiculously fast. In his other hand he was holding pink leggings of some kind. The cloth was thin and quite elastic, ready to stretch to almost any size. They watched him pull it up over the head.

The uterus, DeHaven said, drawing it up over the body, inch by inch. It's like any other muscle, he said. It stretches and it contracts. That's what pushes the baby down. He bunched the loose end in his fist and began to squeeze, like a pâtissier piping cream. The dilation of the cervix *allows* it, he said. The contractions *oblige* it, if you will.

He had put the head into the open jaws. They watched in silence as the doll was piped through. To Morgan this was merely a puppet-show, a bundle of rags bumping against bare bone. There was no flesh, there could be no tearing, no bleeding, no pain. DeHaven had spread his legs a little, the jaws gaping on his lap. Once the head is through, he said, the midwife will normally assist in the extraction first of one shoulder, then the other. He reached his hand down outside his leg, and up under it, to take hold of the head.

The midwife, Morgan said. Or the doctor.

If the lady concerned happens to have a certified physician attending her, she can count herself extremely fortunate, DeHaven said.

The head, he kept saying. The cervix. The shoulders. The

149

uterus. They sounded like specimens, each in their own separate jar.

The hand that had reached up between his legs to catch the doll now pulled it through, brought it back around and sat it on his lap. It had been a quick and simple birth, apparently, taking only the time needed to describe it.

If it's so simple, why does it so often go so wrong? Morgan said.

The great difficulty is the size of the head, DeHaven said. I mean, in relation to the size of the pelvis.

The shark's mouth.

The whale's mouth. Exactly. Some women's hips are simply not big enough.

What about Kitty? She's not exactly the biggest woman in the world.

I've seen worse. I've seen worse that have got away with it.

And if the hole, the gap, whatever you want to call it –

The passage.

If it just isn't big enough?

If that's the case, there's no point whatsoever in trying to force the issue. It's merely a great deal of time and effort wasted, DeHaven said.

The day passed. Again and again he undid the tie and slid the glass through the gap, hoping for a better view of the cairn to the north. It was a useless temptation. The wind was coming on harder than ever now, and there seemed no hope of ever again getting away. They would lie here calmly and dumbly, he told himself, and let themselves be frozen, or slowly buried alive. As always, his mind was rushing ahead, to catastrophe. These were his last companions, it told him, in his final home.

Late in the afternoon the wind died enough to let him crawl out. The low sun came skimming over the ice, let him admire the storm's handiwork. The gale had carried off the youngest layer of snow, and now a long row of footprints led right to the tent door, standing up out of the ground a good six inches, like columns of wind-worn stone. Each a little memorial to their passage, the weight of their boots stamping the snow, step after step, making it far more solid than the powder. What impressed him most was the detail, even to the grooves and grips of each individual sole. The sledge, too, had left raised rails stretching to the southern horizon – curious, useless, and exquisitely tooled.

By midnight the wind had died, but out in the Channel the ice was on the move. Between the explosions, it sounded like an army on the march. He could not sleep. He struck a match. The eyes were glistening in the dark.

By morning the wind was barrelling over the beach again from the northeast, so hard he feared they could not face it. But face it they did. It was the 26th of October. They all leaned into their load as a prop, hauling blind. Step by step they hauled north along the beach, and could not tell – hardly cared – whether or not they had veered off course.

The wind was scorching. Under the scarves and veils, his face felt raw. Inside his head, a small sure voice was mocking his every step. With every step his mind was growing sharper, testing, searching for flaws in his reasoning. Flaws so flagrant as to invite ridicule. It was not resolution but stubbornness, this refusal to cede. And the stubbornness, it said, was the product of a weary, fearful mind. He had to keep reminding himself of the rush of pleasure it would give the others, to hear themselves ordered down. The wind was dying now, the sky beginning to clear, and it was another two hours before he could let himself say those words. They had made about four miles, he judged. In such weather, it was a good day's work, and felt like total defeat. That was the price, apparently.

As they were setting up, he walked out alone to look at a bump on the spit nearby. It was another silly hope he needed to snuff. It was nothing. He stood up on top of it to consider the world. He could see the coast to the north much more clearly now. It was obviously a continuation of the beach. The opening Myer had imagined did not exist. Their cairn seemed no nearer. Lone flakes were wandering through the air, like flakes of ash after a fire. He himself was the tallest thing for miles. Here, there were no more excuses, no version but his own, and for a moment he was thankful that Myer's plan had hustled him so far north. He was the lawmaker here, with what felt like a lawmaker's heart – one now answering gladly to the power of a mute, raging world.

Inside the tent, he found DeHaven kneeling over Cabot, who was laid out on his back.

It's his feet, DeHaven said. Says he cannot feel them either one.

Morgan asked how long it had been.

Perhaps an hour, Cabot said. I thought they might come back. I didn't want to slow you up.

Morgan hung his head, as if in shame. It was not shame, it was anger. He had explained the rules twenty times.

Already DeHaven was drawing out his skinning knife. Banes, he said, boil up a quart of snow. He was wrestling with the laces. His fingers were numb, would not obey. He nodded to Morgan to come and kneel beside him. He touched the tip of the blade to the top of the boot, let it fiddle back and forth. A little V opened up, an invitation, as Morgan pulled the sides apart.

Harder, DeHaven said.

Patiently, the blade worked its way down.

I'm sorry, Cabot said. He was lying on his back, could hear their work. I thought I would certainly feel it. If really it was so very bad.

Exactly the opposite, DeHaven said. Even a Frenchman ought to know that.

The tip of the blade nicked the ankle, and the foot didn't even twitch. Morgan rolled off the sock. The thing looked and felt like soap. Outside, the wind was again beginning to bustle and fret.

An hour's hard rubbing, with no mind for his whimpers, eventually brought the blood back. Afterwards, they wrapped the feet in blanket squares, and stockings, and boot-hose. He would have to wear moccasins from now on.

In a way, Morgan was disappointed. In the kit made up for

the party before they set out, DeHaven had included a small saw. Mortification, amputation, he had explained. It's very simple, really. Morgan remembered the conversation perfectly:

Where do I cut?

There's what's dead and what's not. You try to cut right along the line.

But how do I know where that is?

Again, very simple. Start where you think you should start, and if he screams, just move the blade down a quarter of an inch. There's always going to be a grey area, of course. Between high tide and low tide, if you will. That's where you want to be.

Explaining, he had been bumping the blade up and down Morgan's index finger. The teeth left their print on the skin. Morgan remembered them clearly, those little red marks. There had been a promise in it – of great suffering, of clean hard choices, of sacrifice. But here in the tent the saw was still wrapped up in the medicine chest, with all its tiny little teeth. It was another promise unfulfilled.

By morning the snow was falling so hard he could not see ten feet. It was a deliberate tease. The cairn was not two miles off, and still out of reach. All day and all the next night again they lay in their bags. About ten o'clock on the second day the storm lulled a little, and the same faded spectre as before appeared. Good and loud, Daly offered to go along, if Mr Morgan wanted to push on without the other men. And then the wind lulled a little more, daring him to refuse.

Hard sharp snow, like handfuls of fine gravel, flung through the air. Heads down, eyes closed, feeling their way with their feet, the two men pushed on. About midday they reached the cairn. It was not a cairn. It was nothing at all. It was a lump of rock a little more stubborn than the rest. Without a word they turned around. Already their last footprints were filling up.

The next morning Morgan ordered them to pack up everything. They were heading south. He tried not to catch

DeHaven's eye, not to see his satisfied smile, his vindication.

He had decided to make a depot at Cape Osborn, where they had first made the eastern shore. It would lighten the load, make progress less painful. And give them something to come back to, that was not quite so far, if and when they returned. For almost an hour they bounced the pickaxe off the shingle, until there was a neat crack. The handle had broken. Daly stood there disconsolate, staring down into what looked like nothing so much as a shallow grave. There was nothing for it, they piled in their tins and bags and those sundries sufficiently cheapened by their week's work, and piled all that over with their rubble, and over again with ice and snow, to stay the scent. Then stamped round on top of it, triumphant.

He had done his calculations. He was leaving five days' supplies, no more, to get them home. In a bottle, he left a note that read: 28 Oct. Search party from HM Impetus, currently lying in Lat 75°36' N, Long 94°21' W, NE coast Cornwallis Island, under Capt. Myer. Lt. R. MORGAN, auxiliary command. Essentials here deposited for party's own use. Capt. Austin & other searching vessels currently at Beechey Island. Our intention is to communicate with them.

Myer's orders were to track the coast all the way to Beechey, scouring it for clues of Franklin. This great work of humanity, he called it. But in his journal Morgan wrote: My people's health is my only measure. I will go as far as I safely can.

They kept at it, day after day. They had their routine. Packing up, hauling, pitching the tent. Setting out, he thought they would soon get to know each other, like brothers, every kink and scar. There was nothing of the sort. They were almost always too tired to talk, even on the days they were trapped in the tent.

Day after day they inched their way down the coast. The fabric was being slowly worn down, worn away. Underneath, through the bare threads, a lone word showed through: *Why?* He did not know. Out here, no answer could compete. He was earning the right, perhaps, to talk about what other men had done. Yet with every destroying day, every hour of drudgery, more and more he felt the breach between himself and them, the men of renown. He had read their books. For them, there had been far horizons, all around. He had gone to the windows they had looked through, and found them walled up. They had been lying, or he was a different sort of man. From where he stood, there was never anything further off than the next step, the next sip of water, the prodigious pains in his legs.

They made their camp high up on the shore, in the centre of a stone circle twenty feet across. Morgan sent Banes to scout for driftwood, and a few minutes later they heard him calling, screaming almost. He was up on the ridge, waving his arms. They rushed towards him, sure the mystery had been solved. Day after day, it was the same. Every mound on every headland looked man-made. It seemed nothing could blunt the hope.

Overhead, vertical cliffs. Beyond, clouds of impeccable fleece feathered the sky. Banes was pointing to the next headland, its knob of rock, perfectly turned to tempt them. Beyond it, the coast drifted away to the southeast, as far as they could see.

Morgan lifted the glass to his eye, and let out a long, stale breath, that sounded like a punctured balloon. The thing looked as much of a cairn as the rest. He told them to go back to the tent, set the conjuror going, get themselves into their bags.

He spent almost an hour climbing. The heap of stones was no more than three feet high, but definitely hand-built. At the bottom, for once, to balance against all their efforts, was a little green bottle. It had been left by a search party Austin had sent up the coast. Here turning back, the note said. This was their farthest point north. The disappointment felt familiar, almost reassuring. It was as though a trick were being played, by someone watching, hidden, and always slyly moving ahead of them, determined to draw them on. At the bottom of the sheet he scribbled Morgan, Impetus search party, 31 Oct, continuing S, and shoved the paper back into the bottle, for the next fool.

By morning the wind was barrelling down off the land, and kept them in their bags. It gave them time to mull over the note. Here turning back, it said. It gave the date, and the officer commanding. It said Austin would winter at Beechey, Morgan told the men. He was trying to tell them they were not obliged to go back to the ship. Previously, he'd always pushed that thought from his mind. Now he let it come, with all its arguments prepared. He figured their distance from the *Impetus*. He wrote the figure down, in geographical miles. It was a fantasy, of course, with straight lines – not the scribbled course they would be forced to take, if they went back. The truth was, he was afraid to go on. At Beechey, with food and fuel and shelter, he would not have the courage to about turn and go north again. It would be too far, and too cold, and too stupid, and too brave.

That evening, waiting for his dinner, he read over his journal, to see in black and white the decision he wanted to make. Only two days before, he'd written: We move too slowly, but cannot quicken our pace. We must match our ambitions to our means. Let it be said, I have full faith in the men's desire to pursue our course. However, I believe our efforts might be better directed, over greater distances, with greater chance of success, in the spring. To continue now, in our current state, would not only put at risk our own lives, but also, indirectly, the lives of those it is our purpose here to locate, for the capacities of some of our party, I fear, are likely to be reduced permanently, if we now persist. The food was still not warm, and he read the passage over again. It all sounded so wise and reasonable, yet he had said nothing of any of this to the men, and they had not turned back, but gone on exactly as before, south.

He set the next tin on the scales, began to spoon the mess into it. Watched the scale-pan lift cautiously from the floor.

The spoon in mid-air, waiting. The pans levelled off, settled, and were still.

On the other side of the conjuror, Cabot sat with his eyes closed.

Next, Morgan said, picking up a tin.

Banes, Cabot said.

Morgan handed it on, picked up another.

Next, he said.

And so the food was shared out.

He waited until the last tin had been handed over. They would want to eat while it was still warm, and that let him speak. He asked them what they wanted to do, and gave them their choices. It was time to decide, he said, whether to push on or turn about. If they pushed on and were by some mishap delayed, they might not be able to get back. It was a simple enough calculation, he said. Pounds of meat per mile per man. On the other hand, tempering their ambitions now meant they might be renewed and extended at a later date, he said. He spoke with no great conviction. But to men spent and sore, for the moment that seemed buffer enough against what might be said back at the ship. They offered grunts of acknowledgement, that was all. He had expected more resistance, but they had disappointed him.

If you have a contrary opinion, Banes, now is the time to state it, Morgan said.

I do what I'm told, Banes said. That's what I'm doing this past fortnight, isn't it?

Morgan explained again as simply as he could. The simple fact was, their food and fuel for the outward leg was now consumed. Not only was it credible, it was true. I'm not sure if you've noticed, Morgan said, but we've had an extra mouth to feed, all the way down.

But they can resupply us, said Banes.

Who?

The other ships. You said it yourself, a dozen times.

And if the other ships are gone? If they struck out in September, before it all closed up?

They'll have left supplies. Not necessarily for us, but for Franklin. Surely.

And if they haven't? If they've already found him, and shipped out? How are they to know we've drifted north, and not gone home before them?

I'm not afraid to take that chance.

You think it's just a question of courage? You think you have more of it than me?

Banes did not bother to respond. That made the answer obvious. DeHaven had said nothing either. It sounded like a conspiracy.

You've obviously been talking to Dr DeHaven, Morgan said.

It took Banes a moment to soak this up. I don't know what you mean, he said.

Of course you don't. You think he came along to admire the scenery. Or for the pleasure of our company, perhaps.

That night he lay awake, playing the same scene over again. He had been protecting himself from every imagined accusation, should they push on and not go back. He had been playing the Devil's Advocate, but now wondered had he played it too well.

When they woke, DeHaven was gone. He could not be gone long, Morgan decided. His bag was still warm. Through the glass Morgan watched him climbing the headland. Why he had decided to climb the headland, Morgan did not know. To cut overland? Morgan scanned and found him again. He had already stopped to lean on his knees. He had started off too eagerly, overestimated himself. Before he was halfway up, the wind began to swing round to the northward, and within an hour a gale had come on.

All day the snow came squalling over them, and all day they lay in their bags, sleeping or smoking or cobbling. Morgan was quiet. Visibility was zero. It would be useless to search.

You're just going to leave him out there? Banes said.

Shut your mouth, Cabot said.

If you care so much about the man, Morgan said, why don't you go? Well? What are you waiting for?

By next morning it had calmed enough for Morgan to go out. He told Cabot to soak and set fire to DeHaven's bag, to send up smoke, and stop the smoke if ever DeHaven came back.

Even as he took the first step, he knew he was wasting his time, that this was all just for show. He was loyal to that idea and nothing else. It was almost ten before he reached the top of the headland. He'd not seen the slightest trace in the snow. Far below, the last of the smoke had faded long since. He stood and turned on the spot. He'd learned to look closely, to let himself be distracted by the details, but today that wasn't enough. He stood a long time looking towards Beechey. He could feel, physically, the magnet's lure. Old friends. The old life. A temptation he did not quite know how to resist. Behind him, the *Impetus* and everyone on it were now almost beyond reach.

It was noon. A lone figure came trudging towards them over the tragic snow. They rushed out to meet him, arms flapping, staggering through the drift like men wading into the sea. Afterwards, their disappointment was not easy to hide.

Eight hours later, they were eating their pemmican, warm in their bags. They had hauled all the way round the bay, along the beach, shouting his name. For good measure, every now and then Morgan had clambered up to bellow into a crack in the cliff face.

He's gone to Beechey, Cabot said.

Deserted, you mean, Banes said. He was accusing Cabot of speaking Morgan's lines, and Cabot looked to Morgan to object.

I'll leave that for Captain Myer to decide, Morgan said. He's gone. Very likely he's frozen. They say it's not a particularly unpleasant way to go. A bit like falling asleep, apparently.

The faces soured. This was a new tone, and a new voice. They had a new, strange taste in their mouths.

Morgan could not understand the man, why he'd gone on ahead, alone. Had he really thought Morgan was ready to turn back, so close to their goal? He had merely wanted the explicit endorsement of the other men, and to acknowledge the risk they ran, pushing on now. He wanted it all on record – his alibi – for his superiors to read, if ever he did not return to the ship.

Alone, on foot, pushing hard, a man might make it in a day or a day and a half, if he didn't stop. If he stopped, he would close his eyes, and fall asleep, and freeze. If the ships were still there, he could invent any story he liked. Blame the storm, say he had been lost. In any case, he would be saved. Even if the ships were gone, he might not be condemned. As Banes said, they would have left a cache of supplies for Franklin. Food and fuel, maybe even a boat. All he had to do, to stay alive, was stay on his feet.

Gentlemen, Morgan said, with a false, cheery voice. Tomorrow we have another long day ahead of us, and I am now turning out the lamp. I wish every one of you goodnight.

He woke at six, lit a match, counted the heads. They were all still there. He watched the flame crawling along the wood, feasting on the soft white flesh of it, and the puny black skeleton left behind. He watched the froth riding ahead. He watched the fingertips begin to glisten and brown. They were somebody else's fingers. They were leather now. They would decide for themselves when to let go.

He lit another match, and lit the conjuror. The warmth would wake them one by one. He pulled on his boots and went outside. He walked over to the wall of hummocks, out of sight. Found a niche where he would be sheltered on two sides at least, and that's where he squatted down. It was his first proper movement in a week. Afterwards, he turned to look at the thing and found it already frozen. In the days and months to come he would be leaning into the traces, or lying in his bag, or in a bunk inside a ship, or in his very own feather bed back home, and all the while what had once been inside him would still be lying here in the ice, unseen and soon forgotten, even by Morgan himself, much as it was now – not being slowly absorbed back into the earth, with a life of its own, but frozen in time.

He was grateful, even glad, that DeHaven had gone on ahead. It was a perfect reason now to push all the way to Beechey, and at Beechey who knew what they would find? He was sure Dr DeHaven had got lost and merely gone on ahead of them, he told the tent. They themselves would now temporarily abandon the sledge, the quicker to push on, and catch him up. It ought not to be much more than the matter of a single day. At Beechey, he said, they would recover their friend, make their communication to Austin, renew their supplies, then retreat to the ship, exactly as planned.

5th November

Lancaster House, it was called. The words were burned into the lintel. Morgan stood alone in the doorway. The men were inside, lying on the bare shale. He looked north and south. It was now calm and clear, visibility anything up to seven or eight miles. They'd found no trace of DeHaven here or anywhere else. Offshore, there was no hint of a mast. That put the ships at an impossible distance. Trapped out in the Sound as helpless as themselves, or in some safer haven.

The house itself was empty. Austin had taken everything, left only a few lumps of coal in one corner, a few broken staves, two split tins of hotch-potch. If they did not want to freeze or starve, they had to return to the ship.

In the mute panic of his mind, Morgan struggled to

161

understand. He had imagined how easy it would be not to go back, if the ships were gone. Lancaster House would have food and fuel enough for six months, he'd told the men. If the expedition ships were gone, they could stay all through the winter, in relative comfort. Next summer, a ship would pick them up. They had pushed on to find the missing man, they could say. It would be true. It would be almost the entire truth. They could say they had been trapped. A storm, an accident. The long hard winter would be testimony in their favour, against almost any charge.

All his life, he sometimes thought, he had deliberately courted shame. That was why he had accepted this particular commission, that men ten years younger had turned down. That was why he had accepted command of the sledge. Perhaps, as usual, he had been punishing himself for other failures, or other flaws, or testing for them. It was a young man's vanity that he clung to, or that clung to him – the thought that he could still redeem himself. From what, he didn't know. He presumed it didn't much matter by now. But time and again, year after year, he put himself farther, longer, deeper. So far, he had always managed to come back. And even that, in his ruthless logic, was a mark against him. This time, he'd gone farther than ever before. Coming down the coast, he was putting himself beyond danger, he thought. Every extra step, he thought, was more room for manoeuvre. In any great space, he now saw, the room for manoeuvre was minuscule.

He stepped into the lee of the gable, out of the rising breeze. His face inches from the frozen wall. He closed his eyes, felt himself swaying gently, let himself lean forward until his head touched the stone. Through his head-furs, the thing felt as cold and solid as steel. Arms by his side, body stiff, he leaned into his forehead, confided it all his weight. The pressure grew. His body was trembling. He clenched his teeth, and clenched his throat. Let his head drop back, his mouth open to the sky. Emerged a pitiful sound. It felt as though something was physically draining out of him, something he'd been trying desperately to contain. He had thought it a reserve of strength, but it felt more like a weight, a burden, that he was now being relieved of. He had arrived, he knew, at a very particular moment, a very particular spot. Whether it was a moment of great weakness or of great strength, he could not say. He could not now tell the difference. It was the courage to surrender, perhaps.

Afterwards, as he turned to go back inside, he saw a head at the door, instantly withdrawn. It was Cabot, he thought. It did not trouble him, the discovery. It would do him no harm, he guessed, to be thought a little queer in the head.

6th November

The next morning they had a good breakfast of pork and chocolate, with a double dose of spirits, and at eight o'clock they started for home. They did not look any more to the south. Whatever calamity or miracle each man had secretly hoped to find at Beechey, that was all behind them now.

Until yesterday, every step had been a step farther out, that would have to be paid for a second time, on the way back. He had thought of it bravely, the volte-face, the first unimpeachable step towards home. From then on, he was sure, the steps would be easier to make, as you counted them down. He was wrong. The road was as heavy as ever, the day was calm, and he was soon dripping with sweat. The beach was covered with snow, and they advanced pedantically, step by stupid step. They were heading back to their last campsite, where they'd left the sledge. They were taking the long way round. If DeHaven was still alive, there was still a chance they might meet him, Morgan said. More than once he looked out over the bay. The floe had been shattered by the gale, and every crack stuffed to the brim with snow. In his mind, he saw a lone figure leaping grandly across the cracks. Or scraping his feet along the ground, feeling his way in the dark, blind. No matter how careful you were, every so often you would sink to your knees, or your waist. Sooner or later, you would simply disappear.

At their last campsite, the sledge was still there, but the oilskin cover was badly torn. Each man gave it a shameful glance. The snow roundabout had been trampled flat, and soiled.

It is a bear, Morgan said. It was an official announcement. He was furious at the doubt, the hope. Look at the dung, he said.

On all sides were familiar horizons. From hereon out, whatever he did would not be enough. Whatever they suffered, it would be deserved. He was coming back at least one man short. Already he heard the insinuations, in the captain's cabin, and traded freely amongst the men.

DeHaven had made a kind of burrow for himself, a hundred yards north of the camp. He heard the voices, crawled out, managed a single, strangled cry. His feet were in a bad way. He looked and sounded like a man catatonically drunk. He had lost his goggles and was totally blind.

They set up the tent around him, stripped him naked, began to rub him all over, all five of them, as hard as they could. Every now and then they dribbled a little rum or hot tea into his mouth. They kept at it all evening and much of the night.

The next morning they carried him out in his bag and laid him on top of the sledge, and tied him down. He was mumbling something, Morgan saw. He put his ear right up against the lips.

Of course I will, Morgan answered him, in a knowing voice. That's exactly what I'll do. Good and tight, he told Banes. We don't want him falling off.

Cabot and Banes laid the buffalo skin over him.

Let's try not to smother the man, Morgan said. If I can at all manage it, I intend to bring him in alive.

That first day they were twelve hours under weigh, minus two hours for stoppages, to rub the hands and feet again.

Don't listen to him, Morgan told them. It's for his own good.

They were twelve hours under weigh that day, and that night in the tent he could see the men were in need of consolation. He trawled his mind and found nothing. Yet often that day, even during the worst of it, he'd felt he was precisely where he ought to be. Where the beach was flat, they found the tracks they'd made coming south. It was a purpose-built road, that promised slick, easy pulling, all the way back to the ship. The deep tracks, the flat course, the obstacles nicely navigated – everything was tailor-made. All they had to do was slot themselves in.

About six in the evening on the 12th of November they made the Cape Osborn depot. Their grave had been dug out, wrecked and robbed. The barrels of bread and pork lay in splinters, teethmarks in the frozen wood. A leather glove sat stiff on a rock, a finger pointing at the sky. Nearby, the lump of a Bible was fluttering prettily. Up and down the beach, every few yards, another alien shape was growing under the snow. A tin of potatoes. A tobacco-box. One of the little rum kegs. They strolled back and forth kicking them out. A sheaf of wicks. The spare thermometer. Then a shout from Cabot – he'd found the little chess set. But not a single lump of meat. Eventually Morgan found the bottle, with only the note he himself – that other man – had left in it ten days before.

He felt no rush to indignation. In fact, some sly part of him admired the scene. He was used to being punished for what he did wrong. Justice, he called it, even when it was early or long delayed.

When they woke the next morning, he told them to stay in their bags. He himself worried about the conjuror, the scales.

165

By his reckoning, they had meat enough for two days. The bread might be stretched a little more.

Over and again that day the drift took them to the knees, sometimes even to the neck. Over and again the nose of the sledge took to burrowing. The crust on the new snow out in the Channel was wafer-thin. There was never anything to be done but lift DeHaven off again. So they lifted him off again, and hauled the sledge back up out of the snow. As they loaded him up, Morgan could not help but study the wilderness ahead of them, that nothing could change. His most miserable prophecies were satisfied.

That day they hauled for twelve hours straight, with never more than a few minutes' pause. Even when the sledge was free, they were wading in water, upstream, feet sucking at the river mud. Step by step he began to forget the snow, the sledge, the other men. He was alone, leaning into the pain. Everything was taxed – every breath, every lift of the leg. There was resistance everywhere, in all directions, all the time. It knew in advance what he was going to do. Even by shifting the harness, he could not shirk it for long. It was too shrewd, and too heartless. It wanted its due. Behind his mask, he had already confessed everything – surrender, indifference, despair. But still the hurt kept burrowing, tirelessly, even when there was nothing more to find. It had reached the raw nerve, and was chewing patiently. It wanted its due.

That day they hauled for twelve hours straight, with never more than a few minutes' pause, until finally Cabot collapsed. It was neither exaggeration nor display. Morgan himself stood clinging to the sledge, knew that without it he would fall. Daly too had let himself crumple to the ground, and Petersen was standing over them, ordering them to get up. He was roaring. He was right. It would be better, afterwards, to be able to say you had still been able to stand. Stretched out on the ice was too much of a concession. You were beaten, with no further asylum. It was your back against the wall.

Slowly, Daly rolled onto his side, onto his belly, managed to lift himself onto his hands and knees. But still Cabot lay stretched out on the snow, looking up at them. What he wanted, of course, was mercy. It was now blowing smartly, and already the snow was banking up against his leg on the windward side.

They set up the tent around him. They ate their meal without a word, scraped their fingers round the insides of their tins. 12 hours' labour, he wrote, for 6 miles' gain, at best. The tent was rattling in the wind. In the ancient lamplight, the faces were stupid with fatigue. Before turning out the lamp, he allowed them an extra dose of grog. It was the one thing they still had plenty of.

Exhaustion had calmed him, flushed away what was useless, cleared his head. The decisions, now, were so much simpler than before. They could not bring the sledge farther, he told them when they woke. They could not do again what they had done the previous day. They could not wait for the surface to freeze. They would have to leave everything but bags and food. How far they still had to go, he did not say. He gave them an hour to better their boots.

I can't go, DeHaven said.

I don't care, Morgan said. You're coming with us.

I don't want to.

I don't care. You're coming with us.

I can't see. I can't walk.

I don't care, Morgan said. I'm not leaving you behind.

Why not? DeHaven said. He sounded like he was going to cry.

The whys and the wherefores are no matter now. We're not leaving you behind. Full stop.

Is it for her? Is that it?

Morgan didn't answer.

I refuse, said DeHaven.

You had your chance and you missed it, Morgan said. From now on, I decide.

For the last time, he crawled out of the tent. In the green

167

dawn, he looked back at the Devon Island coast. Day after day, north from Cape Osborn, south almost to Beechey, he had laid it all down. As best I could, he wrote afterwards, in the conditions that obtained, with the tools at my disposal.

He had them balance a tent-pole across his shoulder. Two packs were loaded, compared, corrected. One of those for a standard, until every load was identical, counterweighed. There would be no pack for DeHaven. That was the only concession made.

He had them parcel up everything else on the sledge, tight and tidy, as though they might come back to collect it at their convenience. Everything, he said. Even the buffalo skin. Even his charts and instruments, and the medicine chest, and the scales, and the lamp.

He handed DeHaven the tub of hog's lard. Extreme unction, he said. Ears, nose, eyes, lips. What else? You're a doctor, you should know.

DeHaven said nothing, took his scoop, handed it on.

For staffs, they gave DeHaven two tent-poles with padded feet. At first, the legs simply refused to obey. He was leaning forward, almost falling, and step after step a leg swung out to keep him up. Morgan had once seen an old sailor with two wooden legs and two canes walk in much the same way. It could be done. It would get easier, Morgan said, as the legs came back to life.

Once they had started that day, he refused to consult his watch. He pushed on without portion, as though determined to cripple them, by sheer exhaustion. All day he herded them on as best he could. Promising, or goading, or daring them to give in. There she is, he bragged – the headland directly ahead of them, still seven or eight miles off, on the Cornwallis shore. That's the medal, he said. They could collapse when they reached it, but not before. It was not just for the men. He too fed on the fantasy. It was a screen between himself and the suffering, and the prospect of more.

They had no tent, but lay down that night in the lee of some hummocks, huddled together in the bags. He put DeHaven in the middle, two men on each side, to keep him warm. Even so, like sprinkled sugar, the frost soon covered his bag the same as the rest. They rested about four hours, without sleeping. Without eating, they set out again. They had no food to speak of. The previous day, without the sledge, they had covered some thirteen miles, he judged.

He had been tutoring himself privately with speeches on resilience, on resolve, on untouched reserves. The deep well each man had within him, and drawing the water up. But none of that could dampen the hope that a depot had been laid down for them on the Cornwallis shore. Myer might not have thought of it, but Brooks surely would. Still, he said nothing of that to the men. Already DeHaven and Cabot looked and sounded a little drunk. He knew it as sheer mortal fatigue, and was afraid of what another disappointment might do.

They reached the Cornwallis shore the next morning, staggering into a strong wind from the north, that seemed determined to hold them up. The men huddled up against the cliff face, around the conjuror. Their fuel was almost done. Only the dregs of the bear fat remained. Their boots were falling apart.

He immediately set off up the headland, ordered the others to take their meal without him, right away. Their meal he called it, afraid to call it anything less. Lukewarm tea and a double dose of spirits, that was all. No one proposed to wait for him. As they were drinking it, two hundred feet above them the wind held their commander ridiculous, lopsided, straining in mid-air – like a puppet, wilting, at the end of a string. At precisely the spot where he'd stood and watched DeHaven approach, three short weeks before.

There was no depot, of course. There was no more food. There was light snow. They were pressed up against the bare rock. They lay down on the bare ground, and closed their eyes. They were shivering mechanically. Around five o'clock, one after the other, Morgan and Petersen and Banes and Daly and Cabot got to their feet. They were within forty miles of warm soup and a warm bed, and now DeHaven announced again that he could not go on. No one showed any sign they heard. He was still lying there in his bag.

Ten feet away, around the corner, the drift was coming on so hard it seemed physically impossible they should stand to it. Morgan led the way. A few minutes later he glanced over his shoulder. It was exactly as he expected. They were all there, all five of them, following.

Before, heading down the Devon coast, the effort often seemed pointless, wasted, there was always so far still to go. It seemed to make no difference, pushing on or calling a halt. Now it was the opposite. Now he was afraid to stop. It was a full twenty-four hours since he'd eaten, and by the end of the day his mind was wandering. With his mind wandering, it was easier to go on. He had dropped back again to drive them. Ahead of him he could see the slumped shoulders, the nodding heads. They too were wilting, rehearsing, learning to give in. He was glad of the veils. Here, now, there were no faces, no silent appeals. He was waiting until weakness began to topple them. All he cared about now was that he not be the first.

Just before midnight, with the men stumbling like drunkards, he pulled them up. Cabot and Banes and DeHaven, he saw, were far more damaged than he. They were slowing him down. He wanted to abandon them, push on with Petersen, survive. By his reckoning they had covered some eighteen miles, had twenty-odd to go. They lay down on the frozen shingle, one right up on the other almost, every man. Beside him, DeHaven was whining quietly, like a dog. Worse, he had never known, and could not imagine. This is the worst moment of my life, he promised himself, counting everything to come. It would be a useful memory, he knew, if he survived.

He knew this must be their last stop. He could see they were spent, almost. They had courage enough for only one more start. He was almost relieved. There was no more need for heroics, no choice to make. He ordered everything abandoned, bags and knapsacks and all. For this last leg, he wanted everything neat and clear in their minds. He ordered them to make a pile of every provision they had, and from their pocket seams they turned out loose crumbs of chocolate, broken nuts, and dust and fluff, and mixed it all in with a cold tin of pork he had been holding back. As they ate he made a little speech. It was a speech from another, warmer world, where it was merely a matter of choice whether or not they went on.

There are ten thousand reasons to give up, and all of them good, he said. They're out there right now, waiting for us, all lined up in a nice orderly queue, every single step of the way. He had never heard himself so definite, so determined, so proud with belief. What he heard was the clamour of alarm.

It was a fine speech, that got every one of them to his feet, except DeHaven. Morgan stared down at him, ready for murder. He was giving him one final chance to pretend. DeHaven would not look him in the eye.

In the end he mumbled: My legs.

Daly and Cabot and Petersen were stamping the ground. There were no favours possible now. All along the shore, the surface was like a layer of broken bottles, in outsized chunks and shards. That was the road they had to take.

Get up, Morgan ordered him.

It was his last chance, and still the man did not move. So Morgan turned to the heap of abandoned gear, and with trembling hands undid his sleeping bag. He had baled it with a length of leather from one of the traces. Slowly and carefully, he now wrapped this around his mitt, for a fist, buckle out. He stood over DeHaven, and lifted that fist into the air.

Get up! he roared.

DeHaven was looking him straight in the eye. He seemed perfectly calm, defiant almost.

Get up! Morgan roared again. And then with all the strength and all the rage remaining to him, he gave one murderous punch to the head.

He stood there panting. He had such pains in his legs he

could barely breathe. He unwrapped the thong, then wrapped it around his mitt tighter again.

Get up, he said.

They still had some twenty miles to go. They had a last drink of rum, and then at six o'clock on the 16th of November, 1850, they all six men made their final start for the ship.

PART III

19th November

Morgan was woken by the smell of fried bacon, and the smell of fried bacon today produced a shrewd, mortal pain in his heart. Then, the sound of crockery, cutlery – a table being laid. Then the first voice. It was MacDonald's, a prayer, expressing profound gratitude to their Lord God and Maker, Who in His infinite kindness had spared these five men's lives and delivered them out of the obnoxious wasteland, back to their friends and their ship, where they would henceforth properly appreciate His untold other mercies. Afterwards, the sound of a meal. Knives squealing on the plates. More voices, chat. Morgan showed no sign he heard any of this. He was awake, but in darkness. His eyes were swollen shut, and he made no effort to open them. He made every effort to lie there as still and as quiet as he could, to give no sign of life. It was as though he thought he could somehow defer it further, his return to the ship.

20th November

Dozing, he heard the door-handle. He did not need to open his eyes. He could smell her, the moment she stepped in. Someone had hung a blanket across DeHaven's bunk, to let him sleep. She lifted it back, looked in. She emptied her lungs noisily, let the blanket fall back into place. A chair scraped. She was sitting down. He managed to open his eyes a fraction of an inch. She was knitting, waiting for him to wake. On the table, laid out in order, the contents of her box. A row of clothes for babies of different age and size – as though there were several babies already aboard, or several babies expected. It reminded him of the plate DeHaven had taken at

Aberdeen, of the entire crew lined up in order of height, from Giorgio to Banes.

Eventually she glanced up and caught his stare, set her wool on her lap. Until now, he had never quite believed her. More than once he'd heard the same news from his wife, and it had always righted itself in the end. But looking at her now, that hope was wrecked. Leaving for Beechey, the belly had merely seemed a little swollen, like someone who's eaten too much during the festivities. Now, even under her coat, the shape of the thing could no longer be disguised.

You came back, she said.

Afterwards as best she could she dribbled soup between the shredded lips. He could feel it dribbling down his neck, inside and out. He did his best to swallow, but felt sickened by fatigue. And forcing himself to eat, it seemed, was forcing himself to recruit, as though the trial was still not done. At first he had protested, insisted on trying to feed himself, but he could not even hold the spoon. The hands lying on the blanket were no longer his own. They were the hands of a drowned man, a week in the water. The skin smooth and swollen and shining, stretched tight. At the end of each fat finger, a baby's fingernail was embedded deep in the flesh, ready to pop.

21st November

Today the exhaustion had subsided a little, the better to let the pain push through. Every inch of his flesh was teeming with it, savage loud and savage bright. On the bunk opposite, too, DeHaven was breathing heavily, whimpering every time he had to break wind. Morgan looked over at the battered face. They held each other's stare. In the eyes there was only recognition, no hate. They knew. They had pushed through, survived.

Kitty came and sat with them again. She brought him a jar of preserved peaches, and today he could just about hold the spoon. One spoon at a time, he could just about keep it down. Afterwards she unwrapped his bandages, to rub salve into the broken skin.

As she worked she chatted amiably, about what had happened in the weeks the sledge party had been gone. She was explaining about Myer, how his health had declined. It was now a fortnight since the old man had left his cabin, she said.

Afterwards, as if out of politeness, she asked about the journey to Beechey, the efforts and obstacles, the empty-handed return. Before, he would have been wary of submitting it to her inspection, would have preferred to hoard – as though the thing were so fragile it might crumble on contact with the air, the light. Now, he began to talk. For what felt like the first time ever, he talked freely, to distract himself from what she was doing with his fingers and his toes.

From his bed, he let his mind swing back compass-like to the scene. Often it seemed to him they were still out there, seen from afar – dim, tiny figures, featureless, the merest touch of a paintbrush on a vast backdrop. He didn't know, he said, if they could have done more. They certainly could have done less. It was a first, faltering version of events, of their failure. He too wanted to understand what had happened, explain it, even if culprits had to be found. They seemed to have failed utterly, as though they had not tried at all. He felt it a mere sliver, that separated all their efforts from some kind of success. As though a greater or smarter effort could have brought another result. But what effort exactly, where, and when? And from that sliver, how had the gap grown so impossibly wide?

In Trinidad he'd once seen a water-boa take a week to digest a bird. It had seemed an extremely tedious ritual, but since returning to the ship that was how he felt his mind at work – trying to chew, swallow, and digest the ordeal. Deliberately, almost stupidly, he reminded himself that they had not failed. They had done exactly what they set out to do. They had travelled on foot from the north of Cornwallis all the way to Beechey and back, man-hauling, in the November storms of 1850. It had never been done before. It would never be done again. It was – he hoped – the greatest physical feat they would any of them ever perform. There was no point trying to water it down, or dreaming of some other exploit. This, here, in the Wellington Channel, in the heart of winter, was what had been asked of him, and he had spent every ounce in the task. He had given his all, was beyond reproach. They could say what they liked below decks, he told himself. He had led them safely out and back, pushed no one harder than he had pushed himself. Those were the hard, immutable facts, that he kept rehearsing to himself. Why were they not loud enough to drown the other murmurs out? Because there had been neither success nor failure, only effort and relief. They had found nothing, met no one, exhausted themselves in the process, that was all. They had not returned to safety, but to something else. What that was he could not quite say. There seemed so much more uncertainty now in the ship, and so much more menace. He had to be careful now where he looked. In certain places, he knew, there was some brutal proof he was not yet ready to meet. Perhaps – except the man opposite – that was why he'd thus far avoided those he'd travelled with. He didn't even want to imagine what state they'd been in when the layers all came off – what was hidden underneath. He had been equal to it out there, in utter necessity, the torrent roaring in his ears. But here, with no useful distraction, he was not. He still couldn't face it, whatever gross fact was scalded into their flesh. Even now, in the officers' cabin, when she came to change his dressings, he still looked away.

He'd still not been to see Myer, for something like the same reason. But he could not put that off much longer, he knew.

23rd November

They were all somewhat diminished, Morgan said, but none so much that a little mothering would not revive them. Dr DeHaven had returned of his own free will. His assistance had been invaluable. As ordered, they had proceeded south along the coast to Beechey Island, where they had expected to find the other expedition ships, but did not. Difficult conditions and diminishing supplies there prevented them from searching further. In the course of their travels, no evidence had been found of Franklin.

Myer lay in his bed barely moving. He looked much worse than Morgan had been led to believe. Even so, Morgan felt his silence an accusation, and made the mistake of trying to explain. Given their strait, he said, at Beechey he had simply sounded the other men, as to whether they thought it better to search the neighbouring inlets for Austin's ships, or to return.

You are not telling me it was your subordinates made the decision for you, or should bear the responsibility for it? Myer said. He sounded almost amused. He seemed to be imitating himself. His voice was weakened, but the bluntness and breeding was still there.

No sir, Morgan said. But I respected their experience, and I expected any considerations they might voice would be of value to me.

Did you want a second opinion, Mr Morgan, or did you simply want someone to second the opinion you yourself had already formed? Myer's head was propped up, stared straight ahead. He was addressing the wall just beyond his feet.

It was the very severe reduction in our provisions, Mr Myer, in a worsening climate, on worsening roads, that discouraged me from searching further.

And no one objected?

Captain Myer, Morgan said, I would not for a moment have it understood that any man would have been slow to go on, but we – I – saw little point, and no safety in doing so, and the prospect of endangering others who might afterwards be obliged to search for us, should we be unable to complete our return, for want of supplies. If you cared to go and inspect the men, and saw their condition, you would be obliged to agree, I think, that even another day out would have been the end of us all.

On the 18th of November, Morgan wrote in the captain's journal, Mr Morgan regained the ship with all of his charges, plus Dr DeHaven, having been out one full calendar month, rather than the lunar month their orders had provided for. Several complain themselves a little less in the flesh. I expect them all to resume their duties shortly. There is no evidence whatsoever, he alleges, that Sir John Franklin ever visited the Devon Island coast.

Myer thought he was being shrewd of course, forcing Morgan to take his dictation. He thought he was merely tracing over old lines. But Morgan was quietly pleased with this new task. From now on the ship's journal and log would be in his hand, and already he was reworking some of the words. He would bide his time before adding the first phrase of his own.

26th November

The day was exceptionally mild, and DeHaven and Morgan went up on deck to try to walk a little life back into their legs. Morgan sent the watch below. He wanted to talk without being heard.

What do you think it is? he said.

It's hard to say, DeHaven said. Out here, in this cold, with this food, the symptoms aren't always easy to read.

Do the men know how bad he is?

They know he's confined to bed, but I've been deliberately vague.

They stopped at the Post Office, already out of breath. Morgan rattled the cage, to see were they still alive. We can't have them thinking there's no one in command, he said.

What's there to command? DeHaven said. The little there is to do, I could almost manage it myself. We're like a ship in port, for godsake.

Not quite, Morgan said.

In any case, the man doesn't command, he interferes. The day you left, he was so busy I swear to God I wanted to drug the bastard.

Under the red light of the train-lamp, Morgan sprinkled the seeds through the wire cage. His mind was already hurrying ahead. His captain was dying. Of what he did not know, did not care. The news was neither warning nor chastisement. The thing was already too far gone, as though it had been going on quietly for years. He wanted it over, was all. He wanted it part of the past, of that other world.

Around the ship the ice was stiff as glass. Overhead the moon was gaudy, in a sky the colour of mud. To the south and west, the land was a cobalt slab. It had taken him too long to admit it, that the day was definitely over, that the light had dimmed.

He caught himself thinking about the baby, wondered would Myer last that long. Something in him, that he had not suspected, would be disappointed if Myer never saw it, was never obliged to admire. At the very least, he would like the man to know it was born. At least once to hear the raucous cry slice through the ship.

Afterwards, he thought of his own father. In that direction too, everything was complicated. Deliberately, he asked himself several clear questions, trying to herd himself past the easy answers. Lying had always been a great talent with him.

Would he have been eager to present it to his father, if his father were still alive?

Yes and no.

Why yes? Why no?

There were so many good answers, it was almost impossible not to lie. He tried to tell himself it did not matter, that it was perhaps better this way. To his father – Myer too, he told himself – it would have been no more than a mouth, a charge, a noise. In any kind of company, Morgan suspected, the man would have been mean with his joy. Even so, Morgan imagined handing over the child. He hoped it was not a question of proving anything, of parading, of success. The old man would have to hold it, of course, feel it struggle, tighten his grip. At any other distance, admiration or indifference came too cheap. He would have to relive, perhaps, what he'd felt when Morgan himself had been in his arms. Perhaps that was what Morgan really wanted to see.

27th November

She found him lying on her bed, in his boots, eyes closed. She set the cat down on the floor and instantly it leapt up onto the blankets, to sniff at his bandaged hands. At the first lick, the eyes opened wide. He started to get up but she waved him down. To answer the sickness and the fatigue – Morgan's as much as her own – she now had nothing but care and patience, an endless fund. He was grateful. He still could not stand for long. He could not yet lift his arms above the horizontal.

It was midday. She'd just had a bath. She stood towelling out her hair, in her nightclothes, made no show of getting dressed. Her boots stood side by side against the wall, waiting obediently. There was to be an inspection later, that was why.

Even now, talking to Morgan, she was merely waiting for another admirer to call. That was why she'd had her bath. It was DeHaven. She wanted to be impeccable for him, as though he would be inspecting for flaws.

In his mind Morgan saw the scene. Her lying on the bed, nightdress hoisted, the folds lying nicely about the bump. The rest of the body has been forgotten. She lies motionless, more than docile, strangely eager for whatever is to come.

3rd December

They'd cleared a space in the hold, and brought in two stoves. Even as he stepped inside, his head jerked back, struck. The whole place stank royally of peaches. The jars had exploded months ago, frozen, and now been woken by the heat.

In semi-darkness, actors were shuffling around the stage. Eventually the lights came up. A domestic scene. Kitty at the table, kneading dough. In an armchair, feet up, reading a newspaper and smoking a pipe, a Polar Bear. Then, a loud banging at the door. Bear and wife jumped up, terrified. Much farce and panic as he lumbered left and right looking for a place to hide. He tried the trunk, the giant pot, even the oven, but in each found another man already in place. Eventually she pointed to the floor. The bear splayed himself like a rug. More banging. She opened the door and in stepped an outrageous mound of furs.

'Darling, is that you?' she said.

The furs nodded yes.

She pointed at the clock, annoyed. 'Haven't you seen the time? I was going to send out a search party.'

Veil, hood, hats, scarves, gloves – layer after layer, it all came off. Underneath, it was DeHaven. She tried to lead him inside, but something held him back – a rope looped around his waist, that stretched out the door. She took hold and began to pull, drew three more men through the door. They were snow-blind, and much was made of them staggering around as if in darkness, stumbling over the bear, and feeling everything – Kitty included – with their hands.

Morgan sat watching, entranced, like a child, full of fear. The world had shrunk to the size of the stage. By now, the merest gesture there had magical power over him.

'Did you miss me?' DeHaven said.

'Of course,' Kitty said.

'Then why didn't you write?'

'My word isn't good enough? You have to have it in writing?'

'Yes.'

She began to write, and began to cry, to wipe her eyes, and wrung out her handkerchief – a long stream of water – into a bowl.

DeHaven made to embrace her, but as soon as he laid a hand on her she yelped.

'Oh darling, what is it?' he asked with a tender voice.

'My bedsores!' she moaned. 'It's all the time I've been spending on my back.'

Of all the men in the room, only Morgan showed no sign of having understood. He smiled stupidly, that was all. He should never have come along. Accepting their invitation, he was accepting the role they'd assigned him. But now he refused to be drawn any further into that game. He refused to supply them with even the slightest show of possessiveness.

'Well,' Kitty was saying now, 'I was expecting you much earlier, but I've been keeping your dinner warm.'

She went to the oven, bent to open it. From the table, DeHaven stared shamelessly at her rump, and rubbed his hands together greedily. 'Fresh meat!' he shouted. She came up with a charred lump on a plate, set it before him with a grand smile. Meanwhile, the other men were ransacking the room, eating everything they could lay hands on – and taking every opportunity, of course, to step and stamp on the bearskin rug. To great applause, one was now drinking straight from the lamp. The others were eating candles, and one was eating the pages of a book.

'Easy boys,' the husband shouted, 'your bellies aren't used to such fine fare. It'll go through you like a dose of salts.'

'Oh, you poor things,' she suddenly said, 'you must be starving!'

She brought out a sugar loaf, that looked vaguely like a little snow-covered rock. The men rushed towards it but DeHaven held them back. With great solemnity he took a little paper Union Jack from his pocket, stuck and saluted it, and claimed the loaf for the Crown.

The scene went on like this, in fits and starts. From the crowd, wolf-whistles and abuse. Morgan smiled when he was meant to smile, but could do no more. In his mind now there was no unheckled thought.

'Well, if truth be known – ,' DeHaven was telling Kitty now, ' – it was not the hardship that was hardest to bear.'

'How do you mean?' she said, perfectly naive.

DeHaven nodded at the bed.

'Do you really consider yourself fully fit for the effort?' she asked.

Every man in the audience answered for him.

She stood up, struck an orator's pose, and began to declaim: 'I have no doubt as to the audacity of the undertaking, and the courage required even to attempt it. But however much you might have my admiration, you cannot have my approval. As your commander – as your wife, I mean – I must ask you to defer your hopes, and to reserve your energies for something more useful, something less heroic.'

'I can assure you my condition is very workable,' DeHaven winked at the audience, with a burlesque, half-crazed smile.

By now she was feeling him all over. 'Oh no!' she shouted, 'he's frozen hard!'

The men cheered lustily, barked suggestions on how to warm him up.

Centre stage, they had rigged up something to look like a double bed. Those in furs were standing in line, veils of steam rising from their backs. DeHaven got in first, one by one the other men followed, until the bed was absolutely crammed. Settling herself under the covers, Kitty suddenly noticed her many bedfellows, showed her shock, elbowed DeHaven in the ribs.

'Might I see you a moment?' she said.

'Here I am,' he said.

'In private, I mean.'

'I'm in my nightshirt, in my own bed. How much more private do you want?'

She whispered something in his ear.

'But my dear,' DeHaven explained, 'we prefer to think of ourselves not as a small crew, rather as a numerous family. And a family where one member has unshared privileges cannot be a happy one.'

From the crowd came another stream of profanities, reckless, extravagant. On it went, the blatant farce. Let them spit their bile, Morgan thought. It was a hard enough life, and slow, and long. They had earned the right. He saw only too well why they had invited him, but he let them jeer, and made no objection, as though it were merely one more way of passing the time. There was another play to come, apparently, then festivities, and he was readying to slip away.

On Myer's wall was Myer's favourite portrait. *Sir John Franklin, with his wife.* More than once, Morgan had caught his commander in communion with it. But over the months the faces had retreated behind layers of smoke and grease. Myer had once tried to clean them with alcohol, very clumsily, and by now they were altogether unrecognizable, unless you knew already who they were.

Now Myer lay there motionless, staring at it. Morgan could not tell, at times, what state the old man was in. Whether he was sleeping or not. Morgan himself, Kitty claimed, slept with his eyes half open. A disconcerting sight, apparently. And now he felt Myer's eyes on him, wherever he set his chair.

It's a great manoeuvre, getting old, getting sick, Morgan told him. Perhaps the best move you've ever made. Look at you. You're out of range now. I've missed my chance.

He brought his face right up to Myer's, mirroring it, nose to nose. Until tonight, he'd always got some kind of response. Often barely a grunt, but an acknowledgement nonetheless. Now Myer lay motionless under the blankets, holding Morgan's stare, occasionally opening his mouth, but silent, as though waiting for something worth a reply. It was a priestly role, and to Morgan's mind the man played it well. So Morgan talked, knowing he would not be answered, might not even be heard, probably not be understood. Keep talking, the silence seemed to say. You have not yet got to the heart of the matter. You are still hiding something. You have not said enough.

Quite a legacy you're leaving me, Morgan said. I hope you're proud.

He leaned closer, elbows on his knees, to examine the stupid grey face. The words had every one evaporated in mid-air, between the chair and the bed. He wondered why he came so often and stayed so long, night after night. At first, of course, it had been to listen to Myer dictate the log. But for the past five days Myer had been too tired or too ill to speak. He wondered why he did not simply sit there reading, ignoring the old man. He wondered why he talked so much – or why he talked at all. It felt like something he'd been waiting to do his whole life. No one had ever been obliged to listen to him before. They had always been the ones talking, he the one sitting in silence, forcing himself to understand.

It's not quite the same now, is it? Morgan said. He was goading himself on. He had only to say what he was afraid to say, what he'd been muttering to himself privately all these months.

The eyes went on staring at the wall. Suddenly a crowd

was passing in the corridor and Morgan held his breath the better to hear. He thought he heard the whimsy of a penny-whistle somewhere in the midst of it all. Still the theatricals were going on, though they seemed by now to have broken out of the hold. Then, from Myer's carriage clock came a lone, chill stroke, calling him back. He glanced again at the man in the bed and saw that the lips were moving, rasping, as though about to speak. Morgan shifted his chair, leaned closer, the better to hear. Then Myer started to cough. He coughed long and hard, as to clear something out of the way. Afterwards, he lay with his eyes closed, in silence. The effort had exhausted him. But weak as he was the old man seemed tougher than ever. Unassailable, physically. He was dying, near-comatose, and apparently indifferent to the fact. What further threat could Morgan pose?

You think you're being patient, Morgan said. Maybe you are. But what's the good of being patient when time is running out?

There was no answer, of course. He sat back in Myer's chair. He was weighing a glass of Myer's brandy in his hand. He was reformulating, more perfectly, all his answers and his jibes, and concocting new ones, for interviews to come.

He caught himself listening again for movement out in the corridor, but by now the revels were raging all about the ship, and it was impossible to tell if someone was out there or not. He turned to Myer's mirror, to his own ruined face. The scabs were withering, the edges starting to fleck away. Underneath was a clean, new pink. Part of him would like to have gone up and gone out with them, let himself be herded along with the rest of the crew. They were up there now, the men he'd travelled with. They were out on the ice, dancing about the fire.

His eyes glanced again at the gap under the door, at the flickering light. He pushed the cork into the bottle, pushed the bottle to the far side of the desk. Then suddenly stood up, turned the key, and flung open the door. It was Kitty, in something like a cardinal's costume, visibly happy and visibly drunk. This was how she wanted to confront him, he saw. She pushed her way past.

How's the patient? she said.

Much the same, unfortunately.

Myer was snoring bluntly now. The trunks were full of his clothes. The air full of his very personal smell. She stood closer, looked down at him, with watery eyes. She was swaying slightly on her feet.

Perhaps you'd better go to bed, Morgan said.

He's going to die right there, in that bed, she said. Then it will be your bed, I suppose.

That's life, Morgan said. You're only ever joining the end of the queue.

Captain Morgan, she said. You'll have to wear the hat.

On the rug under her feet was a grotesque stain.

He's not giving up easily, is he? she said.

No, Morgan said. He looked up and looked down again. There were burn marks on the floor all about the foot of the stove.

You have to admire his spirit, she said. I hope I've as much fight in me when my time comes.

He let her talk. He could not yet muster the courage to send her away. She was a well-built woman, that pregnancy had only improved. Even now, under the silk, her breasts stood straight out from her body, as though strapped to it.

I'm not proud of what I've done, she said. I mean putting you in this position. But when it happened I wanted it to happen. I don't regret it. I want you to know that.

What are you talking about? he said, with an anger he'd not expected of himself. Do you mean the play?

The play? she said. She sounded quite confused. That was only a bit of fun.

The arms flapped up and down, bird-like. The purple silk was billowing beautifully. Morgan was lounging against the desk. It was as far as he could put himself from her, in that space. The side of his head was leaning against the wall. Two

189

feet from his brain, a torrent of sound was pumping past. It was one o'clock in the morning and he was waiting for a drunk woman to talk herself out. He did not bother to answer or interrupt. It would all be forgotten tomorrow, by the only person who cared.

The winter is going to be a long one, she said. We are going to be obliged to spend some considerable time in each other's company. So wouldn't it be best, don't you think, if we tried to clear the air?

He remembered lying with her, naked and sweating, in the dark. She had talked about her life before, her life after. She'd burned all her bridges, she said then. Now she was talking again, and all he could think of was whether or not he would try to take her in his arms. He could not decide. He was distracted by desire. In his mind, as though standing again in her brother's house, in the bedroom doorway, he saw his naked body lying on top of hers. Flesh feasting on flesh, raw. He was not sure what it was that excited him most – the sight of his own body in full flight, or the sight of hers.

But this child, she was saying now. It may be a gift. It may be a chance for both of us to . . . redeem ourselves. I know I'm being a bit vague. Perhaps this will help you to understand. She produced a sealed letter from her pocket. She was holding it out. It was fine, bonded paper, his name on the front. He could read it whenever he wanted, she said, and set it on the desk.

Tomorrow she would take off the simple face she'd painted for tonight's performance. She would lean into the mirror, begin to rub. The sharper lips and eyes, the darker skin. It would come off in greasy, shit-coloured streaks. The rubbing would go on patiently, pitilessly, until she was done.

In the end Morgan took her by the elbow and led her out the door. He watched her moving down the dark corridor. She was swaying from side to side, bumping into the walls, as though they were riding a heavy swell. Under her costume, the hips swung back and forth. Watching that, he could not understand why he'd sent her away.

190

Back in Myer's cabin, he was tempted to shove Myer up against the wall and just lie down by his side. The previous night again he'd barely slept for the pains in his legs, and by now he felt aged and sickened by fatigue. He poured himself a nice-sized brandy and put it inside him. He poured another. He looked at her letter. He'd let her finish her speech without interruption. Now he tore the thing into little pieces. He flipped open the lid of the stove with his fingertips – his fingernails almost – a little knack he had, to avoid getting burned.

4th December

The door to Myer's cabin was warped again, and he had to pull on it with all his weight. Bursting open, it felt like a dramatic entrance, a decisive act. Inside, DeHaven was sitting on the hard chair, facing the bed. Morgan put his shoulder to the door and rammed it shut.

How long before we're obliged to say something to the men? he said.

You know, DeHaven said, while we were away Brooks was laid up five days with the flux, and it was MacDonald running the show. When Brooks finally surfaced he says no one had missed him.

Morgan could well believe it, even on so small a ship. Since their return, he mostly kept to the officers' cabin, and in the cabin kept mostly to his bed. He wanted to see no one. He wanted to crawl into a dark corner, to pick at his scabs, root around for blame. Kitty. Myer. The sly tug north. The failure to find any trace of Franklin or Austin. His decision to come back.

The old man lay there unconscious. At night now, whenever the lard-lamp went out, the blankets froze to the outside wall. Some day soon that bed would be empty, but there was no prize in taking his place. It seemed a punishment as much as a test, to inherit a ship lodged so far north, so deep in the ice, with the worst of the winter still to come. To be obliged to keep them all alive until summer, then somehow get them out.

Isn't there any way at all you can keep him alive? he said.

The minute he's dead I can pickle or preserve him, but not before.

Not quite what I had in mind.

Dead or alive, what does it matter? DeHaven said. You go on running the ship the way you've been running it this fortnight past.

In a way, DeHaven was right. Sooner or later, in the coming weeks, he would have to announce that Myer was dead, that he was assuming Myer's role. But there would be no decision for Morgan to make, no possible change of tack. They would wait out the winter here, exactly as Myer had planned. To anyone who grumbled, he could cite their orders, that were nicely vague and nicely clear – namely, to push up into the Wellington Channel, as far as they could. To further objections, he had only to rehearse the facts. They were trapped in a city-sized block of ice, stuck or adrift it did not matter, they were already too far from Beechey to make a retreat. It was too late in the year. They had a pregnant woman aboard. They could not abandon the ship.

With his fingernail, Morgan flicked open the latch of Myer's locker. You don't need any of this for the hospital? he said.

They sat drinking their captain's brandy, watching him breathe.

How's the face? Morgan said.

You tell me. You're the one has to look at it.

It looks fine. Adds character. Like a duelling scar. Not that character was something it ever lacked, Morgan said.

192

Well, character's not something a man can ever have too much of, is it?

No, I suppose not.

Morgan offered the bottle. DeHaven offered his glass. They sipped cautiously, as if tasting the thing for the first time.

I do ask myself, on occasion, however I ended up here, Morgan said. Where exactly it was we drifted off course.

Apparently, all a man's problems derive from the fact that he's unable just to sit quietly in his own living room.

Who says?

I don't know. One of those gentlemen who thinks about these things. A Frenchman, I think. We'll have to ask Cabot.

Whoever it is, it sounds like Kitty's been reading him, Morgan said. He nodded at the partition wall. All day long, she just lies there reading or sewing or sleeping. Morning till night. And not a bother in the world, from what I can see.

In silence, they listened to the noise outside, the craving. Morgan knew he was stupid, in certain ways. There were blind spots. Some people – Kitty included – likely thought him deliberately obtuse. Dishonest, they meant. He was beginning to suspect they – she – might be right. Almost five months in, and he still did not believe. She had always been this size. She had always slept this much, at these times, in this way. When she woke, as always she would potter to the galley to chat with Cabot, tinker with the pots. Afterwards, if the weather was calm, she might shuffle awhile up and down the deck, that they'd finally cleared and housed over from foremast to stern. Very considerate of you, she said, when she saw what he'd done. That was the day after she'd come to confront him, drunk. Morgan said he'd merely relayed the order from Captain Myer, to fix the ship for winter, to house over the deck, and put up the rest of their stoves. Captain Myer has decided, were the words he used, to the men. As though inspired by her example, he had listed out daily duties for each man, a two-week roster, to coach them through all the idle days ahead. I don't see my name on the list, she said. Name your trade, he said, and gave her a column, but left it blank. She didn't need it. She already had her routine, and every arrangement. She woke, and pottered to the galley, and shuffled awhile up and down the deck, then read or sewed or dozed again, until dinner-time, day after day. It felt like a familiar life, where everything had finally found its slot. She was convalescent, slowly mending, the trauma far behind.

7th December

Often Morgan sat with the old man all afternoon. The men would think they were in conference, he told himself. So for hours he sat flapping through Myer's books, sipping at his spirits, slowly draining them down, and sometimes talking aloud to himself.

Back in October, when they ceased to shave, Myer had confiscated the forecastle's mirror, as though to hide all evidence from the men of their decline. Morgan looked down now on the man who'd written that order. The face was wax. The eyes stared stupidly into space. In the end he could stand that face no longer, and laid down one of his silk handkerchiefs to keep it out of sight. For the man without a face, of course, he felt nothing but sympathy. He himself had not been the same since coming back. It was trouble to sleep and trouble to wake. The slightest effort and it was work to breathe. Ten times a day he tested his teeth with his tongue, to see were they still firm.

He stared at the cloth in silence, waiting for the sympathy to drain away. Once it was gone, he knew, something else would take its place. He could feel a new fear inside him unfurling all its arguments, like a sickness coming on. The man's breathing seemed deliberately louder, made to grate. The handkerchief was trembling at each breath. In the end he could stand it no longer, stood up to leave, and stood over the bed. He was stiff with rage. He took hold of the blankets and pulled them right up over the face.

About the ship the floe seemed perfectly solid, yet their nose had definitely swung round to the north. The thing was impossible, he told himself. It was too cold, and too late in the year. Astern, their storehouses were all intact. The row of lamp-posts that led to the shore, all still in place. But deep beneath the surface, something was on the move. He could feel it in his bones, in his teeth. He could feel his excitement mounting. He took a lamp and shuffled down the gangway.

A mile to the south was a clean new crack, a foot wide. He hounded it out into the Channel, then south, then all the way back to the land. By then the doubt was gone. The next high tide would rip them from the shore again, and set them free.

Coming in, he found a bright rind about Myer's door. He turned the handle silently. She was lying beside the old man on the bed, mapped in gold, smug as a cat.

You make quite a couple, Morgan said.

I had to lie down, she said. The minute I came in he started to kick and I thought I was going to collapse. She lay on the covers in her housecoat. I came to see the patient, she said.

And how do you find him?

Find is exactly the word. He was hiding under the blankets. For a moment I thought you'd smothered him.

I won't say I've not been tempted, Morgan said.

You'd be doing everyone a good turn.

Sure, he'd thank me for it afterwards, Morgan said with a smile, that she refused to match. You don't seem too shocked at the notion, he said.

Five years with the natives and the whalers will school all that out of you. And do you honestly believe I never thought of it with my brother?

I won't do it, of course, no more than you did, Morgan said. I won't do anything, only let him go in his own good time.

Why not? I never had my brother as helpless as this. Where you want him, the way you want him, at long last. Suddenly she thought of something. Do you think he can hear us? she asked.

Very likely, yes.

She reached out her hands. He took hold and drew her up. Whatever her trouble, apparently it had passed.

I wouldn't stand up to him when he was hale and hearty. But now he's helpless, I should take my revenge? Quite a heroic role you've picked for me, Morgan said.

It wouldn't take much, she said. The state he's in.

Another blanket or two, you mean? A pillow, perhaps?

Not even that, she said. Forget to load the stove. Forget to feed or water him for a day or two.

Hurry it on, you mean.

Let it happen. Get out of the way.

I'm too much of a coward, Morgan said.

I don't believe that. A man who'd come out here and then do what you did, to Beechey and back?

That's not courage. It's merely a greater fear trumping a lesser one.

That sounds very like courage to me.

It doesn't feel like it.

She nodded at the bed. But you lack, at present, a greater fear.

It seems so.

Nothing comes to mind?

Not for the moment, no.

You'd better start digging. Otherwise you'll be left to live with it afterwards. He's not going to last much longer, you know.

All around them, the timbers were creaking restlessly. He charged the stove, as though to settle here for the day. He went and got them some tea. They talked. These were the stupid, blatant hours of the afternoon.

196

The day before sailing, I went to see my father, he told her. He was very ill. Perhaps that was why I volunteered. Perhaps I simply didn't want to be there when his time came.

He'd been fading month by month, and Morgan had put off going to tell him the news, that he was going away, probably for several years. The unspoken hope was that he would die first, before Morgan was obliged to say goodbye. When I finally saw him, Morgan said, I wanted to turn around and walk straight out again. I stayed, of course. But it was hard to believe that thing, that person, lying there in the bed, was my father. That I was his son. He was so thin, and so old. The worst thing was, his mind was going, and he didn't – couldn't – wouldn't? – recognize me.

Morgan told her the story as dryly as he could.

He was remembering the last night. He found one of his father's men in the kitchen, by the fire. They'd played together as boys, needed no code. Morgan told him to open a bottle and they drank a silent toast. Afterwards he went upstairs to close his trunk. All night they heard him moving about the house, from room to empty room. In one of the wardrobes he found all his father's folded shirts, perfectly smooth and perfectly white, looking like they'd never been worn.

That must have been hard, Kitty said.

It wasn't easy, Morgan said.

She stared at him like a curious child. The dry eyes, the closed face, the dead passionless grief. Outside, the ice groaned and stuttered against the hull.

I'm going to show you something, Morgan said.

Kitty listened to him walking down the corridor. Almost immediately he was back. He'd brought his private journal. He fanned it out, foraging. Eventually he handed her a letter with his name on it. She weighed it in her hand, and looked up at him, impressed.

What's in it? she said.

Open it and see.

As she began to unfold it, something bounced off the floor.

197

It rolled and turned a tight circle, wound its way down. It was a coin, about the size of a half-crown.

Every July I get a card from him, with a little something inside, Morgan said. Every year, like clockwork, since I left home. Over twenty years now. And always the exact same amount, since the year I went away.

When did you get this one?

It was waiting for me at Beechey. It must have been sent about the time I left.

She picked up the coin, folded the paper over it again, handed it back.

To them, that's who we'll always be, he told her. Children. No matter what we do. No matter how far we go. Beyond a certain point, the passage of time can do no more for us. We stay young, and they grow older, and we lose sight of each other in the end.

They went up under the housing for her daily promenade, that DeHaven insisted on. There was some kind of commotion outside, a howling dog. They lifted the flap to look. Banes and Daly carried him in. He'd dug his way into the ice-house and got at a bag of salt cod. They stood watching him suffer. There was nothing to be done.

You need to keep moving, Morgan said. You'll catch cold.

That's another one, she said. How many does that leave?

At this point I'd almost rather it were one of the men, he said.

A man and a shipload of dogs, that's what you want?

Three or four men, yes. As long as there's no sailing to be done.

She mimicked his whimpers, poked at him with her boot.

You get attached to them, Morgan said.

More than to the men?

Well, they have admirable character, some of them. They know how to haul. They know how to starve. They know how to die. And in the meantime they neither drink nor smoke, they need no tents, no stoves . . .

And no sympathy, she said.

Precisely. And when they're done, you can even put them in the pot.

Can you not do that too with a man?

In certain circles it's somewhat frowned upon, I'm told.

The thing went on whimpering, and still no one stepped forward. They were too fond of him. He was one of their bravest dogs.

Wait and see, Morgan told her. I'll have to do it myself.

Dogs are stupid, she said. I could never quite understand the attachment some men form towards them. Likewise with horses. A wonderful memory, but as stupid a beast as you'll ever meet.

Still no one moved. Morgan stepped over and took hold of a spade. In his huge mittens the thing looked both clumsy and frail. He rotated the handle a quarter-turn, the better to deploy the blade.

Go get Cabot, he told her. Tell him tonight I want a good old-fashioned Irish stew.

And easy on the salt, she said.

Indeed.

10th December

The bed was empty. Myer was gone. Morgan quickly closed the door behind him and tried to think. He went and looked in the washroom, in the men's mess. In the officers' cabin, he leaned to look under the bottom bunks.

Lost something? DeHaven said.

Where'd you put him? Morgan said.

I don't know what you're talking about.

Kitty's cabin. The galley. Then all around the deck.

He found him lying by the helm, face down, in full dress uniform, minus his hat. He was not moving, and not yet dead. But there he lay, Captain Gordon Myer, like a bundle of frozen rags. Morgan was afraid to turn him over, for fear his face had stuck to the planks.

DeHaven came with his bag and bent over him. He was barely able to breathe for pain. He seemed to have broken a few ribs, DeHaven said. However he'd managed that. Had he been climbing? They looked up at the mainmast.

Banes hooked his hands under the armpits. They watched Daly take hold of the legs. They carried him down the ladder and along the corridor. Overhead, the red light of the train-lamps poured in the open hatch.

Close that bloody door quick! Morgan roared. Before we lose every bit of heat we have.

That first night, Morgan came to sit once again by his bed.

Is she gone? Myer asked, fearfully. His forehead was sprinkled with sweat, like steam on a window pane.

She's just gone out for a few minutes, Morgan said, with no notion whatsoever who was meant. A fussing mother perhaps, or a fussing wife.

He had only to stand up and he was already at the door. Once he got out, he thought, he would not come back. Here in this cabin, at the old man's bedside, there was nothing but the cunning smell of old bodies and old clothes. The mirror's silver turning to mould. Here the spiral had turned inwards, was now winding tightly about itself. Morgan sipped at his tea, cast his hands about the cup. Myer's stove had gone out, but he did not call anyone to come and set it again.

All day the old man lay motionless, staring at the knots in the planks overhead. The face desperately concentrated, like a man struggling to learn his lines by heart. The short, shallow breaths had something mechanical about them at first. By evening, they had a faintly metallic ring, and when

Morgan woke the next morning they told him Captain Myer had died some time during the night.

At ten o'clock the crew gathered under the housing, around the remains, which had been neatly sewed up in coffee sacks. MacDonald read the Burial Service by their best train-lamp. I am the resurrection and the life, he said. At some point he handed Morgan his Bible, pointed at the passage Morgan should read. Morgan imagined Myer himself reading it, solemn and trusting, and tried to imitate that voice. Even as he spoke, they could hear the clattering in the distance, that sounded like a cotton-mill. It was the floes out in the Channel, on the move again, always dragging them west and northwest. Morgan kept reading, but could not help speaking a little louder, as though to drown that other noise out. When he was done he slapped the book shut and gave a nod.

They hauled the bundle out to the fire-hole. Once the men had gathered round, Morgan nodded again and they tilted the sledge. The canvas was frozen to the wood, and the thing would not slide off. They stood around stamping their feet and thrashing their arms while Cabot ran back to the ship for an axe.

The weather was clear and calm and cold. Wind steady from the south. Morgan looked hard about the whole compass for even the merest hint of a blush. The northern sky, as always, was a deep, inky blue. Overhead the stars were sharp and clean every one. The men watched while he hacked hatefully at the stiff cloth. He did not care. He just wanted to be rid of it. A glaze had already formed again in the fire-hole. The mittens loosened their grip. The bundle wriggled through. Morgan pushed it under with an oar. He turned to the ship and raised his arm. The watch bell rang. They shuffled back the way they'd come, past the line of posts that led to the gangway, each armed with a lantern, that would be lit if ever anyone lost his way in a storm.

Morgan went out again after lunch to see had the hole

201

frozen over, to see if by some mischance the bundle had popped back up. He thought he saw a tint now to the southern horizon, like the green glow of a gas flame. Otherwise, all around, the moon cast a metal sheen on the snow. This was his home and his inheritance. Without the ship, there were no more bears, foxes, or birds. The only life for a thousand miles was now within.

21st December

On the officers' table was a bundle wrapped in crêpe.

I'm sure DeHaven will be deeply touched, Morgan said.

You can't say he hasn't earned it, she said. All the care he's been taking of me.

I don't think a gift is something you can earn, Morgan said. Otherwise it's merely a reward.

She unfolded the paper, held it up, held it against him. You don't think it's too small?

There's really not that much of a difference in size.

What do you think? she asked the other men. Do you think he'll like it?

If he likes you, he'll like it, Morgan said. That's the way it usually works.

Christmas was in four days. He had not seen it creep up. He'd been distracted by the worsening weather, the examinations, Myer's decline. He checked the calendar, again. His fingers counted it out. There seemed something inevitable now about so many things.

As soon as she was gone, Cabot got out his knife and set to work again. He was carving another toy, a horse. The blade stuttered across the wood. The man's face was fierce, the mouth half open, the tongue visibly wiggling a tooth.

Isn't the head a little big? Morgan said.

The wood was polished to a high sheen, every slick crease. In four days' time, Cabot would smuggle it into her cabin and set it on the locker, where it would be visible as soon as she opened the door. As though the child itself might come running in any minute, and he was preparing a surprise. For the first time in decades, Morgan felt excited at the prospect, and frustrated deliciously. It was the mere sight of the presents, the general festive hum and trim. He felt a tightness in his stomach not unlike fear, hesitation – yet simultaneously felt himself tilted forward, ready to rush towards the prize. It was an old habit come rushing back, an echo and an aftertaste. He was learning how to be patient, he supposed, all over again.

At dinner that night he lit a candle, and ordered a universal toast. It was the 21st of December. The best of days, he said.

If you don't mind, I'll wait until Christmas, MacDonald said.

This is my Christmas, Morgan said.

You were too long in Persia, DeHaven said.

Mother's Night, Yalda, what matter, Morgan said. Every day now is a day closer to the sun.

25th December

On Christmas morning, after service, they all crowded into the main mess, and stood before the table in silence. There was fox stew and hare pie. Preserved peas, and roast parsnips, and fried potatoes. There were plum puddings stacked high, ready to fall. There were almond fingers, sugared buns, and an entire crew of gingerbread men ranged about a gingerbread ship.

Morgan did the rounds, moving dutifully from group to group. He made a point of shaking every man's hand. Nearby, he heard DeHaven's group laughing and turned his head. He looked them over proudly, patted Banes's paunch, said he liked to see men who appreciated the good things in life.

Just don't get too fond of it, DeHaven said.

What I think the good doctor is trying to say is, you've got to take it while you can get it, Morgan said. Carpe diem, he told them, plucking the sponge straight out of DeHaven's hands. He tore off a piece and lobbed it into his mouth. Everybody laughed. Seeing his opening, DeHaven reached over and took Morgan's gold-trimmed tricorne, that none of them had ever seen before, and sat it on his own head. Morgan had found it in one of Myer's trunks.

Morgan laid a hand on DeHaven's shoulder and rested it there. Mr Brooks, he said, make a note of that man's name. He's one to watch.

The knot of menace and praise had a private, perverse appeal for almost every man, and they were all laughing again as Morgan moved away.

That afternoon they had a regular shooting-match, a single stake, an ounce of tobacco a man, winner takes all. At a hundred feet, a row of empty pork tins, topped and tailed and laid on their side. Each one housing a candle-stub, alight. The scoring was simple. It was hit or miss, and sudden death. Taking aim, the darkness seemed greater than ever, more definite. One by one the men pulled the triggers. One by one the points of light went out. Eventually Morgan and Brooks went to set them up all again.

Now's our chance, someone shouted. It sounded like Banes.

They had reason enough, Morgan supposed. And they'd been drinking since morning. Afterwards, he stood behind them. The darkness was thickening. They could see nothing now but the lights adrift in the night.

In the galley, Cabot had poked holes in the sausages, and the fat was starting to worm its way out, wriggling free. Below, the smell of cooking soon infiltrated the crowd, and seemed bent on stirring up unrest.

DeHaven was sitting alone at the end of the table, a bottle of brandy in his hand. Morgan watched the man lift it to his mouth and gulp it down, with absolute impunity. Nice of the captain to join us, DeHaven shouted across the room.

Morgan came and sat opposite.

Another year over, almost, DeHaven said. And so much to celebrate.

You're still alive, aren't you? Morgan said. Six weeks ago, you would have settled for that.

A man on the wheel will say anything to save his skin.

Even so, Morgan said, what we cherish in times of trial may be a mark of proper priority. Inside him, one by one, the drink was clearing all obstacles out of its way. It progressed patiently, methodically, with a kind of polite pedantry. It was sure of its course.

Look at the facts, DeHaven said. Where we are, against where we hoped to be. If you ask me, a more perfect failure would be hard to achieve.

Morgan watched the ship's surgeon trying to cut a sausage. Do you want me to get your bag? he said.

God knows where this came from, DeHaven said. Did you check Myer was still all of a piece, when Cabot sewed up the sack?

The door had been propped open with a stool, and out in the corridor he could see the ream of light under her door. Eventually DeHaven went to empty his bladder. As soon as he was gone, Morgan stepped out and stood at her cabin door. Expertly, he turned the handle to peer inside. She was lying under the covers with her eyes closed. The desk was covered with presents. There had been more for the baby than anyone else. The men talked now as if it might arrive in the next few days. Sometimes they talked as though it had already been born. There were toys, wraps, even tiny socks. A bell-shaped rattle. In the corner, the little cradle Cabot had made. A visitor would be looking around for the baby itself.

Are you all right? he asked. He could hear the drink in his own voice.

I'm fine, thanks, she said.

Can I get you anything?

She shook her head.

I'll leave you in peace then, he said, rather sadly.

She nodded her agreement and he pulled the door to. It had not gone quite as he expected.

He went up to empty his bladder, and stepped out onto the floe. The dogs were scrambling about in the darkness, dragging off the bones from dinner, to bury for harder times. He unbuttoned his flies and let it come. He turned slowly on the spot, cutting a deep hole in the ice, three hundred and sixty degrees. As though that might be enough to make it give out from under him. It did not. Under his feet, under a bloodshot moon, the ice glowed white-hot. Behind him, the brig was no more than a pasteboard cut-out laid on a pale ground. He stood listening to the rumours. Some sly hand was still carrying them west and northwest. At what rate he could not properly say. But day and night now the gates were closing quietly behind them. One hundred miles deep into virgin soil, DeHaven had announced again, just minutes before. Where never yet the hand of man has set foot. The other officers had smiled, as usual. It was his ability to imitate himself in better times that they needed and admired. Morgan had made no protest, which DeHaven took as a cue for more.

From the start I knew it was a blessing, poor Captain Myer getting sick, he told them. Never God closes one door but He opens another, as MacDonald says. Richard Spread Morgan at the helm. When I heard that, gentlemen, I knew we were saved.

It was neither brag nor bluff, nor another greedy capitulation. The Cornwallis coastline had sunk ingloriously, day by day – then all at once, in a rush to be done. Ahead of them now, in every direction, were battles they could not win. North and south, east and west, it was endless devastation. Overhead, the rigging was dripped glass. A veil of fog was coming down, blurring the outlines. If he stayed out much longer, it would be transparent shadows, no more. Even so, he was sad to leave it, to go back inside. The night before, in the captain's journal, he had written: We cannot turn back. It was a convenient truth. Might there still be a means to find a haven for the winter and get themselves in? Perhaps, but he had refused to think it out. Some part of him did not want to stop the slide, or try to return – stay close, at least – to what he knew. He was too fond of the notion by now, the growing distance to the known world.

Below, they had begun to sing. DeHaven was leading the chorus, grandly beating time with a fork. Morgan sat with his back to the crowd, hoping they would not see him alone and try to come to his rescue, try to get him to join in. The brandy bottle was empty, but by now his cabin – his own private supply – seemed too far away. He took a drink from his friend's glass, pushed it round his mouth, trying to paint over the taste of Cabot's peculiar beer.

When eventually DeHaven came back, he pointed at where he'd been sitting before. Sir, he said, I regret to inform you that place is in matter of fact occupied.

I know it is, Morgan said. By me.

They were sitting looking at each other when Cabot came by again, carrying a platter piled high with meat. They could have whatever they wanted, he said. Bien cuit, à point, saignant, or bleu.

Where's the blue one? DeHaven said, lifting up the slabs of meat, looking under them, searching. Blue! he said. He was almost shouting now. His fingers were dripping with grease and blood.

207

Cabot looked frightened. He looked like he did not know the word.

B-L-U-E! DeHaven roared at the struggling face. You want us to spell it out for you?

That night they drew lots, noisily, and the men refused to allow that the draw had been fair. If it wasn't done over, there'd be mutiny, shouted Banes. Cabot won a pint of brandy. Hepburn won half a dozen cigars. Morgan had made sure to allow them plenty from the stores. It was another trade. In the half-light, the faces were famous with drink. Champagne! shouted DeHaven. Cabot said there was none left. It was a lie, a two-man conspiracy. Morgan had confiscated the last two cases. They were in his cabin, hidden under the bed. He was keeping them for the birth. When – if – it happened, he wanted to show it was something to celebrate.

31st December

Alone in his cabin, Morgan reviewed the year. Exactly as DeHaven wanted him to do, he set off the evidence against their ambitions. A more perfect failure, he wrote, would be impossible to achieve. He reviewed the ship's stores and equipment, their position and prospects, the crew. Qualities, he wrote. Obedience? For some reason, I have always been wary of a man too willing to obey. There are men who need to follow, and those I cannot trust. Curious qualm for a commander, I know. I prefer a refusal to fail, even to the point of pig-headed stubbornness. For weaklings and cowards are never stubborn, even in their vices. Intelligence, he wrote.

Good up to a point, but no more. Bravery, I find, often is little more than the ability to recognize necessity in advance. He thought stupidity the greatest threat out here. He who thinks himself smarter than all mischief. That man is mortal danger, and not only to himself. One by one he copied the names out of the muster-roll, and gave each his qualities. In any case, he wrote, it matters not how I rate any individual, for there is no one to supply his place. They will serve. The inevitable will temper them, every one.

He read again Ross's advice for choosing an Arctic crew. It said nothing about experience, hardiness, constitution, age. All Ross said was, no married men, if it can be helped. No man who thinks his life worth something to someone else.

12th January

On the 12th an invisible current began to draw them more northerly, and still he did nothing to resist. Higher latitudes. He liked the words. He would take it as a reconnaissance, a chance to bring back news of the living to be had there, the fee.

Waiting, they talked.

C'est longue, she said.

Morgan nodded in sympathy, but already their drift felt to him like a kind of reprieve. Not an exit, but an unearned stay.

During the night of the 16th they crossed another mythical line. The 76th parallel. Morgan did not announce the fact, but with a flutter he felt something wake inside him – the useless pride that they had penetrated farther north than any other ship. He had expected far greater inhibition, far south of this. He was almost disappointed to find the sea here not utterly impenetrable, to find it was still possible to navigate – navigate! – in the legendary north. It cheapened everything he'd read, the blocks of Arctic literature he'd brought along. His disbelief was part flattery, but he knew well they'd done nothing exceptional. They were trapped in a block of ice ten acres in size. That was their little world, the cast of their lamp. Their progress was no fault or feat of their own. It was an accident of currents and winds that let them penetrate so far, he told the crew. He barely heard his own efforts at modesty. Nothing could shout down the applause he heard incessantly now.

17th January

Several times a day, greedily, he went up to try for new bearings, desperate to figure their drift. But for a week now there were no bearings, and no stars. Day after day he scoured the sky with the glass. Then, just for an instant – it was noon, the 17th of January – he thought he saw a more solid spectre – cliffs? – pushing towards them through the veils, directly ahead. The naked eye only brought it closer, all in a surge. Without warning, a ragged wall stood in their way.

That night he did not sleep. He sewed his last letters and log into his tarpaulin bag and waxed the seam. In two minutes he could be fit to jump. The hull was scraping along the shore. Calmly, he imagined the scene of their destruction. He took one last look at the gilding on the mirror, the crumbs on the desk, the bevelled planks of the cabin wall.

25th January

After lunch he watched her waddle more slowly than ever to the bed. He watched her lie back, with an offended sigh. She lay with the blankets folded to her knees, hugging the bump, warding off the danger. The stove was kept going for her now all day long. It was too warm, and Morgan felt oppressed, felt the sweat rolling down the small of his back.

Oh! she said. The word was full of air. It was a plea for sympathy.

Twenty-four, she said. Contractions, she meant. She'd been counting them, miserly, all through the day.

Kitty, he said, you're not even at seven months. This too would pass, he meant, as every crisis did.

But the old sheets were already piled in the corner. They'd been sitting there for weeks. Even if it were born now, DeHaven had said last night. It was a provocation, a test. His friend was merely sounding the surface, Morgan told himself. He needed more time.

It was unsettling, the way time had begun to expand, to make room for what was to come. Looking back, there were entire years he could barely remember. They had been squeezed of all their flesh. In his journal, on the calendar, they were mere numbers on a page. But the ten or twelve weeks remaining now seemed phenomenally wide. It was an obstacle he would have to hack his way through, inch by inch. Progress would be tedious. He could be patient. He could take his time.

You wouldn't prefer to just stay that way indefinitely? he said.

She considered the conundrum, wary of its traps.

I wish it would just be over, she said. That we could skip all the . . .

All the mess, he said.

All the waiting, that's what I hate. Yet there's a part of me wishes it would last for ever, that the end would never come.

It's not something you can rush, he told her, smiling. As DeHaven says, it's like the blooming of a flower. It's like the leaves on a tree. It takes its own time. You plant the seed, and then you wait.

27th January

Day after day the wind drove them north. It drove them past shingle beaches, past frozen quarries, past sheer, stupefying walls of stone. He remembered running along under the cliffs of Greenland, the cliffs of Devon. Those men had been proud of their summons, and the courage it called for. Before them now was an enemy shore.

It was her birthday. He watched the candles gasping. He watched her heave again and blow the last of them out. Cabot brought a better knife, and Morgan cut.

Not for me, MacDonald said.

Cabot put a lot of work into this, Morgan said.

It's too rich, MacDonald said. My stomach won't take it.

He's fasting, DeHaven said. To mitigate his own vile sins, and the sins of every man aboard.

As soon as she went to bed, MacDonald began to complain. All night and longer he'd been holding it in. He spoke bitterly of their situation, their prospects. In his mind there was only one possible outcome. They were going to be crushed. The first proper pressure, he said, she'll crack open like an egg.

Brooks considered the source of the stupidity. Nonsense, he said. The great merit of this lady – he slapped the wall gently, as though slapping the rump of a champion – is she's not only strong, she's flexible.

Thank you Mr Brooks, Morgan said.

The reed that bends and the reed that breaks.

Precisely.

That's not what Banes says, said MacDonald.

What does Banes say? Brooks was smiling, ready to laugh.

He says she's too heavy and too stiff. All those knees and Samson posts below.

What in hell does he know about it? Morgan said.

He's seen more ships than you and me both.

Ten years building them in Greenock, DeHaven said.

You seem to know more about my crew than I do.

Go talk to them once in a while, DeHaven said. Go play a hand of cards with them. You might learn something's not in the Regulations and not in the log.

Go get him. Brooks.

Brooks brought him back. He stood there defiant, wondering what he'd done. They put it to him, what MacDonald had said.

Look at her, Banes told them. The big fat hips and belly on her. She's all fat and fight and nothing else.

They sent him away, then argued it out.

Believe you me, MacDonald said, every one of those timbers is a sin of vanity, committed by men in the dockyards imagine themselves more savvy than the Lord above. Think on it. Should ever He desire to shuffle about His ice, is it a few lengths of Irish oak will stop him? They're stalks of corn in a threshing machine, no more. They serve no purpose whatsoever but to weigh her down, and make it that much harder for her to heft herself up, when comes the final crush.

We've survived every crush so far, haven't we? Brooks said.

MacDonald looked at the man with open disdain. Once His mind is made up, he said, the ice will go over her, or under her, or through her, or whatever way takes His fancy, and the best and wisest thing you can do then is to stand well out of His way.

213

10th February

It's now, she said.

It's not now, Morgan told her. It can't be, not today.

Why not? she said. Have you something else planned?

Yes he had. One more day, was his prayer now. Twenty-four more hours was all he ever asked for, when the contractions came on like this. It seemed so little, for such relief.

Breathe, he said, refusing to be rushed.

Her breathing was audible, shallow, fast.

It's now, she said.

It can't be now, he told her. DeHaven says there ought to be at least a month left.

Ought? she said, and almost managed a smile.

It was just the time he needed to prepare. Having to live through the last day over and again, constantly rally and muster – the process was steadily draining him of all anxiety. The timing, now, seemed admirable. These next few weeks would wear him down perfectly, find him merely resigned when the moment came.

Today, as always, the contractions came and went.

Well? Morgan said.

I wish my other patients knew how to suffer half as well, DeHaven said.

How many have you now? she asked. In the hospital, she meant. She was trying to change the subject, to take her mind off herself.

Her stove was going full blast, and she was lying in only her nightdress, the blankets folded to her knees.

Why are they sick? she said.

Who? DeHaven said.

The ones are sick, and not the rest.

You see how they live, he said. You see what they eat.

She knew well what they liked to eat. She'd spent more than one afternoon with Cabot trying to concoct something more palatable, and still they'd barely touched it. They wanted their salt junk and their hard tack, and nothing vegetable.

Why don't you go down to see them? Morgan said. To the hospital, he meant – that little corner of the men's quarters that had been curtained off. I'm sure they'd appreciate a little mothering.

The two men sat with her, chatting, trying to distract her as best they could. The contractions did not return. Eventually she dozed off. Once his friend was gone, Morgan stared openly. By now her body ought to have been sacred, but was not. Still it stood in the way of everything else. A wall of feeling surged up as he forced his mind towards it, dwindled as he drew back. He could come no nearer than that to the pregnancy, the birth, whatever was on the other side.

That afternoon he shuffled across the ice and stood panting at the edge of the world. He studied the horizon. One day he would spot a lone figure far out on the ice. Staggering. Starving. Blind. One of Franklin's men, come to reproach him for having given up hope. But not today. Today it was too cold. Directly behind him, on a pole planted fifty yards from the ship, the mercury stood at 27°, in the negative. Under his furs, his lungs were tingling, almost pleasantly. In his mouth was the fine taste of blood. He stood a long time trying to fix what he saw. It was noon. The day seemed to be growing clearer, the silt settling, and he thought he saw something sharper pushing through, far to the south. A gargantuan black mass. A bottomless shaft in a violet sky. It was the mountains of their unknown island, he supposed. He would not see it again. Once again – as if corrected – the course of their drift was west and northwest. Meekly, they submitted themselves to the vast, mindless plan.

14th February

On the 14th of February, returning from his walk, Morgan spotted two ravens rummaging in their rubbish heap. He refused to shoot. He was already too fond of them. It was four months since they'd seen another living thing.

Inside, the stoves were kept going day and night, gave off a furious marmalade glow. Apart from meal times and watch duty, most of the men now kept to their beds.

Cabot! they roared. What's on the menu?

By now Cabot knew the routine. He knew their need to torture themselves. Tonight, he announced grandly, for our Saint Valentine's Feast, we start with oyster soup. Followed by roast beef and gravy. Followed by trotters with a white wine sauce. To finish, whipped cream and jelly cake.

Morgan spent hours sketching them. He had them sit. He scrutinized the faces for flaws.

Why don't you draw me? she asked.

She stood naked before the mirror. She turned full face, three-quarter, profile. The distance from that other woman – the rivalry – was narrowing daily. She no longer minded his stare.

Staring, he found he could admire the transformation, but not the thing itself. The breasts were now a preposterous size, shone like polished wood. Her body was ripening. It had become even more pregnant, somehow. She was the only one aboard not visibly in decline.

He remembered DeHaven boasting, a few days after they'd returned to Disko, of his bargain with one of the native girls. Fresh meat, DeHaven said, at once confiding and taunting. When you haven't had it for a few weeks, there's nothing on God's green earth half as good. Think of it, he said. Red, raw, staring up at you. The feel of it, warm, in your mouth. The juices running down your chin. I'm telling you, Dick, it was pure sin.

He's kicking! she said, turning to face him. Look!

There was no need, he was already staring, but the bald

216

fact of it was too big for his mind to fit around. A young child, fully formed, somehow living inside her, that was one day going to come out. Many times he'd imagined a slow deflation. The protuberance, instead of pushing ever farther into his world, would slowly recede. The thing was not impossible. His own clothes hung on him looser than ever. That very morning he had punched a new hole in his belt.

Look! she said again. She meant the skin, stretched bright and shining, and the world within. You can feel it, she said. He was sitting on the edge of the bed now, she stepped towards him, and pulled up his shirt. She was crushing herself against him, flesh against flesh, as hard as she could. She wanted him to feel it as she did. As though she herself, like a Russian doll, were somehow inside him, Morgan, and inside her something smaller again.

20th February

From the Crow's Nest, he was surveying the ruins again. To the west, a ragged horizon, an iron sky. Overhead, he had never seen aurora so bright, meteors so finely etched. But all too brief for comfort. Only the moon was constant, refused to die. Many an hour Morgan had spent studying her through the glass. Under her stare, the world was the colour of ash. That noon, to the south, it had looked to be soaked in piss. That was the sun, he told himself, every day now closer to the horizon. That was what the calendar said, yet it was colder than ever before. On the 18th they had touched minus 40°. And now the wind, he thought, was shuffling about a bit to the east. He stood there swaying, his eyes closed, listening to the voices again. He would not be surprised if tonight the mercury froze.

All night, it sounded like the carpenters gone mad. It sounded like the plates being popped, or bolted home. It was the ice splintering. It was the porcelain cold. Morgan told anyone who would listen that this was a good thing. It was a wonderful way of dispersing the old, tough ice. It would be easier to navigate, he said, when the break-up came. He was smiling, but the hammering had frightened him, knocked something loose. He did not know why he suddenly felt so close to disaster, to shame. He lay awake most of the night. He woke with the taste of fear in his mouth. He felt not weaker but lighter. Something had drained away.

After breakfast he rounded up the other officers, and Petersen. He wanted to be told what to do, when finally they were crushed.

No one spoke.

DeHaven? Morgan said. You've never been shy with suggestions.

DeHaven said he wanted to go home. But it would be better if the thing could be managed without them all freezing or starving to death.

Mr MacDonald, Morgan said. You have some rather strong views, which you have been honest enough to share with me, with regard to the suggestion, my suggestion, that the best course of action may simply be patience.

It is true that I personally believe it unwise to place our hopes in the ship.

Go on, Morgan said. Tell us why.

In my opinion, in view of her construction and current disposition, it is unlikely she will last very much longer. The longer we wait to abandon, the more our health and stores decline. Unless we act promptly, my fear is that when finally the crisis comes, we may be unable to face it.

Mr MacDonald, Morgan said, let us imagine that, on quitting the ship, we want to make for land. In what direction, at

218

what distance? We do not know, but set that consideration aside. Let us imagine we make land due south. There is nothing to suggest animal life ever ranges so far north so early in the year –

Present company excepted, DeHaven said.

By animal life, you mean the natives? said MacDonald.

I don't, but what if I did?

They can feed us, MacDonald said.

Mr MacDonald, let's try not to forget just who and where we are. Do you honestly believe people so far north, so early in the year, could have food enough for strangers, and if so, that they would be willing to share it, and if so, that they could have enough to feed our entire party for anything but the shortest period, before their surplus stocks, and then their essential stocks are run down? Our very best hope, by that plan, is to prolong a little while our misery, and involve others in it to boot. Then what?

The presence of a woman and a child might well encourage the natives' sympathies, MacDonald said. Or a woman with child, according to our schedule.

Do you really think so?

They are not Christian, but by all accounts they are a noble race.

They all glanced at Petersen. He was asleep, as usual, on MacDonald's bunk.

In any case, Mr Morgan, I think you are taking rather the bleakest view of our prospects, MacDonald said. God is good, as Captain Myer liked to say.

No, Mr MacDonald, I am not taking the bleakest view. I am simply trying to determine our ability to overcome the obstacles we are likely to encounter if we all now set out together over the ice, as you so blithely suggest. And having spent four weeks hauling in better weather, with the lightest sledge, and the fittest men, I believe I can judge the matter at least as well as any man aboard.

As you say, that's your own personal opinion, MacDonald said.

219

Just how much do you think we can haul? Morgan said, almost shouting. How long do you think we can last? How many weeks or months of tremendous toil, over uncertain ice, at inhuman temperatures, day after day, until – what? Until the miraculous apparition of an expedition ship, along a stretch of coast where no ship but our own has ever passed? And all this with a woman and newborn baby in tow?

It may be that Franklin's ships preceded us. Is that not why we are here?

We're to be saved by Sir John Franklin? That's your plan? Gentlemen, I rest his case.

You seem to have everything calculated to perfection, MacDonald said. A pity there is no room in your plan for hope.

I hate to agree with my friend, DeHaven told MacDonald, but he's not wrong, as to the child's prospects. The thing is simply not possible, in such cold. Not for the first year, at any rate.

That settles it then, MacDonald said. We wait aboard until we freeze or crush, then we stand out on the ice and wait to freeze or starve. That's our plan. To go on what we're doing now, indefinitely.

Let me ask you a simple question, Morgan said. Why, if you think life aboard so perilous, did you encourage Miss Rink to come along?

MacDonald said nothing.

He thought it would force us to turn back, DeHaven said. He wasn't thinking of you, or her, or even the child. He was thinking of himself.

27th February

He watched her lick her forefinger. It flicked the charts back and forth. The latitudes were marked in red. Afterwards they stared at a map of Denmark. She trailed her finger across the page, pronouncing the names. For no reason he could think of, he showed her a drawing he'd done of his father's house.

You're disappointed, he said. You expected something bigger. Something more substantial.

Let's say, had it been bigger, I wouldn't have been surprised.

That doesn't say much for how I present myself, does it?

Quite the contrary.

That afternoon there had been a light fall of snow. The ice was stuttering dryly against the hull. She'd thought he was out of her range, was what she meant.

At the dinner-table she produced his picture again. MacDonald and Brooks leaned in for a closer look, and he made no effort to parry their insults.

Nice little stables, DeHaven said. But where's the main house?

He remembered the summers there. August. Parties in the garden. Sunsets. Bonfires blazing on top of the maple trees. The swallows shooting overhead, their shadows dripping down the white walls like molten lead. The years had passed. He'd never before felt much attached to the old place. Now he found he was no longer prepared to run it down as he always had. Since his father's death, it was now his own.

Some days the thing was no more than a rumour, that in a week or two or four there would be a child aboard. He had to force himself, consciously, to remember who that child was. Who would one day look to him for attention and affection. Considering the matter as coldly as he could, he did not think he had any to give. Were the choice his alone, he decided, he would not entrust a child to his own care. Taking care of himself already felt an endless chore. It would be sheer presumption to take on another charge. These were sane, measured

221

considerations, he thought. A showcase of self-knowledge and humility. He would muster something, he supposed, to meet the need. All his life, he'd watched other men at it – uncles, cousins, friends. He'd seen his own father try. He might have the measure of the role, as much as they. The child might not be quite so wise as he feared. In certain roles, Morgan knew, he was more convincing than he expected to be. In spite of everything he might find himself adored.

28th February

She was standing up in the bath. The water slid off her like oil. The wet hair was plotted carelessly. She dried herself off. They went together to her room, but as they were going through the doorway she seemed to stumble, propped herself against the jamb. She stood with her eyes closed, looking inwards. Something was wrong, something new. Her entire body had somehow tightened, as though preparing to be hit. Eventually she opened her eyes and found him. He helped her onto the bed. She lay in the heat, in her underthings, and stiffened and softened and stiffened again. There was a new urgency in it now. He locked the door. A minute later she let out a sigh, a little moan, not unlike the protests of pleasure he'd heard so long ago. It had passed.

She hoisted her nightdress. By now the skin seemed dangerously tight, ready to rip. But it had not ripped, it had continued to stretch, week after week. It had a near-transparent quality now. Week after week, he said, as though he had some sense of progress, which he did not. The thing was as new as it had ever been.

Look! she said. Hiccups!

The skin was moving, blatantly. Times he had stared baffled at the artery pulsing happily in his own neck, beating time to a tune he would never hear. This was not the same. The thing was not merely repeating its lessons by rote. Something was in there, trying to get out.

Touch it, she said. Quick!

So far he had always refused. He wanted to take her aside and spell it out brutally – that they were each on their own in this thing. She would disagree. She had the perfect contradiction right under her hands, answering her constantly. She seemed to think he could have it too, had only to do as she did – place the flat of his hand against the warm, tight flesh.

Are you afraid? she said.

He had refused so often that a refusal now could add no offence. But she had accused him of cowardice, and for once he let the notion in. It was his way out. If he accepted the challenge, the threat of a slight, he could surmount it. And so, with a boy's bravery, he reached out his hand.

It had always looked tight and hard, as though there were a solid object underneath. But under his hand now it felt far more generous. He'd often seen sharks hooked and hauled aboard, thumping about the deck, and that was the only thing he could think of that felt similar. The underbelly, tight and heavy and hard. That same sense of bulk, of history.

The thing was definitely warm, like freshly-baked bread. That meant his hand was cold, he supposed. He wondered could whatever was inside feel the chill. The cold spot. The hint of an alien presence.

Then, under his hand, the world jumped.

Lord Jesus, he said, loud and clear.

He had whipped his hand away, as though from a scorching hot plate. He would not have been more surprised had something started under his own shirt. He took her shoulders and turned her into the light. There was something animal, alive, on just the other side of the skin. It was jerking now, to a monstrous pulse. Hiccups, she said, but he looked at her

223

sceptically. The thing was far too frivolous for a baby in the womb under its father's hand. The kick had answered his touch. He was sure of it.

Afterwards, alone in his cabin, he faced the mirror. His beard was as rowdy as a castaway's. His carbine stood in the corner. The shock came slowly, dragging its feet. He could feel his face straining, not to smile. It was going to happen, and here was the first flush of joy. It was a complicated happiness, with so much residue to flush away, that had been building so long. He wondered would there always be so much resistance, so much noise, so much protest from the pipes. He did not know. He could not think.

He read DeHaven's books, most of them. He studied the pictures. He studied his own mind as best he knew how. What he decided was, he was going to be taken by surprise.

When I think of it, he said, I think of the smell. The linen. The soap. The shit. I can never get much farther than that.

Me, DeHaven said, I think of the geography. Think of the American continents, he said. North and south, and the narrow strip of land linking the two. Think of an hourglass, he said. Think of your wineglass, if you prefer.

Morgan turned the thing in his hands, suddenly delicate.

You have the bell, DeHaven said. That's where the baby is for the moment, suspended in a class of soup. It's obviously not as stiff as a wineglass, of course, more like a pigskin, let's say, to maintain the drinking metaphor. You've seen them drinking from wineskins à la Bayonnaise, squirting it straight into their mouths? That squeezing, those are the contractions.

Morgan looked into the glass. The wine looked darker. It no longer looked like something he wanted to put in his mouth.

The finger was pointing to the junction of bell and stem. Of course, it's quite a squeeze, DeHaven said. Yet, what's up here – he flicked a fingernail against the bell, with a nice, clean note – somehow has to make its way down here. He tapped the same nail against the foot. The sound was blunt, dead.

Easier said than done, I suppose, Morgan said.

From the pictures he'd seen, DeHaven's model was not quite right. The stem was too long. Impossibly narrow but mercifully short, one book said. Morgan had already considered the question, with her laid out on the bed. It was a matter of inches at most. But these were real inches, unfortunately – the ones used by surgeons and dentists, on people in great pain. They were not the inches of an Ordnance Survey map.

5th March

She was holding a single finger up in the air, as though performing some complex calculation and warding off distraction. It was what she did, sometimes, when waiting for a contraction to pass.

Finally he dared ask: Should I get DeHaven?

She nodded mutely, severe. This time she was afraid of having gone too far. She was afraid of being forced to give birth now, as punishment.

He found DeHaven in the officers' cabin, found him sitting at the table, cradling the cat. On the table was a tin of their precious preserved milk, that should have been kept to go next door, later, if need be.

I thought we were saving that for the baby, Morgan said. In case.

Dick, we only have the one case of the stuff. It would only be dragging it out.

DeHaven got his bag to go, but stopped at the door and turned back.

She has a doctor at hand, and a very distinguished one at

that, he said. She should count herself lucky. In many ways she's better off having it here than at Disko.

Still Morgan looked unhappy, unconvinced.

Everything's ready. Everything's clean, DeHaven said, but it sounded like pleading.

Morgan pushed the saucer of milk under the cat's nose. She sniffed at it suspiciously. Torture, he reminded himself deliberately. From the inside out. With those attending her doing nothing to relieve or refine the agony, only goading her on. Spectators. Il faut tenir, the French said. Simply face into the pain, and bear it, rather than try to get out of its way.

What if she doesn't survive, but it does? he said. His was an ever-ambitious anxiety.

DeHaven was looking at him curiously. For godsake, Dick, he said. What are you worrying about? No mother, no milk. No milk, no baby. It's as simple as that.

Afterwards he lay down on the bunk to wait and brought the cat with him. Just as she liked it, his fingers caressed the cat's throat, felt it throb. Satisfied, the eyes began to close. The Beast, he boasted, bitterly. The name had been spoiled. Kitty had heard and taken to using it, for the thing squirming inside her. Somewhere in the depths he felt a definite deflation – the soft flag and slump of surrender. The last of the barricades had collapsed. The grand, brassy thoughts could now come marching down the boulevard.

Later, he wrapped himself up well and climbed aloft, all the way up, the ropes shattering under his feet. It was midday. He was trying to steal a glimpse round the corner, to bring back news of the sun. A small red light sat neatly on the horizon. He felt his face tighten, then felt it relax. The hope had lasted a second, no more. In any other sea it would have been a beacon. Here it was merely the Dog Star, on a new round. Sirius, that makes men wane, and women pine, said the Greeks.

Crates flung over the side in the last crush still lay all about the ship, as though nothing had changed since then. Beyond lay the vast, virgin plain. They were cast out and encircled. The stars wheeled loosely overhead.

As long as he could bear the cold, he stayed aloft. There was a new world waiting for him below. Even when he went down he lingered awhile on the deck. About the ship it was now freezing so hard the ice was sizzling, like meat on a spit. It was a full week since the last fall of snow. From the distant floes came a sound that brought him back to his army days, in the East. It was the ice exploding. It was a firing squad, in the quiet dawn.

11th March

March. The last days. The sky was not brightening but being washed clean. The sheet stretched to dry. They were idle, according to a strict routine. He marked nothing in the log but what they read on their instruments. For five days there was wind from the east, steady and strong, one long breath. The Liberator, he called it, when any of the Irish were near. What we need is wind from the north, he wrote.

What we need is wind from the north, DeHaven announced to the dinner-table that night, to usher us to a more genial part of the globe. He had rooted out and been reading Morgan's journal again. *Genial*, meaning that which contributes to propagation, DeHaven explained.

Out of boredom Morgan wrote to his wife – a letter to the wife he would like to have, from the man he wanted to be. He wrote: When last I felt something warm and yielding, or when last I felt warm myself, I would be at pains to say. It was not true. It was another empty appeal. He spent the best

227

part of every morning away from the ship, hoping to fortify himself. It was now not ten degrees below the freezing point. On paper, in black and white, it sounded cold. In the flesh, it was not. Rounding the ship, at a stroll, I tingle, he wrote. Farther or faster, over uneven ground, I begin to sweat.

He went to see her. They went up for her daily stroll. It was strangely calm and strangely mild, and for the first time that year she did not stay under the housing, but came out onto the ice. He bent and drove a finger into the surface, to show how it gave. The finger left a dent, like the neat patter of footprints now scattered all over the floe. His little mark would not last long, of course. Someone would stand on it. Later, it would all melt.

It's like putty, he said. It was a kind of promise. Try it, he said, but she could not bend.

It was almost noon. The sky was like a dirty glass bowl. The glass began to blush. The reddened bar began to glow. Nearby, as they often did now at this time of the day, the men gathered to stare at the same horizon. Slowly, gracelessly, their idol was rising, like some luminous sea creature lifting itself off the ocean floor. Morgan and Kitty stood side by side. Each lifted their veil and let their faces soak up the light.

They turned a slow circuit about the ship. He watched the way she shuffled along, as though managing a deep wound, something any untoward movement might tear open again. She moved like one of those characters in their plays – the wounded soldier, the beggar, the blind king. Every movement a signpost towards the past, saying I was well, I am sick, I was young, I am old.

They talked and he listened. Today she was like someone slightly drunk, with a happiness she was determined to share. Every now and then she stopped to breathe. Waiting, he scanned the ice with the glass. Eventually he found something of interest. Bear. A mother and two cubs.

Now they were ambling along far behind her. Now they were sprinting to catch up. She bent and licked them all over, lavishly. He handed Kitty the glass, let her find them, listened as she let out a wounded groan. She watched them waddling over the ice, skating splay-legged down the hummocks. She turned to him with begging eyes.

I want one, she said.

I think you're going to have your plate quite full as it is.

Please, she said, with the old pain in her voice.

You really think you'll have enough milk? He sounded anxious, sceptical.

You jest, she said. Haven't you noticed? She was puffing out her chest. Even now, she said, I could feed the entire ship.

Once he'd put her to bed, he made the mistake of telling DeHaven, and DeHaven insisted on going out for them, immediately. Fresh meat, he said. For the hospital.

Morgan watched his friend take aim. She sprinted forward a few yards, seemed to trip over, did not get up again. The cubs ran forward, pawed at her impatiently. This was a new game, that they wanted to learn how to play. Afterwards the men stood around grinning and panting, each in a halo of steam. Twenty yards off, the dogs slobbered and scoffed over the steaming entrails. Under a sky that shone like slate, the shadow puppets slid left and right. The night was quiet now but for the sound of Cabot sharpening his knives.

12th March

He wondered what time it was. He hadn't heard the last watch. It didn't matter. It was still the middle of the night. He'd been sleeping but in his sleep had heard her scratching on the wall.

How go you? he whispered to the taut face.

I lost, said a voice ragged and dry. She did not finish the sentence. She was searching for the right words. It was like fumbling in a trunk in the dark. It would have to feel right. Had she lost her waters? Was that what she wanted to say? That it had started at last, and so soon?

The plug, she said. It was not the right word. No such word existed, for her, for this.

The jelly thing, she said. That blocks the . . .

I understand, he said. He turned up the lamp. When?

Just now.

Describe it, he said. You're sure that's what it was?

Sticky. Brown, she said. Like something you blow out of your nose. Like something you cough up out of your throat.

He wished he'd not asked. Now he would have to explain to DeHaven, with words of his own. He turned to go.

Richard, she said.

He halted, but did not turn to face her. What? he said.

Could you take it out?

What? he said. He wanted to hear her say it out loud.

The pot.

Why?

It's just, well, I don't really want him to see it.

The pot was already waiting by the door, with the cover on. He carried it up, to fling over the side, onto their rubbish heap. But first he took the cover off and held it under the lamp. She was not wrong. The glob looked like what they hacked up into the bowls in the hospital. The water was a greenish brown, the surface slick and greasy, as though spilled with train oil. It was another kind of proof. The birth, it said, was a purely physical thing.

230

A corner of the housing had come loose and was flapping frantically. He went over and tied it down. In the galley, he got two cups and set them on the tray. The kettle was beginning to tremble. The cat leapt onto the counter. The props all looked so familiar, so uninclined to change. Then he lifted his head, frowning. He stepped out and lifted the hatch. She was roaring his name, with a new kind of hate in her voice.

Back down into the animal kingdom, down the ladder, step by step. He stood facing the door. He was about to face the judge. He was a child again, and it felt unfair to give someone so helpless so much responsibility.

In the cabin, she had one foot on the floor and one on the bed, knee bent, was leaning back on an elbow, and perfectly still. The pose looked ridiculous. He glanced between her legs, ready to see a mess.

I've just had two, she said.

Two more, he said. How many does that make?

These are different, she said. She sounded slightly out of breath.

Until now the contractions had bloomed and quickly withered, their roots not particularly deep. But tonight they ploughed straight through her, barbed, on their way to another place.

Do you think this is it? he said, and heard both hope and dread in his voice. It was the question he asked himself at every crush. After so many false alarms, he still did not believe. It would pass, as everything passed.

I need – She could not finish the phrase. She had still not moved from her bizarre pose. She looked stuck. She blocked her breath, then used it to blow away the last of the pain. The pot, she said.

He took it from under the bed, held it out. She shook her head.

Do you want me to leave? he said. She wanted to empty her bowels, he knew, not to empty them later, when the time came to push.

She shook her head mutely. It was coming back. Her two

231

fists were gripping the blanket. The knuckles were white. The fingers would have to be peeled away one by one. There was something in them she would never let go.

Tell me what to do, he said. He had stepped over the threshold. From now on, everything would be merely practical. He felt himself strangely calm, as he often was when the actual crisis came. He no longer had to maintain his anxieties with such meticulous care.

She reached an arm towards him. The gesture was operatic, without opera's excess. He stepped closer, let her grab hold of him however she needed to. He put his hands under her armpits, to hold her in place. She hooked her arms around his neck and let it take some of her weight. She tightened her grip. At last she swung her second leg off the bed and onto the floor. He swivelled her around and set her straight.

Good, he said. He wanted her to believe she had the measure of the trial to come. He wanted to believe it himself.

Her head against his chest. Under his hands he could feel her lungs working, managing the pain. The gutters, she said, working to get the words out. The waters, did she mean? The guts? Still she clung to him with both hands. He was something warm, solid, sure. He stroked his hand up and down her back. It seemed to be what she wanted. For the moment it seemed enough. The daily wrestle and dance were done.

The nightdress was up. DeHaven had his hands flat on the bump. Under the pressure, it was ceding readily, like potter's clay. It had the same dull brown colour, the same slick sheen – some kind of oil they had poured on. Morgan watched with horror and admiration. Those first examinations, that other anxiety – that had all happened to someone else, long ago. Three months. Four. Five. He was older now. He was slow. He was more frightened than he'd even been in his life.

He could almost feel those same hands deforming his own insides. The mere thought was sickening, but he forced himself to watch. If he could not watch this polite puppet-show,

how could he hope to sit through the epic hours to come, the raucous stretch and pulp?

That bump, that's the head, DeHaven told her. You see? And there's his little backside. He turned to Morgan, asked: Do you want to feel it?

No thank you, Morgan said, but less from fear now than respect. Inside, he knew, was something more precious than all the rest. A dark, troubled knot of flesh. It was the heart, irrepressible, beating hard. It was something he trusted absolutely. It was tougher than everything. It wanted to live.

Ideally it would be engaged by now, DeHaven said.

What he meant was, the baby still had too far to travel, to reach the outside world. Morgan smiled cheaply at the thought. How often had he told the men that out here distance equalled time? In this room, henceforth, time equalled pain.

DeHaven had put on one of Cabot's white aprons. Now she watched as he rolled up his sleeves. Morgan watched her as discreetly as he could. The more you resist the more you suffer, he reminded himself. For as long as he could remember, this was a lesson he'd wanted to learn. He wanted to catch her eye, to tell her some useful lie, but now she turned her head to stare at the wall, not to see what DeHaven was doing to her bump. It made no difference, of course. She'd had too much practice, and the fear came quickly, effortlessly. It knew the way.

The contractions came and went. Each time felt like it had to be the last, that the very last dregs of pain in her were being drained away. Then she would feel it building again, like a wave far out from the shore. She settled the strap better between her teeth, and waited for it to come.

By now Morgan was kneeling by the bed, holding her hand. He would tell her whatever he thought she needed to hear. How brave she was. How far along. Anything he could think of but the truth. The truth was, there was so much worse in store.

Between contractions, they did their best to kill time. Morgan started to read aloud to her from a magazine.

Let her rest, DeHaven said. She's going to need it.

They went at it, hour by hour. In the end DeHaven put her walking, to try and hurry it on. It was four short paces across the cabin floor. The two men sat up on the bed, out of her way. She waddled back and forth.

About three in the afternoon something suddenly took her in its grip and began to squeeze. Morgan caught her as she collapsed, sat her as best he could on the bed, held her up. In his arms, he could feel something wilt, something cede. He laid her down very carefully, and laid her dressing-gown over her, and the blankets on top of that. Still she was shivering. Morgan said he would bring her some tea.

He went out and went up and was glad to get away. He stayed too long in the galley, letting it come. This was how it would be, he thought. This was older and wiser. This was nothing to be done. It was going to happen, finally. Imagining, he felt sick with anticipation, with the great, complicated success of the hours to come.

It seemed less like a specific time than a specific place they'd been slouching towards, all these months. It was that cabin under his feet. She was down there now, waiting. The legs somehow hitched up and spread. Her face staring madly into the pain. The animal grip of her hand. The desperate, defeated panting. In the corner the stack of neatly-piled cloth, still a sober white. By tonight, he knew, the same cloth would be crumpled in a bucket, glossy and red.

A few minutes later DeHaven followed him up.

It'll be a few minutes before the next one, he said. Cabot will call us if there's need.

He'd come to get his tools, which were boiling in a pot. He lifted the lid and peeked inside, as though to check were they done.

This is how it's going to be, is it? Morgan said.

How do you mean? The birth?

You've been at a few, haven't you? he said.

I've been at plenty. There's no point talking about it until I get a proper look at what way it wants to come out.

He needed a proper look, Morgan thought, but Kitty herself would be in the way. He would struggle to get a proper grip, a direct line of sight, and it would be her own fault for being such an awkward shape.

They seem quite strong now, Morgan said. How much worse do you think it can get?

Well, they're not going to ease off.

That was his friend's answer. There was no use debating the matter now. It was time for everyone to take their punishment.

Eventually DeHaven fished out his tools and dropped them on their tray. Morgan listened to them clatter and settle. They looked merely clean, new, nice to hold, but he knew they were still far too hot to touch.

Well? Morgan said.

In my opinion, it's wiser not to talk too much about it in advance.

I want to know. I want to have some idea of what I'm going to see. I won't say anything to her, I promise.

From what I can see, it's like being murdered, DeHaven said. Although I imagine most murders can't be half as painful and drawn out. And if you ask me, I think I'd prefer to be murdered. At least when you're murdered, right up to the finish you must have some hope of escape. Maybe murder is the wrong word. Tortured is perhaps a better way of putting it. The woman is tortured, and survives. And not only does she survive being killed, but when she comes round she finds someone else – someone completely helpless – it is now her charge to keep alive. Even as she herself tries to recruit.

On the galley door now came the very lightest knock. It was Cabot. He seemed strangely shy.

It's Miss Rink, Cabot said. She's says she's bleeding again.

They went at it hour by hour, scream by scream, and nothing but DeHaven's blue bottle to thin the catastrophe. Listening, Morgan imagined a blank page being slowly torn in two. The rip has a will of its own, wanders off, like a fault line in a solid wall.

Flaws appearing in places she would have sworn were sound. But that solid surface – it is the merest skim of plaster over old cracks. Underneath, all the old wounds are still open, and the pain knows exactly where they are. It knows her better than she knows herself. It has been studying her secretly, all her life.

Good girl, he told her, regardless. That's the way. The next time it comes, you do that again, exactly the same. He didn't know if what he said was true, but it didn't matter. What she needed more than anything was some kind of encouragement.

We need to do something, he whispered to his friend.

Give her another dose, DeHaven said.

Morgan poured a spoon, but she could not lift herself. He brought it closer, but she made a sign with her eyes. He brought the basin. She tilted her head, let it all dribble out. It looked like bits of crushed bone, ashes, dust. She had broken a tooth, biting the strap.

I can see the head, DeHaven announced. I'm going in.

She showed no sign she'd heard. Her hair hung in ropes on her shoulders. She looked drugged or in a daydream. The tears ran down to her jaw.

Wider, DeHaven said, leaning in. He turned and took the forceps from the tray.

Whatever he was searching for was well hidden, but he seemed determined to find and dig it out, regardless of any resistance met on the way. Morgan stood watching, stupefied. He was holding one of her legs. The screams were going right the way through him, to the soles of his feet.

When it came it came almost in a slither, as though to discount all that had gone before. More than anything, Morgan thought, it looked like a mass of liver smeared in something like buttermilk.

Here, DeHaven ordered. Hold it a minute for me.

And Morgan's two massive hands were suddenly weighing the meat-purple lump.

Cabot stood uselessly in the corner, back to the wall, holding the immaculate white wrap.

The thing was warm and slick, whatever it was. To the touch it felt just like the guts of a newly-shot bear, as you cleared him out. But it was moving. It was alive. And at the end of each finger, outrageously, there was a tiny fingernail.

Soon enough DeHaven sent him out. He needed to do some stitching up and didn't want her watching the mirror of Morgan's face. Morgan put on his furs and went out onto the ice. He knelt to wipe his bloody hands on the snow. He was flooded with relief, weighed down with it. He knelt there breathing, still soaking up the essential fact. Often in recent months, he had woken in the morning to a well-earned sense of relief, a reasonable calm, that told him the crisis was past, false alarm. That was how he felt now. It felt like success – his personal share.

For over an hour he circled the ship, refusing to go back in. What he felt now, he did not need or want to share. It was dark, and he kept veering and veering harder, to keep the red lamp on the mainmast in sight. Again and again he passed the gangway, but did not tire. Tonight he was younger than he'd been for many years. Soon enough, he supposed, the feeling of mastery would start to drain away. His legs and lungs would falter, and with them the invincible dream. But for the moment it was a feeling he refused to interrogate, refused to doubt. With nothing to hinder or heckle, images rose to his mind of what he'd seen that day. But none of the labour, the flailing foremath. He saw only the baby, bloody and fierce, cradled in his own outsized hands. The clenched fists, the bright greedy eyes, the mother's champion face. His own childish pride, that someone's survival now depended on him. The devotion he could freely foster on it, without fear and without risk. For a few moments, helplessly, he was determined to be up to the task. For the first time in a long time, he heard a call to his better self.

PART IV

1852

20th February

Their plates were full but untouched. Knives and forks in hand, they sat staring at the table top. They watched the cork trundle towards the edge, falter. Now she seemed to be leaning a little more to port. For a moment the cork lay there motionless, then rolled wearily back to where it had been. She was rocking ever so slightly in her cradle. Suddenly Morgan's hand shot out and snapped up the dawdling thing, turned it ninety degrees, set it down again. They watched it roll happily past his plate and sail straight over the side.

Boats, sledges, and packs were all waiting up on deck. In a matter of minutes they could be off the ship. They would make for the island, he supposed. After that, he did not know. His one hope was that she not be crushed.

Perhaps, MacDonald said, something ought to be said to the men.

What exactly do you propose I tell them? said Morgan.

It's just that this last spell seemed especially violent, and especially long.

Mr MacDonald, Morgan said brightly. You may inform the crew that the captain notes their concern, without sharing it.

Overhead, the boots of the watch swayed back and forth. MacDonald put a forkful of his dinner into his mouth. He looked sullen, accused.

The door opened. She had come for her supper. Am I late? she asked.

They watched her shuffle to the end of the table. Tonight she was wearing her sealskin jacket, that Petersen had shown her how to make. She bowed her head over her plate, pursed her lips, and sucked it up.

The pan was passed from man to man. When it came to him, Morgan took his slice and leaned across her, handed it back to Cabot. It was the last of their frozen blubber. Coddled since morning in a marinade of kitchen-spirit and thaw-water, meant to help the thing go down.

241

Hello, she said brightly. Remember me?

It's not for you, Morgan said.

Why not? I won't be more fussy than anyone else.

I don't think it wise. For your stomach. And for the milk.

Why don't I be the judge of that?

They ate in silence. Outside, the world was changing shape.

I hope I didn't interrupt anything, she said.

Mr MacDonald is a little worried about the weather, Brooks told her.

We are in the Arctic, Mr MacDonald, at the tail-end of winter, Morgan said. It is a storm. That is generally how it goes in the Arctic, at the tail-end of winter. He had not even looked up from his plate. If you don't like it, he said, there's the door.

They came flailing out of the ship as from a house in flames. Some men leaping straight over the gunwale onto the ice. Roaring like drunkards. It sounded like a full-blown revolt. Here at last was the chance they'd been longing for. Every timber was whimpering. It was the end. They had already decided, she would be crushed. With a proud, ponderous groan, she was heeling over. As perfect a heeling over as I ever saw, Morgan said afterwards.

From a safe distance they watched a lump of ice the size of a billiard table topple over the gunwale, slide across the deck, bounce out onto the floe again. Humbled, they watched the main crack ploughing for the bow. A gang was already shovelling it full of snow, hoping the thing might somehow freeze again into a solid block. Any other time, Morgan would have laughed at it as a practical joke, and a shrewd one. Now it dismayed him, the effort wasted, but he did not call them off. It would be a wonderful example to cite, of their own stupidity.

She was standing up against him, in her bearskin boots and her bearskin coat. He opened his own, tried to stretch it around her. The boy was underneath, pressed between them, screaming as loudly as he possibly could. The physical

242

power of the thing was impressive. The depth of the outrage. Simultaneously hopeless and insistent, every lungful milked to the full. He'd not let up since they'd grabbed him from his cot.

Daly and his party were hauling crates across the ice, away from the listing ship. MacDonald was lowering the boats. Cabot was counting the bread bags, over and over, and Morgan wondered was the man drunk again. All set, Brooks came to say. Morgan held her a little tighter. He did not know where to go.

Careful, she ordered. You're crushing him.

They stood face to face by the coal-house, listening to the war. Before, the collisions had always been deep and dull, like distant artillery. This was new. This was clean and brittle, like breaking glass. It was the extreme cold. The vast, mechanical rattling all around. This is what it had sounded like, he reminded himself, before Ghazni. The awkward hundreds on horseback. The thousands in restless gear. The nagging of stirrups, sabres, spurs. It brought him right back. For just an instant, for no good reason, he wanted the thrill of seeing the *Impetus* destroyed.

Half an hour had passed. Where there had been screams, now there were whimpers. To comfort himself, Morgan held the small, warm body against his own, as gently as he could. More than ever, he felt the original, sickening need. It was half-sleep drifting into a well-tailored dream. It felt, at times, like he was falling in love.

By now the moon had come out to watch. Overhead, the spars were etched into a gunmetal sky. Out in the desert, the men were playing at ghosts. The ice had the cold conscience of pearl.

Then the spell was broken. Suddenly Morgan was roaring, ordering the boats hauled back aboard, and ordering everyone off the ice. From every crack now came a cloud of steam. Whatever was beneath the ice had started to simmer. Now it was starting to boil. The world entire was breaking up. Not one square yard was sure, no two in agreement. A boat would have been bucked in seconds. In a minute, it would have been kindling.

They stood by the gangway in their furs, bundles at their feet, looking over the wastes. Out there, somewhere, was their island. On clear days, even in the very best light, it was never more than a sketch. Only six or seven miles off, he goaded himself now. It did not matter. Over such terrain, in such turmoil, they might as well have tried for Peru.

They watched the coal-house, intact, sliding towards the edge of the floe. Afterwards there was only a long black streak, like a lone slur of charcoal on a clean page. They watched the main crack close up again, squeezing its filling like cream from a cake. About eleven o'clock, inexplicably, the pressure eased off. By midnight the ship had begun to right herself, bit by bit. Each concession seemed begrudging, but one followed the other, in fits and starts, and that is how they were reprieved.

21st February

Breakfast was quiet. The faces were grey. Some of the men had slept in their clothes. Some had not slept at all. He had Banes and Leask scrape off the deck to proof the seams. He sent Cabot down into the crawling space, to proof the Samson posts.

Nowhere, strangely, was there any sign of play.

Some of the men seemed relieved. As after every crisis, they seemed to think they had seen something like the worst. To Morgan, the ice had merely been toying with them, and he could not esteem men so fond of hope. But that evening, from his private supply, every man had half a gill of brandy to toast McIntosh & Sons, Shipmakers, of Inverness. It would restore a little swagger, after this latest crush. It would oblige them to absorb a little more the next time, to have boasted how well their ship was built.

Alone in his cabin, he took a book from the shelf, opened a marked page. *Mount Raleigh*, he read. First charted by John Davis himself. *A brave mount, the cliffes whereof are orient as golde.* The words had been written over two hundred and fifty years before. To Morgan the man was a friend and neighbour. Now they too had their own lump of rock.

He had sighted it a week before. The date was marked forever in the log. It had been the quietest day in months, with a noon sky very like the colour of mud. He would hardly have called it brighter, but to his eyes it was decidedly less dark, and he could not resist going out for a walk. An hour later, a full moon in a clear sky suddenly showed him a spectral coastline to the southeast, about four miles off. He should have jumped up and roared Land! but did not dare. He was terrified such presumption might make the thing disappear. He wanted to rush towards it, to touch and grip the thing, to hold it in place. He merely shuffled a few feet closer and stood in silence, as though expecting someone to appear and wave to him from the shore. Even as he stood watching it, the weather was worsening again. Snow of the finest grain now hung in the air. Between him and the island, already, it was someone's breath on the window pane.

Since then – a week ago – no one had gone up but the watch, and even they stayed mostly under the housing, that the latest storms had now set hard as board. Below, lying on his bed, Morgan dreamed of sleeping for months on end, to wake in blatant sunshine, like a bear. More and more, he admired the animal world. He had almost entirely ceased to think of returning home. His mind could not reach further now than the island, the return of the sun. The sun, he knew,

245

was daily closer to the horizon. He read it and repeated it. At noon every day, he went up expecting some sudden break in the weather, some little hint of pink glass, and always found everything the colour of steel.

25th February

The men's natural vigour must be properly husbanded, Morgan said. October twenty-eighth.

Natural vigour, Kitty said. What a wonderful man he was.

They were drinking tea. It was late afternoon. Morgan was reading aloud from Myer's journal again, the best parts. The watch was shuffling back and forth. DeHaven lifted his head. He was next on the roster.

God forbid, he said, that our island should drift away with no one there to wave it goodbye.

The exercise will do you good, Kitty said. You said so yourself.

Want of exercise, Morgan read. Want of light. Salt meat. He flapped over another page. Simple problems with simple solutions, he said. He was very fond of them. Our late, much lamented Captain Gordon Myer.

There was no miracle remedy, he knew. Some men were more susceptible than others, was the useless truth. Maintain their diet, the daily exercise, was DeHaven's own advice. And perhaps a bath per man per week, with a rough towelling afterwards, to get the blood flowing again.

Lemon juice, Morgan said. Correction, *fresh* lemon juice. Cabot! he shouted at the ceiling. Go pick me a dozen!

They say if sorrel doesn't altogether cure, it certainly calms, MacDonald said.

246

Small beer, said Brooks.

You can't say it has Cabot in the best of health. For all the gallons he's drinking.

I don't mean that dross he concocts for himself, Brooks said.

The yeast might in fact do the gut some good, DeHaven said.

I've heard it said there is nothing more effective than a cheerful outlook, said Kitty.

All nonsense. The only thing we need is patience, Morgan said. It had become almost the chief virtue in his mind, because he was so much better at it than most other men.

Does chewing tobacco have anything to recommend it?

A wise choice of race, MacDonald said. Did you ever hear of an Eskimo going down with it?

It hasn't done Petersen much good, has it? Have you been to see him lately?

Pure-blood I mean.

The list went on, suggestions from all sides, and nothing in it untainted by mockery or despair.

The only guaranteed remedy I ever heard of, DeHaven told them, is to take an apartment in London for the summer and take a stroll in St James's Park every afternoon, if the sun is out.

They smiled bitterly. Outside the world was still raging, worse than a sandstorm, and as cold as it was ever likely to be. For months now, they'd lived like monks of a lax but enclosed order, undisturbed by the prospect of change. They spoke to God, and spoke to each other. They wrote and read, and followed the trump. They had nowhere else to go.

They talked of the island, and what they would find there, with the return of the light. But above all they spoke of the release summer should bring. Morgan did not contradict them, but knew they were wrong. It was his own fault, perhaps. All winter the living had been so much better regulated, for the sake of the boy. Below, there were no more gloves, no hats. Even a topcoat often was too much swaddling. They were too

247

snug and too easy, and liked to forget what exactly was on the other side of the wall.

But he himself had not forgotten. He knew well what was going on. As from a great distance overhead, he saw the prodigious cold clotting and closing every lead, every last crack – everything loose, soft, wet – like so many wounds staunched and healed. He tried to sell it to himself. It would stop the drift. It would be easier to traverse, if the ship were crushed. His mind was searching for an exit, something to force his hand. This last crush had squeezed her farther than ever out of the ice, and she now stood lurching a little to port, timbers propping her up, very like a boat beached at high tide. As such, she was now unlikely ever to be destroyed. She was just as unlikely, he thought, ever to sail again.

29th February

It was the last day of February. He was in the washroom, in the bath, in an inch of lukewarm water. There was a scratching on the door, exactly like the scratching of the cat. Calling for an answer, an acknowledgement, from whoever was inside. Morgan's heart was tightening, readying itself for the first blow. He could not even see the door for steam. He did not know what to do.

He put a knuckle to the panel, tapped twice. Wondering would the boy understand what it was, who, how to respond. He sat naked and perfectly still, waiting for the reply. The silence was terrible.

Finally the boy struck again, with all his force and all his weight. Three slow, deliberate blows, and with each blow

Morgan felt something cede. The fear told the true story, as usual. It was a summons he had been waiting for, and dreading, all his life. He touched his hand flat to his chest. There was an animal knot under the ribcage, a muscle tight as a fist. This must be how it felt, he thought – the first great valve faltering, the first trickle of death. In his mouth, this was the taste.

Dadda! the boy shouted.

It was a sharp breath on slumbering coals. Something within him was burning, mortified. There was suddenly life again – glory – in a place that had been iron, grey.

Again he tapped a knuckle against the door, and in answer the boy began to pound. Morgan reached for the walls on either side of the tub, as though to brace himself against another shock. He could feel the whole of the ship, every nerve, trembling in his hands. She was about to be crushed, to fall apart. There was nothing to keep her joints, to stop the planks from clattering loosely onto the floe. But he was not strong enough. The crack between door and jamb began to breathe. The boy was trying to push it open, to get in.

Oh God, he choked. He could not stand this devastating happiness, this pitiless game. His arms were pressing stupidly against the thin walls. He felt faint. He was falling. He was holding himself in place. With short, shallow breaths he was keeping himself alive.

He could not say what the boy wanted or what he wanted himself. He only knew it was painful pleasure, this call and response. There was no way to receive or cheat it. He had been lured and trapped. Somehow he had to get out of this iron-plated room. He had to get into the open air, free, out of range.

1st March

DeHaven made sure now to knock on the cabin door every morning, before he began his hospital round. Morgan was never eager to go. He knew all too well the state of their decline. More than once, coming in from the cold, he himself had fainted dead away. So far, he had always managed to reach his cabin, where the thing could be concealed. He told DeHaven they needed more exercise. DeHaven said they needed fresh meat. At last count, five men had the flux.

It's Petersen now, DeHaven said. He can't even move his legs.

In the forecastle it smelled worse than a stable. They pulled back the hospital curtain and stepped inside.

How do you feel? DeHaven said. Describe it, he said. He was taking notes.

Like I been at the wrong end of a good hiding, the man said.

Open up, DeHaven said. Let's have a look.

The man's tongue looked like he'd been eating blackberries.

DeHaven rolled down the blanket, told the man to undo his johns. Much like a bruised apple, the skin near the armpit was stiff and wrinkled, the flesh beneath dark and soft. DeHaven touched it with his fingertip. Morgan himself had something similar at the top of his thigh, just where he'd caught an arrow, coming into Kandahar. The thing followed no logic that he could see.

They moved along. The next man was Petersen.

It is what? Petersen said.

From a small blue bottle, DeHaven poured a measure onto a soup spoon. Open wide, he said.

Come on now, be good, Morgan said. All the other boys have taken theirs.

The mouth remained shut, obstinately.

You think we're trying to poison you? Morgan said. Carefully he took the spoon, and threw it back in a go. He held the stare a moment, then poured another dose.

250

In the half-light, the other men lay watching. In the end, Petersen did as his captain had done. Even as he swallowed his face crumpled, and they all began to laugh. Morgan too gave a smile, but kept his lips closed. He did not want to admit it, but his own gums were blistered and raw. He felt like he was teething again, decades on. It was a less a moulting than a revival, of all the old woes.

We need fresh meat, DeHaven said. Not just for the hospital, but for the boy.

Morgan said nothing. There was nothing to say. Day and night he had the memory – the foretaste – of it in his mouth. He'd already been to see the hunters. Blacker, Banes, Jones. It was pointless. There was nothing to aim at.

The estate seems hopelessly short of game, DeHaven said. Quite shot out. Present company excepted, of course.

We're not quite come to that, Morgan said. Not yet.

15th March

Kitty was sitting at his desk, writing on an orange slip. The latitude and longitude, the date, the name of the ship. Done, she dropped it in the basket, and took another from the stack of blanks. Five hundred, she announced. Beside her, Morgan didn't answer. He'd done as many himself, as had every man aboard with a legible hand.

During their first winter's drift, on Myer's orders, once a month he'd thrown overboard a special tin with a similar slip inside. He'd done it once a week last summer, as long as the ice was still loose and there was a chance of the tin drifting away. But he'd been wary of it from the off, as he was wary now of launching their last balloon. It was too perfect a picture of futility, the commander who placed his only hope in these useless appeals.

While you were still laid up, late June perhaps, one day Cabot came rushing in all a-fluster with one of the tins, that he'd fished from a lead way out, Morgan said. He knew he shouldn't have been so surprised. The strollers were always scouring, always hoping for some sign they too were now being searched for, that help was on its way.

It might be just what they need, Kitty said.

Morgan didn't see what she meant. The men already knew where their ship lay, at what date. You should have seen Cabot's face, he said, when we opened it up.

What if it were another date? she said. Another ship.

Some other ship, searching for us?

Why not? she said. Let them find it, she meant. Let it give them hope, encourage them to persist. What harm could it do? We could write out a few now. Different-coloured slips, different ink. Smuggle them out, and discreetly tag them to the end. The first to be reached by the fuse, she meant. Those that would fall closest to the ship.

The better to justify an abandon, he thought. With the direction to take. Melville Island would be best, and most plausible. It was not such a bad idea. Afterwards, when they got to Melville Island, they would be safer. No one would mind the fraud. Saved or perished, the deceit would be of no consequence.

When they'd done their quota, she put on her sealskin jacket and her sealskin coat. Their amusements were few and far between, and she wanted to see the thing go up. The boy was napping. She would ask Cabot to keep an ear open, to call her if need be.

They stood their backs up against the hull, out of the wind, and watched DeHaven seal his mixture in the keg. They waited for the reaction. When it was ready, DeHaven ran out the gas through their rubber pipe, to the waiting heap of silk. The tail too was waiting nearby, in an impressive heap. A full

252

five thousand slips of their brightest orange paper, each one handwritten with their details and coordinates.

Morgan remembered playing hide-and-seek in his father's garden, when he was a boy. He told her about it, asked had they that game in Denmark too.

Hide and sick? Kitty said.

Seek. Search. Some children hide, the other children look for them.

Then, he'd always been impatient to be found. But how could he reasonably expect anyone to be troubling over his sort now? It was only eighteen months since they'd last been heard from. Even those aboard, most of them, appeared not to appreciate the essential fact, that they were not lost, but beyond helping. They had pushed too far.

They watched the silk quietly come alive. Something inside was searching, prodding, feeling for a way out. They watched it swell, take shape. Its ambition was clearer now.

Do you remember Myer wanted to send a man up in one? Morgan said. With a rope attached, obviously.

A rope can always be cut, she said.

The idea wasn't as barmy as it sounds, Morgan said. It would have improved our navigation no end. How many days did we waste driving ourselves into dead ends?

He wasn't prepared to go up himself, though, was he?

I don't think the discussion ever got that far.

Would you have gone up in one? DeHaven said. Would you go up now?

That would depend who built it, and did they build it right, and how far up I had to go. How long are our ropes?

We have the ropes. We have the silk. Cabot and Banes could easily knock together the frame. Slick the seams. Coke gas from the stoves run up through the pipes. I watched them do it once in a fairground in the Phoenix Park. The air here as cold as it is, she'd shoot up.

By now the balloon was beginning to stretch and swagger, to lift itself off the ground. The last dent was gone and suddenly the thing looked solid, hard.

How far up does she need to go? Morgan said.

The higher the better, DeHaven said. Once the tickets are loosed, there's only one way they're going to fall.

When he judged it ready, he whipped out the pipe and tied the knot. Already she was leading westward, straining. Banes and Daly were struggling to hold her in place with guy ropes. Another guy was tied to the whaleboat kedge.

DeHaven shouted at them to keep her steady. He was fixing the quick-match tail. Now he had them let her off a little, and the tail uncoiled magically. Its papers were rattling.

A little more, DeHaven said. Easy now. That's enough.

They watched him light and shield his match and heard him curse. He lit another. Eventually he managed to get it alive to the end of the tail. The thing began to crackle, just like a fuse.

Hold her, he shouted, but the wind had risen and she was leading hard, and Banes and Daly had both to come round shipside. As in a tug-of-war, they planted their heels hard in the ground and were leaning backward, not far off forty-five degrees. The tail swung back and forth freely, smoking. DeHaven nodded to let her go. The guys slid through their gloves with a pleasant, rasping sound, fell dead on the snow.

The anchor! Morgan roared, but it was too late.

They watched the anchor bump along the surface, snag and snatch at the hummocks, drag on. Morgan himself went after it, but refused to rush. There was no need. The thing was too light to stall the balloon, and too heavy to lift. He could let it walk ahead of him with no risk of ever being lost.

It was almost a mile before the anchor finally jammed between two blocks and held. He wrapped the guy three and four times around his arm and put all his weight into it, to loosen the draw, the better to unwork the knot.

Free, he did not let the rope go. He could feel its strength, his own measly ballast, the giddy call. Standing up straight he was nearly jerked off the ground, found himself staggering after it. He could not keep his feet, and unless he wanted to be dragged along the ground he had to run, to jump, let himself be lofted into the air. These were giant steps he was taking now, bounding grandly, due west.

He watched it rise and watched it shrink. Very soon it was nothing but a little blue dot. Anchor in his arms, hugged to his chest, he began to slog across the crust. Coming back the wind was against him, and soon he was working hard. Already his arms were trembling, wanted only to drop their load. He drove on. He got angry. Underneath was drift deep enough to swallow him whole.

Every few minutes he dropped the anchor and stood to breathe. He looked south. It was almost noon. He stared fearlessly at the glow. It was not a source of light, but of emotion. It did not warm his skin, but fell directly on something inside. Under its heat, Morgan felt that thing wake, stir, like a seed. He could feel it, physically, planted deep in his flesh, alive. The idea, pure and simple, of abandoning the ship.

1st April

APRIL, the calendar said. The word promised buds, warm breezes, greenery. What they had was raw havoc. It was another promise broken.

He lay on his bed, letting his mind go where it would. It was fantasy. It was confession of a kind. Eyes closed, he heard open sea labouring loose ice.

Writing his journal, he hardly knew how the sentence would end. It seems to me we have attained – he wrote, but struck that. He started over. We have reached – We have met some kind of limit, he wrote. We might persist here longer, or push a little farther by other means, if I thought it useful, which I do not. He held off the pen and read over what he'd written, to see did he agree. He had once dreamed of pushing all the way to the west, coming out somewhere the far side of Melville Island, and from there to Behring's Strait. He had even calculated how many weeks of open sailing might be necessary. It seemed a ridiculous notion now, as did so many of his plans.

They had calm, clear days. They had scorching winds. Overhead, they had lurid green flames, that made the needle frantic. There was more to the days now. There was more light. The eyes stared, working hard to see their former friends. They seemed ashamed of what they saw. They looked like inmates. They were shabby, men and clothes. The weave was wafer-thin in places, failing at the seams.

Then, on the 3rd, at noon, against a blackboard facing south, the spirit thermometer gave them 25°. Under a bell-jar, untouched for thirty minutes, it rose to just above the freezing point. Morgan had already checked the log. It was their first positive since September.

To the men, these first hints of spring were reassuring, earned. They saw the promise of open water, open sails. Morgan envied their faith but could not share it. They were too far north. No matter what moderation, the break-up would never come. Day after day now he tried to shepherd thoughts of an abandon. Day after day, he called himself back, in the hope of being saved some other way.

4th April

That Sunday they woke to a stout wind from the north. After breakfast, Morgan went up to admire it alone. As he passed the galley, he suddenly stopped – mid-stride – to stare at something on the deck. Too late, the fear rushed through him, because he had almost stepped on it. His own shadow. The day was cold, the wind harsh, and under all the layers he was smiling, feeling less like an orphan than he had in years. He sent down the order for the officers all to put on their furs. For the first time in months, he had decided, they would take their coffee up on deck.

A godsend. A veritable godsend, MacDonald told them, almost as soon as he came up.

The lines were stirring overhead, the colours rattling happily.

I wonder why God did not send it before, DeHaven said.

Perhaps He feared we would not appreciate it, said Morgan.

Cabot came and placed the tray on one of the crates, with stern formality. They watched him pour. MacDonald was watching with a kind of wonder. He waited for Morgan to raise the cup to his lips.

I believe that is very close to blasphemy, Mr Morgan, he said. What you have just suggested.

You are right of course, Morgan said. The Lord is watching over us and directing our doom or our salvation, as He sees fit. He dropped a lump of sugar into his cup, stirred it conscientiously.

I do not think we can know His mind, Mr Morgan, and to cast a judgement on His motives and manner and final ends is a terrible vanity, that a man would do well to quell.

That sounds very like a threat to your captain, DeHaven said.

Morgan took another sip. Like tar oil, he announced. It sounded too much like praise for Cabot to take offence. In a way, the chaplain is quite right, Morgan said. All in all, I am a vain man. Complacent too, on many fronts. Although I like to think that, in a private moment, no one knows better than I the depths of my own ignorance. Does it trouble you, MacDonald, having such an incompetent man in command? My immorality, of course, we will not even mention.

We must place our faith in a Higher Power, is all I say, Mr Morgan. Accept that we are not entirely masters of our own fate, nor do we need to be.

Too true, Mr MacDonald. Too true. We are all ignorant and powerless. To a greater or lesser extent, obviously, Morgan said. It was he who was threatening now.

That is what I believe, MacDonald said.

And you believe, too, I suppose, something to the effect that it rests with God to console, or chastise, or care for, or neglect, or even afflict each and every man as He sees fit, according to processes and principles beyond our understanding.

God is good, MacDonald said. That is all we know. I think you must have proof enough of that in the shape of your little boy. He was inching back from the edge.

You must admit that on occasion it is difficult not to doubt. There is a great deal of contrary evidence put in our way.

We are tested every day.

Is that what He has been at, these past eighteen months? Testing us? Morgan said. Stack us one on the next in our little box, and let us brew? Day after day, night after night, staring at each other's faces, and staring at the planks, and breathing each other's stink, two winters and two summers now, and another one coming on? Whatever else may be said of Him, He has patience, I'll give Him that.

I would not presume to say, Mr Morgan. In any case, I don't believe patience is a term that can be properly applied to the Almighty.

Yet, if nothing else, I think we can safely say that we have been tested. Unless of course you think there is some other agency at work?

It has been a trial, yes. The purpose of the trial, I do not know. As I have said, wherever we see the sign of direction, we have no means of judging if it be for a first or final end.

Mr MacDonald, Morgan said, I do not mind being tested.

Only, I think I would like a clear choice, between one thing and the other. One choice would be easy, of course, and wrong. The other painful, and right. That is generally how it works, I believe. But what have I had to choose between, these past two winters? If I knew that, I think, it might have been easier to face.

We must trust, MacDonald said, that will all be revealed in time.

7th April

A lone snow bunting was perched on their main topsail yard. They had last seen him at Beechey, in another life. Since then he had been to America. Within days, Morgan knew, the sky would be alive with them. The thought irritated him profoundly. He could not imagine what lured so many so far, to such an inhospitable place.

They come here to breed, DeHaven said. As you yourself did.

They watched him gorging himself on their piles of filth. The men leaned over the gunwales, flinging down bits of bread and tack. It looked like they were trying to frighten him away.

They'll be an absolute blessing, DeHaven said. And I don't just mean the hospital. The little lad, fresh meat will do him no harm at all. Mince it up good and get those new teeth of his to work. And the men too, as soon as we get enough of it into them, I can get the gymnastics going again.

Morgan spent all the next day out on the ice. Scanning, spotting, taking aim. By late morning everything was wrapped in gauze. By mid-afternoon, he felt he was looking at the world through some kind of window that was at once dirty and bright. By afternoon's end, he had bagged almost fifty, and wandered miles from the ship, almost to the island. He brought his compass up to his nose, cupped his hand as a blinker, to look for the sun. The light blared up off the snow. He could see nothing. He was blind. With the birds strung boa-like about his neck, he shuffled westwards. Every few minutes he roared for help.

They had hoisted their train-lamps onto poles, set them up in two converging lines, that stretched from the ship almost a quarter mile. Banes and Blacker and DeHaven watched their captain groping his way from post to post. Bloated with laughter, they crouched behind one of the whaleboats, as he stared stupidly into the future, calling out was anybody there?

He knew they were watching. He could hear them, was deciding what to do. Since boyhood he'd been able to load his gun in the dark. He loaded it now, and knelt, and fired a shot as level as he could out over the snow. He paused to listen. As far as he could tell, nothing had been touched. He turned a few degrees to his left and started to load again.

10th April

Ba, little Tommy said.

No one seemed to hear. Brooks and MacDonald were lying on their backs, reading and pretending to read. At the table, DeHaven was playing with the numbers in his notebook, as though his calculations were rules to be obeyed.

Ba, he said again. Bread was what he meant. He sat in the chair Cabot had made for him, in what had once been Myer's place. Head of the household, they said. Life was better with him aboard.

Without looking up, DeHaven tore a few scraps from the loaf and flung them down the table.

He's not a bird, Morgan said. Can't you just reach over and put it on his plate?

Today, for the first time in an age, dinner would be something called stew. To celebrate, Cabot had baked a batch of fresh loaves, and the sinister smell of it filled the ship, making them all homesick.

Not the crust, Morgan ordered. The scraps were too big, and too many. Delighted, the boy would grab and shove them all into his mouth. Morgan was terrified of him choking, and he choked at least once a day. He would go red in the face and fall silent, then begin to jerk his head back and forth, trying to cough up the lump wedged in the back of his throat.

20th April

It was the 20th of April, a Friday. They were going to visit the island at last. They were ready. They were better and stronger almost every one. The fresh meat had worked wonders, and DeHaven's exercise drills, and now they were scrambling over the ruins to the threshold of a new world. Overhead, the sky was a fake blue. Their little ice-hole was a pool of gold. All about them the snow fell in lone feathers, that vanished even as they touched ground. As they came to the edge, the leaders pulled up to wait for Morgan, let him come to the fore. Warily, as though it might not bear his weight, he stretched out his foot to step onto the land.

It was worse than threadbare, he would write that night. Yet they had set out for it every man as for a tropical promise, primed for admiration and delight. Now they stared up at the starved, sterile slopes. They stood and stared at the walls of rusted rock, that rose plumb into a pewter sky.

They walked the shore, scanning the skyline, scanning the stones at their feet. If nothing else, he hoped for some scrap of larch or pine, to prove that their drift was not unique. That was what he was reduced to. They did not find enough for a matchstick. They found nothing at all. No one was looking for them. No one had passed this way earlier, hoping to be found.

Then a hundred yards ahead, MacDonald was roaring and waving grandly, like a shipwreck. A campsite, Morgan thought. A signal-post. A skeleton. He stumbled along the shore. The man stood pointing dumbly. As Morgan came up they all stepped back to let him see. He lowered himself to his knees, bent his face almost to ground. It was a lone dropping, not much bigger than buckshot. It was certainly too small for a hare. He rolled it between finger and thumb, crushed it, held it to his nose.

They spent all afternoon hauling themselves to the top of the cliffs, for a better view.

Magnificent, DeHaven said.

They built a cairn, knee-high, tacked one of her old red petticoats to a pole, planted it. It was the loudest flag they had.

Half a mile offshore, Morgan paused to look back at the lump of rock and ice. Already he understood that they could not winter here again, so close to where they had wintered last year. The men could not stand it, stripped now of all prospect of release or relief.

Beside him, the men had stopped to watch the sinking of the sun. It sat on the southern horizon, growing fat. Some unseen weight seemed to be forcing it down, flattening it out.

Morgan watched without shade. The thing was trembling, alive. In the end it went down with quiet dignity, in a sea of flame. They could not have been more solemn had they gathered to watch the scuppering of a ship.

22nd April

It was a lovely thing, that they said had cost Cabot a full week's work. Sound, balanced, trim. The wood neatly carved, the loose grain buffed bright. A seat in front, a standing-rack behind, with handles just the right height. Morgan stood looking at it, warm with gratitude. He had not expected this or anything like it. He had not suspected the source.

They brought the boy out to show him the prize. They set him down and fitted his hands to the push-bar. Leaning into it, he began to plod across the snow. Morgan watched with terror, sure it would shoot away, the boy would topple, strike his head. It did not happen. It was exactly what he needed to help him walk. He was an invalid taking first, miraculous steps.

The men had been at their exercises, but all now stopped to watch. They shouted down from the deck, urging him on. The voices were melodious, home-brewed. It was a joy to listen. The sun drenching everything, warming his face, warming his hair. The quiet, delicious pride. Morgan felt benevolent towards them all.

By now the boy had mastered his technique, was leaning far forward, putting all his weight into it, quick with his feet. A yard behind, Morgan kept his stride. The tracks wandered loosely left and right.

She runs beautifully, he shouted to Cabot. Everyone could hear. Cabot did not answer, was busy with his pipe. After much ritual tapping he put the thing between his lips. A stream of blue smoke poured into the air. Nearby, the gulls were brawling over the garbage.

Morgan stood the boy up on the platform, put himself in front, began to pull on the rope. Almost immediately came the first sounds of complaint. He wanted his father to stop, and did not know how to wait. Already he was trailing a foot behind him, like a man descending from a moving train. As soon as Morgan stopped, the boy let go the bar and fell backward. The head hit the snow with a thump. He lay there offended, splayed. There was a burst of laughter from the men, quickly snuffed. Morgan was rushing to help but Tommy was already rolling onto his front, getting his knees under him, straightening up. He stood and staggered forward, five or six steps, fell over again. Unaided, he still could not manage more than that. Eventually he made it to the front of the sledge.

He stood there swaying, rope in hand. That was the role he wanted now. He looked around for Dadda, wanted Dadda exactly where he himself had been a minute before. So Morgan crouched down and took hold of the bar and duck-shuffled as best he could behind the sledge, as though the boy were pulling him along.

He kept falling over and kept getting up, finding the rope, resuming. An example to us all, Morgan shouted. There was no need, the men were cheering every time he struggled again to his feet. Finally Morgan could stand the lesson no longer. He went and picked him up and sat him on the front.

Stubborn little tike, Brooks said.

That'd come from the father's side, DeHaven said.

Tenacious is the word you're looking for, Morgan said.

Or stubborn, DeHaven said. Or pig-headed. They all sound good to me.

His mother, too, can take a little credit, I think, Morgan said.

Tommy sat up proudly, paraded his smile. Again and again Morgan wheeled about to bring him past the gathered men, to renew the applause. He kicked his legs in delight, revelling.

Morgan felt – He did not know what he felt. His wife had once stuck a knife through every one of his shirts, at the heart. It was the kind of nonsense of which she had always been capable. He had worn them anyway, as punishment. Under his jackets, the slit could not be seen, but he'd felt more vulnerable, physically, in that particular spot. He felt the same thing now. In the armour, an invisible rift. That was the danger. That was where he would be hurt.

He felt himself tapped to the source, the endless supply. He felt glutted and generous. He called Cabot over, held out the rope. Here, he said, I give you my son.

The runners slurring along the ice. The boy stretching his neck, to check his father saw and understood. His smile was perfect, painful to see. Morgan did not think he could stand to watch it much longer. He could not stand to think that some day soon he would be leaving it behind. They passed from sight, behind the ship. Close by, the boy's excited cries had been barbed and sharp. In the distance, they seemed painfully weak.

Morgan listened to the men's voices. They had lost their charm. The faces were leprous and leathery now. They were lounging on the cases. Everything was lazy, as though trapped in a great, thick heat. He stood waiting. Until Cabot and Tommy returned, he had nothing to say. The seconds passed stupidly. Already it was too long. He could feel it flowering, fantastic – the thought that he might never see his son again. Cabot was dragging it out – doing it to tease him, no doubt, but it was a game he did not want to learn how to play. All he heard was an ominous silence. His mind did not know what to do. It was a brilliant afternoon. Inside his head, the voices were whispering desperately in the dark. The noise was impressive, menacing, infantile. They were plotting all the tragedies to come.

Finally they came round the bow and passed under the

bowsprit. The men clapped and roared. Here was the king they had been waiting for, to lead them to victory. Impossibly, the boy seemed happier. The radiant face – the icon – was brimming with joy, life. The tiny teeth, gleaming, painfully white. Hair the colour of honey, now starting to curl. The long eyelashes, pretty as a girl. It was him they had come to see, for him they had made the pilgrimage – he the healer, the maker of miracles. Morgan wanted to rush and seize hold of him, feel his power, his warmth, his weight. But he could not interrupt this moment of glory, the prophet's arrival at the city gates. It was the boy's own life now, his exaltation. Morgan was merely a witness, a slave.

24th April

Out beyond the coal-house, Banes and Cabot were firing at empty meat-cans. Every shot was a bullet less, but Morgan made no objection, he had loosened his grip. All morning he let them at it and did not complain. But about midday she came up to give him a black look, and he went and whistled at them, pointed at the ship, showed them a man cradling a baby, trying to get him to sleep.

He did not go below again, but took his wicker chair and carried it down the gangway. He would go to the amphitheatre. On any calm, clear day, healthy and sick alike now repaired to it from the ship's stench.

By the bottom of the gangway, something was sticking up out of the snow. It was the handle of their ice saw, the eighteen-footer. Morgan walked past without even a glance.

The amphitheatre was a high wall, in a half moon, around a

tilted floor. Inside was shelter from the slightest breeze. It faced south. They were the spectators, basking in the show. Today, half a dozen men were already stretched out on the furs. He looked at them lying there, eyes closed, stern as snakes set to bake on a stone. These were his heroes, his band of brothers. These were the men would haul with him across the desert.

The handle stood six inches above the surface. They had all tried it, one by one, and two by two. Some had tried it three and four and five times. Some tried it every time they passed, as a kind of joke, concrete proof of their dilemma. Now Morgan himself stood astride the thing, lowered himself into a deep squat, like a man going about his necessary business. Both hands gripped the handle. He was straining visibly, and motionless. Cabot and Banes stood watching.

The boy! DeHaven always shouted, whenever he passed it now. Only he shall draw the blade! It was another of his pointless jibes, that Morgan always remembered, to goad himself on.

Not a budge, Banes said.

Cabot shook his head solemnly, to confirm the fact.

A foot from the dead edge of the blade – two yards from the hull – a clutter of wedges had been driven into the cut. The men stood staring, determined to figure it out.

Maybe gunpowder might do the trick, Banes said.

Gunpowder, Morgan said. Certainly. We'll pack gunpowder against the side of the ship. Five hundred miles from any possible aid. And we'll light the fuse and hope the ice gives out before the hull.

Morgan squatted lower, took a better grip. They watched his face turn purple. Like a man in a fit, his whole body began to shake. Eventually he staggered to the nearest crate, sat with his elbows on his knees, panting for air. Every now and then a gull swooped down from the masthead for a quick, smart laugh. When the time came, the birds would all fly away again, in long orderly lines.

How else are we meant to get out? Banes said.

With a studied movement, Morgan drew off his mittens

267

and dropped them to the ground. A scrap of rubble scampered across his lap. He was being ambushed. They stood one on each side. They had waited until he was exhausted and alone, and could no longer dodge. What he himself believed was of no consequence. He had to calculate. He had to tell them what he had decided to do.

Well? Banes said. The man wanted a good answer. The better part of his patience was gone.

Eventually Morgan stood up again, took the sledgehammer from where it lay on the ice. He lifted it high into the air, and with all his weight and all his strength brought it down on the nearest wedge. Lifted it again, brought it down again, and again, until the head was flush with the top of the ice.

Up on deck, sacks of flour lay one on the other like gross folds of flesh. Today all the doors and hatches were open to let in fresh air, begin to leech the ship of its winter stench. On the mainmast, a lone sheet was taking deep, desperate breaths. The door of the galley was propped open with Cabot's toolbox. They were carpenter's tools. Long planes, wheel braces, spokeshaves, with handles worn beautifully smooth from use. Overhead, the sheet suddenly whipped out and snagged on a pole. Somewhere deep inside the ship, a door slammed. It sounded familiar. It sounded like his own.

27th April

They were growing stronger, getting fatter, from all the meat. In the mornings DeHaven had them at their exercises again. In the daytime they shot birds. Cabot boiled and stripped the flesh and bottled them in their own grease. A reserve for the winter, Morgan said. At night they heard the foxes' childish cries. In the morning they found bear tracks at the foot of the gangway. About the ship, as the snow thawed, the garbage flowered miraculously.

Every day now there were new signs of weakness. The world was rotting, had ceased to resist. Every yard was ragged with icicles. Every rope, every edge. Every now and then another lump of snow shuffled off a spar. Beyond the ship, he felt the concession under every step, saw himself suddenly plunging through the surface, into the depths. But even as the ice melted, he knew, there was no longer any chance of their being released. On the surface, true, the glass was turning to jelly, but deep down everything was still solid rock, beyond any hope of a thaw.

The hopes and explanations grew complicated. They would have to be patient, he'd told her. They would have to be patient, he told everyone now. There was no reason the coming summer should be like the previous one. Perhaps the spring storms would destroy everything. It was some extraordinary stroke of luck he hinted at, but he knew full well they could have no luck, nor court any, if they stuck to the ship.

He watched them playing with the boy. They were taking possession. They knew what he wanted, what he liked. They had the cinder-buckets all in a row. With the blades of their shovels they were chopping up the snow. Morgan had rarely seen them so applied, so concerned. The boy too was watching suspiciously. They shovelled in the slush and packed it. With both hands Cabot lifted a bucket into the air. In a single gesture he flipped and brought it down. Now the boy was curious. He wanted to imitate his hero. He shuffled over, put his mittens to the side of the thing.

Look, Cabot told him. Now we do tap-tap-tap.

With the edge of his spade, he tapped the side and the upended butt.

And now Tommy! he ordered.

They had cleaned one of the small stove-shovels for him. Cabot put it in his hand, struck it against the bucket a few

269

times. Then, with the care of a cook removing a mould, he eased the bucket off. Underneath, the shape held perfectly. The boy spent a moment admiring. Then lifted the shovel high over his head, and brought it down. He worked methodically, took his time. It was a judgement from above. When he had destroyed it completely, he looked up at Cabot again. He looked like he was going to cry. He wanted another one.

They were alone on the frozen sea. Overhead, the sky was stretched unbearably tight. In the full stare of the sun, the piles of ice were whispering. He tried to sell it to himself. Of course it would be held against him, abandoning. In a way, he was relieved the retreat would be so difficult. The long overland – overland! – trek would be to their credit perhaps.

Spring meant snowstorms, but those would soon be done. Late summer meant sludge. Ross himself – the accepted authority – had preferred the autumn road. But Morgan had not the courage to wait that long. He feared the shrinking days. He feared the men. What he meant was, he doubted them. Their ability to trust and to obey. Their capacity to punish themselves, to soak up the cold, to starve. Besides, he had to be able to promise he would be back for her before winter. May was probably the best time to start.

29th April

There was a little boat. Cabot had hollowed it from a single block. It sat proud on the surface. Cabot had fixed it a keel. Now they were watching it fill. It was like watching a branch in quicksand. Unhurried, but irreversible. There would be no miracle. Underwater, it continued to sink at the same rate, until a giant hand slid under and raised and emptied and set it on the surface again. Tommy refilled his jar. He was holding it with both hands, ready to pour.

He was naked in the bath. He lay on his belly, the better to thrash. He was flailing wildly, as in a tantrum or protest of some sort. Smiling, Morgan wiped the water from his face. The legs flexed and pushed like the legs of a frog. He slid forward beautifully. Morgan wanted to see him in a river, a pond, hear the clean grey gravel rattle and crack.

The boy lay on his back, satisfied. The water came to his chin. It was as though he'd been laughing long and hard. His smile was sheer relief. He lay in the shadow of some great task. Something had been proved or achieved. It was worth nothing now it was done.

Morgan watched closely. There was something he had to learn. They were joined. They were breathing the same air. He could feel the sweat trickling down the small of his back, into his waistband. The stove was going full blast now. In places the iron was a dirty pink. He had watched the water being poured. He'd watched Cabot shovel the coal.

The skin was glistening, polished, like fruit. Underneath was his sacred flesh. Morgan dared not touch it, did not want to leave the slightest trace. Very gently, he drew the hair back out of his son's eyes. It was darker now. It hung like little lengths of frayed twine. In a room nearby was a slop-pot, soiled napkins, dirt. There were stray hairs, parings, snot. All these things were evidence of some kind, and all false.

There were little nails somehow planted into the end of his toes. The flesh was swelling around them, perfect and strange. All his life, all the useless hours – nothing had prepared him. He had merely trained himself to want, disdain, and indifference. He had nothing to meet this. Somehow he had opened the wrong book, the wrong page. It was a picture he was forced to stare at, to recognize. The boy was blinking, oblivious. He was like an animal wandered onto the stage, at just the right time, in just the right way.

271

1st May

Brooks was back from the island. He threw his canvas bag up on the table, let it sound. Already Cabot was reaching for it.

Don't open it, Brooks said. Just guess.

A bottle, MacDonald said.

No.

Gold, DeHaven said.

No.

Fossils.

No.

A skull. A man's skull. Bones.

No.

Brooks undid the straps and upended the bag, let it rumble out onto the table. They stared at it stupidly. Morgan took a lump in his hands. They watched him tighten his grip, the knuckles pale. The fist slackened. The table was scattered with chunks and crumbs.

Bear shit? Musk ox?

Sadly, Morgan shook his head. It was turf.

Is there much of it?

A whole mountain, Brooks said.

It was more treachery, the worst yet. Now there was no reason not to go. There was nothing to hold him back. The ship was now entirely out of the ice, impossible to crush. With an endless supply of turf, those left behind could live in something like total comfort, warm and dry, for years to come.

2nd May

They were up on deck, in the afternoon. Tommy was asleep in the hand-cradle, in the sun. In the wicker chair beside him, Morgan was patching the knees of a pair of trousers, as best he could.

DeHaven sighed grandly. A woman's work is never done, he said.

Morgan looked at him bitterly. In his other life, he'd done his sewing in secret, by Myer's sickbed, in Myer's cabin, afraid of what the men might say. Like so much else, that fear too had withered away.

Tropic or Arctic? DeHaven proposed. By now it was an age-old debate, an excuse to argue. They were facing south.

In the Arctic a man suffers more, Morgan said.

But lasts longer.

Apparently.

So if you were offered two years in the tropics against two years here, DeHaven said. He was trying to force his captain to contradict himself.

The thing is, Morgan said, in the tropics the first two years are far and away the worst. Past that marker, freaks and accidents apart, you start to feel safe.

You can live long, if you don't die.

Exactly, Morgan said. Whereas here, to be perfectly blunt about the matter, I think that after two winters it's time to go home.

Somewhere under the mainmast, a chunk of ice bounced off the deck. They looked up and caught Cabot studying them from the galley. On the stove behind him, steaming, was the stew-pot.

Chef André, what's on the menu? shouted DeHaven.

Napkins, Cabot said.

Hail the conquering heroes, Morgan said. Two useless years and counting adrift in the ice.

DeHaven was smiling. Louder, he said, lifting his head. Maybe they'll overhear. Maybe they're ready to bargain.

273

DeHaven was right, it was a fantasy. The ignominious return. In a moment of weakness, Morgan's ambition had shrunk to that. It was a sacrifice, to appease the gods. A disappointment he was prepared to live with, if in exchange they would sanction and orchestrate his release.

From near the mainmast came another wicked thump. Morgan set his sewing onto his basket and stood over the cradle. I'd better take him down, he said. Some of those are two and three pounds weight.

Many times he'd imagined going to her cabin, to tell her what he had decided for them all. He would have to tell her first, of course, before anyone else. For weeks now he'd fretted over the scene, as something he had to get right. He knew his steps, his lines. He had rehearsed it out on the ice, where it all made perfect sense. Spoken aloud of the weeks and months already wasted, and the months and years ahead, to be spent in much the same way, moping about in the ice, making little or no progress, even losing ground, pushing them further than ever from the prospect of rescue or release. He played the scene over. Time and again, out and back, his mind was working the same ground, trying to make himself a smoother road. He was trying to convince her in advance. He was trying to make it come out right. Now, alone in his cabin, he unrolled again the blank chart, as though he might yet find there some solution that would spare him the task.

At first he'd thought of loading her into the boat with the boy, and covering the boat, and trying somehow to keep them warm. But the boy was too fragile still. The slightest sickness, out there, was death. The first severe storm. He could not fight it off. He could not soak it up. He was too small. Everything was on the surface, exposed. Morgan tried not to imagine the specifics – and then he would catch himself, like a child sneaking a treat from the pantry, gulping it down, every possible horror. He could hardly bear to think of it even in the abstract. He knew well he would not be able to watch it in the flesh. He himself was no longer strong enough for

274

that. Before the boy was born he had considered himself an explorer of sorts. By now he felt himself a mere passenger.

As with any situation in life, he wrote, a man's strategy must be shaped by his own strengths and deficiencies, and by the obstacles he expects to meet. I resign, therefore, all further hope of navigation. We are now almost two years beset in the ice, a schooling sufficiently long to teach us that we are no longer masters of our fate. Here, we have learned, no force counts which is not exerted by the floe itself. Nothing human even registers on the scales. The longer we wait, the farther we drift, the weaker we become, and the poorer our prospects. If we wait another year, I am convinced we shall all be lost. As matters currently stand, however, there remains the possibility of a reduced party, namely the strongest amongst us, reaching our friends by our own means, and the hope that with their aid we may return to the ship to retrieve those we must temporarily leave behind. This is what he wrote in the captain's journal. This was his official defence. Still he had announced his decision to no one.

3rd May

He was standing alone in the cabin, leaning forward, arms locked, hands flat on the door. Once he took that first step, he could never take it back. On the other side was an older man. For whom exceptions and excuses would be made. Less expected. Falterings and failings forgiven. Everything he had always refused. Leaving the cabin, he was leaving behind him a long trail of useless sacrifice. To say useless was perhaps saying too much. Along the way there had

275

been moments of glory, of rightful arrogance. Times when the dream of domination seemed to be already flowering. But once he stepped out the door those moments would be history. The milestones would all be behind him, staring in silent reproach. Whatever heroics he'd performed out here, he knew, would be overshadowed by the fact of abandoning the ship. Heroics was the wrong word. The word could no longer wield the power it once had. He had the trip to Beechey to thank for that. Then, leaving the ship, he thought he was stepping out of the mire, into a spare, clean space. But the thing had not been neater, only more exposed. Setting out for Beechey, he thought he might get a glimpse of his true character, whatever was hidden under all the layers. He'd thought to test himself, sure that something definite must emerge from the trial – as though afterwards he would be stamped by it, his mettle proved, visibly. There had been nothing in it but quiet, confused misery. All he'd brought back were the shrivelled certainties of old. So he knew better this time what he was going to, out there. This time, if he left the ship it was not to bring back evidence, proof. He had enough of that. After thirty-seven years, he was finally giving up the search that had tormented him so long. He was quitting the game. He was walking away from all those familiar, childish devices, and their relentless appeal. He was not only turning away, he was turning back towards that shabby place that was his childhood, to find another way of living there.

In the corner, the empty chair rocked back and forth. It was another thing Cabot had made for her, to make the feeding more comfortable.

You've come to say goodbye, she told him, and showed him a smile, that he was obliged to admire.

Not quite, he said. Not yet.

And that was it, the thing was done, the news was old.

Heavy blue drapes hung over the door. The narrow bed, and the cot, that had replaced the desk. A locker, and under the bed a chest for clothes. Bookshelves on the wall. This was her room. With the boy, this was her life. He was asleep. They would have to talk quietly.

The breaths were measured in and measured out. The face was serious but calm, carved. As always, it had been transformed. Somehow, he was more beautiful than before. Looming over him, his father looked neglected, spent.

She leaned back in the chair, settled the wool on her lap. He sat opposite, on the edge of the bed.

I know you'll come back, she said. You don't have to argue it out.

She took up her needles, to busy her hands.

I want you to go, she said. I know it's our only chance.

Out there, he said, there's an invisible line. And once you cross that line, every danger is mortal.

I know, she said.

Dud matches, he told her. A dud lamp. The simple fact is, you're safer here. Both of you.

I know, she said.

An entire heating system, he said. An endless supply of fuel. There's many a poor man at home, I tell you, would be plenty happy to trade.

Several years' supplies, he said. Cabot's been working like a black.

Richard, she said. You know well I can't argue with any of that.

The bargain is yours, if you ask me. You and the men who get to stay behind.

I'm sure you're right.

The trouble, of course, will be finding volunteers. Not to go, but to stay behind. No matter how black a picture I paint. You know what they're like. They're like children. They'll think we're abandoning them. You've seen them, all mad keen to do their gymnastics now, to get into better trim. Even Petersen says he's going to try to come up.

In her hands, the needles meddled tirelessly. Behind her back, the boy's arm was dangling out the bars.

He's too fragile, is the long and short of it, Morgan said. Perhaps in the most exceptionally favourable circumstances imaginable. Easy hauling, no storms, no winds. The open water not too far. The sailing clear. But that's too many ifs. I can't take that risk.

In the distance, the bell shyly summoned the next watch.

DeHaven says it's waving the white flag, quitting the ship, Morgan said. The entire expedition, he means. Total failure.

What do you think?

I think he just wants to go home. He doesn't give a damn about the expedition. Never did. I've often wondered why he came out. It wasn't from love for his brother, I'm sure. I don't think he's mentioned him twice the whole time.

What about you? What do you think? What do you want?

Morgan shrugged. For months now, far beneath the surface, the work had been going on. Anxiety and expectation, in continual, quiet conflict, had worn each other down. They now fitted smoothly together. The joint was difficult to see.

Perhaps they've already been found, she said. Perhaps even now they're all sitting by the fire in London, drinking hot chocolate, and fretting over our sort.

Perhaps, Morgan said. The thought had often occurred to him.

He looked into the cot. Every morning a new child stretched out its arms. The words were piling up, the talents. He knew less and less every day who this boy would be.

Other men have abandoned, in their time, she said. Men quite as good as yourself, if I may say so. Your hero. Ross.

I'm not abandoning, he said. I'm coming back.

I know you are, she said. You already said that. She was fussing once more with her wool, perhaps to avoid looking him in the face. Je ne reviens pas, je viens, she said.

What's that?

It's what they say, the French. At least, it's what one of them said to me, one time. I do not come back, I come.

I understand the words, he said. But what they actually mean, put together like that, seems deliberately vague.

When next I come, she said, it will be for the first time. Something like that.

He had lain awake in the dark arguing all the alternatives out of himself, making it sound inevitable, but he could not completely staunch the doubt. He pressed down hard, stopped the flow, and already it was leaking out at some other joint.

You hear them talking about it, he said, like it's nothing at all. It's just gritting your teeth, and tightening your belt, and toughing it out, apparently. As though these are choices a man makes. They're choices a man makes when he's snug and well fed in a well-heated ship.

He looked over at her, but she seemed not to have heard. She was too busy admiring her sleeping son. Afterwards he stayed on with her, to pass a little time, to shorten the afternoon. They sat in silence, listening. In the tiny nostrils, the air rustled like silk.

That evening he called DeHaven, and they worked their way through the list.

Cullen, he said.

Lungs, DeHaven answered.

Morgan wrote the word down.

Bonsall.

Shaking fits.

Galvin, Morgan said.

DeHaven lifted his head, lifted his eyebrows.

Morgan made a mark on his page. Blacker, he said.

Rheumatism. Chronic, but not severe.

Line by line they went through the schedule, scouring for flaws. Later, the landscape and the weather would be too hard a judge. Here, now, he had to play their part. In any case, they could not all go. Someone had to stay to look after the ship. Someone had to stay to look after Kitty and Tommy.

Cabot, Morgan said.

Drunk or sober?

I'll talk to him, Morgan said.

Do you think he even remembers what sober is?

279

Anderson, Morgan said.

Which one is he?

The one always licks his bowl.

There's more than one of those.

The mangy red whiskers.

That lazy bastard, DeHaven said. Constipated again, he says. What that means is, he can't be bothered to push. I'd almost be tempted to take him, for a lesson.

Leask.

Leaks, DeHaven said.

They went down through the list. Then the officers' muster-roll. Half the names, he could not understand how Myer had been convinced to take them on. Most he rated as bodies to warm and mouths to feed, nothing more.

4th May

The days were endless, their long sodden march, that finally brought them round again to Sunday. The bell called them up on deck. MacDonald stood on a crate to make his sermon.

Providence – , he announced, in a loud, clear voice.

Below him, the men looked pious but unconvinced.

Afterwards, Morgan took MacDonald's place on the crate and told them their story, for the months to come. He made sure to give the perils in great detail. He told them there was no guarantee they would reach their destination. There was no guarantee they could return to the ship. We must hope the trials of the past two winters have better inured us to hardship, he said.

The men stood bareheaded and shivering. The iron flakes drifted down. It was Pompeii.

The preparations began. Fitting and mending, counting and stacking, as for a siege more than a retreat. They hauled twenty barrels of bread all the way to the island. These they stacked neatly in the new stone house they'd built there, as a refuge for those they were leaving behind, should ever the *Impetus* crush, collapse, or burn. They would leave tons of fuel and flour, tons of tinned meat, tons of coal. In the same house, in a lead case Banes would water- and weather-tight, he would leave copies of every single survey made since Beechey. Which I hope, he wrote, (if ever we do not succeed in bringing the originals to Cape Dundas) will enable others not only to trace the voyage we ourselves have undergone, but indeed to enlarge the map of the world. They were also leaving a copy of the log and the ship's journals, Myer's and his own. And the postbag they'd been given for Franklin's crews, so long ago, at Aberdeen.

The manner would be simple, but not easy. They would put one of the whaleboats on runners, load it with gear and supplies, and nine men would haul it behind them, much as he and the others had hauled the sledge. Due south, over the floe, until they met open water, then launch and sail to Melville Island. Overland, then, to Cape Dundas, where there was a depot and a winter house, and perhaps relief. That is our object, he wrote. Nothing else matters from the moment we step off the ship. Every man of us is now going to amnesty or annihilation, and needs to fix that thought in his mind. Well and good if, on the coast of Melville, or on one of the many islands said to adjoin it, we meet the other searchers, or the lost men, or depots laid down for them, but we should not expect it. Well and good if, with our hunting pieces, we have the occasional happy accident, he wrote. He scratched all that out and started afresh. To stiffen my calculations, he told his journal, I must imagine that we are going together into an empty room, where

281

we must remain for an undefined period of time. We must not hope for sustenance beyond what we ourselves bring in. We must not plan to bring anything out. We must simply survive.

One way or another, he judged, their fate would be resolved by the end of July. They would have to arrive at the open water at just the right moment. Too early would be too far to haul the boat. Too late, whatever open water was out there would have begun to freeze over again, soon be too thick to sail through, and too thin to bear their weight.

6th May

Listen to this, he told her. And take note. He was reading another of the letters from Parker's postbag. It spoke of Lady Franklin, with keen reverence, for pages on end. Her unstinting courage, it said. She has given everything to her husband's cause. She has counted nothing, neither health nor wealth. It is impossible to imagine a more selfless or substantial devotion.

An example to us all, Kitty said.

Indeed.

They compared sacrifices. It was a pleasant little parlour game, guaranteed to produce a nice inner glow. He said he wanted her out here with them, the heroic Lady Jane Franklin, watching the tip of her index finger being sawed away. He wanted her out in the traces. He could only imagine her in a vast dress of tulle and crinoline, dainty little dance slippers shuffling across the ice, lace flapping uselessly at her wrist.

That night they put him down a little earlier than usual. She wanted to get him used to being in his cot alone, awake. Half an hour later, in the middle of their meal, Morgan looked up from his plate, frowning. He lifted a finger. They listened, frozen, readying their fear.

What is it? DeHaven said.

Morgan dropped his napkin on his chair, went out. In the half-darkness of the corridor, he put his ear to her cabin door. The night was calm, did not interfere. Alone in his room, trapped in his cot, the boy was chatting to himself. It sounded like compliment and it sounded like shy complaint.

Bopopop, the boy said. boPOP.

It sounded musical. In the dark, for a friendly mind, it was something pleasant to listen to.

DaDEE, he said.

Morgan closed his eyes. The hour was sacred, the place. It was the ante-room. He was about to enter, to begin. Outside, listening, what he felt was a fierce physical craving, as for fresh meat.

DaDEE, the voice said again, a little brighter, a little anxious, as though waiting for a reply.

Morgan tilted forward, until his forehead touched the door. There were songs the men sang, lines he'd known since childhood, open wounds. Sometimes he heard them from afar, coming in. What he was hearing now was older and stronger than any of that.

Under his feet, he could feel the entire ship moving, a quarter of an inch. Suddenly he was afraid of it all, every plank, like a creaking stairs in the night. He was jealous – the ship seemed at such ease with itself. Like the ship, the boy would drift into a lively sleep. He was unknowing, full, without flaws. His mind had not yet turned on itself. It was floating gently to the surface, towards the blazing light.

Outside, his father's head was still pressed against the door, penitent. He wanted to go down, to drift and swim. To loosen his grip, let slip, and let the current bear him away, his entire stupid weight.

So often before, going to answer the screams, he'd found the boy in a rage, abandoned, hurt. Tonight he heard someone

283

else. Now there was joy where there had been grief. It was not progress but metamorphosis, unaccountable.

The minutes passed. Still no one came to get him, to check why he was taking so long. Perhaps she knew what was going on. Perhaps she was giving him time to soak it up, let it bleed through the outer layers, reach the core.

Popi basha! the boy was shouting now. Perfectly aware of his power, his unbearable charm. He had begun to repeat himself. BA-SHA! BA-SHA! It was an incantation, that Morgan wanted never to end. BA-SHA! BA-SHA! he was chanting, and Morgan's mind nodded along like an idiot, desperate to agree. Both hands pressed flat against the door, as though to hold it in place. He felt slightly drunk. Something inside him was working itself loose, working itself free. Something was flowing through him like memory, like blood, warm and slick. It was filling his stomach, his lungs, his throat. He could taste it now. He was quietly drowning. He could not leave.

7th May

Morgan was hanging from the beam, by both arms. Beside him, Daly and Blacker and Cabot and Banes. The arms were starting to tremble. DeHaven stood watching, chronometer in hand, shouting them through the drills. Knees up. Nails in. Nails out. He had another beam almost waist-high, and set them hopping over and back, over and back, until they crumpled. They squatted low and leapt, frog-like, into the empty air. They moved like poorly-mastered puppets, arms and legs grotesque, lifting stiffly up and down. To keep them quick, DeHaven played out his orders with a pack of cards.

Clubs were frog-leaps, as many as there were spots on the card. Hearts were handstands, diamonds pull-ups, spades hopping the low bar. Any Jack put them hanging again.

One by one, the bodies dropped. They made no effort to rise. Only Morgan was still clinging to the bar. The fingers were starting to slide. Below him, the others all lay panting.

DeHaven gave them time for water. He called them back again. He was on his hands and knees, ready to start. It was two o'clock in the afternoon, the 7th of May. All over the deck, men were lying on the boards, chests heaving. One by one they got to their feet. They stood over him, looking down. The arms began to bend, ridiculously slow, until he was holding himself only inches from the planks. The veins in his neck were bulging horribly. There were sickened groans, grimaces, pantomime incredulity at what was being asked of them. There were splutters of laughter. The man was asking the impossible, and showing how it was done.

Morgan stood on the deck moving his arms back and forth, mechanically, in an empty embrace. He was trying to interrogate the pain, to discover its roots and its reach. What it wanted. How clever it was.

You don't want to go, is that it? DeHaven said.

The hospital is full of men can barely walk, Morgan said. I don't have the right to suffer a little too? I'm obliged to be immune, am I? Because I'm the captain?

Dick, almost every time we go through the drills now, there's something wrong with you. If you don't want to go, you have only to say so. There's not a man aboard won't understand.

I have a pain in my back, Morgan said. I've had it before, I'll likely have it again. The thing goes no deeper than that. He began to wheel his arms again.

Stop, DeHaven said.

He put the flat of his hand between the shoulder blades. It was like a hand stilling a restless dog. There, he said. He touched his other hand to the base of Morgan's sternum.

285

But the pain is in my back, Morgan said.

That's where it surfaces. But this is where it's coming from. Trust me.

Firmly, he pushed Morgan towards the open hatch door, put him standing between the jambs, hands shoulder-high on the wall on either side.

Now lean forward, DeHaven said. Into the darkness of the stairwell, he meant. As far as you can without falling.

At first it was only a kind of tightness. Morgan tilted forward a few inches more, found the pain and leaned into it, let it hold him there, upright, testing, as though it might flag or cede. After the brightness of the deck, for a few seconds he could see nothing, not so much as an outline. He leaned forward a little more. And a little more. From somewhere behind his ribcage, suddenly, there was unexpected news.

9th May

He lay on his bed with his journal in his hands. A number of men are willing to stay aboard, he read, to guard over the ship, and guide her as best they can to safety, should she be freed next year and I not to return in the meantime to resume my command. I have thanked them sincerely, and more than an order consider it an offer I am obliged to accept. In material terms, I have no fear for them. There are several good years' living in what we leave behind. He read it over again. He was reassuring himself, learning his lines by heart. From the locker came his watch's endless trim.

Patience, he read. An unlimited reserve. A good fund of

shame. Utter devotion to the ordained object, even if one cannot say quite what that object is. He was rereading his journal of the previous year. The date, shortly before the birth. A free run of just three little weeks, if we get it, would bring us almost to Behring's Strait, he had written then. It made Morgan smile, to read over his old self. That man was luck and bluff. He had resolve and indignation, but no particular plan.

There was a gentle knock on the door, and instantly he was on his feet. It was Petersen, as he knew it would be. DeHaven had sent him a warning.

You seem better, Morgan told him. I'm glad to see it. For a while there, we were a little concerned.

Petersen did not answer. He had his meagre few lines held tight in his mind, and he did not want to loosen his grip.

What's on your mind, Carl? Morgan asked. He opened his arms.

I want the promise you leave no man behind, when you go away.

I don't think I quite understand, Morgan said. What man exactly are you thinking of?

I think the man is not in very good health, just now, maybe. Maybe the man is not the very best for hard work, just now.

Do you think we should take them along, such men? Men that can't haul? Men that aren't in the best of health?

I will not stay to live and die in this ship. This I know.

Listen to me now, Morgan said. Certain individuals are going out on a sledge journey, and certain individuals are remaining aboard, to oversee the ship. You know well there's no question of an abandon.

You cannot say you are coming back, Petersen said. Even if you want. Even if you say you do it. The ice it changes, every day. You know this.

Do you honestly believe I intend to leave Kitty behind, and my own son? That I'm planning to head south and never return? Do you really think I'm capable of that?

Petersen didn't answer.

287

I've obviously been a harder man than I thought, Morgan said.

I am strong, Petersen said. I am strong like any of you.

Didn't we come back from Beechey? Morgan said.

Yes.

And that was in the height of winter.

Yes.

Miss Rink and the baby, do you expect them to haul in the traces?

No.

Nor do I. That would be plain stupid. Anyone incapable of hauling all their own share of the load is going to stay and oversee the ship until our return, that's all. It's only common sense. Any other course of action would be reckless and irresponsible.

The man's smock-front, Morgan noticed, was dribbled with soup. It was another fact come to join the line, to argue against him.

Carl, he said. No one under my command will ever be abandoned. Full stop. He sounded annoyed, offended by something unseemly in what had been said.

When Petersen left, Morgan shut the door as quietly as he could. He was waiting for the man to die. For the illness, these last weeks had been a triumph. The spots were softening and darkening, like windfallen fruit. They could not leave him behind, and they could not bring him along. Death, Morgan had decided, would be the politest solution of all.

10th May

The high life, for everyone, for a little while, he told the men. They should enjoy it as best they could.

Like prodigals, he said. Like the prodigal son.

The prodigal son mended his ways and came back home, DeHaven said.

The way he lived when he was away, Morgan said. Before.

Gentlemen, he would say, looking at what they were leaving on their plates. Our chef will be offended. You know what a sensitive soul he is.

The bottles were left open on the table, here and in the main mess. The wicks were left high, night and day. It was as though the order had gone out, to pirate their own ship. It was part of the price. It was telling those left behind they would not have long to wait. There would be food and fuel enough in the meantime. There was no longer any need to scrimp and spare, to think of the future, the uncounted years to come.

After dinner they sifted one more time through Franklin's postbag, and whoever found a passage of interest set it aside, to be read aloud. They were bored of their books and their Bibles. They were killing time.

You would be surprised to see how young Eliza is improved, Morgan read. This last year and her growing have mended her health entirely. She now plays and sings very well and greatly enjoys company. You may be assured as to her behaviour, which is neither shy nor pert but perfectly modulated.

Is there any picture of her? DeHaven said. Does it say how much she'll have a year?

You're finally looking to settle down? Kitty said.

Everyone else seems to be at it, said DeHaven.

Brooks handed him another and pointed at the passage to read. He read the name and date and read out the greetings. Then: Your sister got a good situation in a draper's shop but lost it for what reason she would not tell.

Well now, DeHaven said. I wonder what that might be.

Now she is thinking of emigrating to Australia, Morgan read, from where she has news there is great demand for teaching school. The priest thinks the place is wild and fast for a lady but we are confident of her character so we are encouraging her. Otherwise we fear nothing but disappointment awaits her here. There is no department of labour in which she is not able and willing, as you must know. She has good testimonials and letters of introduction, but of course her passage must be paid and we are asking all her family to help, for if only we can get her out we are sure she will succeed.

The poor girl, Kitty said. They're trying to get rid of her.

Dear Con, said Morgan's voice. Things are very bad in the country still. We could better bear it and every other trial if you were home. How your long silence has weighed on our hearts. Your poor mother has only one hope now which is some information of her son's safety. But she bears her trial with resignation and she has been a great lesson to us all. Our father has been less better able to bear the absence of all his sons. The priest has often been here to remonstrate with him and each time he has sworn a solemn oath he will reform but ere long he has fallen again into dissolution. You would be frightened to see the change. God forgive me but sometimes I think it would be a great mercy if he were taken. I am helping as best I can but I have my own family now and can not do as much as I would like or always be on hand when need is most. My two boys are getting to be fine big lads now both of them, you would not recognize them. Some of the people in the town are very good towards us, though we would not take it if we could help it as there is no more bitter bread than the bread of charity. But what can not be cured must be endured I suppose, and as Fr Lyons says there is better in store for us all surely. I pray to the Father of Orphans that He be Father to you far from your parents and kin and see to it you stay safe and in health and do not wander. He will not forsake you if you entrust yourself to His care. If we do

290

not meet again in this world we will surely meet in the next beyond all separation trouble and misfortune around the foot of His throne forever.

There is great faith in that letter, MacDonald said.

Who was it for? said Brooks.

A man called Hickey, Morgan said. Cornelius Hickey.

In all the cabin there was silence, respect or shame. Only DeHaven seemed not to have heard. Already he was sifting through the bag for another one.

That's enough, Morgan said. He folded the letter away. Afterwards he got out the *London Illustrated* and began reading aloud from the very first page, even if they had heard it many times before. It was the latest news of the Piraeus blockade. Palmerston was holding firm, but the French ambassador had now withdrawn from London, and that threatened to complicate matters quite seriously.

12th May

He was listening to the boastful knocks of a mallet, as Banes knocked the pins from the housing mainframe. He could feel the thing deep in his chest. They'd found a fault-line, and a wedge was being driven in, opening it up, letting in air and light. The housing had already been rolled up and tidied away. Above was a calm, clear sky. Clothes-lines looped from mast to mast. The yards were strewn with shirts and smalls and every sundry. They'd had their first great wash.

You wouldn't want to leave a mess behind you, she said.

Of course not. What kind of a man do you think I am?

Below and above, almost every man was on his knees,

Bible in hand, scrubbing hard. They would leave her as they'd found her, he had announced. Mint clean and mint bright. To some of the men, it was perfect proof their captain never expected to see her again.

13th May

Morgan carried him down the gangway, upside down, the head flopping, squeals of terrified delight. He carried him around to the far side of the ship, into the long iron shadow, where he wanted him to play. The instant he set him down, of course, the boy made for the blazing snow. Morgan let him wander, strut. He had lived in fetters too long. The snow was soft now, he had his mittens on, it did not matter where he fell. Giant hands always picked him up and set him back on his feet.

The world sloped downwards in every direction, drawing him on. The boy was luring his father out into the open, into the light, where all the old certainties would shrink and crumble. There was something out there he needed to find, and Morgan followed, striding, trying always to keep between him and the sun. There was a time when he had prized such light. Not now. The shadows were too sharp and too deep. They slurred reptile along the ground. Still Morgan loomed, his fathomless silhouette. His shadow was flat and solid. The boy stood in the middle of it, as in a pool of dirty water. He dragged it along the ground like a cape.

In the distance the shadows were bottle-green. A lone gull drifted down like a windstolen handkerchief. The boy watched it with admiration, wobbled off in pursuit. The gull lifted into the air, set down again a little farther off. Morgan watched the hunt.

No! he shouted, but it was too late, Tommy had veered under the hull, run straight into one of the props that held the ship upright. He bounced off. He sat stunned on the ice. He wrestled himself to his feet and set off again. He wanted with purpose, not whimsy. He had no interest in sympathy. Morgan watched with no small esteem. Here was the man he himself would like to be.

The men were leaning over the taffrail. Below was what looked like a frontier atrocity – a dozen bears spliced and stretched on the ice. The clatter of voices. The brilliant, savage light. On its southern face, the whole of the hull was splattered with shirts and smalls. The floe was strewn, treasure everywhere – bales, bottles, planks. The boy wanted it all.

Then Morgan saw the bear. Standing shyly at the corner of the coal-house. She seemed curious, and a little confused. The boy hadn't seen her yet, but was wandering in her direction. Suddenly he lifted his head, and stopped dead in his tracks. He turned his head to search for his father, to check did his father see. His arm was pointing.

Ca! he shouted, grinning beautifully, with great pride.

He was waddling towards her now as fast as he could.

In the belly of the ship, in the still afternoon, Petersen was struggling to breathe. Beneath them lay twenty-seven feet of ice. On the surface, Morgan was frozen in time, in temptation. If, for another few seconds, he did nothing at all, everyone could go home together, once and for all. He stood watching, sick. These were the final moments, the final breaths. Time was flowing around his body, like a river around a stone. He could hear it rushing past.

He put a ball into her just under the left ear. She was already turning to move away. A ripple ran through her from head to haunch. The boy was screaming, on account of the noise. A single step, then she toppled clumsily, like a drunk on his hands and knees trying to get up.

293

14th May

A spoon and a pair of blinkers, Morgan said. One spare pair of drawers, one spare shirt. He was proud and dismayed, that he could be reduced to this.

Opposite, DeHaven was folding and refolding a pile of clothes on his bunk.

I keep hammering it home, Morgan told the room. No et ceteras. And I keep finding little trinkets and other nonsense in their bags.

He set a pack of cards on the scales, and noted the weight. The same for the little bundle of books. They were for the boat generally, to help pass the time. His concern with every little detail, the men regarded as mere fuss, a sign of nervousness. He himself knew it as a lack of confidence in his scheme, and in the crew.

In the forecastle they were sewing in silence. Patching. Doubling seams. That morning he had ordered them to replace all their buttons with buttons twice the size. They were tailors now, making clothes for other men.

He thought freely of Melville Island, its northern coast. It was a callous hope. He wondered where the real attraction lay – in the prospect of relief, or in the trial itself?

He read his latest list aloud, for the ship's surgeon to perfect. Boiled pork and pemmican. Candied ginger and chocolate. Coffee and rum. More than almost anything else, the coffee was sacred. He had seen its miraculous powers with his own two eyes. Coming back from Beechey, every morning it had raised the men from the dead.

To save weight, he would have anything tinned turned out and put in bags. Have each week's ration separately packed, with the sacks for later weeks a little heavier, to give them something to look forward to.

15th May

The galley door was wide open. She was in there with Cabot. Morgan put a stool under him and leaned back against the door. The man's evening was obviously well under way. He moved only when he had to, and the words came out one at a time.

Say your goodbye, Cabot told her now. Say it to his face and not just to the back of him.

Your goodbyes, Morgan said. Plural.

Why should he come back? said Cabot's voice. Why? Tell me for what reason.

Whatever was said, Morgan made sure it made no dent in his face. He watched Cabot pour again. There were several bottles on the counter, but he made no remark. For the first time in his life, he refused to count. It was a city they were abandoning, an entire civilisation. By morning the Cossacks would be galloping through the church.

Cabot was still searching for the cork, and Morgan watched him sway.

Perhaps you'd better go to bed, Cabot, Morgan said.

Why?

Because you're drunk and you're talking nonsense and you're embarrassing me and Miss Rink with every word you say, and if you succeed in remembering any of this tomorrow I sincerely believe that in recollection you will be an embarrassment to yourself.

Richard, Kitty said, and managed to make this some kind of plea. She still wanted to be the man's friend, and Morgan was angry at her, too easily. He was too ready to condemn. He was still struggling to convince himself to leave Cabot behind.

It's like a holiday, Cabot said. Your life. Did you ever think of it in such a way? You do what you want, and afterwards nothing of it matters at all.

That is one way of considering the matter, Morgan said.

That is the reason I like it so much out here. Up here. It's not real, everything that happens. It's just like a holiday. When I go home, everything will be the same as it was when I went away. And for now I can do as I prefer, and later it is forgotten, it disappears. I just leave it all behind.

You're not coming with us, Cabot, Morgan said. You're staying with the ship.

Cabot gave no sign of having heard. Morgan studied the face, that the drink and the cold and the lack of light had turned to cheap meat.

Why would I bring you, given your physical state? he said. Why would I want you along, more than one of the other men?

Richard, Kitty said.

Look at you, Morgan said. You're a weight and a liability and nothing else. How much hauling do you honestly think you could stand?

I'm sick, I know it, Cabot said. But I'm not the only one. There are plenty in the hospital. Petersen.

There's healthier than you will be left behind.

I got all the way to Beechey, didn't I?

We're going a lot farther than we went to Beechey. And besides, that was a long time ago. You've done a great deal of harm to yourself since then.

Cabot struck himself in the chest, very hard. I'm still a good man, he said. You'll see.

No you're not.

You have decided to punish me, is that it?

I'm not in the business of punishing. I want men that can haul hard and long and won't be looking for any special consideration. I want to get to Melville.

Cabot reached for and tilted the bottle for a better look. He seemed tempted to finish it off. The captain decides, he said. I'm not going to beg. He poured another dose and put it inside him. The empty glass struck the surface with a solid, decisive knock.

There's something inside me, Cabot said, more quietly. Something alive. He was talking to the floor.

What is it? Kitty said.

I don't know. But sometimes I'm glad it's there. Sometimes I feel I would like to wake it up. This does that, sometimes, for a little while. He showed them the empty glass. And sometimes I wish I could kill it, I could rip it out. Sometimes I think it wants to kill me. I can't explain. I myself, I find it hard to comprehend.

Cabot, you're not well, Kitty said.

Have you been eating properly? said Morgan.

I'm the chef, Cabot said.

You're the chef and your clothes are hanging off you, Morgan said.

When Cabot was gone, she talked and Morgan listened.

He's not making it any easier for himself, is he? she said.

No, Morgan said. He looked up at her and looked down again. The galley floor was caked with filth, all about the foot of the stove.

Are you really going to leave him behind, or are you merely trying to scare him?

If I leave him behind, I don't like to think what he'll do to himself.

I could take care of him, Kitty said.

I know you could. But I think you'll have enough on your plate. In any case he's not fit to bring along, as matters stand. You see the state he's in.

But if he stops drinking?

I don't know. I don't think he wants to. I don't think he can.

They talked of Disko, of before. Those people seem like strangers to me now, she said. Living a very strange life. Doesn't it seem that way to you?

I don't think of it too often, he said. It's hard to imagine, out here.

I sometimes wonder how it would appear to me, if ever I was able to go back.

Perhaps you will, some day.

Perhaps, she said.

297

We live in hope.

I thought you said hope is not a strategy.

It's not. Not a good one, at least. Not advisable, but inevitable, I suppose.

I've been thinking of it recently. Of what happened there, between us.

What's done is done, Morgan said. What's the use of going over all that again?

She was looking him straight in the eye, had something she had rehearsed, and was waiting to say.

Perhaps you thought you were doing what you did for my own good, she said. Leaving me behind, I mean. I can see that now, but at the time I couldn't help asking myself if in some way I did not deserve it. As if it wasn't in some way a judgement or a punishment.

Kitty, I gave you no great thought in those days. It was an entirely selfish decision, I can assure you.

What I'm trying to say, she said, is that before I was sure I was with child, and I thought I would allow you leave Disko without me, I felt not just betrayed and abandoned, but totally destroyed, by everything that had taken place between us.

Destroyed? he said.

I don't know if that's exactly the right word. But it feels right to me.

Rather strong, Morgan said. Humiliated, I might understand.

It was more than that. And it wasn't merely at Disko. It stayed with me for a long time after coming aboard. I don't feel that way anymore.

I'm glad to hear it. I know well it hasn't always been easy, with me. I know I haven't been much of a help.

Now I'm glad it happened, she said, even the way it did.

When Morgan said nothing she asked him directly: Aren't you? Hasn't it all worked out for the best?

I'd hardly say that. Given our circumstances. They could be better, to say the least.

But are you not glad it happened? she said. Are you not glad he is alive?

Yes I am, Morgan said.

Despite everything else.

Yes.

But you don't like saying it.

I don't need to say it. Not for you and not for him. Haven't I shown it a thousand times, in a thousand different ways? Is that not enough?

He was now standing by the stove, leaning forward, both hands flat on the wall, as though to support it. As though there were a storm outside, as in the old days, and he needed to feel it, physically, every twinge. But there was no storm. For months now there had been nothing new to her tilt. There was no more creaking, no complaint. She sat proud on the surface now, safe from all immediate harm.

Why are you asking me all this? he said. Why are you forcing me to say it out loud? Do you want me to stay, is that it? I thought we'd been over all that twenty times. I don't want to go, but in my heart I know it's the best and maybe the only chance he has.

16th May

Before he even opened his cabin door he could tell something was wrong. There was too much fresh air. The voices were too loud. They had left the hatch open again. Climbing up, he could hear a dozen voices chanting, stamping uselessly on the boards. He stood watching. Tommy was in the middle of the circle, swaying on his feet. Kitty, Cabot, DeHaven. A slow handclap, all together, as he started to dance. The handclap quickly wilted and died. Tommy had staggered into the mast.

He stood hugging it with both arms, drunk with fame and fright. The men were laughing. They seemed outraged at their own audacity, at how easy the boy would be charmed. Now they grabbed his arms and legs and carried him wriggling across the deck. They were going to throw him over the side. The little body swung back and forth. There were shrieks of terror, brilliant shrieks of delight. All at once, the hands let go.

17th May

For days now Petersen had lain unconscious. In the main mess, in quiet moments, they could hear every amateur breath. In the evening the men flung down their cards more noisily. For once they were glad when Tommy cried. Otherwise, someone was always tinkering on a whistle, or tinkering with a song. They were smothering the dying man. They were shouting him down.

Finally, on the morning of the 17th, they woke to a sinister silence, and no one said a word, afraid to disturb it, as often they had been afraid to wake the sleeping child. They said it was a relief, a deliverance. They reminded themselves of how much he had suffered. They said he was better off now.

They hauled the bundle ashore. They stood in silence facing the wall of rock. Inland, the first bruises showed now on the south-facing slopes. MacDonald read something from the Bible and improvised a speech. The man had been a brother in adversity, he said. He had been party not only to their fleeting doubts, but to their enduring hope. They planted a small marker deep in the pile of rocks, almost to the cross-tree, to keep it straight.

20th May

Waking early, he felt a nice kind of tiredness, one that wanted to be indulged, and he would have liked to stay in bed all day. But that was a bachelor's fantasy. He could hear her already fluttering about next door. He could hear the fuss of hammers and saws, too – last adjustments to the sledge – that came gnawing through the ship, calling him up. Still he did not move from his bed. He had not the courage yet. He remembered the haul to Beechey, and hardly knew how to approach it, the idea of starting anew, of making a like effort all over again. It seemed a mockery of what they'd done on that trip, to presume it could be reproduced, mechanically. There would be nothing new out there, the second time. Only the same scenery, the same weather, the same work. The thousand tiny laws of that other empire, and the rigour with which they were imposed. And here, now, in a warm ship, in a warm bed, it felt harder than ever to brush the thing up, make it shine. Here, now, his body believed it had found its final home, its final comfort and its reward. Even as it tried to tell him so, he knew it was wrong. On the far side of the planks The Pack was alive, gathering strength. The world was circling the sun. The clock was counting down, rushing towards consequence, as it had been for the past two years. A mere two years of his life, but it felt now like a squandered inheritance.

He left her door ajar, to let in a little light. He stood watching a long time. Tommy had rolled onto his back. A hand was clawing at the empty air. The mimic of a dream? Morgan stood in silence, listening. Soon he too was drawing in deep, greedy breaths. The air of that room was flavoured with something deeply familiar, that he could not name. He could not separate it from the rest. Even from his own clothes now there came a troubled song.

The hair was longer now, starting to darken, and starting to curl. Morgan leaned closer, approached the knife. The hand that held it was trembling. Fear was bearing its lamp into all the dark corners, driving every living thing before it, out into the open. He touched the edge of the blade to the little tress, began to saw back and forth. The first strands curled into the air. Gently, he told himself. Another minute was all he needed, before she came back.

He had brought one of DeHaven's tiny glass specimen jars. 'No luxuries' had been their new commandment for the past several weeks. Ever so gently, he lifted the curl of hair. He had succeeded. Still the boy slept carelessly. Outside, the sun was rising, and the world was in decline. On the maps, in the drawers, the vast unfolded space. The long days and nights, the seasons, had brought him to bloom. He was floating in the darkness. The solid world had fallen away.

And then all that was spoiled.

Morgan heard it even as he spotted it, in the very corner of his eye. A fly. Here. Now. It was not possible, he thought. It was perfectly possible of course. He listened, tried to find it in the dark. It was a worn metallic spinning, meant to irk, to chafe.

He watched it drift down. It wandered blindly back and forth across the face, the eye. Morgan watched it feel its way. He could hardly believe its audacity, its contempt. He wanted to crush it, to hear that tactful little noise. He took a towel from the bed, knotted the end, but he could not strike. It had settled on the forehead. The legs were working fiendishly. The boy refused to notice, could accept everything, even this indignity. He lay perfectly still, poised, as for an illustration. He would wake easily, in a familiar place, needing nobody, enjoying himself. Morgan stared helplessly. It could not sting, could not feed, could not lay. How many days had it left? What was the point?

His hand swept silently past, and the threat lifted it into the air. It swam frantically on the undertow. He willed it to quiet and settle again. He found it on the locker, the marble top. He slid closer, assassin. He began to lift his arm – a crisp thump, he thought, a purple streak – but it was too late, the fly was gone.

He pulled the door full open. The light might draw it out. Maybe he could herd it – waving comically, like a shipwreck – out into the corridor.

The crew were all gathered out on the ice. The sledge party all in furs. Several with gutta-percha masks. Banes and Blacker and DeHaven were stamping around in a circle, laughing at the tracks they made. Their new boots looked like the boots of giant men. Morgan stood apart looking south, at their new home. He knew what was waiting for him. The space was vast, made them small. The rewards seemed more doubtful than ever now. All he had to cheapen the bitterness was the trial to come. At least they could not be accused of taking the easy way out.

This trial now before us – , he announced. He could not see their faces. They could not see his. As we turn to face it together, he said, I call on every man now fully to indulge his faith in the resilience and courage of his companions and captain, and reassure himself that whatsoever men can do to attain their object will be done by them. The rest we leave to powers higher than our own.

He could hear the boy crying, felt himself begin to gag. She had gone back down to see to him. It was as good a moment as any to start.

PART V

20th May

They had whitewashed the name of the ship on the cliff face, in letters twenty feet high. The word was waiting for them, soaking through the twilight, as they approached. The ice lay in devastation all along the shore. The best path, he had decided, would be along the bottom of the cliffs. That narrow ledge was scattered with boulders and broken slabs of ice, so much rubbish deposited there by the last, incomparable storm. Nothing was level and nothing straight. It would have been easier, of course, to abandon the boat and carry everything on their backs, except that they would need the boat when they came to the open sea.

As a general rule, he wrote, the mornings are worst. The great thirst, he wrote. The great pains in the soles of our feet. Offshore, great pillars of steam rose up out of the cracked floe. They slouched along at once resentful and penitent, and the sweat froze on their faces even as they pulled. The horizon marched ahead of them, at whatever pace they set. Already, he wrote, it seems a ridiculous way to proceed. Time after time we must empty the boat. Time after time we have to hack our way through a solid wall. Often, at such moments, I have been tempted to pipe them down. He did not. He was desperate, those first days, to put as much distance as possible between himself and the ship.

They stood straining in the traces, mouths pumping smoke. From every footprint, steam. The fine slick coating on everything was very like sieved flour. The frozen air rustled incessantly. With an endless groan the runners dragged over the hard snow. They were all waiting for the first man to complain. Then there would be a chorus, he knew.

He usually called a halt about midday, for about an hour. He would have preferred a shorter stop, but they needed all that time to erect the tent and get their food at least lukewarm. Had they brought her along, he told himself, they could have set up the conjuror in the boat, under the housing, let her

307

nurse the flame even as they were on the move, to have the food heated by the time they stopped. They could have given her the frozen tins to keep under her furs with the boy, to thaw.

This afternoon, he wrote, at the moment of departure by some shrewd instinct I turned around. The man directly behind me was Cabot, and at just that instant he was pushing a handful of snow into the middle of his face. The picture softened me an instant, I confess. I have experienced personally the dry heat of the Afghan desert, and now rate the Arctic a fair rival.

He could not help but stare hatefully at what was being stuffed into the open mouth. Cabot froze, and the snow scattered down the front of his smock. Morgan made no comment. There was no point. It would soon be running out of the man. It is everything their precious religion tries to teach them, he wrote that night. Desire and surrender, fleeting joy, then long painful punishment.

Three times that day the men had to gather around Cabot, to form a shelter from the wind. They turned their backs on him, and listened as he emptied his bowels again. By the end he could barely stand, and could not haul, regardless of any threats Morgan might concoct. Neither then nor subsequently did I make the slightest rebuke, Morgan wrote. I am no longer the enemy. They have enemies enough out here, is what I want them to understand.

23rd May

They would halt at the next headland and put up in the lee of it, he announced. To continue due south from there would take them off the island, and out onto the floe. This would be their last chance of proper shelter for some time.

The day was clear. Under the cliffs, the shadows were blue. To the west a sprawl of fog. At the foot of the cliff they found a circle of stones about as wide as the tent, each stone about the size of a man's head. Placed there ten or a thousand years before. To date, it was the only evidence the land had ever before hosted any of their own kind.

As it was still early, he might have ordered a snow-house built for better comfort, but he did not want them familiar with better comfort out here. In any case, he liked the notion of doing exactly as their predecessors had done, setting up tent in the same spot, weighing down the edges with the same stones. As a boy he had liked to sneak into his father's bed, as soon as his father was gone and sure not to return. He enjoyed the warmth, and the perverse satisfaction that it was somehow stolen. His father, in a certain condition, always slept on his back, arms and legs spread, star-shaped, and the boy he had been always liked to spread himself similarly, stretching to try to find and fit the trace left by the larger man. Shifting a foot here, a hand there, always trying to map himself faithfully to the heat that other body had left in the sheet. Now the temptation was the same, a fond voice saying it must be warmer here, where other men had once slept. The real warmth, of course, would be afterwards. The memory of the shared bed, a bolster for days to come.

The next morning, beaded on a frozen rope, he and Daly and Banes crawled up the slope. This was the most prominent piece of land they'd seen in a year, and had Franklin passed this way here was where he would have left word. Also, Morgan wanted to reconnoitre their road for the day. The road, he called it. It was the word and nothing else. It was

309

whatever lay between them and where he wanted the land to be.

The snow about them glowed pink. As the sun lifted off the horizon, they watched the colour soak down the slope, towards the tent, like cordial through crushed ice. The smudge he'd seen yesterday – what he wanted to be another island – was now gone. In its place, a lone grey hair had drifted down from the heavens, settled on the surface. It looked like the slightest breath of wind would carry it off. It did not matter, he told himself. It was due south. The rest of the page was blank. There was no other way home.

Far below, back at the tent, he could see the little specks moving about. They seemed of little consequence, destined to be crushed. He admired and pitied them.

With no small trouble, he wrote, we built a cairn to house a short narrative of how we came hither, and why. It is posted with hope overreaching expectation, in a place known by Christian or pagan neither one, and must remain unread until others' emulation of the trials we ourselves have undergone. HM brig Impetus wintered these two years past some 50 miles north of this point, the note read. On the 20th of May, 9 of the crew left the vessel with the purpose of seeking aid for those remaining aboard, who have not the means to quit it independently. Since leaving Beechey Island in September of 1850, in the course of our travels north and west of the Wellington Channel, we have seen no sign of any vessel except our own. From here we travel due south, by boat and sledge, in the hope of striking the northern shore of Melville Island, and travelling from there to the depot at Cape Dundas, which we believe is our closest relief.

By the time they got back to the tent, his right hand was dead. There was no pain at first, no feeling at all. It seemed someone else's hand, that was all. The fingers were the colour and consistency of cheese, and looked so strange – so unlike flesh – that he was tempted to hold the thing up to his nose. It was not altogether unlike waking up with a dead arm. It would be hours before the first furious tingling began.

With his left hand, he slipped a chunk of frozen meat into his mouth. He sat there grinding it down. In his mind, he saw her secretly slipping just such a chunk into her mouth, letting it take her own heat, to blood temperature. He saw her chewing patiently, before feeding the pulp to the boy, as to a baby bird. He could imagine – himself almost taste – the thing as it thawed, gave, came to life. What he tasted was warm blood. It would not be the first time the ragged edges had cut him open. Perhaps it was not her mouth imagined, but his own.

As he chewed and swallowed, he watched Banes eating sullenly. To make the cairn, to hold the note, it had taken almost an hour to hack enough stones from the frozen ground. It may direct others to the ship, Morgan told the man. Should we ourselves, by some misfortune, be unable to do so.

24th May

The next morning he was first to wake. He dressed quietly, crawled out. Ahead of them the ragged crust was a mouldy pewter. To the far south it was crushed green glass. Day by day since setting out, his urine had darkened. By now it was the colour of claret. He would have been afraid he was somehow injured, but that the other men all left similar stains in the snow.

They packed up. He watched Cabot trying to lift a bread bag. Back at the ship, he had been able to lift one alone. Now, without his even asking, Daly came and took the other end. It was as simple as that. They were weaker than before, from cold and want and work.

It was the 24th of May. The spring tides had not yet

managed to boost and burst the bay-ice, and they could head straight out from the land, due south.

At noon they stopped by a block of ice that the wind had sculpted to a distinctly human shape. While they were eating, someone put a hat on his head, gave him goggles, a nose-shield, a pipe.

Ask him has he seen any other sailors pass by, Blacker said.

Ask him how he got so goddamned gross and healthy-looking, said Banes. Ask him where's he squirrelled away all his grub.

Ask him has he seen any women, Leask said. Christian, heathen or pagan. Tell him we're in no way particular.

Just then a flock of geese came cruising low over the derelict floes, braying, mourning. They had been summoned north. Morgan lifted his head to watch, and for a moment left off chewing, out of respect.

Today the road was too hard and too dry, and the runners stuttered along, a dry finger on a polished table top. Their steps echoed loudly on the hard crust.

It sounds like tympani, Cabot announced. Don't you find? In France, he said, you know how they make them, those drums? No one answered, but no one objected, and he seemed determined to talk. They have two even four horses pulling the skin, he said. In all the opposite directions.

Sounds more like a medieval torture, DeHaven said.

To make it so tight, Cabot explained. He seemed over-excited. I have seen it done, he said.

To Morgan, their steps on the surface didn't sound like a drum. It sounded like other men marching nearby, in greater numbers, with greater purpose.

They made their road through the rubble and waste. By noon it was all they could do to keep upright, but for another eight hours that day they drove on. It is far worse than I ever conceived, he wrote. I have always considered myself ruthlessly honest, the enemy of deluded hope, yet today's landscape has

312

showed me my mistake. Contrary to everything I ever believed, I must consider that until now I have been an optimist.

That night he studied the faces. They were now the faces of older men. A fine white dust had found wrinkles everywhere. Beards and eyebrows and lashes all were stiff and grey. They lay hugged one to the other in their common bag. They would have put her and the boy in the middle, he supposed, with the best furs and the hot-water flasks.

Men's strength already impaired, he wrote. He and DeHaven lay side by side, as they now did every night. In his own journal, DeHaven began to write. With this wind, it was too cold to talk outside.

More rations, DeHaven wrote.

Too soon. Too slow, wrote Morgan.

False economy. Failing men = slower progress = more rations consumed.

On the other side of him, Daly was squirming ridiculously. He was not looking for sympathy, Morgan knew. He was flexing his muscles, moving his limbs, trying to keep them alive.

As they slept the false flush of the hot food drained away, and the cold came soaking up out of the ground, to claim them. About one o'clock Morgan sat up and lit a candle. Some of the men were shaking mechanically, like men asleep on a moving train. The tent walls looked as stiff as card. He dared not look at the thermometer, but the severe cold brought a strange sense of relief. He felt justified, vindicated. He was right to have left them behind.

Several times already he had dreamed the boy was out here with them, living as they did. He saw the scene: he'd woken suddenly, wondering was the boy breathing, was he smothered, was he stiff. In the tent's twilight he found the little head, pulled away a flap that had fallen on it. The lips looked blue. He leant closer, held his breath, but it was impossible to hear anything over the general labour. He brought the flame nearer, held it right up to the mouth. The flame wavered and settled, then wavered again.

313

He kicked Cabot awake. Grog, he whispered. It was a voice with ragged edges, close to tears.

He listened to the man fumbling with the matches. One by one, the terrified hands managed to light all the wicks.

We were in very real danger of freezing, he wrote. We were in mortal danger of falling into a sleep from which we should never wake. We were cold almost to the core. I told Cabot I wanted it scalding. I told him I wanted it steeled with rum.

In his dream, he dipped his finger in it, rubbed it on the boy's lips, as they had wet with fine wine the lips of the new-born kings of France.

25th May

All morning a bear tracked them. No man was to so much as turn his head, Morgan ordered, even if she came alongside. He wanted to encourage an attack. But the next time he looked, she'd fallen back, was almost out of sight.

Before he could stop the man, Cabot was out of the traces and striding back the way they'd come. Immediately, the bear halted her retreat.

Then she was bounding towards them, towards Cabot, at about four hundred yards. And still the man kept striding on to meet her.

Hold, Morgan told the guns.

Remind me which one is Cabot, said DeHaven.

He's the big mass of fur.

She was sprinting now.

Hold, Morgan said again.

Afterwards, they watched as she tried to lift herself up off the snow. They laid into her with their rifle-butts, about the head.

Like a cook testing a cake, Cabot eased his carving knife into the gut. Looking on, the men were stepping from foot to foot in a bizarre dressage, to spare their feet. He cut out the tongue, and split her from crotch to thrapple with the axe. The stomach was empty. They left the offal steaming and blubbering on the ice. The birds had already heard the news.

The liver is the best part, Morgan told them, but not a man was willing to try. So he forced himself, to give the example. A minute later he was retching grandly onto the ice a yard from the tent door.

There he was, on his hands and knees, the steam of his own sick rising up into his face. He raked up a handful of clean snow, pushed it into his mouth, chewed it round, spat it out.

Commander Morgan, he said out loud. At your service.

For four days solid, breakfast, dinner and supper, they ate nothing else. Not one man liked it and not one man complained. At supper on the third day, DeHaven told the tent:

He who suffers most in the Arctic is the man with a refined palate.

Only Morgan looked up from his tin. The others were too busy eating, seemed not to have heard. Morgan knew he had only a few seconds to speak. Afterwards, the moment would be gone, and their interminable evening resume.

I am not altogether sure I can agree with you, Doctor, he said.

DeHaven stirred his hand in the air. He was giving his friend permission to make a fool of himself.

For example, Morgan said, Arctic hare I personally find not merely inoffensive, but quite as appetizing as pheasant, as I remember it.

Perfect proof, DeHaven said, that you've been away too long.

You're saying memory deceives?

Isn't that its prime purpose?

315

But Morgan refused to take the bait. The marrow of the musk ox, you must admit, is a great treat, he said. From what I remember, these boys here nearly came to blows over it, last time round.

They'd eat rotten offal if sufficiently starved, DeHaven said. Wouldn't you Banes?

Banes considered him hatefully, the man who worked so hard to keep them all in good hauling health.

Eat a bloody lizard in India, one time, he said. Out in the desert. Eyes and all and glad to get them. Warn't nothing else.

And Cabot's whale chumps in red wine. Close your eyes and you'd take it for boeuf à la Bourguignonne. You'd almost think you were back in Paris, wouldn't you, Geoff?

Bear, DeHaven said. It was a glove thrown down. Tell us how delicious bear can be.

Bear, I will concede, is an acquired taste.

Acquired or imposed? Leask put in.

This was good. They were listening. Some were even interested now.

Necessity is a fine gravy, of course, Morgan said.

The others sat chewing their lumps of meat. It might as well have been opium, Morgan thought. The conversation had lifted the heads a few minutes, but they were withdrawing again, one by one, each to his own private world. Cabot had closed his eyes just for a moment, nodded off, but did not topple. He sat propped inside the hard shell of his coat.

30th May

Cabot was holding a canvas boot in the air over the lamp, turning it painfully slow. The night before, he had forgotten to take them with him into the bag, and now they were frozen. One by one, the drops were sucked down into the flame.

Higher, Morgan said. That's the last pair you have.

His own were starting to crack at the folds, like his hands and his feet. He rubbed them all with the same fat. Most of the other boots were as bad. They would have to be renewed. They would have to start cutting up the sail.

While they packed up the boat, Morgan walked out a little way alone. Dotted here and there on the ice were banks of bloody steam. Finally he let his eyes settle on a smudge due south, trying to decide what it deserved. He would have to be wary, he knew. In this light, in this landscape, everything you stared at quickly came to life.

They had five minutes every hour to breathe, and to take a dose of rum. They knew the ritual by now. As soon as he piped them down, they all gathered in a tight circle in the lee of the boat. Each man in turn stepped into the centre, slipped his mask, raised his face, and opened wide his mouth. As he brought the bottle close, Morgan's hands trembled – as though the danger were all for him. But he enjoyed the trust. If flesh and tin touched for even an instant, they would have to be ripped apart.

Starting again after lunch, he wrote, I could not help but notice the bizarre efforts employed by Cabot in his attempts to walk. At first I wondered whether this might not be an unwelcome effect of the severe cold combined with the quantities of rum, which in our deadened state we drink down like milk. This was wishful thinking, of a sort. Cabot's feet were obviously freezing. He could barely stand, yet somehow the man managed to stagger forward. His knees would not bend. He was like a man walking on stilts – falling forward beautifully slow, one step at a time, rolling his hips to always

317

get the next leg in front of him, left and right, to prop himself up.

Today I piped them down early, he wrote, out of consideration for Cabot. We cut off his boots and for a full hour all hands were engaged in vigorously rubbing his legs and his feet. The things were white and waxy halfway to the knees. With a courage and dignity I confess I did not expect of the man, he did not much complain.

Afterwards Cabot lay there in silence. Morgan had him served first, but he barely looked at his food. With a kind of cruelty, a coolness, he watched the others chew. It was as though he now knew something they did not.

1st June

June 1st. I am beginning to suspect my charts, my compass, and my plan. We are now almost two weeks hauling without the first hint of land. It did not particularly matter. He did not have to justify his course. The shortest way to land or open water had to be due south.

Saturday 2nd. That the ground slopes upwards in every direction, is an impression many of us share.

Tuesday 5th. Another difficult march, with no visible change. It is as though day after day we wake to find ourselves returned to the same point of departure, to travel all day every day over the same ground.

The drift came roaring along the surface, wave after wave, blowing their legs out from under them. Had they been any length of time at all on their march, he would have ordered them down. Eyes closed, joined and spaced by the frozen

318

traces, they staggered on. Morgan their leader, with his long white cane, always sounding for the next trap. They were fat and featureless, silted up. The chests were heaving against the weight. The veils crackling with ice. Leaning forward preposterously, whenever they had to stop.

Six hours later, they planted the tent as best they could on the stone-hard ice, crawled inside, lit the lamp. They watched Cabot prying away bits of the block, dropping them into the pot. It was like splitting shale. Afterwards, in total silence, they stared at the conjuror. Evening worship, DeHaven called it. One by one, he inspected the corns and the blisters, the noses and ears. Their mouths were watering. Morgan thought he saw tears in Cabot's eyes. The hunger was worse now than it had ever been. Morgan himself had stomach cramps. The smell of meat filled the air.

You'd eat bear now, I wager, Mr Banes, DeHaven said.

A bear, said Daly.

Would you eat it raw? Would you eat the liver?

Banes did not answer. The bodies were beginning to drip and steam. That day the wind had shrivelled further the remains of their purpose, their defiance, their hate. They lay there watching the conjuror, watching Cabot, waiting for the first sign that the food was nearly done. Morgan lay in his bag like the rest, cursing his stupid fingers, forcing himself to write. To protect our eyes from the general brightness, and from the frozen particles hurled at us by the wind, we are now obliged to advance almost entirely blindfolded, he wrote. 'Advance.' He was smiling grimly even as the word drained from his pen. Eyes shut or blinded, we shuffle forward in total obscurity, arms outstretched to meet the innumerable obstacles set in our way.

He lay in the bag between Cabot and DeHaven, wondering where he would find the strength. Cabot's lips were murmuring again. Under the eyelids, great scenes were taking place. Harmless revels, Morgan told himself. They were all breathing heavily, still at work. They were beasts of burden. At full rations, they had enough for perhaps another month.

6th June

The men were marching on the spot, like soldiers on the stage. As usual, their boots were stiff as tin, and they were all desperate to be on the move. Already the drift had them shapeless. There was an occasional half-hearted effort to shake it off. The last bag was stuffed under the tarp. They leaned into the weight, leaned out over the frozen sea. I have several times now lightened the load, he wrote, yet it feels heavier at every start. The morning is always the worst, I tell them, but I wonder is this true. As soon as joints and lungs warm up, he told himself, the feet will find their slot. As though a party had preceded them, dragging the same sledge, the runners leaving two tracks the same depth, the same width apart. Sooner or later, he promised himself, they would slide into line. The track was out there, laid down in advance.

Every so often, with a great cough, an entire drift ceded under the weight of the boat. A good hint there was open water locally, he announced. Higher temperature, thinner ice, softer snow. It was good news, he told them, trying to trade.

By late morning he was so exhausted he felt quite drunk. Relentlessly, his feet fell into place. He was searching for a rhythm to help him forget the fatigue, the constant nagging strain, the needless shock of every step. Lulling him into a kind of half-sleep. His mind become soft and malleable, unbraked, spinning loose and free. Where it imposed nothing and did not defend itself.

About eleven the wind hoisted the drapes to show what lay ahead. Line after line of waves, frozen at full tilt. They would have to hack a way through it, by shovel and pick. Beside him, Cabot was already bent over, hands on his knees, scrounging for breath. The sweat was dripping from his face down into the snow.

I can't, Cabot said.

Morgan believed him. Both his own shoulders were raw.

I had hoped the daily march would eventually inure us to fatigue, he wrote, or make it sufficiently familiar that we could accept it callously. This idea, like so many others, has proved a fantasy, bred and nourished by other men's accounts of hardship, and my own willingness to believe.

The next morning, when Morgan left the tent to empty his bladder, Cabot crawled out after him. For the past two days, Morgan had refused to notice the man's limp. Now that limp was on display.

What is it, Cabot?

My foot.

What about it?

It is not in such good shape.

How so? You're standing on it now, aren't you?

It's blown up, very big.

So are mine. What do you want me to do about it?

Well, it's because today I can't quite put my boot.

Morgan had so far avoided looking at the thing. He looked at it now. It was a fat parcel of fox-skin.

So, you let it get bitten and didn't tell anyone, is that it?

Yes.

And now you want us to put you in the boat and haul you along like the Queen of Sheba, is that it?

No.

You want us to sit around here eating our way through the last of the food, until it suits you a little better to go on?

No.

You want to be left behind?

No.

You want Papa to carry you on his shoulders, is that it?

Non.

What is it you want, then? You want to be nice and snug back in the ship with Kitty and Tommy and all the rest of them, is that it? You want me to wave my magic wand? You want everything the way it was before?

321

Cabot didn't answer.
Is there anything else?
No, sir.
Very good then, Morgan said.

10th June

Morgan was lying on his back, blindfolded.

Tuck your hands inside your trousers, DeHaven ordered him.

They watched the gentle struggle inside the bag, and DeHaven nodded to the man kneeling on each side. They leaned forward and leaned into it, all their weight, to hold him down.

DeHaven was kneeling behind the head. Ready? he said.

No.

Layer by layer, the fingers peeled the blindfold away. DeHaven bent a little closer, touched his fingertips to the clenched right eye, as he'd once seen a faith healer do. Beside him, Cabot was holding the eyedropper in mid-air, reverently, as though it risked exploding at the slightest jerk, like pyroglycerine.

Now, DeHaven ordered, as his fingers pried the eyelids apart. The dropper twitched once, twice, and each time – the synchronization perfect – Morgan gave a whimper that sounded exactly like a little child.

The next day, the noon sun gave him 78°08′ for a latitude. One or even two minutes of that might be credited to the glare and the mist and the sorry state of his eyes. But that was all the leeway he could in good conscience allow himself. He wrote the figure on the page, closed over the cover of his journal, told himself that later he would look at it properly.

That evening again he'd seen bruises on the southern horizon. Clouds, perhaps. And clouds meant water, in his scheme. At the very least a mess of leads, possibly a chance to wet the boat, maze a way south to the open sea. He could see it to the smallest detail. If he closed his eyes he could even hear it, the brutal scraping of the keel as it ran over the edge. He watched her sliding into the water, settling, sitting proudly, over and over again.

Beside him the men were snoring. From outside came the valiant grunts of the ice. From inside his chest, half smothered, came a steady, righteous industry. He breathed in and out calmly, expertly, just like a sleeper, but sleep wouldn't come. He was too excited and too afraid, at the prospect of finally getting away.

It was the 12th of June. An early morning mist had burned off to show a thin brown shadow on the southern horizon. It held his stare. It was nothing, or it was land. He handed the glass to DeHaven, whose eyes were in far better shape. It was land, DeHaven said. Morgan took the glass again. To his mind the line of the horizon was slightly smudged, that was all. Even so, he let DeHaven broadcast the news. It was meant as an encouragement, should have quickened their efforts, but they were beyond such gallantries now. It was all they could do, at almost any moment of the day, not to collapse.

When they paused at noon, he had the men form a pyramid, triple tier, as they had so often done for DeHaven's gymnastics, back at the ship. Three, three, and two. He struggled to the top, and stood swaying ceremoniously on the upper men's shoulders. To the horizon the floe seemed as solid as ever, as patient and as wise. Overhead, the moon was bright as a saucer of milk. What we took this morning for land now looked distinctly like a herd of musk oxen, he wrote. I shall veer a little more to the southeast, to meet them. I am putting off any decision until then.

They were nothing but chunks of a berg which had once been rolled in the dirt.

16th June

He made a list of what they would take, what they would leave. Sextant, he wrote. Caulking Iron. Lamp. Beside Anchor, he wrote an X. Unarguable necessity, was the standard. What will enable us to advance, or to persist, and nothing else. For the moment he preferred not to calculate the total load. In any case, it was useless to tell the men what weight they must haul, if it could not be reduced.

Blue Rockets, he wrote. Fishing Gear. Harpoon. Rope. He changed his mind, and began to add it all up, pound by pound. There ought to be a direct translation, he wrote. So much less to haul, he wrote, so much more to the march, each day. He was flailing and grabbing. Every thought was now tainted with the cheapest hope. He wanted to be saved.

The floe had been shattered, but overnight the snow had grown up out of the ground to cover the cracks. He had them fan out in the traces, as wide as they could, to spread their weight. He had strapped two tent-poles together for a feeler, twelve feet long. His blind man's cane. He wandered left and right, divining. Somewhere under the surface, invisible, was a safe way.

17th June

The distant floes were a solid blue. Overhead was a hard bright sky. Underfoot, it was like dragging through liquid mud. At noon, with his instruments, he located himself as best he could. 78°04', the instruments said. What the instruments said was that a week's killing labour had somehow pushed them backward, several miles closer to the ship.

After lunch, he had them unload another case of ammunition, the second conjuror, the common sleeping bag.

What do you want us to do with them? Banes said.

Pack it all up properly, he said. Rainproof it as best you can.

I had them hack out a place for it in the side of a broken berg, he wrote, as though we might collect it on our return.

Afterwards, the load felt no lighter, and throughout the afternoon every few minutes he was obliged to call a pause. Perhaps it is pretending we might go on as long as we like, he wrote. I do not know. Even Daly, our hardiest man, today touched his knee to the ground. He did not complain, but it is plain to see that even he is almost useless by now. The other men appeared shrunken and wild-eyed. In the evening they swallowed their meat lump by lump. The useless food. The useless sleep. The relentless work. Every one of them was under the spell. Morgan could think of no way to rally them. I can think of no way to rally them, he wrote. They are failing every one. Today, for the first time, I begin to suspect my own determination, that it is compulsion more than resolve.

Is anyone out? Cabot said. He was scanning again with the glass, and it had snagged on something odd. Unseen, Morgan shook his head. In any case, Cabot answered himself, it is much too little. It is more like a little bear, or even a … dwarf. It's starting to crawl!

Morgan took his turn to look. It was not a young bear, he said. Nor a fox. Nor a tiny man. He set no store by the sudden shifting. In the end, if studied long enough, at any

325

distance everything out here came to life. It was nothing. It was the skewed optics, and the lack of a frame. Likely just a little bird, he told Cabot. It's gone. Flown off. Just a trick of the light, he said, and crammed down the glass.

No, Cabot said. It was not nothing. Give it. I know what I saw.

Morgan watched him scouting again. Look long enough, you'll find it, he thought. It was the distance in-between that was alive.

It's up on its legs! Cabot shouted. It is no furred animal – it walks!

Morgan watched the man rushing and tumbling across the snow. He would have preferred an easy scorn, at Cabot's easy elation. But it warmed him, to think of the man's heart – however briefly – flooded with hope, pumping it joyfully through every vessel and vein. Even to think of it now had his own heart awake. He was jealous, he realized.

He found Cabot's track, and started to follow, but made sure not to run. It was a lone nomad, perhaps, from some unknown tribe. It was the survivor of a wreck, that had spotted their boat, their smoke, received one of the many messages sent out from the ship, and was heading north to find it. It was Franklin himself, or one of Franklin's men. Come staggering across the ice, sure he was saved.

Halfway out, Morgan stood to lift the glass again. He found Cabot far ahead, queerly stretched and suspended, then suddenly found the thing that was drawing them on. It was an elbow-length mitten, perhaps a fur hat, apparently abandoned in the course of a march. It was warmer now, of course. The man who'd dropped it thought perhaps he would never need it again. Morgan walked on, calmer. Soon he spotted a square blue bottle lying on the snow, that Cabot must have rushed past. Then what looked very like a leather face-guard. It looked like the trail of another party, as worsened as their own. All at once Morgan felt a rush of pity for those men, for the futility of their task. For what they must have endured to get here, for all that lay ahead, and for the state in which they must face into it. It was as though he were hovering overhead, immune and uninvolved, looking down. He wanted to admire the hardship, but merely felt baffled by it.

That evening, back at the boat, Morgan mimicked the version of Cabot he'd seen in the glass. He made himself taller, and stretched out his arms. He flapped his arms elegantly, and tried to fly away. Now giant, he said. Now very small.

21st June

The better to husband our strength, he wrote, but did not finish it. He wondered what decision it was he was trying to obtain, by what roundabout route. Except the pretence of irritation, he knew no other way to decide. We have now been a full month in the traces, he wrote, and have used up half of our supplies, the better part of our patience, and the better part of our strength. Today is Midsummer's Day. It is a milestone I wish were ahead of me yet. Millstone, he almost wrote. From now on the sun will every day be a little lower in the sky.

The sail, he wrote. 6 light oars + 1 steering. The mast. He was making a list. It told him where he still wanted to go. He was no longer reckoning what weight they could haul, but what weight they could float.

Sledge & Boat & Tackle, he wrote. Guns & Axes. Kettles & Pans. He totted it all up. TOTAL DEAD WEIGHT. The figure meant nothing. It would have been too heavy at half as much.

It is impossible to know what to jettison and what to keep,

he wrote. Every object and instrument seems vital in one or other scenario. Without it, I imagine, we will be lost.

Again he went through his own affairs, discovered that she'd put her lambswool shawl in the bottom of his bag – the shawl she'd often used to wrap up the boy, and worn herself all through the spring. Unfolding it, he woke the smell of her soap, her hair, and the smell of something else. He lifted it to his face. Deeper down, stale and sure, was a darker tone – a hint of sweat, perhaps. Perhaps a hint of baby's shit. He folded the thing over and set it back in his bag. He was not done with those memories, that calling. They were not done with him.

24th June

Finally, the boat stood at the water's edge. Somehow they managed to slide it in. They drew it back and held it tight against the ice. DeHaven crawled out and slid in. He staggered onto a bench, pulled on one of the oars, and pulled the boat out into the middle of the lead. From the floe, they watched him take hold of his own hand, flop it up and down as he had so often done with the boy's.

Bye-bye, he sang prettily. Bye-bye. Bye-bye.

Morgan watched another sack handed across, watched the boat sink another eighth of an inch. The gunwale was too low. Two more bodies would have put them under, he told himself. They'd brought too much. Apparently he'd expected them to have consumed more by now, or to weigh less. Apparently he'd been planning for worse.

They drove themselves forward with the oars and poles, in

the manner of gondoliers. The lead was filled with rubbish. Then the floes were suddenly closer again. The sides of the boat began to bump and drag. The faces turned to him. They wanted to know what to do, where to go.

By morning the lead had closed over completely. The banks were slowly sliding past, wearing each other smooth, as though to make a better fit. After breakfast, Morgan went to the edge to judge their prospects. What he saw was a chastening. Had they not drawn up onto the floe the night before, the boat would have been crushed like an egg.

They hauled the boat to the floe's southern edge, where they completely unloaded it. They then lowered the boat into the lead as best they knew how. Then they loaded it up again. Twenty yards farther, they passed every one of the packages up onto the ice once more, and crawled up out of the boat, and drew up the ropes, and hauled the boat up after them onto the neighbouring floe. Gain: one eighth of an English mile.

The first flakes of snow trickled idly through the air. In the southeast was a bruise-blue sky. They sat in the boat, under the cover, all the rest of the day. They played whist. They read *The Vicar of Wakefield*, again. They asked Cabot to tell them about France, the French. He told them of his days as a furniture-maker, as a *compagnon*. They listed the names of the prophets, the names of their children, the cities of India. They recited lavish menus. With great solemnity and ornament, like *seanchaidhthe*, they described the women they'd known. Like men turning puppets, they mocked their own efforts with their hands. After dinner, as much for distraction as anything else, Morgan asked Cabot to cut his hair.

30th June

The weather was clear. He felt it an omen. It was noon. He took his latitude, got 78°02', and did not double-check his calculations for fear it might be worse. He wrote the figure down. It was nothing but the scratch of a pen, and official confirmation that all the heartbreak of the past fortnight had been for nought. That even as they advanced, the very ground they were hauling over was moving under them, invisibly and silently, carrying them backward, north.

That afternoon: four hours, one crack. Not a man refused to participate in the farce. They were beyond that now. Outlook unimproved, he wrote. There is not the slightest prospect of navigation without the proper wind to clear us a way.

They drifted uselessly in the trash. Not enough like water to let them row. Not enough like a floe to sledge the boat. They sat in total silence for hours at a time. All around, the ceaseless rattle of thaw-water feeding the sea. Occasionally someone gave another useless pull on the oars. It was not the days lost per se which vexed him. It was the provisions swallowed without return. It was the counting down. It was the earth's orbit about the sun.

On the 1st they had a good day, with several wide floes and long leads, and covered almost two miles, he judged. Then all night and all the next morning, it blew hard and steady from the south. To the naked eye the world held its ground, with the wind as mere dressing, but his noon observations put them markedly closer to the ship than before.

With what must have looked from any distance like unshakeable purpose, they hauled their whaleboat to the edge, unloaded it, roped it up coffin-like, carefully let it down, clambered in as best they could, loaded it up again, rowed the few yards to the edge opposite.

They waded through the sweet-water lakes now with little complaint. It was July. I now make my observations with fear *in my heart*, he wrote. *It is reading a judgement. I have said nothing yet to the men of our Sisyphean task.* He was afraid even to write the figure alongside yesterday's, to compare. For the moment he preferred to keep it inside his head, where nothing was ever quite as definite as it would be elsewhere.

They lay in the boat, talking about nothing and everything. They watched DeHaven tamp a sprig into the bowl of his pipe. Soon he was smoking happily. His rivals watched and breathed in silence, craving those sly delights. They had long since smoked all of their own. He made no effort to hide his pleasure, and afterwards they seemed to show him a greater deference, in almost everything.

Today the shadows were sheet metal. The sky was definitely blue. The ice lay flat to the horizon, sparkling, like a vast salt lake. In the cracks, the water was molten lead. In the distance, the leads looked wide enough to navigate.

What we need is a steamer, DeHaven said.

Cabot! Morgan shouted. Did you pack the steamer like I told you to?

After what passed for breakfast, they lifted the oars. They rolled and pulled, one single stroke. They rolled and pulled, once more. Outside it was floating ice and freezing water. It was a forgotten kingdom, a watercolour sky over thickened scraps of ocean, and at the back of the boat a sad Frenchman baling, baling, baling incessantly. They were under siege. Everything was dwindling. Their stunted imaginations, their natural strength, their patience. Ambition and anxiety had given way to bored misery.

He listened to them bickering again. As usual, it was someone else's turn to bury the slops, to lard the tarp, to pick lice. Every day without fail, someone was conned out of an ounce of bread. Today, Banes had cut Cabot's string instead of unravelling it. That was the grief. His excuse, that the thing was not possible – what he'd done fifty times before. His fingers were numb, he said, lying there in his shirtsleeves. The knot was too tight.

331

There was a time, Morgan wrote, when I obliged myself always to make the peace. Now I let them concoct their grudges and flourish them. Previously, I feared they might come to blows, and that nothing could be worse. Now, between Cabot and Banes, I am merely curious to see how they go about the thing. They can kill each other for all I care.

6th July

They parked up a whole day to parch their bread. The daily traffic had by now fairly ground it down. They scattered the crumbs over the sail, and stood guard, in case the wind rose or the gulls got bold.

Baa, baa, baa, Tommy had taught them. It was his latest, favourite bird-call. He opened his mouth as wide as he possibly could. He was as proud as a young drunkard. Baa, baa, baa, he said grandly. Baa, baa, baa, echoed all the ventriloquists now, as the gulls came down. The memory was sickening. All in a rush, Morgan felt tears welling in the pipes.

Do you feel that? DeHaven asked.

What? Morgan said.

The wind. The air.

What about it?

It's definitely warmer. That's air has passed over open water.

Morgan insisted he felt nothing, no difference, but it did not matter what he felt. His instruments did not lie, and his instruments that day put them back at 78°03'. The plot had been perfectly devised. They could not win.

By the boat, Cabot was shaving the last of the meat from their last bear hock. Beside him, the men had piked oars askew in the fleshy ice, to rig clothes-lines for damp smalls and socks. One by one, Cabot draped his long wafer-thin strips amongst them, in full face of the sun. The men sat underneath, propped against the bales in their shirtsleeves, to themselves soak up a little heat.

The minutes passed, but not the day. The vault was a timeless, porcelain blue. The ice a glowing, porcelain white. The phantoms had formed ranks on the horizon. Morgan took a giant stride forward, a giant stride back, watched them reappear, melt away again. It was a flexible landscape, at his command. At his slightest whim, it seemed, he could set or stop the dance.

Leask was reading aloud again. *The Pilgrim's Progress.* It took a deliberate effort to listen. All around, water was trickling endlessly.

In my humble opinion, DeHaven announced loudly, your money might have been better spent. A bit of The Bard. A bit of Byron. Anything but that tripe.

They gathered and ate. They listened to the gulls squabbling over the rests of their bear. By morning it would all be gone, even the bones.

The food seemed to have giddied Cabot a little. As the other men lit their pipes, he began to sing. It was his one and only contribution to the repertoire. They all knew the tune, and hummed along, but only DeHaven and Morgan knew the words.

Il était un petit navire, they sang. Fifteen two-line verses and the refrain cheering uselessly all along the way. They sang it right to the end, Cabot and DeHaven and Morgan, because they knew what the words meant. Afterwards, the sailors interrogated them, for the sake of something to talk about. So Morgan sang it again in the silence of his mind, and translated aloud what he heard.

There was a little ship, he explained. Which had never sailed the sea. And then the song goes, Ohé! Ohé! Matelot

– sailor – Matelot sail upon the sea. It's funny, because the word they use for sea is *flots*, F-L-O-T-S, meaning more properly *stream* I suppose. And the English *floe*, well – He waved his hand at the world about the boat. Anyway. Matelot, Matelot sail upon the sea. The ship set off on a long voyage, on the Mediterranean sea. After five or six weeks, food was in short supply. They drew straws to see who would be eaten. Morgan paused to check the effect. And again, Ohé! Ohé! Matelot, Matelot sail upon the sea. It fell to the youngest, he who had never sailed the sea. So they argued as to what sauce, with what sauce I suppose, the poor child would be served. One wanted to fry him, another to make a stew. While they talked it over, he climbed to the top of the mast. He – Morgan turned to Cabot: En haut du grand hunier, et la suite?

Il fait au ciel une prière.

From atop the mast, he prayed to heaven, Morgan said, and pleaded with the, literally it would be 'the great immensity,' but in English? I don't know. Anyway, it goes on, the boy looked over the sea and he saw waves on all sides. O Virgin Mother, cried the poor misfortunate, if I have sinned, forgiveness, and stop them from eating me. Ohé! Ohé! et cetera. And at that very instant, a great miracle for the child. Little fish into the ship leapt in their thousands. They took them up, put them in the pan, and the lad was saved. Ohé! Ohé! Matelot, Matelot sail upon the sea.

Nice bit of luck, DeHaven said.

And it's *that* they sing the French garsoons? Banes said. Very cheery. No wonder they haven't a navy worth the name.

But you don't understand, Cabot said. In French it is I think much, much nicer to hear. It has in it a great amount of charm. It is not at all violent or even cruel like you think. The children, they adore.

The sides of the tent were black with grime, from the conjuror, the lamps, the pipes. You could scrape it away with your fingernail. You could write on it, black on black.

Morgan lay there with his eyes open, staring up. It was a song she'd often sung to the boy, rocking him back and forth, holding him tight to her flesh – her own greedy body and the little body it had produced.

10th July

All day a storm kept them huddled in the boat, under the covers, listening to the rowdy clatter of the rain. The next morning, through the canvas, they listened to DeHaven in raptures. He was roaring like a madman for them to come out and see – quick! – the rain had melted all the ice! All gone! Vanished! he shouted. Nothing but open water as far as you can see! They smiled bitterly, afraid to lift the flap.

Later, Cabot doled out the food.

Cabot, DeHaven moaned, with his spoon in his mouth. The face was rapt. The eyes were closed. He sighed with a profound and fearful joy. He could not believe so perfect a pleasure had been be so close at hand.

Cabot went on fussing with the wicks. Everything was soft and damp. The men smelled foul, old. They ate in silence. The ration now was fourteen ounces per diem, with five ounces of meat, bulked out by whatever they managed to shoot.

And when the birds are all gone, DeHaven said. Then what are you going to do?

Then, Morgan thought, you cede. You turn your back on the ridiculous dream, that has fired you for so long. You turn and with a brave heart you take that first step north.

Could I wave my magic wand and make it appear on a plate, DeHaven said. It was an old, wicked game.

A cup of warm milk, Banes said. It seemed both pain and pleasure to say.

The máthair's boiled bacon and cabbage, Daly said.

Boiled potatoes, swimming in butter and parched with salt, said Leask.

Fried onions, with pepper, said Galvin.

Fish-head soup, Blacker said.

White bread, said Anderson. Fresh white bread and strawberry jam.

Cabot doled it out and they passed the plates along, each man secretly weighing it as he did so, to compare with his own.

Or her battered tripe, Daly said.

Charlotte à la Russe, said Leask.

Roast mutton with caper sauce, said Banes.

Turkey and Boiled Oysters.

Goose Galantine.

Tapioca Pudding with Brandy sauce.

Madeira Jelly, drownded with fancy cream.

And Mr Morgan? Daly said.

None of it, Morgan said.

That's difficult to credit, Banes said. With all due respect, sir.

Why so? Many's the time I've had it piled on my plate, all that.

You didn't like it?

Of course I liked it. I'd be a liar if I held the contrary. But I can't say it ever made much of a difference.

Maybe you should've had seconds.

I could get as much and as often as I liked. And still it didn't fill the hole.

What hole?

The hole I wanted to fill. Wanted or needed, whichever you prefer.

What was it you wanted, so?

I don't know.

Women? Was that your vice?

No. Not to say I didn't – don't – appreciate those pleasures as much as the next man, but the end result is the same as all the fine living.

If I may be so bold, sir, Banes said, I think I may be obliged to present to you some of the ladies of my intimate acquaintance, when we get back to Cork.

I appreciate the offer, Mr Banes. But without wishing to cast even a shadow of a doubt on the talents of the mademoiselles in question, I fear that even they may not have the remedy.

Outside, with a charming music, the thaw-water made its way to the sea.

DeHaven nodded at the flap. Another few days of this, he said, and we'll have to start building the Ark. It was an old joke, come true. Their world was thoroughly rotten by now. All around them, edges were continually collapsing. They had not yet collapsed under a man, but Morgan had no doubt that moment would come.

13th July

He found himself clinging to a rope in mid-air, gently swinging back and forth. Above him, most of the crew were draped over the taffrail, cheering heartily. He trapped the rope between his legs, and reached left hand over right to hoist himself up. Inch by inch, it seemed to him, he was pulling himself towards the top of the rope, yet when he looked at the side of the ship, a few feet away, it was obvious he was making no progress at all. Those up on deck, he realized, were slyly letting the rope slip, to keep him where he was. They were

337

even gauging the rate, to always leave him no lower or higher than before, but always midway between water and deck. In the end he loosened his grip a little and allowed himself to slide, to confound them, and as quickly they started to haul him in. His only proper choice, he understood, was to let go the rope entirely. Everything else left him at the mercy of those above.

The nights are long, it is hard to sleep, he wrote in the captain's log. Life is short but the nights are long, my grandmother used to say. This is what he wrote in his private book. I often think of her now as I lie here awake in the early hours. I often think back twelve months exactly, of how my life was then.

So much and so little has changed, when in his mind he sends himself back to the ship. It is late evening, very mild. The shadows are soft, milky almost, as if seen through old man's eyes. The sunset ice is the colour of flesh. Their new ice-hole, mercury. Everything is so perfect, they forget. There is no wind. Still, the water is a nervous witness, with its own fearful version of the world. He prefers it to the heroic versions he reads in his books, alone in his cabin, night after night. They have been motionless for weeks. They are bored, but are learning to play. This evening Cabot comes running, excited, like a boy. Quick! he orders. Come and see! It sounds like an emergency. And bring Tommy! he shouts back.

The ice-hole is a hundred yards square, off the starboard bow. A line now leads to it across the snow, like a single locomotive rail. It is the track of the keel of the whaleboat. Morgan watches the men ease it into the water. They are strangely gentle. They have made hardly a ripple. He watches them run to the far side of the hole with a long rope, the end of which is attached to the boat. Hand over hand they draw the boat across, with the same great care, not to worry the glass too much. The boat is not halfway across when the whale comes up.

He comes up first to quarrel, then to sing. It is a Biblical sound, a vast assembly of battered brass. It is a lookout on

338

a hilltop, a call to war, the lonely sounding of a retreat. There in the desert, there is no other sound and no possible reply. But it is too big and too loud, and in Morgan's arms Tommy begins to scream. The men are delighted and slightly ashamed. They hadn't meant to frighten him. They are not quite sure what to do. They do not know how to make the whale go away.

Morgan has turned him away from the world, is holding him tighter, chest to chest. The boy's wails are sawing right through his flesh, but he is still smiling bravely, in the presence of the men. He will not need to endure it much longer. His son's mother hears everything. He knows she is on her way.

Afterwards, the ragged ball of flame teeters on the horizon. The boy's father and mother are staring straight into it, wide-eyed. It is midnight. They stand shoulder to shoulder in silence, for a minute or two. It is no later, but the red ball is somehow better nested now, more solid, at ease. The matter seems decided, once and for all: it need never lift again. He puts his arm around her, but still they do not speak. There is no sound now but the measured saw of Cabot's snoring, up on deck. After an hour's wailing the boy has finally gone to sleep, and it feels like a great victory, after a long campaign.

16th July

For the past three days, we have had a constant sprinkling of snow. The ice-holes are turning to sponge. If it were only a little later in the year, a little colder, I tell the men. If only it were September or October, the sponge would stiffen and in time toughen sufficiently to bear our weight. But it is not September, it is July, and we have not the means of surviving in situ until then.

He wrote out a list of questions to ask himself. He wrote out the answers yes and no. Is it possible that. Is it probable that. Given the means at our disposal. Given the weather. Given the time. He did the sums, pound per day per man. Pound per pound. Beyond all the questions, the answer he wanted was still waiting for him. They would never reach the open sea.

Even so, in moments of silence, he often thought he heard a distant rumour. The sound seemed to come from every direction at once. He could sometimes be seen standing alone on the floe, eyes closed, trying to locate it, turning slowly on the spot but otherwise perfectly still, like a dancer on a music box.

I thank God that the earth is not, in fact, flat, Morgan said.

This is wondrous news, DeHaven declared. But a heresy, surely?

Imagine the discouragement, Morgan said, if a single glance gave us the full extent of all that intervenes –

He lifted the glass to his eye again.

That's not south, DeHaven said, but Morgan paid him no mind.

You wonder, Morgan said. Once a thing is proved beyond doubt and accepted generally – you wonder how it could ever have been otherwise.

For instance.

For instance, the shape and form of the earth. Were the earth flat, and the sea with it, how is it a man could never see more than five or eight or ten miles on the level, but so much

340

farther from a height? The answer seems so obvious now. You wonder how they managed to deny it so long.

People don't like to change, DeHaven said. They don't like to admit they were wrong.

They always seem so stupid, Morgan said. Those who inhabit the past. Be it a month or a year or a thousand years ago. And I put myself, my older – younger – self top of the list. So many delusions, all so alike and all so obvious, now we can see what came afterwards.

They had Morgan's birthday. Cabot made him an oatcake sprinkled with crushed hazelnuts. They planted a thick candle in the middle of the thing. A hand brought a taper. The lone flame trembled. Leaning in, the faces glowed.

Make a wish, came the prompt.

He remembered birthdays as a boy. The parcel waiting on the mantel. The tightness in his chest. That morning he'd shot a seal and watched it sink. Far to the south, through the glass, he'd watched the divers drop out of the air, like they were dropping dead to the ground. Now, he imagined gifting Tommy – the same but somehow bigger, older – his first gun. Imagined standing behind him, arms reaching around his shoulders, teaching him to aim.

Come on, someone said.

Globs of wax were crawling down the side of the candle, mettle-thick and mettle-white, and still he refused to blow it out.

July 20th. Today again I had the men transfer all our worldly belongings to the far edge of the neighbouring floe, a distance of perhaps a furlong at best. In the men's minds and muscles, effort equalled progress. On the page of his journal, too, his words made it sound like an advance. On a map of the world, lined and numbered, it was not. Afterwards, naturally, Dr DeHaven made a show of admiring the view, he wrote. A change of scenery, he called it, and said he approved. He said it would do us good.

341

Every morning now there is a new skin on the pools of thaw-water that blot the floe. It is partly this new wind, I believe, and partly proof that the sun's power is now in decline. Today again the pieces of the puzzle seem closer than before. In perhaps another month the general cohesion will begin, and proceed until the Arctic Ocean is again one single solid block. Somehow, I find this a comforting thought.

One by one they stood out their empty tins to collect the rain, and one by one he threw his sealed tins into the water, with his latest report of their progress. In thus acquainting the reader with our endeavours, he wrote. He had not acquainted anyone with anything yet. Thus far, not a single other soul had seen a word he'd written. He was merely setting his words adrift in the world, hoping some friendly force would carry them to a proper destination. He performed the ritual but no longer believed. Screwing down the lid of the tin, he felt he was condemning it. This note would never be read, no more than those which preceded it. As though to be rid of the thing, he flung it as far out into the water as he could, with all his remaining strength. He heard it drop, watched the birds lift into the air. He watched them settle again. In the awkward canals, the water was alive, gem-like. The world was ablaze. The air as bland as a June evening in the old world, the garden, the regiment.

Still this southerly wind has not failed, he wrote. Only he seemed to know the consequence. The men seem blissfully ignorant of the true nature of our predicament, he wrote, that we are being constantly carried back towards the ship, despite our Trojan labours at pushing south. Today I totted up my columns again. *Travel* now 58 days. What is opposite, under *Gain*, I hesitate to write a second time, but Kitty, it seems tantalizingly near.

24th July

They had a proper fight, in a proper ring. Cabot and Banes. Morgan didn't ask why. He didn't want to have to untangle the knot. It was cold and damp. They were hungry and half blind. They were lost. He was surprised there was not trouble more often.

Now Cabot was sitting on a crate with his shirt front pressed to his face. Younger, Morgan had boxed no few proper contests, and recognized Cabot's disappointment, how fierce it was. He himself had renounced such exposure. He stood by the boat contemplating the man. This was his turn, Morgan thought. This was the watershed. Henceforth he would only ever put in a respectable effort, never again a phenomenal one. Henceforth there would be some extra element of measure in everything he did. Orderly advance or orderly retreat, in another world, where winning and losing were not quite so far apart.

With considerable effort, Cabot was now trying to pull his shirt over his head. The cloth was wet with sweat, almost transparent, pasted to the skin. It was too tight. Cabot could not manage it. Suddenly he was flailing and thrashing, ripping wildly at the thing clinging to him. There was a long wretched rip. Then another. Still Cabot was struggling, trapped.

Morgan could stand it no longer. He stepped over, to help pull the man free. The shirt ceded with a generous sigh. The wallop and smack, as Cabot flung it down. Afterwards he sat sobbing, face hidden in his hands.

Someone had set soap and a bucket of water nearby. It was for both men, to work themselves over, then work themselves over with snow. Banes was still standing a little way off, waiting politely. He caught Morgan's eye and raised his eyebrows, but Morgan quickly shook his head.

Cabot should have known better, of course, than to make the challenge. Morgan should have known better than to let it run. Banes was so much the harder man. But Cabot

343

had nursed a reckless hope, as though anger must be ballast enough.

Morgan hunkered down in front of him, a hand on each shoulder, trying to look him straight in the eye. Cabot was staring at the ice between his feet. Mumbling to himself. As though he alone of all the men could not hear the kind and wise father's voice. Listen to me, Morgan was saying, trying to sound severe. Listen to me now. It's over. Finished. Done. You have to swallow it, that's all. He sounded like he knew what he was talking about. As though he himself had been in the ring. As though he too, tomorrow, would be pissing red on white.

26th July

From outside came the sound of a foghorn, and not a man so much as lifted his head. It was not a foghorn. It was the wind in the mouth of an empty tin. Not distant but local, and no summons, but mere noise. They knew the difference by now.

They were now in the last part of July. By now their stories were all well bled, and they ate their breakfast without a word. It was a solid silence, but for the sound of each spoon scraping its own little tin pot. The soup was a rude mix of barley and bread-dust, and other scraps and sundries he tried not to recognize. They prodded the stuff with their spoons. They bowed their heads. Obediently, the spoons ferried the stuff to their mouths.

Cabot, DeHaven said. Yet another triumph. He had closed his eyes for ecstasy.

They sat all day in the boat, not quite sure what they were

waiting for. Officially, they were waiting for more heat, or more cold, or more wind, or wind from some other quarter, to melt, or freeze, or open up the floe, or properly close it.

You are Agamemnon at Aulis, DeHaven told his friend.

He was waiting to set out, Morgan said. We're trying to go home.

They tried again to shove the enormous blocks aside with their poles. This useless porridge, he wrote, in which element we can neither properly sail nor push nor row. The hours passed peacefully, unhindered. Only the misers had any shred of tobacco left. For weeks now the majority had been smoking tea-leaves. The more adventurous had taken to smoking Promethean primers, mixed with regular match-paper, rolled in pages of the Bible. It was another of Cabot's concoctions, to which Morgan refused to object, as long as the tarp was folded back.

They played whist. They played casino. With their catapults, the men bombarded their former camp. Cabot sat alone in the stern mechanically baling out onto the ice. He looked a deeply unhappy man. He no longer knew where to rig his faith. Nothing had changed, and their crisis was come.

What's the secret? Morgan asked.

There's no secret, DeHaven said. He was gathering. Play the cards in your hand and the cards on the blanket, that's all. Stop trying to play everyone else's cards too.

The wind was swinging round to the east, setting them in a slow clockwise spin. The men stood motionless, shut their eyes, but their orbit could not be felt. Morgan told them to line up something on the boat with something much farther off.

31st July

From close by came a gnawing, mechanical sound, that seemed very nearly to be coming from inside his own head. It was Cabot, grinding his teeth again. Morgan drew his hand up out of his bag, groped at the dark until he found the right face, and touched his fingertip to the jaw. It was quiet, instantly.

Afterwards he slept. In the early morning, he began to dream. In the depths of his dream a man was shouting, but even as he dreamed he knew to pay it no mind. They were always too ready to see a new lead, land, a water-sky. The slightest hint of anything strange – even bear droppings – still sent them galloping across the snow. They were too ready to be saved. It's nothing, he promised himself, already too anxious to stay asleep. Because there was something else under the shouting, that was not quite right. It was a softer layer – a kind of a gentle, mechanical whirr. Soon it was a ferocious metallic clattering, boring past the tent. By the time Morgan woke properly, it was the only sound in the world.

Rats! Cabot was screaming. Rats!

That's not rats! shouted someone else.

Morgan parted the flap, pulling on his boots. The entire floe was shimmering, like a field of wheat. They seemed not to be advancing, merely swarming over the ground, like bees on a bush. He could smell them, he thought. The day was noticeably darker. That was how many they were.

He tried to fix his eyes on a single one, to follow its progress. It was impossible. They were too many, too crowded and too busy, and all too alike. Many had stopped to sniff at their boat, their crates, their slops. He watched one creeping along the gunwale, at the bow. It reached its forepaw over the edge and sadly drew it back. He watched the little whiskers working, the little claws. Soon it was testing the air again, stretching farther. Suddenly it fell.

The men were thrashing at them with blankets, with knotted shirts, trying to keep them away from the tent. Cabot had hoisted the open food bags into the air, on the steering-oar, to keep them safe. But they were scampering up the man's body, his raised arms, and on up the wood. Morgan listened to his scream.

Within ten minutes they were gone. The ground looked trampled, soiled. In the distance, the gulls were swooping down to carry them off. He watched one struggle in the beak, drop and fall and bounce.

They look like they know where they're going, DeHaven said.

Do they? said Morgan. Perhaps you want to follow them?

They can't run forever without food.

Maybe they'll run till they drop.

Do you honestly imagine they've left food and land to run mindlessly over the ice, and on into the open sea?

Morgan shrugged. Who could say? Who knew what promise they'd overheard?

They themselves had been wandering aimlessly. It was the favourite occupation of their race. He saw it now with arrogant clarity. The lemmings showed him something else. What that was, he did not know. But he envied their sense of urgency and purpose.

1st August

Daly stood at the door of the tent.

It's Cabot, sir, he said.

What about him?

He's out beyond the hummocks.

Doing for himself what no other man can do, Morgan said.

No, sir. He's took your fowling piece.

Morgan was suddenly interested. A bear? he said – but even as he said it he knew the shotgun was useless against a bear. Still, in the first, nice panic he was scanning left and right, wondering where the rifle was, thinking only of how the flesh would be a resurrection.

You'd better come, Daly said. I believe he's a mind to use it on himself.

He was sitting on a block of ice. He held the gun by the barrel, with both hands. He'd made a deep dent in the snow between his feet, to lodge the stock. He'd obviously heard them coming, but did not look up.

Suddenly DeHaven stepped forward and yanked the gun from Cabot's grip. Cabot made no special effort to keep it, to resist.

That wasn't so hard, was it? DeHaven said brightly. He balanced the thing in his hands, and seemed to be admiring the weight. He tucked the stock to his shoulder, held it level and wheeled slowly, as though scouting for game. The tip stopped six inches from Cabot's face. Cabot refused to look away. He was looking right up through the sights.

Would you like me to do it for you? DeHaven said.

Cabot showed no sign he'd heard.

You're hoping we'll beg you not to, is that it? Dear old Cabot, that we couldn't possibly manage without? Him and his wondrous knack of splitting a tin of pork. Is that it? Is that what's behind this whole song and dance?

Still Cabot did not react. It was a private conspiracy.

One less mouth to feed, is all it will be, DeHaven said. One less body to warm.

The barrel tip by now was right up to the mouth. As it touched the lips, both Cabot's hands came up instinctively, to hold it off.

No dithering now, DeHaven ordered. Be quick about it, at least. You press the trigger, you won't even hear the shot. He sounded angry. He flicked the wing. The action was loud and clear. He shifted his weight to his front foot, shoving the barrel right up against Cabot's teeth. Still Cabot refused to cede. In the end DeHaven stepped back and left him holding the gun to his own face.

They watched and waited. Then Cabot was doubled over. They watched him retch and watched it steam. Afterwards they watched the pool of vomit burrowing.

Leave him be, Morgan said. He turned and walked away, back towards the tent.

He could not feel as sorry for Cabot as he might. It was too easy to imagine the strange buoyancy the man must now feel, the relief. Morgan himself knew it too well, from his drinking days. This was always the best time, these first few minutes, when you felt cleaned out and calm. This, now, was your reward. You'd done your penance, and were ready anew to meet the world head-on.

Back at the boat Morgan got the rum keg and poured. Somehow he felt he'd earned it. He was on his third drink when DeHaven arrived. Morgan watched him help himself, then raise his cup as for toast or celebration.

Well, he said, that's that nonsense settled for good. As I always say, nothing like a gun-barrel in the mouth to clear a man's mind.

Morgan made no remark. I used to hope he might consider me a friend, he would write later. Since leaving the ship, somehow that hope had drained away. I naively supposed that by quiet attention, and by my own uncomplaining example, I might gain the man's confidence and respect, that the immediate presence of qualities he himself sorely lacked

349

might prove a positive influence. Morgan wondered why, and for whom, he wrote such elegant lies. He had merely wanted Cabot to work and obey, and not complain. Until now he thought he'd managed the man rather well.

The noise was neat but dull, and soon smothered by the dumb horizons. It was the sound of a single shot.

Someone go quick, Morgan said. See what the fool is after doing to himself.

No one moved.

You, he told DeHaven. You're the one was cheering him on.

DeHaven began to button his coat. Knowing Cabot, he's probably missed, he told the tent.

About three minutes later, DeHaven came strolling back. They were all waiting outside.

Well, he said, I stand corrected. I didn't think he had the spunk.

Already they could see the birds wheeling beyond the hummocks, dropping down out of sight, lifting up again, carrying the precious flesh away. Only Daly did not look up. He was greasing his leather, and apparently deeply taken with the task.

Mr Daly, Morgan said, would you please go and cover him up, quickly. Take the sail, the groundsheet, whatever you need.

They watched Daly rummaging in the boat.

What are we going to do with do with it? DeHaven said, when Daly was gone.

It?

The body.

Cabot, you mean?

I mean Cabot's body. His mortal remains.

I don't think I understand your question.

Well, I presume we can't eat it. That would never do. We ate every one of the dogs, but we can't lay a finger on him, on it.

He's not a dog, Morgan said.

Unfortunately.

This is Cabot you're talking about.

I know, DeHaven said. Good fresh meat, that's perfectly fine for the birds to feast on, but not a starving man.

We're not starving yet.

No, but we very soon will be. And even then we couldn't touch it, you're right. And why? Because certain ladies and certain gentlemen in London, if ever they got word of it, might disapprove. What a world we live in.

That's the world you're rushing back to, Morgan said.

DeHaven sighed grandly. Well, he said, we should at least post a man out there with the rifle. It might well draw in a bear.

The others walked out after Daly, to have a look. Morgan lingered in the tent. The stench there was sickening. For weeks now the faces had been black with grease. God knows what they would become without me, he thought. Bit by bit, he began to fling Cabot's gear out onto the ice. As though it somehow smelled worse than the rest. A spare shirt, a spare collar – the man had brought a collar! – mittens, boot-hose. He would have to burn the man's letters before the others got their hands on them. He turned up Cabot's sack and shook everything out. Everywhere his mind turned, it was ready to understand. He might have helped, he supposed. Of course there was no helping someone like that. Still, he could not quite manage to condemn the man, except the inconvenience. It was nothing he had not many times thought of for himself.

When he was done he went to check the parcel. Approaching, he lifted his gun and fired into the air, to frighten off the birds. It was like a pillow exploding. He stood over it awhile. He did not know where the men had gone. All around he could hear the ice at work. The real world wasting away. A few feet ahead of him, he watched a long tongue of ice politely detach itself from the main. It touched the surface and slid under with a stifled laugh, like a doused torch.

The distant world made a very fine picture indeed. But the beauty and strangeness of it could not quite disguise the simple truth. They stood before an abyss. The mess went on forever. Cabot was dead. Almost every promise now seemed false. Two months, he reminded himself. It had been a credible attempt. *Creditable*, even. He could do whatever he wanted now.

For dinner that night they had cold pork and chocolate and made no attempt to light the conjuror. No one was yet ready to take Cabot's place. Afterwards he watched them making themselves comfortable, settling in. Tonight there was little chat. What's done is done, DeHaven said.

Even had the hauling gone tolerably well, it was too narrow a calculation, leaving the ship so late, he wrote. It was too far to ask, in such little time, in such a landscape, of such men. However painful a concession it may be to make, we are left with no choice but to recognize these unforgiving facts. To do so would be the bravest action yet from men who have never once shirked – With the policy of a lacemaker, he lifted his pen a fraction of an inch off the page. He raked the nib through what he'd written and began again. Following a tedious sequence of privations and hardship, in the course of which, on a thousand occasions, the company's tenacity, their humility, and their powers of abnegation have been proven beyond a shadow of a doubt, we are now obliged to concede our adversary's supremacy. That concession made, it would be both foolish and useless to persist longer with our current plan. In my opinion the only proper course of action is now to retreat to the ship. We have given our all, and for the present must agree to trade hope for patience.

He put up his pen again. There was perhaps too much resignation in it, too much failure, and he knew well the thing was more complicated than that.

2nd August

Out there, Morgan said, there's a certain line.

The famous line, DeHaven said. I thought we'd already reached it. I thought that's why we stopped.

What I mean is, beyond a certain point, you can't change your mind anymore. You lose that luxury. You can't just turn about and come back.

Dick, I went with you to Beechey. I know as well as anyone where it goes. Banes too, and Daly. And we're all ready to face it. Doesn't that tell you anything?

And what about Tommy? What about Kitty? It's not just our own lives we're playing with now.

The rules have changed, DeHaven said. As though they had merely stepped from one court onto another, to play a different game.

Every man for himself now, is that it?

It was a pure miracle she ever got so far north, DeHaven said. You know well she'll never again sail.

Perhaps next year, Morgan said.

Why would next year be any better? Why not worse?

Possibly, Morgan said.

So you'll trek south as far as you can, then trek all the way back to the ship, again?

If I have to.

And how many times are you going to do that?

As many times as I have to.

You can't, DeHaven said. You can't keep doing that year after year, the rest of your life.

Why not? Morgan said.

It was still early morning, but already the day was glaring, severe. The dream was gone. The sun drenched everything in its brilliant, bitter logic. Under their feet, the ice was sizzling incessantly. They were standing at the edge of the floe. Against bears, Morgan had brought the gun.

A return to the ship is not necessarily a concession of defeat, I told him, Morgan wrote. It is merely deferring hope, not abandoning it. It is reserving our energies for something less heroic, and more likely to succeed. I implored him to consider the matter from that perspective. In the stores, I reminded him, not counting what we might shoot, at full rations we still had sufficient for two full years. Tinned meat. Tinned fruit. The very best preserves. Chocolate and jam. Beer and spirits and wine. You saw the way we were living before we came out, I said. How bad would it be?

A cheap enough ransom, if you ask me, for a year or two years of a man's life, DeHaven said. A few spoonfuls of jam, a few tins of salt meat. He looked north. The horizon there was still a little troubled. Everywhere else it was clear, clean day. It's not the food or the cold is killing me, he said. It's this endless waiting. Whatever's out there, why not at least walk out to meet the damned thing head-on?

Look at them, Morgan told him. Look at me. The evidence was there for all to see. The grey hair. The grey faces. The bodies thin like never before.

But it was no good argument. Trumping everything, from the tent came the wicked smell of warm chocolate. It was the old world calling. DeHaven took a good deep breath of it and held it in.

What about Tommy? Morgan said. It had always seemed DeHaven was fairly fond of the boy. This was as close to pleading with him as I could in dignity allow myself, he wrote afterwards. If ever the child fell ill, I told him, I would not know what to do.

He's your son, DeHaven said. Your charge, not mine.

My charge? Morgan said. The pronunciation seemed difficult. His skin was tingling, tight, no longer fit. The gun was too heavy in his hands.

They stood listening to what sounded like the fussing of fat in a hot pan. It came from the edge of the floe.

All I want, DeHaven said, is to make a decent shove for it. To give myself that chance. Instead of sitting around here like a fugitive, waiting to starve or freeze to death.

You want to walk all the way home, is that it? Morgan

said. Just point your nose in vaguely the right direction and keep going on sheer bloody-mindedness. Keep putting one foot in front of the other, and hop across the cracks?

Exactly.

Morgan could not see if the man was smiling. The beards now masked almost every hint of humanity, good or ill.

And the boat? Morgan said.

The boat is what's holding us back. We take what we can carry, no more.

And when you come to open water? You're planning to swim?

It hasn't helped us cross much water so far. It's been more of a brake than anything.

Morgan took a step closer to the edge, touched the barrel tip to the surface, to test it. He lifted his left leg an inch off the ground. The ice under his right foot began to cede, with a vulgar sucking sound.

The thing is physically impossible, Morgan said. The state of the ice. The state of the men. I know it and you know it. The thing simply cannot be done. You do know that, don't you?

No I don't.

And when there are no more floes, what will you do? When it's young ice like this, or no ice at all. You'll walk across the water, is it? Like Jesus himself? You and your disciples? All the way to Melville?

Yes, DeHaven said. If that's what it takes. Yes.

Morgan was staring down at his own boots, apparently shy or unsure. Inside those boots, his feet had finally shrunk again to something approaching a normal size.

Go on, then, he said.

Close along the edge, the new ice looked like unpolished glass. Farther out it shone more brilliantly, in places seemed almost wet. The thing was too well painted. It looked like a perfect match.

Morgan lifted the gun and pointed it at DeHaven's face, and nodded at the lake of young ice before them.

Go on, he said. Now's your chance, once and for all, to make me shut my mouth. Back on the floe, wreaths of snow-dust like spun sugar were lifting into the air. DeHaven stood at the edge, with Morgan just behind him, and the gun in-between. He cocked the wing. The sound of it was very clear. He shifted his weight to his front foot, pushing the barrel right up against DeHaven's teeth, and as he did so DeHaven's hands came up to save himself. But Morgan jabbed the tip hard at the face, and sent him sprawling backward.

DeHaven stood at the edge, the tip of his fingers at his bloodied lip.

One foot in front of the other, Morgan said. That's how you start and that's how you go on.

DeHaven slid his foot onto the young ice. He shuffled forward, several yards. Stood there swaying slightly, like a drunk. He twisted his head to look back. But Morgan too had stepped out from the edge, and was closing in again.

Since morning the ice had been basking in the sun and in places was now glossed with a slick film. Still DeHaven inched his way forward. Every now and then he glanced over his shoulder, to check was Morgan still following, still pointing the gun. Morgan tracked him through the sights, and tried his best to keep up. Any moment he expected the man to disappear, as through a conjuror's trap. He did not. He was there still, far out, ever farther ahead, trying to get out of range or trying to draw him on.

Morgan's own boots sloshed along like a mop on a flooded floor. Beneath them, he felt the ice working to take his weight. In the end he slowed and stopped and stood watching the miracle. A lone man, far from the edge, walking on water. Under that distant figure, sea and sky rippled and shone, silver and blue.

In the mirror under him was a world muddled and bled. He watched the dream settle, resolve. He saw the choices made. They seemed so simple now, so obvious. He squatted down, drew out his knife. It went right to the handle, like a skewer into a hot cake. He didn't dare draw it out again. He didn't dare move. He was trying to think, and trying to breathe. He was waiting for the terror to drain away. The ice under him was as rotten as damp card and had no good reason to bear his weight.

He thought of how far it was back to the floe – what he took for solid ground. A fanatical voice was telling him he'd already gone too far. But other thoughts, too, were careering through his brain. Behind his eyes, the clockworks were turning as fiercely as they ever had. There was something alive in his flesh, like the first thrill of sickness. It was a deep, abiding ambition, that only he could properly appreciate. Its magnetic pull, downwards. Its mute tenacity. It had stayed with him when so much else had abandoned or faltered. It had not taken root. It was not new. It was the rage to fail.

In the end he gave a good long roar for help. He stood listening to the better silence. The day was fading at last. Any second he expected to see a pinpoint of light floating in the distance, in the direction of the boat. It hardly mattered. At that distance he could not summon it. He had no whistle, no bell, and feared a shot would send him through. He roared again as loud as he could. The fool stood waiting for an echo. The other man was ready to renounce.

DeHaven was far ahead of him now, at the very limit of his range. But Morgan himself could not take another step. It was as though he were physically carrying the boy on his back. He stood there sickened with longing and love. He understood it now. The thing was not a gift but a burden. It had weight.

Under him, the sea entire started to creak, then to crack. It did so carefully, crazily, with a long luxurious rip. It sounded like the leisurely fall of a tall tree. It felt like the entire solid world beginning to cede.

2nd August

DeHaven heated the seal blood over the lamp, then poured it out. Don't think about it, he said. Just get it inside you. It'll do the rest itself.

Morgan looked at his cup as though at something he'd hidden and hoped never to see again.

Drink it while it's warm, you fool, DeHaven said. That's half the good of it.

It tasted not unlike raw eggs.

The Eskimos drink it don't they? DeHaven said.

I'm not an Eskimo, Morgan said. He could barely whisper. He sounded aged, hoarse. At just that moment, he wrote later, I was as weak as I had ever been in the presence of those in my command. I considered them in their bags. Many refused to catch my eye.

How was I to know I'd go all the way through? he said.

The laws of physics, DeHaven said. You've heard of them, haven't you? Or maybe you thought they didn't apply to you personally?

When he woke the next day, it was with the body of an older, weaker man. He felt sick to his stomach, and cold to the core, with knowing pains in every muscle and joint. A caricature by some unknown hand was pinned to the pole by his head. It was his portrait, in Franklin's pose, with Franklin's uniform and hat. The thing was very well done. They said nothing, of course, until he reached to take it down. Then they roared like madmen.

After breakfast DeHaven ordered him to sit up as best he could. He held Morgan's bare wrist between his fingers and studied his watch. He pressed the flared end of his tube to Morgan's bare back. The wood was cold.

Breathe in, he ordered. Now hold it. Now breathe out.

Inch by inch, breath by breath, he shuffled around Morgan's back, searching for something, that Morgan was convinced he would find. He looked into his ears, his eyes, down his throat. To Morgan it felt as though he was looking much farther. Finally, DeHaven told him to put on his shirt.

How long do you give me? Morgan asked.

The flap had been rolled back. Outside, towards the horizon, the sea entire was filled with blood. In Morgan's portfolio, mocking, was a letter of recommendation from Her Majesty to the Chinese.

For three days he lay quaking under the covers, letting his mind drift where it would. Hour by hour, breath by breath, something essential was draining away. He could not even sit up, they had to slide the pan under him, and feed him spoon by stupid spoon.

Good boy, DeHaven jeered. *Very* good.

5th August

The years had passed. They had all grown older, each in his own way. The life and the weather had done its work. The faces looked like parchment now. In the end Morgan asked them directly, one by one, who wanted to push on.

Banes, he said. I suppose you'll be leading the charge.

Banes would not look at him. Morgan still looked quite weak and quite ill. It was another reason not to stay. He was the worst of their prospects, in the flesh.

Leask, Morgan said.

Sorry sir.

Mr Daly.

Yes sir.

Yes what? Yes you want to push on, or yes you want to return to the ship?

I want to push on sir. But we'll come back for you and

Miss Rink and Tommy, sir. Be sure of it. Just as soon as we possibly can.

Thank you Daly, Morgan said.

John Daly, he wrote. Without a shadow of a doubt the hardiest individual I have ever known bar none, and the most faithful. I do not mean to embarrass him by this accolade, which is free of all exaggeration. He is a model for diligence, devotion, and toughness. He is more man than any of us, and he too wants to go on.

They had a quiet dinner. Morgan did his best to get them to talk, to show he held no grudge.

What will you do afterwards? he asked. When you get back. Do you think you'll sign up again?

I don't think so, no sir, Daly said. I think I've done my stint.

Where will you live? Back home?

Very likely, yes sir.

The Mammy's cooking, Morgan said. It's been the downfall of many a great man.

Afterwards, he walked out alone for a smoke. Even when he was done he lingered, half-heartedly tidying the empty tins, checking the straps, the halters. For the moment, he refused to go back inside. There was nothing in there for him now but looks of condolence. Eventually DeHaven followed him out.

It's hard to stomach, I suppose, for some of them, Morgan said. But I understand.

What's there to understand? DeHaven said. They want to survive, that's all. They want to go home.

What Morgan meant was, he understood why they had been obliged to wait. The thing no longer looked quite so much like an abandon. They needed it to look like bravery. They needed a good fund of hardship – a long, harrowing tale – to buffer and blur the capitulation. Morgan himself, of course, minded a contrary logic, had always loved the choice everyone else refused to understand.

They stood at the edge. The lake had all been painted over again. A few days before falling in, he'd seen a vast, sly shadow, deep down.

They say the whale's closest relative is the hippopotamus,

Morgan said. Naturally, when you hear that first, you dismiss it out of hand. But you get used to the idea, after a while. And you end by saying to yourself, why not?

If I wanted the joys of family life, DeHaven said, I would have stayed at home. That's what I tell the men.

By now the sky blushed orange, pink, pearl. The cracks spidered their way towards the horizon, north and south. DeHaven was headed back to the boat. Morgan watched the man leap. The huge pans were shifting under him as he made his way.

To this point, he wrote, I always considered the decision to go back a concession, nothing else. The rest was mere fuss and pantomime – salvage, I thought. I thought that by persisting, day after day, I could put myself beyond their reach. I was wrong. The bond is stronger – the call louder – the farther I go and the longer I stay away.

6th August

He spread one of the oilskins. As at a market, he set out his wares. He laid out the smallest compass and one of the sextants. I don't suppose they'll save you if you run into any great difficulty, he said. But it will be some comfort to know you have them at hand.

To you or to us? DeHaven asked.

To us both, I hope.

He brought out his watch. He sprung open the cover to check it still ran. He handed the thing to Daly. It felt as though he was confiding to their trust something precious, that he expected to be returned intact.

I watched them pack, he wrote. Banes and Leask were giddy as schoolboys. I wanted to see them humbled. A few days travelling will see to that, I promised myself. But for the moment, in their minds they are still the chosen. So be it. I will admit to being as jealous as ever of such men, but I will make no more efforts to emulate them.

The party continuing south has been given food for 10 days. I have totted up the weight per man. I am also giving them the spare shotgun, that in all honesty I never cared for. I believe I have been generous with the ammunition too, of which I note we have no shortage. Perhaps I was always expecting or indeed hoping for a separation of some kind. Who can honestly know what one has been hatching secretly?

He looked up. Banes had their mirror on his knee, had his razor open, was splitting matches lengthwise.

They are taking the mast, he wrote. It is the longest piece of wood we have. Also, the grappling hook and ropes. They will move from floe to floe as best they can until the mess begins to congeal. They say they will draw the floating fragments to them and hop across, where the mess has not yet frozen, or is yet too thin to take their weight. Where necessary, they shall use the mast as a sort of bridge or plank. In any case, that is their stated plan. I think it ludicrous, but confess I did not prod it too hard. I was perhaps afraid they would change their minds.

When they left this morning, he wrote, their packs looked pitifully small. I took care to note the details of the scene. Even as they moved away, a dozen gulls came down to heckle. As they came to the first line of hummocks, without breaking his stride Dr DeHaven raised his arm and held it aloft a moment, no doubt a last signal of his defiance to those he flattered himself were watching him go. Long after the last of them had walked into the labyrinth, the sea-birds could still be seen wheeling overhead, as over a fishing boat.

Morgan had already written out his latest sheet of paper and slipped it into a bottle. He put it in the boat. This is our furthest point south, it read. Necessity caused us to abandon our ship, lying as she did entirely confined in ice and inept for navigation. Greater necessity now obliges us to return to her; namely, increasing weakness, decreasing supplies, the advancing season, and our perfect lack of progress. We shall pass the coming winter aboard as best we can, in the hope of more propitious conditions next spring, when we will attempt once more to return home, by the means available to us. August 6th 1852. RICHARD SPREAD MORGAN, Acting Commander, HMS Impetus.

After breakfast, he gathered those who had chosen to return with him to the ship. He made a little speech. The sky was fraught with birds, directly overhead. All through his own speech, Morgan heard only their garrulous banter. They seemed determined to shout him down. They seemed ready to celebrate. Their time had come. They hung in the air, waiting for the men to be gone.

They piled the boat with all they were leaving behind. They knotted their Union Jack to the steering-oar and jammed it in the tabernacle. Flushed with a strange kind of joy, they leaned forward into the raging light. Of the flag, he wrote: It is no boast or claim. It marks a limit, that is all, and testifies to the efforts we have made to rejoin our former life, which even now seems to lie directly before us. More, it testifies to our reluctance to admit the unattainable. Could it have been otherwise? I do not know. I confess I did not expect obstacles so perfectly conceived to frustrate us.

Last night, Morgan wrote, as I was drifting into sleep, I distinctly remembered an event I had previously blanked from my mind, involving those two musk oxen we managed to round up last summer. You may not remember them, as you were even then much confined to bed. My hope, I confess now, was to keep them for milk, for Tommy, if you died. For two months we kept them in the coal-house, but the situation was obviously ill-adapted to their habits or needs, and they did not thrive. By September they were dying, and

I decided they should be released. Whether or not this was out of kindness I cannot say. I suspect it was only in order to spare us the sorry spectacle of their lingering death. Also, you were by then much improved, and DeHaven was confident the danger was past. I myself undid the ropes and unblocked the door. The creatures looked at me curiously but made no move. After waiting for a minute or two, I took one by the halter and pulled it outside, in the direction of the island where we had happened upon them. I managed to lead or more properly pull it perhaps half a mile. The other followed at some distance. In the end, growing cold and tired and not a little irritated, I let go the rope and started back for the ship. When I looked around, the animal had dropped to its foreknees. I watched as it bent its head to the ground, then toppled onto its side, as though it had been shot. I went back and stood over the thing, watching the steam rising from its flank, and watching its nostrils slowly flare and pinch. As well you may imagine, there was nothing I could do. I could not even put it out of its misery, as I had not brought my gun. After a time the nostrils were still. Its fellow had finally caught us up and came to stand close by. It too stared down at the dead ox, from whose body the steam continued to rise. I do not know how long we stood there together, but in the end I began to walk back towards the ship. The surviving ox turned to follow me, like a lovesick puppy, and I must say I was not really surprised. The thing was alone in the world now – for an animal, surely an unappealing thought. As I walked along I could hear distinctly the beast labouring behind me. It was blowing hard, but scraping its way patiently over the ice. I did not go directly up the gangway, rather stood by the door of the coal-house waiting for it to arrive. I remember DeHaven saying afterwards that when his own time came he hoped he would face it as well. What he meant was, just as quietly, with equal resignation or indifference. 'I thought you wanted to die like a soldier, spitting and swearing,' I answered him, for that is what he had proudly asserted many times. But he denied this and maintained what he said. I have often thought about the matter since, especially during my last sickness here, and during the many other moments of idleness our travels have afforded me. What I realize is that I want not to die but to live like an animal, to face into it all just as quietly, with resignation or a comparable indifference, to use DeHaven's words.

Assuming she lies exactly where we left her, from our current position it is not much more than 100 miles to the ship, due north. Between us and her, it is hard to know what exactly keeps the pieces in place. They seem the fragments of a gigantic puzzle forced together, made to fit. What I fear most is a sudden blast from the north, which would scatter them, or inspire a drift that would bear us south, ever farther from the ship we are now trying to regain, even as it previously drew us backward, as we struggled to advance. I believe, however, that time is now on my side. It is growing colder again by the day. This morning, there was a thin veneer in our water-cask. It wrinkled to the touch, like the skin on cold soup. Soon there will be young ice again in every lead. Soon the nights will begin the simple task of gluing together again all the fragments of summer. Tomorrow morning or the morning after, I know, when we go to wash we will have to smash the surface with our pans. This is not a prediction but a certainty. All of a sudden, even in its humblest details, the future appears to me more definite and reliable than the past.

This evening, he wrote, I have been reading again to the men, from DeHaven's journal, which he was obliged to abandon on account of its weight. I treat them to at least one instalment daily. The men receive it as news not of another time but another place. What I mean is, they talk as though what is described occurred quite recently, but far, far away. I can hardly quibble. To me, likewise, the events referred to are no more real now than those of a storybook. The transformations have begun. With reminiscence and silence, we are consigning ourselves to the past.

May 17th, 1852, Morgan read. Today we bid adieu to Petersen. To the end he kept faith with the old dream, that we would push through to Cathay, as he liked to name it, and round the world again all the way to Disko, to fame and fortune and a good wife. But here he will stay, his corpse perfectly preserved for all eternity, a heathen laid under a wooden cross, a fitting monument in my opinion to the inanity of mortal ambition and design.

This was the turnstile, he knew. Every next step was for exile. In two little weeks, if all went well, they might be looking again at the ship, if the ship was where they left it. At this remove she remains a source of hope, even of unexpected feelings of nostalgia, he wrote. Speaking of her, the men speak as of the gift of a benevolent power. To every one of them, just now, she is a warmer, better life. This morning I stood atop the berg I have chosen as a home for this my last letter to the world. I had a clear view, in all its fullness, of what lies ahead. It was one white tract. It is blind ream, to every point. From that vantage, I myself thought of her with a sort of giddy caution. I hardly dare believe that, in such a hostile setting, something so fragile can continue to preserve us, and perhaps one day be the means of our salvation. Yet I cannot help but hear the promise farther north. North, there will be no more grand or petty ambitions to harass me, only an endless roster of little miseries. To balance all that, when finally we arrive, there may be a smile of recognition from my son. Then the lad will probably want to climb up on the sledge, to play. I know that ought to suffice me, just as I know it will not. I want more. I want to hold him in my arms. I want to press him hard against me, his warm living flesh. I want to feel it beating, my other heart.

ACKNOWLEDGEMENTS:

For many details and a number of incidents I am indebted to first-hand accounts of the search for Franklin, and of 19th-century Arctic exploration. The most important sources are listed below.

The Surfacing is a work of fiction but takes as a template a general historical context and specific historical events. In 1850, ten British and American ships converged on Beechey Island and found the famous traces of Franklin there. From there they dispersed to different zones (mostly unmapped) of the Canadian archipelago to pursue the search. Their route to Beechey and beyond was often similar, but the *Impetus* broadly follows the itinerary and methods of the *Advance* and *Rescue* from Disko through the ice to Cape York, to Beechey then Griffith Islands, then up into the Wellington Channel, as given in Kane and Carter. From there, aficionados will know, no ship ever managed to go so far north and west of the Queen's Channel as the *Impetus*. That said, Belcher ascended the Wellington and Queen's Channels to c. 77° N (and sledged far beyond); and Franklin himself, in 1847, got about as far in much bigger ships; they had their unexpected drifts, and I want mine. Besides Kane, Carter and Belcher, the general drift north also takes as a model the drift of the *Fox* in Baffin Bay in 1857–58.

I am greatly indebted to the numerous accounts of sledge travel in the Wellington Channel and on Somerset Island given by Sutherland and Kennedy respectively. These have provided me with detail specific to sledging in those conditions and that geography; I have reworked several incidents related in those accounts. (I am also indebted to accounts of McClintock's sledging on Melville Island and Somerset Island/the Boothia Peninsula; and of the sledge journeys out from the *Resolute*, *Enterprise* and *Investigator*.) The 'retreat' with the whaleboat of Part V takes as models the retreat south to Cape Sabine of Greely in 1883, the retreat from the *Advance* of the 2nd

Grinnell expedition in 1855, and the retreat of Payer from the *Tegetthoff* in 1874.

Cape Dundas was an agreed point of rendezvous and refuge for all the Franklin searchers. Parker and Deuchars were whaling captains McClintock and others met in Baffin Bay, and who advised them. As told to McClintock, the *Princess Charlotte* went down off Cape York in 1856, much like the wreck Kitty describes. The character DeHaven has nothing to do with the commander of the 1st Grinnell expedition (I just liked the name). There is an Offshore/Inshore table in Collinson; a sun-house in Payer; a bird-man mirage in Kane; a present of coffee and seeds in McClintock; a balloon with tail-papers in McDougall; and many other little debts too numerous to mention. The phrase 'Je ne reviens pas, je viens' is from an interview with the Palestinian poet Mahmoud Darwich. All temperatures are in Fahrenheit. Where known facts have not suited my narrative, I have ignored them.

SOURCES:

Personal Narrative of the Discovery of the Northwest Passage, Armstrong; *Last of The Arctic Voyages*, Belcher; *Searching for the Franklin Expedition (Arctic Journal)*, Robert Randolph Carter; *Journal of HMS Enterprise 1850–55*, Collinson; *Narrative of the Last Grinnell Expedition*, Godfrey; *Three Years of Arctic Service*, Greely; *Ghosts of Cape Sabine*, Leonard F. Guttridge; *The US Grinnell Expedition*, Kane; *The Eventful Voyage of the Resolute*, Kellett; *Short Narrative of the 2nd Voyage of the Prince Albert*, Kennedy; *Voyage of The Fox*, McClintock; *Voyage of HM Discovery Ship Resolute*, McDougall; *Frozen Ships (Arctic Diary 1850–54)*, Miertsching; *Discovery of the North-West Passage by HMS Investigator*, Osborn; *New Lands Within The Arctic Circle*, Payer; *Journal of a Voyage in Baffin's Bay & Barrow Straits*, Sutherland; *Abandoned*, Alden Todd; *Dr Kane's Voyage to the Polar Lands*, Villarejo.

For more details, photographs, etc., visit *cormacjames.com*

THANKS:

Thanks to Isobel Dixon for her faith and tenacity, and to all at Blake Friedmann. Thanks to Robert Davidson, Moira Forsyth, and all at Sandstone Press. Special thanks to Jerry Page for reading, advising, photos, and much more. Thanks for keen reading and comments to Fin Keegan, Greg Flanders and Brian Hanrahan. Thanks to Kirstin Chappell and Marie-Martine Khamassi for help on visuals. Thanks to Colum McCann, Rose Tremain and John Boyne for their generous encouragement and support.